Dare Not Desire

Dare Not Desire

Shenlee Luketic

XULON PRESS

Xulon Press
2301 Lucien Way #415
Maitland, FL 32751
407.339.4217
www.xulonpress.com

Editor: Michelle Schacht
https://www.wordofmouthediting.com

Unless otherwise indicated, Scripture quotations taken from the Holy Bible, New International Version (NIV). Copyright © 1973, 1978, 1984, 2011 by Biblica, Inc.™. Used by permission. All rights reserved.

Scripture quotations taken from the King James Version (KJV)–public domain.

Scripture quotations taken from the English Standard Version (ESV). Copyright © 2001 by Crossway, a publishing ministry of Good News Publishers. Used by permission. All rights reserved.

Scripture quotations taken from the Holy Bible, New Living Translation (NLT). Copyright ©1996, 2004, 2007 by Tyndale House Foundation. Used by permission of Tyndale House Publishers, Inc.

Paperback ISBN-13: 978-1-66285-524-5
Ebook ISBN-13: 978-1-66285-525-2

In honor of my mother.

"Yet God has made everything beautiful for its own time. He has planted eternity in the human heart, but even so, people cannot see the whole scope of God's work from beginning to end."

~ Ecclesiastes 3:11 NLT

The Preseason

Romans 8:28 NIV

And we know that in all things God works for the good of those who love him, who have been called according to his purpose.

The Dung Beetle

There are three types of dung beetles in creation, but all have one thing in common—they find animal feces and feed off it. Some dung beetles feed only on feces while others feed on mushrooms, decaying leaves, and fruit.

Many dung beetles are known as "rollers" because they roll dung into round balls. Despite all obstacles, they roll the ball in a straight line to their desired location. Sometimes, other dung beetles will attempt to steal the dung ball, so the original owner has to move quickly away from the dung pile to prevent its treasure from being stolen.

The male beetles are strong, pulling over 1,140 times their own body weight, the equivalent of an average man pulling six double-decker buses full of people. Both the male and female are involved in the rolling process. Usually, the male rolls the ball as the female hitchhikes on top or follows behind. In some cases, they roll together. When they locate a soft spot in the soil, they bury the ball. After mating, the female lays her eggs in the dung ball, which serves as an incubator and food source. Most parents stay together to protect their offspring.

The second type of dung beetles are labeled "tunnelers" for burying the dung wherever they find it. The third type is called "dwellers" for they neither roll nor burrow; they simply live in the manure.[1]

Which type of dung beetle are you?

We all have stepped in, have relationships that are, or been born in… for lack of a better word…shit.

What do you do with the shit you have in your life?

---

[1] "Dung beetle," Wikipedia, accessed April 18, 2022, https://en.wikipedia.org/w/index.php?title=Dung_beetle&oldid=1082662289.

Chapter 1

Game Day

The score was 24-21 with less than two minutes in the fourth quarter. David's team was losing. This was what he lived for, though, his favorite place to be. He loved the two-minute drill; the emotions that came with it, the feeling that he could do anything, the fans going crazy, and his teammates motivating each other as a supportive family. It gave him a confidence that could never be duplicated off the field. This moment was almost every little boy's fantasy, their dream: to get the ball and take his team down the field for a winning touchdown. No one made it look as flawless or exciting as David. He could never get enough of this game.

"Huddle up!" David yelled, making a circle with his hands indicating gathering together, for the roar of the rival team's fans was deafening. "Huddle up!" Patting his teammates on the helmet as they ran to the huddle, he clapped, capturing their attention. With twenty seconds left, on third-and-ten, his teammates eagerly looked into a set of laser-focused, blue, passionate eyes and believed in their leader. David never faltered under pressure; he never quit, doubted, or gave up. Time and time again, David reached down to a place that the common man rarely dared to travel. He understood negativity in any form could kill even the smallest sprouted seedling. David's core had to deliver the message that they could win if only their hearts believed. Shouting over the crowd's voices, he bellowed, "We need to rise up. Take it to another level. We aren't laying down. Let's fight!

Let's go win this one!" Calling the play, walking up to the line of scrimmage, they were set as the 40-second play clock struck one. David yelled, "Hut! Hut!" The ball was snapped to David as he dropped back in the pocket, confident his offensive line could hold off the defense long enough to allow his go-to receiver to run to the end zone. But the man-on-man coverage was too heavy for David's typical quick release of the football and the defense, eager to sack David to end the play, broke through the offensive line. David had to run out of the pocket as two 300-pound linemen's hands obstructed the view of his favorite tight end. As David scrambled away from the defense's grasps, he was able to silence the crowd's thunderous sound and set his sights on the end zone. Seeing the slightest opening, with precision timing, he delivered the winning touchdown. Pointing first to the tight end in acknowledgement, David raised his arms in victory and joyously shouted, "Unbelievable! What an unbelievable catch!"

As little boys, his entire team ran into the end zone, jumping onto one another, then falling down in a massive heap rejoicing in their hard fought victory. In all his years of playing the game, David never tired of the feeling that came with winning. Last year, his team had just missed getting to the playoffs, and he believed this was the year that would see them there and further.

The Luka Family

Humming along with the birds, Sharon opened the oversized sliding glass doors allowing the gentle breeze and the slight scent of Lake Erie to fill her beloved home with the pleasures of nature. Looking out over the horizon, the lake was a vivid blue today as the sun shone brightly, and the sound of the wind ruffling through the trees gave her already peaceful heart just a little bit more gratitude. She enjoyed the simple joys of life that money could never buy.

Many believed that Sharon's joyful heart came from the vast wealth her husband, Michael, had amassed from his investments. A self-made billionaire, he had sort of walked backwards into his business while managing his retirement portfolio, adding sizable gains as he purchased and sold stocks. Eventually his hobby lead him to take a step of faith, and he left his corporate American job to co-found a small but mighty Cleveland-based firm. But those who truly knew Sharon, knew her contentment came from her never-wavering belief in Jesus Christ. A small, mustard seed-like commitment she professed at the tender age of nineteen grew into an abundant crop, yielding good fruits of labor into her now mature, but not too mature, stage of life.

Hearing the timer, she quickly went to the oven, shutting it off. Upon opening the door, the cheesy, hot, bubbling scalloped potatoes hit her senses, causing her mouth to water. "Looks good," she said, carefully taking it out and placing the potatoes on the massive island, then going back to the double wall oven to ensure the meat was roasting to the perfect temperature. All was on track for dinner with her family, and before setting the table, she decided to quickly peek out the window to see if anyone had arrived. Smiling brightly, Sharon watched as her oldest daughter, Katherine, pulled into the driveway, waving happily.

Sharon hurried through the kitchen to the mudroom and opened the garage storm door, calling out, "Hello!"

"Hi, Mom!" Katherine smiled getting out of her car.

Holding the door open further, Sharon said, "Come in, come in."

Chuckling delightfully, Katherine walked through the six-car garage and up the three small steps leading into the mudroom, hugging and kissing her mother hello as soon as she reached her. Almost rolling her eyes, although she would never be that disrespectful, she smiled delightfully as her mother bent over and kissed her belly saying, "Hello, my little one."

Tickled by this new greeting that was fast becoming tradition, Katherine joked with her mother saying, "I'm not even showing yet."

Standing straight up, she smiled at her daughter and asked, "Do you really think that will stop me from kissing my little grandbaby?"

"You and James's mother will spoil this child," Katherine said.

Taking her daughter by the arm, Sharon walked her into the kitchen. "Of course, we will. That's what grandmothers do, sweetie."

Katherine smiled, knowing her mother and mother-in-law would pamper their little bundle of joy. She removed her purse, hanging it over a table chair as she sat, asking, "Where's Dad?"

Pointing, Sharon said, "In the office." Katherine looked towards the closed doors as her mother continued. "He shouldn't be much longer."

"James and his parents are running a little late," Katherine said.

"No problem, sweetie," Sharon said as she gathered plates from the cabinet. "Lana and Eric will be here soon and are bringing a cake."

"Oh really?" Katherine asked, resting her chin on her hand. "I don't think I'll have any."

Sharon spun toward her daughter. "Are you feeling morning sickness?"

With her big, dark brown eyes, she quickly answered "No, not at all."

Slowly, walking towards the table, her mother asked, "Are you hungry?"

"I guess I can eat," Katherine replied.

Placing the plates down, she sat in the chair across from her daughter. "Are you feeling okay, sweetie?"

"Yes, why?" she wondered.

"Well," her mother countered, "You don't seem interested in eating."

Katherine shrugged her shoulders. "Isn't that okay?"

Looking lovingly at her daughter, Sharon said "Lana is making her cake and you don't want any? That's not like you. Are you concerned you will gain too much weight?"

Katherine took a deep breath, shifted her eyes away from her mother's gaze, then whispered, "What if I'm a bad mother?" Sharon reached out and took her daughter's hand. "What if I mess this baby up? What if I'm a push over? What if I'm too harsh?" Moist tears wet Katherine's eyes. "I don't know how to change a diaper. I don't even feel comfortable holding a newborn. What if I drop it? What if my baby doesn't like me?"

"Your child will adore you," her mother reassured.

Shaking her head no, Katherine admitted, "I'm not you."

The look-alike sat across from her idol, a pillar of a woman and an indescribable blessing that Katherine had the privilege of calling mother. Sharon was a beautiful, classy woman who was revered by her daughters and loved by her husband. She also was a quiet yet talented businesswoman whom Katherine looked up to in all ways. Sharon had taught both her daughters the art of loving others as they would want to be loved—the eternal biblical commandment. Sharon was a woman who could equally stun at a black-tie affair and get into the trenches with those in need, having taken to heart the Bible verse "too much is given, much will be expected."

"Katherine, sweetie, you are so much more mature than I was at your age," Sharon said. "Both you and your sister are in a much better place than I was."

"That's because of you, Mom," she stressed. "It was like you knew me better than I knew myself. I can't raise a baby. I can't send my child over here for you to teach it. That's my job and I don't think I can do it."

"Of course you can," Sharon replied.

"No, I can't," Katherine insisted. "Poor James. I'm lucky that man even wanted to marry me after all those years."

Sharon grinned, reminding, "James was ten years old when he told you he would marry you."

"Yes, but I didn't want to marry him."

"Katherine, honey, you were only five," Sharon said.

"When I was in college, Mom," Katherine clarified.

"You weren't ready for marriage," her mother said.

"I'm not too sure I'm ready to be a mother," Katherine confessed.

Squeezing her hand lovingly, Sharon said, "Who is? Your father and I waited seven years and I still wasn't ready. You can prepare and plan but honestly, until this newborn comes into this world, you'll never know the capacity God has placed within your heart."

Katherine's chin quivered as she wiped away her tears.

"I'm so very thankful for you and your sister," Sharon said, rubbing Katherine's hand affectionately. "You both are such an incredible blessing from God. I was terrified to have children, you know. And I prayed earnestly to understand how to love you both and raise you as God designed and created. God answers prayers. God answered my prayer for wisdom, and He'll answer my prayer that you will have far greater wisdom to raise your own children."

Soaking up her mother's words, knowing that God would deliver, Katherine said, "Thanks, Mom."

Chuckling slightly, she said. "Your father is right, you are so much like me, but let's keep that between us."

Grinning, Katherine had to say, "It's no secret."

Standing up to set the table, Sharon said with a wink, "Your sister is too."

Katherine walked to the utensil drawer to help her mother continue to set the table. "It scares you, doesn't it?"

"Like you have no idea," Sharon laughed. "It's what keeps me on my knees."

Unfortunately, Sharon had experienced a traumatic childhood. Being raised by a mentally unstable mother and a cold, distant father had left many wounds and scars to battle. Like so many, healing didn't come easy for her. Sharon had been headed down the road of destruction until God grabbed a hold of her and placed her on a different path. Committing her life to Jesus Christ, although transformational, still came with years of challenges as she began the long, tedious process to work through the horrifying abuse she suffered as a child. But God was faithful and just, using her pain to give her an understanding of others' anguish and an abundant amount of wisdom to discern, analyze, and care for the brokenhearted.

But those years of destruction from her anger and resentment lead to a shameful sin that still haunted her to this day. She was fearful her daughters would follow her footsteps since we all, like sheep, go astray. It was one of the many reasons she remained on her knees praying to her Creator and Maker. Prayer was her constant companion. After accepting Jesus Christ as her Savior, Sharon's first prayer was asking God for a nice man. Within a year, God fulfilled by bringing Michael into her life. She often said it was the greatest prayer ever answered by God.

"Something smells good," Michael said walking through the kitchen. He kissed his daughter on the cheek before grabbing a fork and tasting the potatoes.

"Dad, it's hot," Katherine warned. "I already burned my lips."

Shoving a fork full in his mouth before he could heed the warning, he waved his hand over his mouth, saying "Hot!"

"But good, isn't it?" Katherine asked, taking another fork full but blowing on it first.

"They are great," Michael said as he stood next to his daughter, trying to cool off the piping hot goodness to enjoy together.

Michael, a well-respected, full-of-life man, loved God and his family unconditionally. Anyone who had been in his presence even for a mere moment knew this man would lay down his life for his family, protecting them at all cost. And because of it, his wife and daughters honored him accordingly. His eyes, like the Earth colored in shades of blue, brown, and green, were joyful like his fun-natured personality. His smile lit up his entire face. He stood polished and distinguished, from his full, peppered hair to his solid and well-kept frame that seemed to be meant for a suit, even a tuxedo for the many charity events they hosted.

"Eric and Lana are here!" Sharon announced as she ran to the garage door with Katherine tagging along. "Hello."

"Hey!" Lana called out, carrying a rather large cake box. She wore a party hat and was blowing on a paper horn as the women chuckled. After giving kisses all around, including one to her husband, Eric, she said, "Okay, I got a little carried away."

Lifting the lid off the box, Katherine licked her lips, saying "Wow! This is amazing."

"Maybe too much frosting?" Lana asked.

"Never," Katherine protested, scooping up a finger full and popping it in her mouth, looking at the Noah's Ark themed cake.

"I know the baby shower is months away and this isn't the theme, but I couldn't stop once I got started." Lana giggled.

"Like Katherine is going to pass up on one of your cakes," Eric teased the sisters, walking into the kitchen to greet his father-in-law.

The sisters were in their early twenties and only nineteen months apart. Lana was the youngest daughter, Katherine's best friend, and another look-alike of Sharon. The three women were very similar. All had dark brown hair, although Lana's was straight and long while Katherine's was wavy. Sharon kept hers a medium length to highlight her rosy, apple cheeks, full lips, and brown eyes beautifully frame by her naturally high arched, thick eyebrows.

Lana, was slender, like a ballerina, very fit even for a pastry chef. Sharon was more voluptuous and Katherine had a muscular build but petite frame with a tiny waist and bosom. Their eyes were all varying shades of brown, but Katherine's were huge, deep, dark chocolate and innocent like a doe. They each were graced with full lips, supple skin, and smiles that lit up their faces. They were beautiful, elegant, and graceful women, inside and out.

"Hi, Dad," Eric said, hugging his father-in-law. A man hand-selected by Michael, presenting to his younger daughter and marrying within a couple years, Eric was the son of Michael's business partner and prince charming would best describe his looks, personality, and overall nature. A chef like his wife, he owned with her a little bistro in the heart of downtown Cleveland where the family often hung out. He and Lana aided the family mission by preparing gourmet dinners for the charity events, which were frequently grand affairs.

"They're here," Sharon said, moving to greet Katherine's in-laws, actually the pastor of their church and his wife. They were an amazing couple whom Michael and Sharon had known for years, becoming more like family than friends.

And then, James.

James, a man Katherine had known since she was five years old and he ten. Ever since they met, James knew he would marry her, telling her often, until one day he did. He and Katherine had had a connection since they were little; they loved each other and enjoyed being together.

She was a flag girl, and he a football player. Neither was above average in their sportsmanship, but both loved football, and so did their families.

James went on to college, afterward working for a sports management company. There he climbed the ladder until he decided to open his own company. With the blessings from their family and the financial backing from their home, he and Katherine set out on that adventure together. They established a little company, firmly planted among the large corporations, and made quite a solid, reputable presence.

Now all present and accounted for. The usual group gathered together to celebrate life and today was an especially jovial occasion since Katherine and James had only recently announced they were expecting. And plans for a baby shower was the reason for this tight-knit family to congregate. Although, they needed no event to pull them together. The family adored one another and shared such a strong bond that even a few days apart seemed far too long to be away from one another.

Chapter 2

David Mann

David was an extremely athletic, handsome, and charismatic mid-twenty year old. The tall, blue-eyed, dark thick brunette was perfectly built to be a professional quarterback. His grandma had often said he grabbed his first football before walking and never let it go. David was a natural. Beginning the season with a winning drive down the field, he couldn't help but think of how far he had come. His mother, an alcoholic and prescription drug abuser, had been in and out of his life. His father, angry because of it, made David his favorite target for his wrath. So at the age of fifteen, David decided to leave home to live with his grandma, who took care of him as best she could. Football was his only savior. When he played, nothing else mattered. It didn't matter that his father kept telling him he'd never amount to anything or his mom reiterated that he was a mistake, nor was he bothered by her many trips to the hospital for overdoses.

He was a winner when he threw the ball and knew he would spend his life playing and coaching the sport. The game removed him from reality, so he immersed himself in it, spending hours upon hours studying strategy, players, and quarterbacks. It paid off. He won the state championship in high school, received a full scholarship to college, and won the Sugar Bowl. He even became a first-round pick going to Miami, leaving the city he was born in, never to return. Joyous, he packed his bags, grateful to be out of that childhood and never having to deal with his parents again.

Within the first three years of his professional career, David made a name for himself and was on his way to becoming one of the greatest football players in recent times. However, in the second game of his fourth season, as David threw a pass in the third quarter, he was blindsided by a sack that knocked him out cold. Silence fell on the stadium. After several minutes of the trainers hovering over him, David awoke to a broken collar bone. Taken to the hospital and sidelined for the rest of the season, depression made a home within him.

For the first time in his life, football couldn't take him out of reality. His despair overwhelmed his entire being. Although the doctors told him not to throw a football, he couldn't resist the feeling it gave him, throwing one too soon, which only aggravated his collarbone and prolonged the healing. David became furious, bitter, and distant.

In his glory days, he was an occasional drinker at a trendy bar which included dancing and he enjoyed the attention he drew. The women loved him, and as it was since his high school days, he had his choice. He relished the attention he got from the ladies but never wanted to settle down. He'd seen his dad's life ruined because of his mother. He often wondered why his Dad hadn't been able to control his mom or why he allowed a woman to treat him so poorly. He couldn't be a real man, that's for sure. David would never let that happen to him, so his only option was to hold women at arm's length.

Interestingly, he found women wanted him even more since he was a prized possession—something not everyone could have. Therefore, as a good-looking, successful quarterback, he felt he had the right to be extremely selective. He treated women as if he was indeed a gift. They were lucky to be chosen to have a "relationship" with him. But now his depression dimmed his trophy-status, attractive appearance and curbed his lifestyle. Then, unable to take any more of his darkness, the one woman whom he'd partially allowed in his life left him.

Then he was all alone.

The Storm

It wasn't even three months into Katherine's pregnancy when tragedy struck head-on. With plans in full motion, including a waiting nursery and mailed shower invitations, a drunk driver ran a red light into their car, killing her husband and leaving her with a miscarriage.

And the Earth stood still.

Chapter 3

The Healing

For three months, Katherine remained in her old bedroom at her parents' home. Her mother fed and bathed her, for she didn't have the ability to carry on with life. She couldn't comprehend why God had allowed this tragedy, and when she attempted to talk about her feelings, she broke down sobbing, exhausting herself to sleep.

Pain overtook Sharon as she watched her daughter battle unbelievable heartache. She was unsure how to help her through the myriad of emotions. So Sharon poured out her personal suffering to Michael and God, deciding the best thing to do was to remain strong for her daughter, pray continually, and serve in actions, not words. No one even knew if Katherine was aware of her mom treating her like a newborn baby; she was so dead inside she didn't fight her mother taking care of her every need.

Michael took a leave of absence from his firm to run James's company. At this point in life, he could retire exceptionally comfortable but believed it was best to run James's business until Katherine decided what, if anything, to do with it.

Lana lost her sense of living and vibrant personality since the tragedy struck the family's foundation and she wasn't too sure how to interact with them as usual. She felt guilty her life was carrying on normally, and feared that something horrible would happen to her and Eric. This family that loved and cherished one another had taken a hit, with each one desperately trying to understand how to find some normalcy because it seemed as if they would never again be joyful or unite as the fun-loving family they'd created from the beginning.

Then, one day, Michael called Lana over to the house, and together they went to Katherine's room. Michael looked at both his daughters, held his wife's hand, and said, "Your mother has breast cancer, stage two."

It was as if both girls' hearts stopped at once. Nobody said a word.

Michael, always a rock for his wife, said, "We don't know why God is allowing these things in our lives, but His Word says that He will use all things for our good and His glory, and I hope at a later time we will come to understand that. But right now, as a family, we need to pull together and step through this time in our lives believing God will be faithful."

Tears ran down Lana's cheeks.

"I've decided to retire early from my firm and continue to work at James's company until we decide what to do with it," Michael said. Placing up his hand to quiet their protests, he assured, "I've been discussing this with your mother for the past year. I've been sensing a nudging from God to move on, and this confirms that time has come."

Katherine, who had spoken little up to this point, sat up and said, "Mom, I want to take care of you. I will take you to all your appointments."

Katherine loved her mother, and to lose James was beyond any pain she had ever suffered, but her mom was her rock. The thought of losing her mother terrified her beyond anything she could imagine. Their relationship wasn't strained or riddled with misunderstandings. Their mother-daughter relationship was built on trust, forgiveness, and love. Of course, they'd gone through her awkward teenage rebellious years, but Katherine knew God used her mom to speak to her. Her mom knew Katherine better than she knew herself. She was her encourager and motivated her to be her best, live for God, and go after her dreams.

Thankful that Katherine hadn't collapse hearing the news, and out of fearful emotions, Michael said, "Let's do what we do together as a family and kneel before God to pray for this painful time in our lives."

And with that, in Katherine's room, they all knelt beside the bed as Michael prayed for his family. Finding the words in his heart, he poured forth, "Lord, we know that Your Word says we should consider it pure joy whenever we face trials of any kind because they test our faith, making us complete. But Lord, it's so absolutely unrealistic to look at what we are going through and find any joy. We all have been in constant pain, confusion, and tears. The anger is so overwhelming at times that it is scary. But Your Word also says we should not be anxious about anything, that we need to be in constant prayer and ask You for Your strength, and You, Lord, will give us a peace that we don't understand. And Lord, there is no way I can't say we haven't experienced Your peace during this time, and for that, we thank you.

We pray as we look back on this one day, we will see Your hand firmly upon our family, leading us to where You want us to go. Lord, even though we've lost our son-in-law and our grandchild, we know they are rejoicing in heaven with You. And we thank you for that. We pray for Katherine's in-laws, that You are with them and give them peace. We thank you and are so incredibly grateful for sparing our daughter, and even though this is a devastating time for all of us, words cannot express how grateful we are that she's still alive."

Taking a deep breath, hardly able to continue with his heart heavy and terrified, Michael proceeded, "We pray for my wife, their mother, that we together as a family walk through this sickness. Of course, we pray for healing. But above all, we want Your will to be done. Lord, we thank you for the time You have already given us, and You know the greatest desire of my heart is that my wife and I live well into our eighties, relatively healthy, married, living together, and watching our grandchildren grow. We know, though, our desires are completely in Your hands. Please give us wisdom, strength, and the ability to trust You. We pray to be fully open and honest with You, confessing our thoughts, feelings, and sins to You and one another. We ask this in Your name Jesus. Amen."

And with that, the family rose to begin the healing process together.

Even in his death, James took care of his wife, providing a life insurance policy that meant Katherine didn't need to work for at least a year. She decided to use the time off to care for her mother. At some point, a decision about James's company would have to be made, but for now, her focus could only be on living each moment. Right now, her pain was so severe she didn't know if she could even breathe from one moment to the next, let alone think about her husband's company. So instead of shopping for maternity clothes, she went shopping with her mom for wigs as her lovely hair fell out. Instead of morning sickness, she was there for her mom as she was sick from treatments. And, as she focused on her mother, Katherine began to heal and understand that the greatest gift she could give her mother was not to act or pretend to be strong but to be real and honest. In sharing her feelings and thoughts with God and having a genuine relationship with Him, she was able to come back to life and care for her mother so that Sharon could concentrate on healing from her illness and not worry about Katherine's fragile condition.

Her parents had an almost intimidating relationship with God. They weren't "Polly Anna" Christians who said all the right things and always had a Bible verse handy. No, her parents truly believed in God. Theirs was a real relationship with Him. It wasn't always a pretty relationship because they were what were called "first generation" Christians, so they made many mistakes and wrong choices. However, as they grew in Christ and followed His commands, it became a beloved investment, and God paid well. Sharon and Michael always insisted on waiting on the Lord, which at times caused much confusion and frustration, but they taught their girls that God's way was the only way.

And because of this, both girls came to faith in Christ at thirteen. Yet, for the first time, they were both facing the stark reality of whether they wanted to live their lives for God even though they weren't sure of the outcome. They held anger toward God, especially Katherine. That's what Sharon truly feared because she remembered once having what she thought was righteous anger toward God and sinning in a way that at times still caused her complete shame and hurt.

Chapter 4

David's Healing

As David's collarbone healed, his intense love for football drove him to stop living his life out of the bottle. It wasn't difficult since he'd seen the consequences of his mother's choices. David had spent the last year trying to recover from his injury only to begin reliving horrible childhood memories. Since David physically was incapacitated with no one to care for him at home, his depressed mind wandered to his unloving parents. He relived his feelings of abandonment and neglect, believing he was worthless. Even after his collarbone healed, mentally, he couldn't get his head back in the game, causing his once precise passes to fall inaccurate and sloppy.

His loss of confidence led to him becoming average at best. When Miami didn't renew his contract, critics had a field day with him, especially when no other team readily picked him up. David lashed out at the reporters, making excuses for his poor performance, blaming his teammates and the coaching staff. Now he stood as a national joke, which only made his game even worse. He was no longer the glory boy and he hated it.

Women saw him as a loser, which left David with hardly a selection of choice. Only those who wanted his money gave him any attention, and he resented being used to shell out cash. His outward appearance reflected his inward thoughts. His once rugged, manly looks and boyish charm, which had made women swoon, transformed into something ugly. His dark, thick, wavy locks of hair were now unruly, greasy, and in dire need of a cut. Eyes formerly an intense shade of blue with piercing determination were now gray and bitter. He no longer had a smile that lit up his entire face; in fact, now he never smiled. An overgrown beard hid most of his face and a hat hid his awful hair. David's lean, well-proportioned, muscular frame, which touted a massive barrel chest, disappeared since he hunched over weakly. Covering himself in hoodies and sweats, he hid from the world and himself.

Out of everything going on within, what bothered him the most was a fear he now had of life. He never thought that losing his confidence on the field would become a factor he'd need to deal with, and it ultimately paralyzed his mental ability to perform at his previous stature. Of course, he had known one day his career would end, but he figured he would coach. That future was in jeopardy too because his once laser focus was now gone and he could no longer read the field.

David shut down, talking to no one, although, in truth, he had no one to talk to. His grandmother at this point had passed away, and his parents, well, were being his parents who couldn't care less. Worn out from answering the same questions from reporters, hearing people tell him they felt sorry for his injury, caused him to isolate even more. Maybe this happens to players when they retire, he thought. The only thing David looked forward to was getting home to shut off the world.

When he was sent to California as back-up quarterback, the last of his passion drained away, and now he hardly ever played. In an unhealthy state of mind, sitting on the bench for three years made the young almost thirty-year-old look like a washed-up old man.

Chapter 5

The Rejuvenation

God was faithful to the family. They had prayed consistently through the past three years, and God made Himself real, guiding them through the valley so each discovered their heart again.

Lana's personality sparkled once more. No longer the depressed household, it was instead filled with laughter from her comedic outbursts, and she was often found imitating her father's crazy dancing in the kitchen. Missed and welcomed, Lana's humor connected the family. And her role developed as she took over the cooking responsibilities from her mother. Her time following Sharon around the kitchen as a child paid off as she found her craft creating incredibly tasty meals. But now Lana decided on only healthy, organic meals for her family, employing food as an effective prevention and life-giving alternate. No, she didn't stop creating luscious desserts, but the family was not eating them daily any longer.

Her efforts in the kitchen paid off. Sharon remained strong and healthy, even during her treatments. Her dad lost the fifteen pounds he'd always complained about, and Katherine gained back the healthy weight she had lost during her grieving. The family teased Lana that she had landed Eric through his stomach, and he agreed. Following her mother's example, the two fed the homeless and those in need.

Sharon had a full recovery. Since she didn't like to sit around feeling sorry for herself, she redecorated a few rooms during her illness, which encouraged Katherine go back to her home and clean out James's belongings. She only kept some of his shirts as pajamas and donated everything else, including their bed, for she couldn't bear to sleep in it without him.

Finished with treatments, Sharon felt like her old self again, so she went to work with Michael at James's sports management company since they were losing contracts. The athletes weren't comfortable not knowing the company's future, and even though Michael was a renowned businessman, it was not his area of expertise.

As Sharon went to the office to help with administration work, Katherine began to join her. At first, she only stayed for lunch, but eventually remained longer and longer to help her mom, taking on small tasks. Sharon knew her daughter and gave her projects which she was sure would light a flame inside Katherine for the first time since the death of her husband.

Sharon was proud of her girls and told them often. But Katherine was proud of her mother and wanted to be just like her. God used Sharon to heal Katherine. By taking care of her mom, Katherine couldn't focus on her problems, which somehow lessened the pain. Now, even more thankful to God for the gift of her parents, she couldn't imagine where she would be without them. To Katherine, it seemed as if God had allowed her mother's illness to teach her how to recover from a devastating loss. Although she wouldn't be so arrogant to think she knew God's plans or understood His ways, the thought gave her comfort and moved her closer to Him.

Thus, the family stood firmly planted in their relationship with God.

The Company

James's company dwindled to four clients—two in basketball and two in baseball. These athletes were not stars or household names that could keep the company afloat, but Katherine and her parents weren't ready to shut down the business just yet. Since they had wealth, keeping the doors open wasn't about making money. However, they didn't want to lose money either. There was just a sense that they should continue on for some unknown reason.

Around this time, Reggie Johnson, an established Cleveland receiver, was arrested and convicted of drug possession, which sent him to jail for eight months. He lost everything, but an unexpected event happened while he was there. Through a prison ministry, Reggie became a man of God, accepting Jesus Christ as his Savior. Reggie wasn't sure what would happen once he was released. He asked God to restore his family and allow him a couple more years to play with Cleveland. Hearing his heart, God answered those prayers, and more.

Not a single management company wanted to represent Reggie since he was at the end of his career and a maintenance nightmare to boot. No one wanted a "born again" deadbeat who wasn't talented and possibly passing off a fake conversion story, likely to eventually fall from grace. Who could blame the skepticism?

But Michael took an interest in Reggie. Along with Sharon and Katherine, they met with the football player and his wife, Grace, spending hours talking. It was an unconventional meeting where Reggie spoke about his conversion in prison and hopes that God would use his story to show kids how God changed his life. Katherine saw the tears of a broken and repented man. They weren't sure how it would all work out, but the family decided to take Reggie on as their client.

Katherine still needed to pick up where James left off, despite not having James's usual business contacts and his firm grip on running the company. Since she didn't know what to do, Michael taught her the art of negotiation along with other aspects, setting her on the path of becoming a strong businesswoman.

Sharon knew sports was a man's world, so she concentrated on teaching Katherine how to interact with men who might demean, ridicule, and treat her as a sex object. Afraid she couldn't cut it, Katherine asked her parents to take over while remaining their assistant. Not one to allow fear to overtake her girls, Sharon pulled Katherine aside and looked her in the eyes. "If you listen and learn from your father and allow me to strengthen your weakness, there's no doubt you will succeed."

Intimidation was rooted deeply in Katherine's heart. "I'm not you," she said to her mother. "There's no way I can ever interact with people the way you do. I don't have your wit. You think so fast on your feet. I can't."

"You can. And you will," Sharon insisted.

Katherine, of course, protested. But she had a fire to pursue this venture. As her mother continued to encourage her, Katherine wrestled with understanding if this was God's will for her life. If she took charge of the business, would she be walking down the wrong path, and if so, what would God do to redirect her steps?

Even though Katherine had recovered from the devastating loss of her husband and baby, she was still unsettled spiritually, not always having peace with God. Her deep-seated struggle was understanding her desires versus God's plans for her life and if she was following His lead. Katherine had had her life planned out until the accident completely shattered her dreams. Once the constant goal-setter and dream-chaser, she now attempted to only live for each day because she knew all too well that life was short. She wanted to try and enjoy each day being content.

But her mother had been watching Katherine, knowing she was limiting her world and settling for status quo. Sharon would never do anything less than bring the best out of her daughters. Yes, her girls should live each day content, but Sharon knew God didn't create people to live life on auto pilot, fearful of taking risks or allowing life altering moments to halt their divine trajectory. Sharon always knew one day she would share her shameful past and believed now was the time to show how God was faithful to those whom He loved.

Chapter 6

The Sin

Later that afternoon, because of her conversation with Katherine that day and after talking with Michael, Sharon called her girls and son-in-law over for dinner. Moving to the living room afterward, Sharon began, "I need to tell you something, a story."

The girls looked at one another, fearing the worse. Lana asked, "Do you have cancer again?"

"No," her father answered. "Your mother wants to tell you a story that no one else knows except a pastor's wife and the two of us."

The words didn't comfort the girls since their mother's face showed deep sadness.

Sharon searched for words to begin. Tears stung her eyes, her chin quivered, but she chuckled slightly. "You know I was afraid to have children…let alone girls." Her eye twinkled even through the obvious pain. "God gave me you two, anyway. A blessing that I can't even put in words."

Even though they both already knew her fear of being a mother, especially to girls, this didn't help ease Katherine and Lana's concern.

"In any family, there are certain struggles—sins and fears that should remain between a select group of people, only friends who would give good Godly advice, speak the truth, and not gossip."

This was nothing new; even Eric recalled these conversations. It was confusing why their mother was reiterating common knowledge, but they'd known since they were little that sharing the truth was a practice that created their nurturing family unit.

"There are also certain conversations that should be kept between a husband and wife only, like arguments, disagreements, and struggles which children should not be privy to. It builds a strong marriage, trust, and a deep bond."

The girls looked at one another, burrowing their eyebrows and tilting their heads, trying to understand what their mother was attempting to say. Of course, they knew their parents loved each other and had disagreements, but they weren't sure what this had to do with anything.

"I want to tell you the reason I was afraid to have girls," Sharon confessed. "You already know my mom was deemed…uh, mentally ill. And you know about the abuse and my fear of becoming like her, possibly abusing you. But there is something I haven't shared."

It was not a secret their grandmother had been admitted into three mental hospitals at different times of her life, sending Sharon and her siblings to three foster homes since they had no one to care for them. They also knew their mother's dad had checked out, leaving them after marrying and divorcing her mom twice. The explosive arguments involving police or the violent physical assaults were nothing compared to the mental and emotional slander Sharon suffered. It all combined to riddle their mother with anxiety, guilt, and doubt for most of her life.

Looking to understand how to tell her story, Sharon silently prayed, for she was full of shame. "I was molested very young." Closing her eyes to keep tears intact and steady herself, she said again, "Very young."

"Oh, Mom!" Katherine breathed and reached out for her hand, which her father was already holding, followed by Lana.

"I'm not making excuses," she said as tears leaked out.

"Who, Mom?" Lana asked.

Shaking her head, Sharon proceeded. "It doesn't matter. Maybe one day I can tell you, but I'm not ready…just let me get through this."

Her daughters understood and settled back. Eric held his wife's hand.

Sharon wanted to get through her story quickly, get it off her shoulders since she knew her girls thought she was without sin. Yes, sometimes she didn't speak in love or had to apologize for a sin, which they viewed as minor, but she knew in their minds she always seemed to talk, console, and respond correctly in every situation, which wasn't always the case.

"I couldn't have been more than four years old when it began." Painful humiliation made itself known with a whisper. "It continued until I was sixteen."

Katherine grabbed her heart.

"It was by a female."

"Who?" the girls demanded.

"Girls, let your mother tell the story. She's not ready for that yet," Michael said.

22

Sharon could barely talk, couldn't see through her tears, but wanted to get through the excruciating past. "At first, being so young, I didn't understand, but eventually I realized it was abnormal."

Her daughters were instantly at her feet, tears flooding everyone's face. Even Eric couldn't hold back his emotions.

Pulling herself together, almost chuckling, she went on. Making direct eye contact with her girls, she lovingly smiled. "I knew I wasn't gay. From a young age, I was always attracted to men, and I believe by God's grace I knew they liked me too."

"They still like her," Michael said, making his daughters laugh since they knew all too well that their mother, even at her age, had a remarkable sensuality that men desired.

"Those memories tortured me, even though I buried them deep. I was, and still am, ashamed. Of course, confused and angry too." Reaching out, she lovingly stroked her girl's hair then got down to their level, sitting on the floor with them, leaning against the sofa. "That was one reason I was so angry at God and why it appalled me that I had to believe I was a sinner, ask for forgiveness, and accept Jesus as my Savior."

Kathrine and Lana already knew that three days after Sharon turned eighteen, she packed up her belongings, transferred schools, and left home to move in with her grandma. Being the last one home after her sister and brother fled, she was the only target for her mother's abuse and it was not something she would stand for any longer. After barely graduating, she found a job and an apartment with her sister. And within a year of being away from her mother, she accepted Jesus Christ as her Savior.

"Anyway, I became in bondage to men," she revealed. "It's something I never told you, but I struggled with men. It was obsessive. Mostly, internally. I was too insecure to show a man my feelings because I never thought I was good enough to date. So they became friends. I didn't date a lot. You know I didn't want to marry, but deep down, I wanted a family."

They grinned and adored their mother.

Touching Michael's hand, his smile delighting in his wife, she knew she was fully loved. "I felt like a new creation in Christ after I accepted Him as my Savior. I asked God to bring me a nice man, not to marry," she chuckled, "but just a nice man. That was my first prayer, and God answered by giving me your father."

Lana looked at Eric as he got on the floor next to her, listening intently.

"You already know that came with years of struggles before we married." Smiling brightly, she said, "Our wedding was beautiful. Such an answered prayer. The wedding night, I felt set apart." Blushing, she said, "You already know we remained pure before God, but our honeymoon was painful."

This confused the girls. They didn't know this side of the story. Of course, they knew their parents remained virgins until marriage, but their painful honeymoon hadn't been mentioned.

"Your father pulled away from me almost immediately on our wedding night, although at first I didn't notice and he continued to distance himself until we came home, neither of us speaking to one another."

"I was afraid," Michael said. "It wasn't until years later that I realized I feared your Mom leaving me. You know my parents aren't very nurturing." Katherine nodded, remembering how she told her parents at three years old she didn't feel like Michael's parents loved her. "I didn't understand that sort of love or intimacy," Michael confessed.

"I tried to talk to your dad, but he shut down, and to make things worse, he started looking at other women. I know, it sounds…I don't know…maybe silly? But to me, it was a devastating three days after we married."

Despising her past, desiring a different outcome than her childhood, Sharon determined her marriage wouldn't repeat her parents' disaster. It wasn't the case. Her attempts to create a normal bond with Michael turned ugly. As she reached out to discuss their problems, he blamed her, arguing and criticizing her efforts to establish a warm connection. Eventually, she kept him at a distance, and over time, Sharon shut down emotionally. Therefore, lovemaking was tense since her body wouldn't blossom naturally for him, infuriating Michael further.

At a young stage in her marriage, the loneliness and hatred she felt for her husband and God fueled the anger planted in Sharon's heart. To believe Michael was a gift from Him became a joke that wasn't funny. To finally marry after not having a desire to for so many years only to end up in a loveless, hostile relationship magnified her belief she was worthless. Hardly an education, no parents who cared, and a husband who sneered about life—what a situation. Again, she was the target of abuse.

Things only turned worse as Michael lost his job and his side business fell apart. That landed him on the sofa, deep in depression with even more reason to spew out hate. She wondered what kept them married. He never laid a hand on her. Instead, he destroyed her with words, attacking her joyful spirit and grateful outlook on life. Drawing on survival methods learned in her youth, Sharon remained away from home and hardly spoke when she was there. Her personality shined at work, though, naturally leading to advancement.

"We were married just a couple years when I got promoted," Sharon said. "I met a man, felt attracted to him. I prayed for help." She wept. "I couldn't tell your father. I knew I was being tempted but didn't know what to do. I struggled for a year, and finally I told God if He wouldn't help me overcome my feelings, then to give me over to my sin, and that's what happened."

Confused, Katherine asked, "Are you telling us you had an affair?"

"Yes."

The girls were shocked. Katherine moved slightly away to comprehend what she just heard, removing her hand from her mother's. Lana leaned into Eric. It was so unbelievable. Their mother, their role model, had just confessed to committing adultery. A deeply committed believer and follower of God had cheated on their dad. It had appeared the model marriage.

Michael caught their attention. "I don't want you to look at your mom any differently. We were both different people back then. You girls weren't born, and we didn't have a clue how to love one another. We brought so much baggage into our marriage and expected each other to fix it."

"How long, Mom? How long was the affair?" Katherine asked.

"A year."

Katherine's voice didn't hide her dismay. "One year?" she trembled.

Sharon knew the next part of her confession wouldn't help much, but she continued. "It would have been longer if God hadn't step in," she said. "I didn't…we didn't, um, have sex…but we did other things. Thankfully God preserved that for your father. But we were headed in that direction." Joyful tears for God's goodness and gratitude for His protection of her even while she sinned slipped down Sharon's cheeks. Even the sisters were relieved, softening their faces and letting out a sigh.

"Then, one day, when I was coming home from work, I began to shake since I knew God was speaking to my heart and I was ignoring Him. For a week, I trembled, and then God directed. You know His voice. He wanted me to confess to your father, but of course, I didn't. I settled on ending the affair and keeping it a secret. But God wanted more." Her eyes sparkled even through tears, saying, "It was as if God said, 'Either you tell Michael or I will, and you don't want Me to tell him.'" So I confessed."

"What happened, Dad?" Lana asked.

Sharon answered for him. "He took it much better than I ever expected."

"God was working on my heart," Michael said. "You know the story. I had found a job an hour away from home. There was hardly any work to keep me busy and I had too much time on my hands. God was intervening on our behalf since I used that time to listen to gospel radio."

"God protected us," Sharon said with a thankful heart.

"Yes, He did," Michael agreed.

"But it wasn't easy. I didn't end the affair willingly. I did, though, out of fear and obligation. My heart wasn't into our marriage or my relationship with God. I was ready to leave your father. I was fed up with life, abuse, and following God, which seemed only to lead to hurt. So I continued on with the affair."

"Wow," Katherine whispered, moving further away from her mother.

"I was defiant and, in my way, sticking up for myself for the first time in my life." They heard her chuckling mixed with sadness. "Ridiculously, I was blaming your Father."

"I was in pain, but I listened and prayed," Michael said. "I had no intentions of leaving your mother. I loved her from the moment I met her and knew I wanted to marry her."

"God used your father as a sounding board. He wasn't argumentative, even when he continually showed me I was sinning. He was loving, and eventually, I loved him too."

"We went to counseling, and she no longer hid the secrets of her past. I saw your mother weak, understanding how the abuse had taken over her life. My heart became tender as I watched her work through the shame she'd never revealed."

"Your dad helped me to see clearly my full-blown sin. I know that sounds crazy, but ask anyone you know who is alcoholic or a thief and you'll see they can justify their behavior." Then she looked directly at Katherine and said, "Just ask Reggie how he justified his addiction and he'll give you his story."

Katherine understood.

"When I finally was convicted, I cried and couldn't stop for what seemed like months. I took a leave of absence from my job and eventually went to work with your father. My heart literally felt like it was broken, like it actually had a tear in it. I was an adulterer. My mom cheated on my dad several times, something I never thought I would do. That guy had a wife and children, and I was absolutely horrified by what I did to the family, your father, and God."

Michael caressed her hand.

"I was in counseling for years. It took a long time to heal from my past." Looking at her husband, Sharon added, "And from our broken marriage."

"Some areas are still in repair," he said.

With a light laugh, she answered, "I think that will always be the case. We are sinners and will always need to work through all the problems that arise from our sin nature."

"Why, Mom?" Katherine asked. "Why are you telling us this now? Did something happen?

"Well, I always knew I would tell you girls," she said. "I put it off for years. Obviously, not something I'm proud of. Hardly anyone knows."

"At that time in our lives, there were too many Christian family members and friends who were rather judgmental," Michael said. "It was important for your mother to focus on healing rather than deal with judgment from others. It was no one's business, and I didn't want anyone looking at your mother any differently. We told you this because we trust you. We aren't trying to portray a perfect marriage, and you know that. But, just like we don't discuss our business matters with those we don't trust or who aren't at a level where they can give us wise counsel, we don't discuss our personal life either."

Looking at Katherine, Sharon said, "I wanted you to know." Switching her gaze to Lana, "And I couldn't leave you out." Making eye contact with Katherine again, she added, "I understand your doubt...maybe resistance...in taking James's place but God is frugal. He promises in Joel 2:25, 'I will repay you for the years eaten by locusts.'"

Michael whispered, "Amen."

Tears spilled freely. "I should have been a lesbian. I should have been an alcoholic, drug-addict, or promiscuous. I should be divorced several times and have children from multiple men. I should have been married to someone who beats me, cheats on me, or living in jail. I was hardly educated to work in an office, let alone support myself and not go on welfare, thus repeating my childhood."

Still sitting on the floor, huddled around their mother, the siblings thanked God for breaking the generational cycle. Both girls were grateful, breathing peacefully.

"I should have abused you," she whispered.

"You aren't your mother," Katherine reminded, holding her hand.

"By the grace of God!" Sharon praised.

Michael nodded.

"By the grace of God, I came out of that sin, planted firmly in His word," she hailed. "By the grace of God, our marriage survived. And by the grace of God, I learned how to love."

Katherine moved closer.

"That sin, my sin, revealed my heart and its pride. I hadn't forgiven anyone for their sins, yet God and your father not only forgave me but wrapped their arms around me tenderly. I thought I was better than others since I didn't repeat the dysfunction, but I was just turning a blind eye to my behavior, justifying its existence," Sharon confessed. "My heart was hard, and God used my folly to humble and soften it. If God and your father can forgive and still love me, I have no excuse not to do so for myself. There are so many hurting people in this world who will do anything to deaden the pain. Because your father opened his heart to me and helped me through my bondage, I can't help but extend a hand to others who are hurting and believing their bondage will relieve pain. That's how God began a ministry within me."

Katherine smiled for her mother always brought life to God's saving grace.

"I know God will use you too, and I know you will continue in James's place."

Katherine sniffled, agreeing, "Okay."

Sharon then specifically addressed Eric and Lana saying, "We are here for you if you ever need to talk to us about anything. You can trust us and know we will fight to help you through whatever you are struggling with as individuals or as a married couple."

Eric and Lana's smiles showed they already knew this.

"I've always told you both that you are better than me. I was in complete fear when you lost James and your baby because of the anger you would experience and what it might cause you to do. But I can see you are working through those emotions. I'm so thankful to God that you didn't take a sinful path the way I did. And my pain was not nearly as intense or as sudden as yours."

"Mom, it's because you didn't push me. I had to rest."

"That's what I believed God led me to do, and I believe He will lead you now too."

Katherine felt a closer bond with her mother since confession in their family led to deeper intimacy. She always had viewed her mother as intimidating, having a wealth of wisdom. Who could live up to that pillar? But now, she understood her mother's entanglement in sin exposed her weakness, her reliance on herself rather than God. And God, being frugal, used that sin in her life to meet others exactly where they were in theirs—with a woman who wasn't judging, forcing, or criticizing, but who boldly prayed, serving as needed.

"Okay, let's figure this out together," Katherine said. "Let's see where I can go with James's business."

Relief flooded over Sharon that God once again had used her past to help those she loved. The family talked through details of the affair, their respective struggles, and their fears in life, ending the evening in prayer.

God is indeed frugal.

Chapter 7

The Transformation

Sharon spent the next three years teaching her daughter the art of conversation. Katherine entered a man's world, feeling out of place. To be skilled when speaking to any individual was essential, but responding to those challenging, undermining, or objectifying types took a level of sophistication beyond her age.

Both Sharon's daughters were beautiful, but it was their personalities that set them apart from every other pretty face. And because Katherine had a such dynamite personality, her beauty was all that more attractive to men, especially since she was single. Yet Katherine had no interest in dating and felt called to remain single even though she was young, stylish, and in the prime of life. Rather, she was eager to immerse herself into the business as a tribute to her late husband.

She studied her competition, both men and women. She analyzed as if she was playing the game of football on the field herself. She fast was becoming an expert as she listened to journalists question players and coaches, making mental notes of responses and reactions, often predicting the outcome of the questions. Marketing Reggie Johnson became her playground. She brainstormed with her parents, dreaming, creating, and analyzing how to turn around his career, establish his name, and give credence to his testimony. All authentic, nothing fake. Reggie's aim wasn't to make money but to make good on God's character and grace upon his transformation. He and the family were a close-knit team, and it paid off immensely.

There were plenty of wonderful women in the industry who'd paved the road for her, and she desired to earn their respect, which she did. Katherine had no interest in riding on her father's coattails, often neglecting to mention her maiden name. Michael was a highly sought-after, deeply respected man, but Katherine's calling was to stand on her own merits, firmly rooted in her Savior's plan.

It took time, and certainly wasn't easy, but she earned her way up the ladder. Like anyone hired newly into a company, it took time to establish trust, credentials, and identity. Yes, it was her business, but as in any place in life, she knew it was more important to love others according to the golden rule. And how did she desire to love? Respectfully, courteously, and thoughtfully mixed with much laughter. Her strides paid off as she became well-esteemed, building a worthy list of business contacts along the way. Of course, they were only local, but they were solid, productive, and profitable. And her favorite part? Working with her male counterparts, for she adored their playful, bantering interactions.

Katherine divided the company, keeping 51 percent ownership and giving the remaining to her parents. Since her father loved baseball, he headed up that division while Katherine's devotion to football kept her busy. Sharon had no problem looking after basketball, but they all worked closely together, collaborating daily, looking out for the best interest of the eight clients entrusted to them.

Since the family was charitable, they expanded their giving opportunities by organizing a local foundation. Involving their clients and teaming up with generous Cleveland athletes and business executives, they held four major fundraising events a year, raising millions of dollars for worthy causes. Lana and Eric pitched in their expertise, catering the festive events, which had the added benefit of placing their restaurant on the Cleveland map.

They created one of the finest "mom and pop" management companies around. They were known as trustworthy professionals who built deep relationships with their clients, business associates, and colleagues. The eight athletes under contract weren't elite by any means; mainly players who did their job but weren't established household names. Except for Reggie, who was born, raised, and devoted to Cleveland.

Michael, an investor by trade, taught their client athletes to invest wisely for the future and expounded on the benefits of giving. He knew the value of being as debt-free as possible and not being a slave to possessions that weren't lasting. He explained the burden of debt would prohibit them from taking advantage of opportunities that could better their lives, and those of others. These men reaped the benefit of his teachings, massing wealth tenfold.

All in all, Katherine was proud of her little company, and knew James would be too. It was her love, her baby, and she cared for it as a special gift from God. Often, late in the day, Katherine paused in her office overlooking Lake Erie as the sun was setting and all went home for the evening. She'd wonder just how far God would take her in the business. As usual, her heart leaped for joy in these moments before she quickly realized she was dreaming. Better to stop and be content for the day and not think about tomorrow. She knew all too well how brief life was.

Chapter 8

The City

Almost five years after his injury, sitting on the bench, there was another change. This time, David was going to Cleveland. No athlete wanted to go to that team or the city. The team had never gone to the Super Bowl since its inception back in 1967 and had only appeared in a handful of playoffs. All Cleveland sports were losing teams. The only good thing the city was known for was its stellar hospitals. Outside of that, David felt there was no reason to visit the town. Plus, he wasn't even going to be the starting quarterback. He felt like a loser going to a loser city.

So now David headed to the Mistake by the Lake, as the city frequently was known. Cleveland fans were loyal, because what else could they do with their time. The weather wasn't all that tremendous; only half the year was sunny. Downtown was a joke, had hardly any life at all. In his opinion, Cleveland was a deadbeat city no one wanted to call home, and now he had to leave beautiful California to continue with his career. Moving early April to be ready for team activities was his only option if he still wanted to be on the field.

Plus, he was required to be involved with the community. David didn't mind working with children or helping charities, but he didn't enjoy hearing fans tell him how great he used to be or listening to their pep talks to "help" him get back to his game. Even interviewers asked the same questions: "When do you see your game improving" or "How hard is it to be a back-up when you were on the fast track to becoming one of the greatest quarterbacks of your time?" He hated people feeling sorry for him and hated answering the same old stupid questions. That's why he remained home. No way would he go out with his football buddies and listen to them brag about their stellar performance. At least in Cleveland, he didn't know anyone, so it wouldn't be hard to hide.

The News

Word about David coming to Cleveland spread like wildfire. It split many fans. Some were very excited about his addition to the team and others thought his washed up self was a waste of time. Local radio personality, Mike Trino, was less than thrilled and in no way hid his sentiments. Trino had amassed a rather large following because of his frankness regarding local, newsworthy content concerning his beloved home, Cleveland. No matter how admired or talented an athlete, especially a celebrity athlete, played for any team if they were disrespectful to his hometown, Trino called them out.

Once again, Trino was lighting up the phone lines with his comments about David coming to Cleveland. "He's a washed-up head case who will only harm the team with his attitude." Trino was right. David was miserable, and it openly showed. He hated Cleveland and barely hid the fact that he wasn't pleased with the trade, but what was he to do? No other teams had made him offers. Even in interviews, David cut reporters off mid-sentence and came across as cocky to mask his inadequacy on the field and also in life. David was not looking forward to any interviews with Trino and planned to avoid him at all costs.

The Introduction

It was a big day at the stadium, not to the public perhaps, but to the journalists and local news. Today the media had access to the locker room to interview the players and coaches. They packed the place. Katherine was on her way to see Reggie who was scheduled to speak with Trino. She knew it would be intense.

She dressed professionally, as always. Both daughters followed their mother's style. All loved lipstick and high heels, and today was no exception. Katherine wore a pretty, lady-like, pure white dress with matching white patent leather belt and spectacular heels. The outfit screamed class, elegance, and sophistication. Only she knew it was a steal; she'd found it on the clearance rack, which was where most of her wardrobe was purchased. She'd swept her long, wavy hair up in a modern French twist that showcased her big, chocolate, doe eyes. The perfect shade of lipstick highlighted her creamy skin, completing the look flawlessly. Even though she worked in a predominately male industry, her attire was always feminine and tailored to suit her figure, though she revealed no cleavage or excessive leg. She wasn't comfortable in such pieces. Her tastes ran to interesting neck and hemlines which highlighted her naturally beautiful face and sculpted calves. And, of course, her small waist held its own merits.

Even before showing her credentials, she hugged the security guard, happily talking up a storm. Joe was someone she had gotten to know through the years. Katherine had established friendships and relationships with those who worked within the Cleveland organization at varying levels. She was no snob; she just truly enjoyed being around people and loved talking about the game of football.

Upon entering the locker room, her heart beat rapidly. She loved this place, all its excitement, energy, and warmth. She was greeted by plenty. It was so crowded that it was nearly impossible to navigate through the space, so she went around to the physical therapy room to get to Reggie's locker. It wasn't much of an easier trek since she bumped into many familiar faces, one being Evan, a player she has gotten to know. News had been announced only minutes ago that he would be making his home in Seattle, and Katherine was glad she had the opportunity to say goodbye for now.

As soon as he noticed Katherine, Evan stopped talking to a player and grabbed her tightly, hugging and kissing her cheek. It was their typical greeting, common among many players, colleagues, and even some coaching staff.

"I'm so sad to see you go to Seattle. I will miss you so much!" Katherine said.

Evan was not a client, however, they had a genuine affection for each other, though it was nothing more than that. Katherine made it clear to all she had no intentions of dating, which she conveyed professionally yet firmly every time. It was accepted since everyone knew losing her husband had had a profound impact on that part of her life. Katherine wasn't lonely since she had her family, specifically her mother to talk through her inmost thoughts. She was perfectly content remaining single.

"I will miss your smiling face too!" Evan said touching her cheek. "But this is a good move for me. I wasn't getting a lot of play here and will more often in Seattle."

She could feel his excitement. It was true Cleveland didn't play him, something she didn't understand. Now he had his shot to reach his full potential.

Always a gentleman, which was the actual reason she was fond of him, Evan said, "I'm not sure if you've ever met Dave Mann. As you know, he's come here as a quarterback."

Katherine turned toward the man next to Evan to shake his hand yet could barely recognize the star player. She had no idea it was him. Sure, she'd seen him on TV sitting on the sidelines, but this was not the David Mann she remembered watching when he was leading a team. He looked so different with his overgrown hair and beard, both making it hard to see his face, but she was no less excited to meet him. She cherished the memories of watching him in his heyday with James and her family. He was such a fascinating player.

Lighting her face with a fantastic smile, willing everything within her to remain calm, she tried not to sound like some obsessive fanatic. "Hi, I'm Katherine. It's so nice to meet you!"

David shook Katherine's hand, and before he spoke a word, Evan said, "Katherine is the owner of CMI Sports Agency." Smiling at her, Evan asked, "Cleveland Management Institute, right?"

Blushing profusely, she said, "Yes," quickly adding, "My parents are also owners." She wanted to give them credit for their hard work and dedication because there simply wouldn't be a company without them. "We are so excited that you are part of this team. I was so sorry to hear about your broken collarbone and was hoping it wouldn't affect your game…"

Immediately, David grew irritated and tense. Here it is again, he thought, someone else feeling sorry for him and ready to give him advice about his game. He cut her off. "Look, I'm not interested in becoming a client of yours, so you can knock off the act of kindness."

Katherine was stunned. His comment actually made her step back from him. She was blindsided, and her usual quick-witted response failed to come. Her feelings hurt that somehow he misinterpreted her kindness as a sales pitch.

Re-centering herself, not looking to prolong the conversation, she spoke her heart. "I'm sorry if it came across as if I was trying to sign you on as a client. I only wanted to welcome you to Cleveland and let you know we are excited to have you here."

"Cleveland? Cleveland?" he said with hostile contempt. "You are trying to welcome me to this dump of a city? Do you actually think I want to be here? Who wants to come to Cleveland?"

And at that, Evan spoke up, but the professional side of Katherine that had dealt with these types of personalities countless times took over. She looked right into David's eyes with her big, brown, sad beauties and said the truth. "You are right, not a lot of athletes want to come to Cleveland."

Evan's mouth dropped open.

"I'm sorry to be rude, but I'm meeting Reggie for an interview." She hugged Evan one last time, saying, "Good luck at Seattle. I'll miss you. Let's keep in touch." Looking back at David, she said simply, "It was nice to meet you."

As she walked away, she couldn't believe how nasty David was to her and how disappointed she was. Seeing Reggie, she cleared her mind, not giving her recent conversation a further thought so she could be there for her client.

After Katherine left, Evan hit David. "You are an idiot, Mann!"

"Come on! You can't wait to get out of Cleveland and go to Seattle!"

"I'm not talking about that, you moron! You treated her like a complete fool! She wasn't trying to sign you up at her firm. That family doesn't operate like that."

"Please! You are naïve if you think she wasn't going to give me a sales pitch."

"Dude, you aren't that good of a player anymore." This silenced him. Evan went onto tell David about Katherine and her parents, pointing out, "This community and these teams have a significant amount of respect for that family."

He also told David about Katherine's devastating loss. He praised Sharon's involvement in charitable work and how she invited top-ranking athletes to Cleveland to be part of the family's fund-raising events. Through their company, they'd opened up connections to extend outreach, raising millions of dollars for notable causes and needy families.

David felt guilty for reacting to Katherine the way he had, especially after hearing she lost her husband and child. But he was already prepared for the media to blast him with the same questions, well wishes, and comments about being washed-up. He reasoned he'd just stopped her before she could go down that same road.

Finally, Katherine made her way over to Reggie. Grace, his wife, and children were with him too. She was glad. Greeting them warmly, she enjoyed catching up on their life since she'd seen them last. "Are you ready for your interview?" she said, focusing on Reggie.

"Yeah," he said as his heartbeat spiked, but he reminded himself out loud. "I got my family here, and you know God will help me through this."

Reggie was not shy to talk about God. This interview was important since he was announcing his retirement, effectively making this his last season. Reggie knew saying those words would be emotional since he loved the game, but his heart told him it was time to move on to another chapter in life, one of which he was uncertain of at this point.

The Interview

David dreaded going out to his locker and dealing with the media. Just as he was about to enter the locker room, David glimpsed Mike Trino hugging and kissing Katherine. That caught him as strange since Trino was known as such a hard-ass. No time to analyze his thoughts, however, since the media quickly swarmed him, firing off questions.

There was quite a commotion over David. Even Katherine couldn't help but look over at the scene, though only for a moment since she wanted to focus all her attention on Reggie and was happy to see Trino. Over the years, Katherine had formed a solid working relationship with the sports caster. He respected the family for their charitable work, but he was still Trino, giving her a hard time. Katherine was one of the few who knew how to handle him, and they enjoyed their bantering moments.

They got down to business. Reggie followed Trino's welcome with "First, I want to thank God, my Lord and Savior, for giving me the ability to stand here with my family and to play this game for one more year." Then, the interview underway, Trino asked, "So Reggie, what are your thoughts about having Dave as a back-up quarterback? I heard he was less than pleased to come to Cleveland."

Reggie was tickled by the question but answered, "I'm sure Dave will do fine. You know, I haven't heard those rumors." Reggie's smile lit up his face as he pointed at the mob surrounding David. "You are more than welcome to go ask him yourself."

Katherine and his family chuckled, amusing Trino. "Point taken, Reggie. I know there are still several months before the first official game but do you have any predictions for this upcoming season?"

"I expect this will be one of the greatest seasons of my career since I will retire after this one." Tears wet his eyes as the admission touched his heart. "I am so thankful God has allowed me to play this game for all these years and even return to it after I spent time in prison. I will always wish we could have given the fans more than we did, but I'm grateful I've had the opportunity to play for them. These are the most devoted fans anywhere."

Trino agreed.

"I want to go out on that field each Sunday cherishing the time and really give it my all."

"Are you saying you haven't given it your all in the past?" Trino asked, raising his eyebrows.

"No," Reggie said, "I only want to remember this last season and have no regrets."

"Do you have regrets?"

"Well, of course. I regret not playing at 100 percent before going to jail," Reggie admitted, "but since I've been back, I've given everything in me, and I won't let up in this last season."

"The fans know you have given it your all," Trino said. "I know you've never held back."

"Then how come you've blasted me over the years?"

Chuckling delightfully, Trino exclaimed, "Well, I have a job to do!"

The interview continued flawlessly with much respect and light-hearted discussion between the two. Reggie expressed sadness over leaving his football team, however, he wasn't shy or embarrassed to thank God for all His wonders.

News traveled fast around town, cycling between David's being less than pleased to come to Cleveland and Reggie's retirement plans. It was a busy day, but Katherine enjoyed being part of the hustle and bustle. Afterward, she went to her parents' for dinner and to confirm plans for tomorrow's event.

Meanwhile, the press pounded on David. They were relentless, as were the fans. When he left the stadium at the end of the press event, fans gathered to boo and heckle him, even throwing tomatoes at his car. David didn't realize how much his comment would cause him to backpedal and attempt to right the wrong. He just wanted to get to his condo and be alone. He hated this town.

Chapter 9

The Parents

Katherine never tired of going to her parents' home, and tonight was no exception. Their place was wonderfully welcoming and warm, always something cooking on the stove. She walked into the house calling, "Mom? Dad?"

"We are in the kitchen!" her father answered.

Immediately the smell of Italian food filled Katherine's nose, causing her mouth to water. After hugging and kissing her parents, she went to the stove to see what was cooking. Spaghetti and meatballs, one of her favorites. "Oh, yummy," she said. Upon seeing a salad waiting on the counter, she wondered if there was any dessert. Then spotting fruit, she smiled. "Perfect."

"I heard Reggie's interview," Michael said. "It seemed great."

"Did you hear him get emotional?" Katherine asked, pulling out dishes for their dinner.

"Yes. It only shows the fans how much he loves the team."

"I think Trino actually took it easy on him."

"I think Trino likes Reggie and that's why," her father smiled.

Katherine laughed as she helped her parents set the table, discussing Trino's past interviews. He never was starstruck and didn't avoid hard questions when an athlete wasn't playing to his full potential.

Removing garlic bread from the oven and placing it on the island, Sharon said, "Oh, I watched David Mann's interview and they weren't letting him get away with his remarks about Cleveland."

"Good, he's a jackass!" she blurted.

"KATHERINE!" her parents both yelled.

Neither could believe she'd sworn. Their daughter never swore. It was so unlike her to say anything unkind about anyone, and she had encountered plenty of arrogant men who gave just cause for such a word. But profanity wasn't part of her language.

Katherine was even surprised by her remark, immediately saying, "I'm sorry." She also whispered an apology to God. Even before her parents could ask what happened, Katherine said, "I met him. He was talking to Evan and he introduced us. I had no idea it was him." Looking at her mother, she asked, "You saw him, doesn't he look so different?"

She nodded in agreement.

"I mean...I know he has a beard now; I've seen him on TV. But to see him in person was shocking." Walking to the bar, she grabbed a bottle of water, taking a sip before saying, "But I was still excited to meet him." She took another drink, trying to preserve her emotions. "How many years did we watch him play? James really liked him."

Not missing the tremor in their girl's voice, her parents remembered the games they watched together as a family and their son-in-law's belief in David's talent.

"So I shook his hand," Katherine said "and I introduced myself. Evan told him I owned CMI, and of course I said you both owned it too."

Her parents leaned into the island seeing their daughter wasn't ready to eat.

"I told him we were excited to have him as part of the team and how sorry I was that he broke his collarbone. I believe his game will improve." Putting her hand on her hip, making direct eye contact with her dad, her nostrils then flared. "He completely cut me off and said—and I'm not joking around at all, this is pretty much what he said to me—'I'm not interested in becoming your client, you can knock off the act of kindness.'"

"What?" Michael shouted.

Only addressing her father, moving closer to him, she said, "I know! I couldn't believe he thought I wanted him as a client. I mean, what in the world was going through his mind when all I did was tell him we were glad he was here and I felt bad about the injury."

"How did you respond, Katherine?" Sharon asked.

"At first, I couldn't speak. I was so shocked I didn't even know what to say, but, thank God, my instincts kicked in. I told him I was sorry if he thought I was trying to somehow recruit him but I only wanted to welcome him here."

"Perfect, honey!" her mother said, happy her daughter had handled the situation properly.

Looking at her father, Katherine took another sip of water, pointed, and said, "But wait until you hear this!" Now her face turned red, but she shook her head, taking a deep breath to calm herself for she didn't want to call David Mann another name. "He said 'Cleveland? You want to welcome me to this dump of a city? Nobody wants to come to Cleveland.' Can you believe he said that?"

"He is a jackass!"

"Michael!" Sharon yelled.

"See, I told you!" Katherine said, smiling victoriously.

"Well, he is. What a loser."

"Okay, both of you hold on," her mother said, then asked Katherine, "How did you respond?"

"Well, I went into work mode and told him he was right, not that many people want to come here."

"Then what happened?" Sharon asked.

"I left. I hugged Evan goodbye and told David it was nice to meet him and left."

"And Evan said nothing?" Michael asked.

"He tried," Katherine said, "but my response was so quick it prevented the conversation from continuing. I just thought what a loser."

"See," Michael looked at Sharon, trying to justify his comment to his wife.

"Okay, both of you," Sharon said again. "This guy has been through a lot, and we have no idea what is going on in his mind."

"Mom, I know, that's what I was trying to tell him," she whined.

"Katherine, I know you, and I know you were probably just being yourself, but you have no idea how that man really feels."

Crossing her arms, leaning up against the counter, Katherine questioned, "Are you blaming me?"

"Oh, gosh, no, sweetie!" her mother said, "I'm so sorry if you thought I was implying this was your fault. And by no means do I think what he said to you was right. I'm just trying to help you look at things from his perspective. He's a second-string quarterback coming here because no other team wants him. I'm sure he's depressed. You didn't even recognize him. He obviously doesn't have any good influences in his life or he would have bounced back by now."

Katherine's heart softened toward David a little because it was her parents who'd helped her through her struggle five years ago.

Michael's was a different case. "I don't care what in the hell this guy has been through, he's not going to treat my daughter that way."

"Dad," Katherine said, "it's no big deal, really. How many times have I handled these types of guys, and even some women? It's completely fine."

"It's not fine. I never like it when anyone is rude or disrespectful to you, your sister, or your mother, and I'll be damned if some punk is going to talk to you like that."

She adored her father. She grinned and hugged him dearly. "Dad, this is exactly what I love about you. It's fine, really it is. Plus, Mom is right, as much as I hate to admit it." She smirked. "I need to see this guy as I would anyone else who is going through a tough time. And Dad, let's not forget how hard the fans and press will be on him." Eyes sparkling as she delighted in these thoughts, and with her signature mischievous grin, she said, "I sort of feel sorry for him."

Her mother knew that grin so well, and it actually tickled her because she hadn't seen it in quite a while.

Katherine's ringing phone halted their conversation. "It's Julie, the event coordinator."

"Good," her mother replied, "Everything is ready for tomorrow."

Katherine nodded while answering her phone. "Hello?" She motioned to her parents that she would be in the office reviewing details for tomorrow's event with the children.

Michael waited until his daughter disappeared, watching her close the office doors. "Wait until I see that fool."

"Honey, Katherine already took care of herself, and like she said, the media is going to be ruthless with him." She touched his arm lovingly, looking deeply in his eyes and guiding him gently. "And you know as well as anyone how hard it was when your career and business fell apart. You didn't handle it very well either."

Hanging down his head, Michael knew his wife was right, but he instantly stood up since none of that mattered now. "You handle things your way, but you need to let me handle things my way. I love you, Sharon, but this guy is a punk and someone needs to let him know that."

Eyes sparkling, Sharon's smirk almost covered her laughter. "Well, just be careful, honey, because he is twice your size."

The intensity that flashed in his eyes told Sharon her husband was in no mood to joke around. "I don't care how big this guy is, I'm not afraid of him."

Sharon knew that tone of voice and became concerned. Michael wasn't the type to back down from anyone no matter their size. Being together for over forty years should have taught her this topic was no joking matter.

Katherine emerged from the office, rattling off tomorrow's details and effectively ending the couple's conversation, including any other mention of the newly acquired Cleveland quarterback.

Chapter 10

The Rescue

Katherine was back at the stadium meeting Julie, a coordinator from an area organization that provided support services and programs for disabled children and their families. The nonprofit company worked with a wide range of physical, emotional, neurological, and developmental disabilities to help children achieve their full potential in life. The family was in favor of the charity since it provided therapy, education, and sports to families regardless of their ability to pay.

The kids ran happily around the team shop, selecting jerseys of their favorite players and other memorabilia prior to setting out on the junket. The children and their families were to tour the stadium, meet Reggie and a few other players, and enjoy a special appearance from Trino before the event ended in lunch.

Katherine delighted in watching the parents out on the field with the kids, throwing footballs and running into the end zone for a touchdown. Usually, the grass was off-limits to the public, but this was a private event, and the team's owner didn't mind the kids playing a football game. Afterward came the meet-and-greet with Reggie and his teammates in the locker room. The children waited patiently as the players signed autographs, posed for pictures, and talked with them. Some players shared personal stories of family members with disabilities, encouraging the children to enjoy life, study hard, and strive for their goals and dreams.

Loud cheers erupted all around the room when Trino showed up with chocolate radio microphones. Some kids didn't wait, ripping open the plastic wrapper and taking a big bite before their parents could stop them.

"My kind of kids," Katherine laughed as she unwrapped one herself and savored a taste.

Trino captivated the group with his many stories of Cleveland athletes and the elite players he had befriended throughout his profession. As usual, Katherine became misty, watching the children's innocence and joy of life. Everyone in the Cleveland organization took pleasure in providing an experience for these families, hopefully helping to relieve a burden, even if only for a moment.

They were just about complete in the locker room, the staff rounding up everyone for lunch just before Reggie led the guests marching out the door. Katherine remained an extra couple of minutes and was thanking those who volunteered their time and aligning their schedules for the next event when David walked in, went to his locker, and put away some of his belongings. Trino was the first to notice.

Without hesitating, Trino approached him. It was exactly what he wanted, to be one-on-one with David and do what he did best, get to the heart of things. No way was he going to stand in line to interview David like all those clowns did yesterday.

"Hey, Mann," he shouted.

His outburst shook David. He knew other people were in the locker room, but he couldn't care less. He hadn't even bothered to look around to see who they were to say hello. His physical therapy had just ended, and all he wanted was to get home as soon as possible.

Trino couldn't get to him fast enough. Red-faced, spit flying out of his mouth, he backed David in a corner, pointing in his face. "If you hate Cleveland so much, why the hell did you come here? Who else wants you? Did you get any other offers? Why the hell are you still playing anyway? You are nothing but a headcase who doesn't even deserve to be our third string quarterback, let alone our backup!"

David retreated into the corner with nothing to say as the abuse continued. Trino barely paused as he rallied on. "You are a no-good bum..."

Suddenly, Katherine appeared out of nowhere, and the words died off. She put her arm around Trino, batted her eyelashes, and sweetly smiled at him. "I don't mean to be rude and interrupt your interview with David, but I told the kids you know the Drew brothers, and they want to hear stories about them over lunch."

Katherine immediately brought Trino back to his senses since he hadn't realized how close he was to David, nor how harsh his words were. Backing off, he put his arm around Katherine's waist, kissed her cheek, and said, "Anything for you and those kids."

He walked away with Katherine following until David reached out and grabbed hold of her arm, stopping her. Feeling her tense up, he immediately let go since he didn't like anyone touching him either. "Thank you. I know what you just did, and I want to say thank you."

"You're welcome," she replied.

Before she could leave, he said, "Hey, I'm sorry for acting like a jackass to you yesterday."

Puzzled, she asked, "Did my father talk to you?"

"Who's your father?"

Changing the subject, her heart warmed. "Thank you for apologizing, but I wasn't trying to sell you a contract."

David's blue eyes were full of sadness, his heart sorrowful. "I know that now."

"I just wanted to let you know how bad I felt for you because of your injury..." Right before her eyes, she saw his demeanor change. He hung his head low, staring at the floor, backing away further until he bumped into the locker, blocking out her words. Katherine hadn't picked up on this yesterday because of her excitement of meeting him, but now she could read it loud and clear. So she stopped speaking mid-sentence, which she wasn't even too sure he noticed, and she said, "Here's a little tip on Trino."

He popped up his head, looking confused, although she had his attention.

"Trino has an enormous heart. He's very charitable. Donate to his foundation. It will benefit the kids, but do it discretely. Make it anonymous. If you attach your name to the donation, it may come across as insincere or fake. As if you are trying to 'buy' his approval. He'll find out it was you, but I warn you, make sure you donate from your heart and see what happens."

Trying to make sense of her tip somehow, he asked, "Of course it would benefit the kids, but what's your point?"

Katherine surprised herself, saying, "There is a proverb in the Bible that says if your enemy is hungry feed him, if he's thirsty give him something to drink, and by doing this you will heap burning coals on his head, and the Lord will reward you."

She wasn't the type to go slinging around Bible verses, but this was pouring out of her, much to her surprise.

David's head snapped back while he tried to move even further from her. He couldn't even attempt to hide his confusion. Thinking she was an absolute freak, he said, "What?"

So she put it in her own words. "Look, you have said harsh words about Cleveland and have been rude to the media. You have made enemies."

Dave couldn't argue, but he still thought she was weird, like really odd.

"The burning coals are a way of saying you are throwing off your enemy. It's unexpected. It's not that you are trying to hurt him, but to use your words, it's an act of kindness and as long as you are sincere, the results will be good."

David could barely contain himself and he actually laughed right in her face because he thought she was a freak. "So are you telling me that Trino will want to be my friend?"

"No," she said, "I'm not saying that at all. What I am saying is that your current approach isn't working, so you need to use another method."

His arrogant smile didn't suit his face. Scratching his forehead, mocking her suggestion, he said, "Okay, I'll try your approach and see just how much good that does me."

And in a way, that was Katherine. Not her mother, not her father, but precisely how God created her, eyes sparkling and tickled. Her killer smile flashing bright. She looked directly into David's eyes, lightly chuckled, and said, "It worked on you. You apologized to me. So you may just want to take my advice."

David's mouth dropped open. Katherine's smile displayed her mischievous grin as she walked away, leaving him speechless. She was so thankful to God for His Word and how many times that proverb had proven true.

David stood stunned in silence. Not only was she right, but he had no response as he watched her leave the locker room. Hearing, "Hi, Dad!" he swallowed and backed up in the corner again when he realized it was her father she was greeting.

Katherine hugged and kissed her dad, saying, "We are about ready for lunch."

"I'll be right up. I want to say hello to some of the guys."

"Okay. See you soon," Katherine said, but Michael didn't pay much attention since he was looking for one person, and as soon as he spotted David, he walked right up to him.

When David saw Katherine's father coming straight toward him with anger piercing from his eyes, his only thought was "Oh, shit!"

Although Michael was smaller than David, he was a pit bull and a force not reckoned with. He didn't have a lot of fear when it came to protecting his family. Getting right in David's face, pointing his finger, he started, "Listen, you punk, I don't know who the hell you think you are or who you think you were talking with yesterday, but if you are ever disrespectful to my daughter again, you better hide. And don't even think for a moment that I won't come after you. I don't care what kind of monkey steroids you are taking, I won't back down and will make sure you know that I mean business. You got it, sonny?"

David couldn't hide his fear but still made eye contact, saying, "Sir, I just apologized to your daughter for how I acted yesterday."

"What?" Michael asked, not thinking he heard David correctly.

"I was just talking with your daughter and told her I was sorry for how I treated her yesterday."

Michael backed up. Blood ran to his face and shame took over. "I didn't know you apologized to her. Thank you for being a man." Heeding his own words, he added "I'm sorry to come across so harsh, but when it comes to my family, I'm not very tolerant."

Relief washed through David. "I understand. And just so you know, I'm not on any monkey steroids or any other steroids for that matter."

For whatever reason, Michael burst out laughing, causing David to join him. The oddness of the situation struck David. It seemed like years since he'd laughed so hard, and he welcomed it.

"Yeah, I probably shouldn't have said that either. I'm sorry, son." Michael's heart softened toward the young man and he started to take a liking. He respected David for owning up to his mistake and making amends. "Well, how about if I start again?" His handsome eyes twinkled and his smile lit up his face as he extended his hand. "I'm Michael Luka."

David couldn't help but chuckle. He shook a hand which felt warm, robust, and fatherly. "Nice to meet you. I'm Dave Mann."

Michael placed his hand on David's shoulder, asking, "Are you finding everything you need here in Cleveland?"

Sad, lonely eyes avoided Michael's gaze. The topic of Cleveland clearly destroyed him. "Yeah, it's okay."

Patting him on the shoulder, Michael said friendly, "Are you finding any good restaurants?"

"I've found a couple of good places to eat right around the corner." David named some, and Michael agreed with his choices.

"How about your drive? Have you found the best routes to the training facilities?"

David felt comfortable, more relaxed in years when having a conversation with anyone. "Since I've been in town for less than a week, I'm using a car service until I'm a little more settled and familiar with this location."

"That's a good idea." Michael smiled. "How are your workouts? Are they working you hard? They just revamped the weight room."

David smiled genuinely for the first time in who knows how long. "Yes, they have been working me hard."

He felt like a kid around Michael. Not that Michael was talking down to him, but he could sense that the man cared about his surroundings, proper training, and nutrition. Even cared about his commute. Michael was a father. He wasn't asking the same old questions as everyone else. David truly felt like Michael was interested in his well-being, and it made him feel good.

"I need to meet some others for lunch. Again, I'm sorry about the misunderstanding. It was nice to meet you, David," Michael said, shaking his hand goodbye.

As he walked away, David surprised himself by speaking up. "Mr. Luka?"

Turning around, Michael answered, "Yes, son?"

"Are there any private jogging paths close by, sir?" Taking a couple of steps closer to Michael, he said, "I like to jog outside, but I'm not sure where to go that…"

"There's one right by my house," Michael jumped in "How about I pick you up tomorrow at 6 a.m.? I'll go jogging with you. Is that too early?"

Now his comfort turned uncomfortable since David wasn't expecting Michael to go jogging with him. "I don't want to inconvenience you."

"It will be my pleasure. I'll meet you at the front of your condo building at 6 a.m."

Dave had no choice but to say "okay", and then raised his voice so Michael could hear him since he was walking away once more. "I need to give you my address."

Michael stopped, turned, and made direct eye contact with David. Smiling, he said, "I already know where you live. If I didn't find you here today, I was coming to your condo." And then he left.

David sank on the bench. A lot had transpired over the last thirty minutes with Trino, then Katherine, and now her father. It was a lot to take in, and he needed rest. But David noticed how eerily silent it was when he realized he was all alone. Usually, he welcomed the quiet and empty room, but David felt lonely for the first time in…forever. The thought of going home to an empty place now bothered him. He shook it off, chalking the feeling up to being in a city he didn't like. Nevertheless, it was odd for him to feel lonely.

When he finally reached his condo, David, exhausted, fell asleep for the night, even though it was still early in the evening.

Chapter 11

The Jog

David woke, confused. Where was he, and what was the time? Drained from yesterday, and belatedly remembering that Michael was picking him up for a jog, caused panic. He didn't want to go. David located his phone to check the time, feeling better upon learning he had an hour before Michael arrived. He'd use the time to come up with some excuse to give Michael for why he wasn't going jogging. Although he didn't have Michael's phone number, so now what?

David recalled Katherine's comments calling for an alternative approach, so he jumped in the shower to wake up, deciding he would go with her father after all. He was nervous because they would be alone, and David wasn't too sure what they would talk about. He hadn't been around anyone outside of his team and coaches. He felt uncomfortable around people.

On the way down in the elevator, David took deep breaths to calm his nerves. His heart raced while thoughts flew through his mind trying to figure out what sort of conversation they could have outside of football. As he walked outside, David saw Michael waiting for him at the curb in his car, and fear reigned supreme.

Michael's face lit up. He rolled down the window even before David could get in the vehicle, saying, "I thought you might cancel. Maybe too early for you?"

David offered a slightly embarrassed smile as he got in the car. "Well, I thought about it."

Shaking hands, then smoothly accelerating, Michael asked, "Did you sleep well last night, David?"

Again that fatherly tone comforted. "Yes, sir, I did. How about you?"

"Well, yes, I feel very refreshed and ready for a jog. By the way, you can call me Michael."

"Okay, Michael, it is. You can call me Dave if you like."

"If you don't mind, I'll call you David. It's a powerful name. One of my favorite men in the Bible is David."

"No, I don't mind at all."

He was glad because he enjoyed being called David. It was only after his broken collarbone that he started introducing himself as Dave. He wasn't sure why. Maybe he felt like just using a nickname. Or maybe because he wanted to communicate as little as possible with people. But here's this thing again with the Bible. Katherine did it yesterday, and now today, her father brought it up. He was hoping they weren't trying to pull him into some type of cult.

As they were driving, Michael pointed out locations that held memories, taking a longer way around town to show David some highlights: the hospital where his girls were born, his high school, a building he used to work in.

"Tell me about your parents," Michael asked.

David hesitated and struggled for the right words to describe his relationship with his parents. "They don't live around here."

"How long have they been married?" Michael questioned.

David sort of figured out that Michael would continue to ask him questions about his family since he was a family man after all. So David found himself laying it out, embarrassed by his own story. "My mom and dad are married, but they don't live together. My mother is an alcoholic and a user. My dad hasn't had a job in years; he lives on disability. I lived with my grandmother and have had no contact with my parents in years."

David was fully expecting Michael to give him a lecture on how he should contact his parents, letting the past be in the past. From everything David had experienced first-hand, he knew Michael put his family first.

Michael's voice softened. "Good thing you had football to occupy your attention while you were growing up. You turned out to be a fine young man."

David looked out the window to hide the warm moisture gathering in his eyes.

"I had good parents. My wife didn't. But you know what's interesting? My wife taught me so much about people and life because she had to grow up quickly when she was a young child. It sounds like you and my wife have some things in common."

David eased into a grin. Michael was comforting.

"Well, here we are," Michael said as he pulled up to a gated community.

David was confused. He assumed they were going to a park but this was a charming, wealthy neighborhood.

"Where are we?"

"This is my neighborhood," Michael said, driving down the street.

David could see the lake. The street was beautiful with its mature trees. Michael waved to some neighbors and pointed out, "That's my house." Driving past several more homes, Michael pointed to another and said, "That's where your boss lives."

David didn't quite understand. "Excuse me?"

"The owner of the football team lives there."

David was in disbelief, suddenly uncomfortable. Was it because Michael was so wealthy? Maybe he feared Michael would talk to the owner about him? Or perhaps he thought he couldn't trust Michael? Whatever it was, David just wanted to get back home to be alone, but he knew that wouldn't do him any good.

"Ready to go? I normally jog down here but I wanted to show you the neighborhood. Come on, let's get moving."

David got out of the car, viewing a beautifully appointed private park with a jogging path. It overlooked the lake.

"If we run the whole path, it's three miles. If you include the neighborhood, it's about five miles. Let's start with the path and then finish with the stairs."

David looked. "Where are the stairs?"

"They are by the lake. I'll show you later."

They set out on their jog with little fuss. It was a brisk morning, and the sun was just rising. The path took them right by the lake, and they watched beautiful sun rays hit the water. The sky had that morning blush of pink, blue, and orange clouds. Their breath appeared in the air's cold. David missed this. He loved to jog outside. He loved being in nature. It's was probably one of the biggest reasons he loved playing football; he enjoyed being out in all different types of weather.

The path was busy but not crowded. As they passed by walkers and joggers, Michael greeted them, telling David who they were. Yet he was not gossiping or giving out personal information. Michael simply told him where they lived, their occupation, or family size. Once in a while, Michael told a funny story involving his neighbor, but not in any way making fun of them. It was mainly stories about how they helped one another on a project around the house, getting the car out of a snowbank, or some fun party. David enjoyed the tales, laughing along with Michael in between breaths.

David knew Michael loved his neighbors and could imagine how nice it was to grow up living in this area. He felt relaxed and enjoyed Katherine's father. Michael wasn't talking about his injury. Actually, they weren't talking about football or their careers. They were appreciating the beauty of their surroundings and laughing at funny stories.

After almost forty-five minutes, Michael took them to the stairs. "I only do these once in a while," he said patting David's shoulder, "because they are tough!"

The stairs were not at all what David was expecting. They were built into the side of a massive cliff overlooking Lake Erie. The stairs led down to a huge covered patio with an outdoor kitchen and barbeque area. A firepit, picnic tables, and a playground were nearby to keep families entertained. There was even a ramp for anyone with physical limitations.

Michael explained the neighbors came together about fifteen years back, adding this area for all the families to enjoy. It was an outdoor party center which accommodated block parties, Fourth of July celebrations, and social events.

There were about forty steps on each side. Michael pointed. "Why don't you run them? You are in pretty good shape."

David reluctantly agreed. Truthfully, he wasn't in that good of shape anymore. He'd probably put on fifteen to twenty pounds since his diet wasn't as impeccable as it once was.

As he started running the stairs, Michael yelled out, "You're like Rocky!" and then sang the Rocky theme. David smiled thinking Michael probably did this with his neighbor buddies all the time.

Within five minutes, David was winded. He was upset he had allowed himself to get so out of shape. After another five minutes, he was depressed over his stamina because in his prime he could have run stairs for thirty minutes straight. Not even another couple of minutes later, David stopped. He no longer had it in him. He choked back his emotions as best as possible.

But when he heard Michael's voice, his emotions quickly turned to merriment. "If you ran those steps any longer, I may have had to jump over this railing. I didn't expect you to last five minutes, let alone fifteen. Come on, let's get something to eat. You're making me look bad."

"You are in pretty good shape for your age," David countered.

"For my age? How old do you think I am?"

"You don't look a day over seventy!" David shouted with a wide smile.

"What? I should have kicked your ass yesterday when I had the chance!"

David trotted up to Michael and put his arm around him, joking all the way to the car until Michael asked, "Do you mind if I stop at home?"

David tensed up. This wasn't part of the plan, and he wasn't sure of Michael's reason.

"I'd like to take a shower, then drop you off before I head to the office."

David had little choice. "Sure."

Driving down the street, David could see the beautiful, red-brick home majestically overlooked Lake Erie. A stone-paved walkway led to the front door. Floor to ceiling windows invited the sun to light up the rooms naturally. The house was regal, yet comfortable. It was a home.

Michael pulled into his garage, and the two entered the house. "Honey, I'm home!"

"Good, I was getting worried."

And appearing around the corner, kissing her husband hello, was an older version of Katherine.

"I'm sorry I was gone longer than expected. I was showing David the patio area."

"Did he make you run those stairs? He tells everyone that he can run them for fifteen minutes, yet I haven't seen him do more than three flights."

"My wife is a liar," Michael winked. "Sharon, this is David Mann. And this is my wife Sharon."

"Nice to meet you," Sharon said warmly, shaking his hand. "Come on in. I have breakfast waiting. I hope you're hungry."

"Sharon, do you mind if I take a shower first? I'm all sweaty, and it will only take a couple of minutes to get cleaned up."

"Not at all. Take your time, sweetie." She looked at David. "Do you need a shower before you eat?"

"No, I didn't sweat as much as your husband."

"That's because I worked out harder than you." Michael smiled and flexed his muscles, making them laugh as he jogged off to the shower.

Walking David to the kitchen, Sharon naturally eased into being the hostess. "I hope you like eggs. I also have turkey bacon, fresh fruit, and some toast. I don't know if you eat carbs, but I made some hash browns just in case you wanted some."

"I pretty much eat anything." He smiled and could tell she had been expecting him. She made him feel at ease since she was so attentive.

"Well, good. Sit down and I'll get you a plate. I like a lot of vegetables in my scrambled eggs, so if you don't like that, I can make you just plain eggs."

"No, whatever you have is fine with me." It had been a long time since David had had a home-cooked meal or someone who cared to accommodate his needs.

As she was preparing him a plate, David took in the beauty of the home. It was pretty substantial. The kitchen was enormous—a chef's paradise—and opened into two different, oversized family rooms, each hosting a fireplace and large-size TVs. The décor was classy but comfortable. The house wasn't a museum nor was it flashy, trendy, or dull. It simply pulled you in and made you feel welcomed. It was a showpiece, yet it was built to comfortably entertain. The home could easily be in a magazine, and David would later find out that it had been many times.

As Sharon served David, he said, "I like that light." He pointed to a crystal chandelier hanging over the kitchen island.

It wasn't a typical light fixture with a traditional shape. The chandelier was five feet in length with hundreds of round crystals illuminating brilliant light. It was spectacular and sparkled beautifully up against the dark walnut, ceiling-height cabinets. It was the perfect centerpiece for the room.

"Thank you," Sharon replied. "I love that fixture more for the meaning than anything else."

David was interested.

"When my husband started to dabble in the stock market, our conversations at that time were focused around what to buy, when to sell, and what would be our long-term investments." Sitting next to him with a plate of food, she continued. "I noticed a stock that was about twenty-two cents and I asked Michael to buy me one thousand shares, which he did. He also bought a couple more thousand shares for our retirement. Well, that little stock increased to over four dollars, which may not seem like a lot, but it was enough to purchase that chandelier. I always get compliments on that light, and from time to time I tell this story. It's a reminder to me that no matter how little I invest in something, when I'm sincere, it will always return a profit. I've had that light for over twenty years and that principal has never returned void."

David could see where Katherine had gotten her wisdom from, and he immediately felt comfortable with her mother. He smiled. "You're a good cook."

Seeing he had nearly eaten all his food, she asked, "Can I get you some more eggs and fruit?"

He blushed but decided not to allow his embarrassment to keep him from speaking. "Yes," he said politely, "and would it be okay if I have some more bacon?"

"Absolutely. How about something to drink? We have coffee, orange juice, grapefruit juice."

"Just water is fine," he answered.

"Yep, that's pretty much all that I drink too."

Still looking around, David couldn't help but say, "Your home is beautiful."

She put her hand on his shoulder as she served him. "Thank you." She could feel him tense when she touched him. She knew from experience it might mean he didn't have close, meaningful relationships. So wanting to be sure that he felt relaxed, Sharon continued to stay on the safe topic of her home.

Getting them each a bottle of water, she said, "We have lived here about twenty-one years. We love this house. It has given us of ton of great memories and helped us through some that weren't so good. We entertain quite often. It's not as easy to do it by myself anymore, so both my girls help along with some other good friends."

Feeling relieved that she wasn't asking about his injury or football, he asked, "Did you build or was it already built?"

"No, we built this house," she replied. "We actually modeled it after our first home as a married couple, a tiny bungalow. We entertained in the basement of that house because we couldn't fit very many in the kitchen and we didn't have a dining room."

David grinned wide when Sharon's smile delighted her face. "I wanted to create a home that would feel as if everyone was together even though they were in different rooms. For most of our parties, the older folks solve world peace and politics sitting at this table," she said, tapping on the tabletop. "The younger ones watch football or baseball games over there," she said, pointing to one of the rooms off the kitchen. "And the kids like to hang out in that room to watch cartoons or play video games."

David was almost finished eating, but discovered himself in no rush to leave.

"I always wanted to be near the water. One day, Michael found this lot and we both fell in love with it. We weren't expecting to move, and this was an enormous step for us. But we felt at peace with the decision and bought the land. We worked to save for a down payment and eventually paid it off. It took us almost eleven years to get here," Sharon chuckled delightfully, "even though it was a five-year goal."

David smiled over the humor Sharon found in the goal taking more than double the time.

"This home has become more of a blessing to me than I would have ever expected. It has helped foster some of the best relationships of my life."

Just then, Michael walked into the kitchen, saying, "Something smells good."

"I can fix you a plate," Sharon stood.

"No, that's okay, I can grab one myself," Michael responded.

Since David had finished eating, he got up to put away his dishes.

"Let me get that for you," Sharon said. "Come on, I'll show you around." She looked at Michael, asking, "Are you okay eating by yourself while I give David a tour?"

Winking, he replied, "What, do I look like a two-year-old who needs someone to feed him?"

"Do you want to take this one or would you like me to have the honor?" Sharon asked David.

Smiling brightly, he answered "It's too easy. You can go right ahead."

Conspiratorially, she whispered to David, "Knowing my husband, he was probably thinking of something funny to say while he was taking a shower. We'll just let this one go."

Loading up his plate with food, Michael called back, "You two don't know what you are talking about."

Sharon grabbed David's arm to show him their home, laughing lightly as they strolled away. Each room appeared more beautiful than the last one. Then she took him outside to the outdoor living space, pointing out aspects of the lake. He watched her facial expressions as she described her home and its view. Sharon was not showing off or bragging; she wasn't a woman who did that. She simply was filled with gratitude, thankfulness, and a humbleness that he was not used to seeing. He knew it was about those who gathered together within this home and not the building.

David noticed a smaller house on the property, asking, "Is that a pool house?"

"No. My mom stayed there when she was sick. She suffered from a mental illness, so it made it very difficult to be around her. It was tough on me emotionally, but I didn't want to put her in a nursing home. So Michael got approval from the homeowner's association, and we built this home for her to stay in and hired a full-time nurse. I visited her every day and showed her how much I loved her."

David could see her eyes well up with tears. "That little house has been home to several other people who needed a place to stay for a few months, including Katherine when she was transitioning out of our house back into her own home."

Remembering Katherine's story, he whispered, "I'm sorry to hear about her loss."

"Thank you," she responded. "It was a hell of a couple years, but by the grace of God we have all pulled through it together."

Then David surprised himself by asking, "How? How were any of you able to get through that?" It had been his experience that those he knew who went through some type of hardship didn't recover very well, and Katherine's was an absolute tragedy. He couldn't grasp how anyone could come back from that.

"Well, it was by far one of the most difficult times in our lives, that's for sure. And something I would want no one to ever endure. But God was faithful to us."

Again with the whole God thing, David thought. What is with these people? Was this a crutch for them? Maybe a superstition so no more tragedies would happen in their lives?

"It was really scary there for the first couple months. I didn't think Katherine would make it another day," Sharon said. "Then, I found out I had breast cancer, and it was as if someone was playing a cruel joke on our family. I didn't want to let Katherine know, but with all the appointments and side effects from the treatments, there was no way I could hide it from her. So Michael gathered the girls and told them about my illness. I feared that Katherine wouldn't be able to handle any more bad news, and I really wasn't sure if she was capable of living one more day."

Not even attempting to fight back the tears, just wiping them away, Sharon smiled, saying, "But it was as if God used my cancer to pull Katherine out of her darkness. I was completely surprised by her reaction. She had laid in bed for months, but that day she got up and starting taking care of me."

David hadn't heard this part of the story from Evan. "Amazing."

"Yes, God is truly amazing," she said. "He's not a wasteful God."

David looked puzzled.

"We will probably never know why James and our grandchild were taken from us. But because my husband was created to be a good steward with our finances, God blessed him, giving him the ability to leave his company and carry on with the management company. And because of CMI, we have been able to connect with athletes to raise money for families in need. And the company gave my daughter a purpose and a focus. It gave her something she loved, which is to be part of a team." With a wink and nudge of his arm, she added. "And it has taught her how to work with people no matter how difficult they can be."

David turned beet red, saying, "I'm sorry about treating her so rudely."

Sharon assured him it was okay, saying, "But here again is where God is not wasteful. If you weren't rude to my daughter, Trino wouldn't have yelled at you, Katherine wouldn't have interrupted him, and you wouldn't have said you were sorry. And if my husband had listened to me when I told him not to confront you, would you be standing here right now?"

David was thrown back. He had been vulgar to Katherine. Would he have apologized to her if Trino hadn't yelled at him? And how would he have treated Michael when he was confronted?

Sharon gently touched the scar on his collarbone and lovingly said, "God won't allow this to be wasted either."

And David was overcome with emotion, though he tried to fight it back best he could.

Placing her arm around him, she said, "Come on, I'm sure that husband of mine is ready to get to work."

As they entered the house, Michael was loading the dishwasher. "Thank you for cleaning up for me," Sharon said.

"Well, thank you for making us breakfast."

Immediately, David agreed. "Yes, thank you very much. I really appreciated it."

Michael asked, "Do you want me to drop you off at the training facility or your home?"

Checking the time, David answered, "You can take me home. I'll get cleaned up and head out."

Walking them to the mudroom where Michael put on his shoes and suit jacket, Sharon fondly said, "I never get tired of seeing my husband in a suit."

David enjoyed how these two interacted with one another. There was genuine love, affection, and friendship that he hadn't witnessed ever in another marriage.

"What would you two like to eat for breakfast tomorrow?" Sharon asked.

David wanted to spend more time with them but remained silent, looking at Michael, for he didn't want to seem too eager.

"I'm up for another run if you are?"

David was relieved, then joked, "Do you think you can keep up this time?"

Michael smiled brightly at his wife. "Can you believe this guy?"

Standing in the mudroom, laughing as they talked through the details of the next morning, David felt like he was home. It had been years since he felt welcomed by anyone.

Michael and Sharon kissed one another goodbye, not being shy. "I love you," they shared.

Sharon looked at David. "Well, you better get used to this." Then she gave him a big hug and a kiss on the cheek.

At first, David tensed his back and shoulders. He wasn't expecting a hug or kiss. But Sharon was warm and motherly, and he realized how long it had been since he'd been held by anyone in any way. He enjoyed the moment. Yes, there were women in the past, particularly Gretchen, but she'd walked out on him years ago. Who could blame her? David had treated her with contempt, like he had everyone else. But this wasn't that type of hug; this was the loving embrace of a mother, which told David she cared for him.

This became the routine. David now drove over to Sharon and Michael's home for an early morning run or to lift weights several times a week. The men mostly joked around with one another, talking politics and the stock market. Then, while Michael was getting ready, David had breakfast with Sharon and they spoke about their love of food. She would even give him leftovers to take home for dinner if there were any. They never discussed his game or talked about his accident. The married couple sensed it was not time to approach that topic. And so David looked forward to going to their home. He felt wonderfully warm and welcomed.

Chapter 12

The Party

Memorial Day was approaching, time for the family's annual party. The Lukas held several parties a year, but this one kicked off the summer. It wasn't a fundraiser, just an excuse to pull together family, friends, and colleagues.

During a morning run, Michael invited David to the party. He didn't want to go. He enjoyed spending time with Sharon and Michael, but their attention would be focused on other guests, and he had no interest in making small talk with people he didn't know. Not wanting to come across as childish and having to confess the true reason he had no interest in attending, he worked to think of an excuse.

David wasn't a good liar, so he had a hard time convincing Michael he had other plans. Michael had gotten to know him well over the last couple of months, and he knew there wasn't anyone else David hung around, so he said, "No pressure, come if you can. Stop over around 2 p.m. for lunch. It's an open house, so people come and go throughout the day." Michael nudged him as they jogged, grinning as usual. "Although, since I am grilling, you may want to remain home. My cooking has caused sickness."

David chuckled. "I can hardly wait to eat your cooking."

On their jog, Michael shared his many cooking disasters and funny party moments from over the years. Of course, David realized, he would go to their home for Memorial Day. How couldn't he? He couldn't be that juvenile and stay away for fear of interacting with people.

The weather in Cleveland was always a mystery. There had to be hope and prayer around the climate. But the day of the cookout was an exception—an unseasonably warm Memorial Day around 72 degrees, which was the perfect temperature for a late May celebration.

David pulled into the Lukas's development and, upon seeing the cars lining the street, he realized this was not a typical Memorial Day party. There were at least fifty to sixty cars parked in the street. It took him a while, but he located a parking spot, walking quite a distance to the family's home. He was extremely nervous. Outside of Michael and Sharon, he didn't know anyone else. Where would he sit, who would he interact with, and how long would he stay? Walking up the driveway, hearing music and people talking and laughing didn't help. He felt out of place and didn't want to be there since he wasn't good in these sort of social events.

Sharon spotted David as soon as he entered the backyard, immediately greeting him with a hug and kiss. Intertwining her arm in his, she led them along, introducing him to her neighbors, family, and guests.

David laughed when he spotted Michael grilling, wearing an apron and an oversized chef's hat. Michael shook his hand heartily, and David handed him a bag with several expensive bottles of wine. The two men were happy to see one another. David occasionally shared a glass of wine with Michael and knew his price limit was around $30 a bottle. He wasn't the type to waste money, so David had splurged, wanting his friend to taste some real wine.

Katherine appeared with a tray of hot dogs and buns. "Here you go, Dad."

David had almost forgotten how beautiful Katherine was. She was like a breath of fresh air. He was nervous since he hadn't seen her since he'd apologized and wasn't too sure how she would treat him.

"Honey, you remember David," Sharon said.

"Yes, of course I do," she replied pleasantly. "I'm glad to see you again. I hear you are giving my Dad quite the workout."

"Please, he can't keep up with me!" Michael interjected, flexing his muscles as the others mocked him.

Before David could respond to Katherine, Sharon said, "I want you to meet Lana and her husband, Eric." Finding them in the crowd was no simple task, but Eric and David immediately hit it off once introduced.

Eric was a great guy, and David found they had much in common. They talked nonstop about their college days, Michael's sense of humor, and Florida. Both of them had lived in the same location at some point in their lives. David missed Florida and wanted to return, both to the sunny state and that time in life when he would have been the one hosting a party instead of secluding himself from the world.

Michael rang the dinner bell to the sounds of people cheering and heckling him simultaneously. It was time to eat. There was a massive tent with a multitude of tables and chairs to accommodate everyone. A line formed quickly to select from the grand buffet, but before anyone ate, Michael spoke up. "Let me pray before we eat."

Everyone stopped, bowing their heads. David was used to hearing Michael and Sharon talk about God, but to pray in public didn't seem unusual to those gathered. David didn't mind, but he never remembered a common man praying prior to eating at such a large gathering as a party like this. It seemed out of place and not normal to him, but he liked Michael so much that it didn't totally freak him out.

"Lord, thank you for bringing us all together. Thank you for those who You created to serve our country and fight for our freedom, and for those who have given their lives for us. Thank you for the sacrifice military families make in order for our men and women to do their jobs. Thank you for our country, which we love so much. Please continue to protect our country. I pray for those who You have raised up and for the next generation to continue to submit to You and Your Word. I thank you for all who have gathered here today: our family, friends, and the new friends You have put in our path. I thank you for the food and pray for a safe trip home. In Your name Jesus, amen."

David heard Reggie Johnson call out a resounding "Amen!" He hadn't realized the man was standing right next to him.

"Come and eat!" Michael called. "If it's not good or you get sick, blame my wife, she made it!" And while some people booed him, Michael quickly grabbed Sharon, hugging and kissing her as she laughed the entire time. It was something David was accustomed to seeing.

While David stood in line to get his meal, he again felt uncomfortable since he didn't know where he would sit. He shuffled along quietly, being polite as he waited for Michael and Sharon to serve, thanking them kindly. He then felt a warm hand on his shoulder. It was Lana, who pointed to Eric. "We saved you a seat over by us." The tightness in David's face softened and he nodded as he followed.

David sat at the main table with the family. Michael sat at the head of the table with Sharon beside him, their daughters, Eric, Reggie, his wife, Grace, and their two boys. He had been inserted into the family and felt somewhat intimidated. He wasn't used to a family gathering. But David hid his feelings and joined in the conversation every so often.

He mostly sat back, watching them interact. Michael, as usual, made people laugh. The ladies engaged in a conversation, about what he didn't know. Eric and Reggie talked about football and some trades, a simple discussion for David to join.

Soon the kids broke out a couple of footballs, begging the guys to toss the ball around while clean up began. No need to twist David, Reggie, and even Eric's arms too hard; they wanted to work off the food.

From a distance, David snuck a glance at Katherine from time to time. He noticed her confidence and enjoyed watching her talk with people. She was funny like her dad and warm and caring like her mother. He could see why Michael was so protective of his family. This was the first time David had seen them together, and there was no denying their love for one another. But it was more than that. This family seemed to treat Reggie, his wife, their kids, and their son-in-law as their own flesh and blood. David was starting to feel the inclusion too.

Some guests were leaving as the guys finished throwing around the ball. Michael called David over. "Are you able to stick around a little longer? I would like to bring out your wine and have a glass with you."

David was in no rush to leave. "Sure, absolutely. I'll grab it." Entering the house, he got the bottles but couldn't remember where his hosts kept the wine glasses. He began looking through the cabinets.

"Do you need help finding something?" Katherine asked kindly, placing down a tray full of dirty dishes on the counter as she moved to begin loading the dishwasher.

David, always surprised by her presence, turned bright red, showing her the wine bottles. "I was looking for some glasses."

"I'll get them. There's a bunch of glasses outside," she said, walking away.

David was embarrassed he hadn't recalled the table full of stemware right by the drinks, but he thanked Katherine, running away as quickly as possible. He'd only had three interactions with her, and each time he'd felt like a fool.

After everything was cleaned up and most of the crowd gone, the family sat down together. Michael patted the seat right next to him, saying, "Okay, show me what some $50 bottle of wine has over this $25 bottle of wine."

Chuckling as he sat, David corrected, "Try $500 bottle of wine."

"What! Are you crazy? Why in the world would you spend $500 on a bottle of wine?"

"It's okay, just calm down. I know what you are thinking, this is not an investment and once I drink it, it's gone and it's a waste of money." David opened several bottles of wine to let them breathe, smiling at Michael. "First, I didn't buy all these bottles. Most were given to me. Second, I only drink them on special occasions and today seems like as suitable an occasion as any. Third, I don't drink a lot and never alone, so that's why I brought them with me today."

Michael put his hand on his shoulder. "I'm glad our talk about finances is rubbing off on you."

"Well, that's about all I learned from you," David teased once more.

Sitting at the table, Katherine watched their interaction, noticing how different David was around her father. She knew they worked out together, but she hadn't realized they'd formed a friendship and truly enjoyed one another's company. David came out of his shell around her father. He was the person she remembered seeing on TV long ago. Even watching David with Reggie and Eric, he became his old self. It seemed only when he was in public and around others was he awkward and quiet.

It was now David's turn to serve. Walking around the table, he first poured the ladies a glass, ending with Michael. But before they drank, David opened a bottle of sparkling grape juice for Reggie's boys, serving it in wine glasses, which they loved. Katherine could tell David was seasoned in this setting.

Holding his glass in the air, David said, "Here's to good friends and good times!"

"And many more!" others shouted.

Michael took a sip of the wine, saying, "Yuck, that's horrible!" Everyone laughed. Michael tasted the wine again and inspected the bottle, asking, "Is there enough for me to drink a couple of glasses?"

"Yes," David smiled, enjoying their camaraderie. Over the next hour, David treated everyone at the table to a wine tasting. He compared several bottles of lesser expensive wines to moderately priced ones, concluding with a top-end nectar. They received an excellent education.

The night grew on with plenty of laughter, and soon darkness made its presence. However, no one wanted the party to end. Eric built a fire to keep them warm and cozy in the cool spring evening.

Talk of Reggie's retirement and how much he would miss the game quickly turned into a discussion of Cleveland sports, football in general, and the team's many losses. Rumblings, snickering, and side conversations sounded among them, with "Only Cleveland" stories told, each with their own name.

"There's a name?" David asked.

"Names," Eric corrected.

"There's more the one?"

"There's The Fumble and The Drive," Michael answered, describing how Cleveland was a game away from going to the Super Bowl but fumbled the ball within the final minutes or how the guys couldn't stop their opponent from driving down the field 98 yards, scoring a touchdown.

Jumping in, Eric said, "The Hit and The Shot!" Now they were telling the tales of heartbreaking losses for baseball and basketball in the same fashion, teams being in the final few minutes and steps away from the win.

David laughed at how everyone tried to top each other with another sad loss.

"Going way back, Red Right 88," Michael said.

"Oh yeah, I forgot," Eric chuckled, trying to piece together that devastating loss.

Looking off in the distance, Michael next recalled, "The Move."

"The Move?" David questioned.

"Hey Dad, what year was that?" Eric asked.

"It was 1996, son," Michael replied.

David noticed that he called Eric son too. It made David feel special that Michael called him son, treating him like a welcome addition to the family. David reclined back, watching the family react to their beloved Cleveland football team being yanked out of downtown, moved to Baltimore, and then winning the big title within a few short years. It was devastating for the city and fans. Football in Cleveland had never been the same, the organization going through plenty of coaches, quarterbacks, and general managers.

"There's a curse," Eric chided after listening to story after story of the three major league teams' heartbreaking losses.

"Cleveland fans are loyal. They love their teams, especially football," Michael said. "One time, the fans threw so many beer bottles on the field over a bad call that the officials had to stop the game with maybe fifty seconds left." Everyone laughed. "There were thousands of beer bottles, plastic cups, and other garbage thrown onto the field. The players and officials had to run for safety. It took thirty minutes to regain control to finish the game."

David laughed now too. "There's no way I believe that."

"I'll find it for you," Lana said, searching on her phone for the old story.

"We are telling you, this city loves their teams," Eric said.

"Yes," Michael agreed, "but it's obsessed with football."

Eric and Reggie raised their glasses in agreement.

"Is this city cursed?" David asked.

"Sometimes we feel that it is," Eric smiled.

"What's with the names? The Drive, The Shot, The Fumble," David asked.

"With every major loss, there is always one play that leaves the game with a nickname," Michael answered.

"But wait until you see the fans," Reggie said. "They are one of the largest fan bases in the world. Football started right here. Just around the corner in Canton. These fans are devoted."

"No matter if Cleveland won the World Series, and even when we won the NBA Finals, it wouldn't compare to winning the Super Bowl. Of course, we have our share of fair-weathered fans, but this is without a doubt a football town, and it would be like New Year's Eve in New York City if we won that trophy. One day it will happen," Michael said.

Everyone was having a fantastic time reminiscing, and David was eager to listen to all their stories. Katherine hadn't remembered laughing this hard for this long in quite a while. She was shocked when she looked at her phone, seeing the time. "I have to go, Mom, it's getting late."

"Wow!" Sharon said, noticing the hour. "I can't believe it's so late. What a great time it has been. I hate to see it end. Do you really have to go?"

"Yes, I'm getting up early to work out and then head to the office."

"Are you okay to drive? Do you want me to take you home?" Reggie asked.

"Oh, no thank you. I'm fine," she replied. "I didn't have more than a glass."

David had noticed that she wouldn't allow him to refill her glass of wine.

"That's because she talks dirty when she's had more than one," Lana smirked.

A rosy hue flushed over Katherine's face immediately. "Please. Look who's talking. Eric, tame your woman!"

Batting her eyelashes, nuzzling Eric's neck, Lana asked, "Do you want to tame me?"

"Yuck. Dad!" Katherine protested.

"Don't blame me, she's got your mother's blood," Michael said, taking another sip of wine. "Your mother is the tiger in the family."

Sharon giggled. "Honey, you are the one that brings it out in me."

And then this low, sexy growl came from David, causing Katherine to take notice. Everyone laughed, trying to growl like tigers too.

"Okay, you've all had too much to drink," Katherine chuckled.

"Don't worry, Katherine, we won't defile the marriage bed." Reggie reassured her that the conversation would not go any further than just a couple of laughs. The Lukas weren't the type of a family that took things to the gutter. They enjoyed laughing, but they knew there was a line and hardly ever stepped over it.

Katherine hugged and kissed everyone goodbye, except David, to whom she only offered her hand. "It was nice seeing you again. Thank you for the wine."

"Nice seeing you too."

Sharon walked her daughter to her car, allowing Katherine to evaluate with her mom in private. "I didn't realize how close Dad was to David."

"Yeah, he really likes him. I actually think they are a lot alike," Sharon replied.

That statement left Katherine feeling odd. She didn't press her mother for specifics, but she was annoyed with how well the two got along. She didn't know why either. Katherine loved her parents and was protective of them, so maybe on some level she thought David was using them. Or perhaps it was the wine—she did hardly ever drink. Regardless, she wasn't feeling like herself tonight.

Katherine's leaving didn't prompt anyone else to go. They remained at least a couple more hours, with Reggie and Grace eventually carrying their sleeping boys to the car, followed by Eric and Lana. Finally, it was just David, Sharon, and Michael. They enjoyed the chilly night and their conversation. It was when David felt the most relaxed.

"It's so late, David, why don't you just spend the night? You will be back in the morning to work out with Michael anyway, just spend the night instead of driving home," Sharon said.

"No, I don't want to be any trouble and get in your way in the morning," David replied.

"Nonsense, you are staying the night. It's too late for you to drive home. We have some of Reggie's old clothes that you can wear. You two are about the same size," Michael said.

And they settled it. David spent the night, getting the best night's sleep he'd had in years. Now it felt like his home too. Soon enough it became a habit, where David's visit would turn into a sleepover in which he relished every moment.

Chapter 13

The Charity Event

June brought another charity event. This one was to raise money for abused children, a cause near and dear to Sharon's heart. Their events were like weddings—very festive with black-tie attire and plenty of dancing. Tonight several premium brand liquors, ports, and cognacs kept the guests entertained during cocktail hour while Oyster Rockefeller, Wagyu Beef Satay and imported cheeses, to name a few of the delicious appetizers, were served on silver platters. Naturally, the entrees and desserts were also created from the finest culinary delights to ensure the well-to-do guests discriminating palettes were exceptionally satisfied.

Of course, David was invited. As usual, he felt uncomfortable and didn't look forward to going. Even though he knew he would sit within the comfortable circle of Michael, Sharon, and their kids, he didn't want to be around a crowd of people.

When he arrived, David stood in the receiving line, realizing his attire wasn't appropriate for the occasion. He wore his typical outfit: unpressed, worn-out, faded khaki-colored pants; yellow casual button-down shirt, yellow and blue striped tie, and a blue blazer. He stood out like a sore thumb compared to the men wearing tuxedos or three-piece suits. He looked like he was going to a high school banquet.

The women were also dressed to the nines as this event had become the marquee socialite gathering of the year. It was apparent their hair and makeup had been professionally done, and they paraded in nothing less than glamorous ball gowns. All the expensive jewels shone brightly, sparkling in the dramatic lighting.

As the line moved closer to Michael and Sharon, who were greeting people, David spotted Katherine next to her father, also receiving guests. She looked elegant. Her hair was swept up romantically in a way that emphasized her big, beautiful, brown eyes, and her pale lip gloss highlighted her full lips. Her face had such a natural glow about it. She wore no jewelry because her dress was the show stopper. Gracing her shoulders, emphasizing her lovely neck, the black gown hit the floor at the perfect length. The material was lace and chiffon with a black satin ribbon highlighting her tiny waist. It was tailored to fit her like a glove, displaying the silhouette of her figure perfectly. She wasn't attempting to show off her shape, for the dress only hugged her upper body and waist to accentuate her curves, not to put them on display. She was too classy for that. The rest of the dress draped beautifully over her hips. Even though she wasn't showing a lot of skin, anyone could see that Katherine was fit.

David greeted Sharon. "I am way underdressed," he apologized.

"You are fine, honey. I should have told you what to wear. I'm sorry, I thought you would have known since the invitation read black-tie." She loved on him. "Eventually everyone removes their jacket, so you will fit right in."

Of course, she would put him at ease.

"I didn't notice," David said, feeling foolish he hadn't read the invitation. Knowing he would escape as soon as possible, he added, "I probably won't stay too long."

"David!" Michael shouted, grabbing and hugging him. "We are sitting at table number three. We saved you a seat."

Trying to sound as manly as possible since Katherine was within earshot, he said, "I know, I overdressed for the occasion, but I didn't want to upstage you."

"If it was my choice, we wouldn't be wearing tuxedos at all, but my wife makes me put on this monkey suit."

Sharon smiled, touching her husband's arm. "You know how much I love to see you all dressed up."

"See what I do for love." Michael winked at David.

David's heart raced as he greeted Katherine. He feared she would make fun of his attire. As soon as she finished her conversation with the guest ahead of him, she greeted David, shaking his hand, "Did my parents tell you they saved you a seat at our table?"

"Yes."

She pointed. "Reggie and Grace are over by the bar. Eric and Lana are running around in the kitchen making sure the food is ready."

As he went to mock his outfit and compliment her beauty, someone yelled, "Katherine!"

Everyone looked over as she lit up. "Steven!" It was another Cleveland player whom Katherine had not seen this year. The two of them quickly pushed David out of the way.

David had never had a full conversation with her. She was always pleasant to him, but she never sat down and talked with him the way she did with many others. Maybe she was still upset about their initial introduction? Perhaps he was uncomfortable because she was kind even after he was rude to her? Or maybe the opportunity had never presented itself. Whatever the reason, he wasn't one hundred percent comfortable around her anyway, especially now that she was so beautifully dressed and he looked like a high school football player going to an awards banquet. Besides, what would they talk about?

Moving to Reggie and Grace to order a glass of wine, he heard, "Nice duds, man."

Grace smacked her husband. "Leave him alone!" She hugged and kissed David.

"I didn't know it was black tie," David replied with embarrassment, trying to smooth out the wrinkled creases in his pants.

Now Reggie understood why David felt out of place. "You're fine. Everyone will be looking at me anyway." David couldn't help but smile as Reggie opened his suit coat, twirling around to model his look.

The event officially kicked off as Sharon thanked all attending and presented the statistics on abused children. She kept it moderately short, asking her guests to give from their heart and not out of guilt. Ninety-five percent of their donations would go directly to the children for education, clothing, food, shelter, and extra-curricular activities. The remaining five percent would go toward administration. All monies were accounted for, saving the remaining funds for the kids' college tuition. Sharon highlighted the children's progression and how they were benefiting from the program, next introducing a few families who wanted to publicly thank those who'd helped bring them out of poverty so they could stand on their own two feet. Sharon then asked one of the children to pray before they ate. It was beautiful to hear the prayer of a child.

When Sharon returned to the table, she addressed David. "I hope you don't mind waiting, but we like to serve our guests first. We appreciate the gracious giving and this is just a small way we like to thank them."

"No problem," David said, wondering if he should help too. Luckily, Reggie and Grace remained seated, and since they didn't help, neither did David.

After serving, Michael raised his glass. "Cheers!" Everyone followed, toasting to the worthy cause. Dinner conversation was mainly around the sponsored children. A couple of them sat at their table, making them all laugh with their innocent words.

After dinner was cleared, a tempting dessert tray was served to each table. The family certainly knew how to dine in style. In his years, David had eaten at some high-end, popular restaurants, but this meal rivaled most of them. Lana and Eric had a special gift of creating mouthwatering cuisine.

Soon guests mingled about, with the band heating up the dance floor. Several of David's teammates were dancing to some oldies and smoothly transitioned to current hits. Sharon and Michael socialized, again thanking their guests for their generosity. Eric and Lana managed the cleanup but weren't stuck in the kitchen by any means. Katherine seemed to work the room, but she wasn't. She just thoroughly enjoyed the company of her family and friends. David hung out by the bar, not talking to anyone, realizing all those happily gathered made him feel lonely for connection. It was not an emotion he felt comfortable with, and it was why he was looking for the perfect opportunity to slip out the door. Of course, he would say goodbye to the family, but probably only one or two others.

The dance floor was crowded and rowdy. Even Michael and Sharon were dancing. David watched the married couple, enjoying the show. They were still in love after years of marriage, and they couldn't help but show it. Anyone could tell they'd been dancing together since they first met. It wasn't a choreographed dance. No, they had their own rhythm which suited and complimented them. Not overtly sensual, but in a way that read they were satisfied with one another.

Michael looked around and spotted David. "Come on!"

David waved him off with a small smile. David hadn't danced in over four years. That had been the primary reason he'd gone out with his past teammates. He didn't enjoy the bar atmosphere, but he loved to get on the floor and dance. It was physical. But also sexy. Which of course got women's attention, which he loved.

Although most of the time he'd gone out dancing, he was with Gretchen.

Gretchen wasn't a fan or groupie; she was a career woman. A college sports journalist who became one of the most popular women's sports journalists in professional football. She was a tall, leggy, beautiful, blonde, and rail-thin. They had been committed to one other, even though they put their careers first. That was one reason he'd been attracted to her.

They met their senior year of college. He was the famous starting quarterback. Gretchen was majoring in journalism and dreamt of reporting on professional athletes, particularly football players since the game was her love. She knew the stats on pretty much any player. Interviewing college athletes as required, she became a familiar face around campus. When she finally sat down with David for an article, they hit it off instantly, becoming a couple. They were like Ken and Barbie—very well-suited for one another, but they weren't inseparable. Each led their own life while maintaining their exclusive relationship. At times, it would be weeks before they saw one another, but it didn't bother either of them since they were so focused on their careers.

After graduation, David was drafted, and Gretchen remained covering collegiate teams. Gretchen flew to see him every so often, spending a few days, hanging out with his team, and ending up on the dance floor. Dancing wasn't really her thing, though. David had such good rhythm, but she couldn't keep up and often felt awkward. Yet he made her feel at ease, so she couldn't help but move with him.

Their relationship worked exceptionally well for David. He saw her just enough to keep him satisfied, and since she had aggressive goals, she put no pressure on him to get married. Gretchen was only his third girlfriend, and by far the most serious relationship for him. As he rose to stardom, she did too. However, when he took a hit and was out for the season, she got promoted to covering professional football, and that's when it all changed.

As her career took off and his stalled, he became jealous of her success, taking his anger out on her. She attempted to encourage him and help him out of his depression, but the more she tried, the angrier he became and the worse their relationship got. She came to see him less, making excuses about why she couldn't come for a visit. And no way would he go see her, since her popularity had skyrocketed. Now he was known as her boyfriend, not something that sat well with him. The sexual attraction wore off, with nothing left to salvage, and in the heat of the moment after another slathering remark, Gretchen grabbed her things and walked out the door, never to return.

That was over four years ago, and David wasn't sure how he felt about it now. Occasionally, he would see her while she was interviewing a teammate, and they only greeted one another from afar then. They had never had any closing conversations about the end of their relationship. No apologies, no reconciliation, no communication. She successfully reached all her goals and desires. David missed that time of his life, being an elite Quarterback and having a girlfriend with no strings attached, and it was why he desired to return to Florida. He loved that state, and now he was sitting on a bench in one of the worse cities in America. Could it get any worse, he thought?

As David leaned over the bar railing, watching those dancing, an old familiar song played and the crowd cheered. The floor quickly was packed; even Eric and Lana were dancing. Such an incredible dance tune, it was hard not to move to the beat. And the lyrics, well to be polite, the man wanted to make love to his desire.

"Katherine!" Lana yelled. "Katherine!"

She was waving for her sister to come dance, but Katherine was stuck talking to someone. Yet anyone could see her body was slightly moving; she wanted to exit the conversation and get out on the floor. David could read her lips. "I'm sorry to be so rude, but I want to go dance with my sister."

He'd heard Katherine say those exact words on multiple occasions, begging an apology. When she needed to excuse herself from a conversation, she'd say sorry for what might make her seem rude. It intrigued David, but in truth, Katherine was never disrespectful.

David watched Katherine squeeze her way onto the dance floor, joining the latest line dance with his teammates. But her interest was not to continue line dancing, it was to get near her family. There were high fives all around when she finally made it to them. They were a dancing family. Several men attempted to dance with Katherine, but David could sense frustration. She wanted to be left alone and feel the music. And that's exactly what she did.

Katherine loved to dance. However, the dance floor was the place she missed James the most. Like her parents, James and Katherine had

had their own rhythm. And since dancing can be an intimate thing, she never felt comfortable dancing with anyone else. Katherine now held back while dancing, careful not to entice or become too suggestive. She wasn't interested in attracting attention, but she couldn't help but move when she felt a song. Often she felt frustrated because she longed to dance with no restrictions or repercussions.

David watched. Katherine was so alluring. Her eyes were closed, feeling the beat. She wasn't in any way in your face with her moves or trying to be sexy. It just oozed out of her naturally. Her body hit each beat perfectly. Katherine was in her own world. David noticed his leg moved to the same beat. It amazed him since he hadn't had any interest in music for quite some time. As the song was nearing its end, David stood straight up as he witnessed Katherine completely immerse herself into the flow, swaying her body in such a way that it was signaling to any man that she was good in bed.

Katherine was actually surprised because she usually had such good control over herself. When she realized she was getting a little too sexually involved, she pulled back and opened her eyes, only to find she was making direct eye contact with David, who couldn't keep his eyes off her. She immediately flushed red and turned away from him. She was embarrassed, slightly ashamed, and worried about her Christian testimony. The lyrics weren't in any way glorifying God. Quite the opposite. It was about a guy wanting to have sex with a woman. As she tried to finish dancing to the rest of the song, frustration set in. She hated feeling stifled. She honestly didn't know how to dance any other way, but she truly wasn't attempting to attract any man's attention. However, she couldn't resist moving the way she did, and she desperately missed her dance partner.

When the song ended, a slow one began. David watched several men approach Katherine but interestingly, Michael grabbed her hand as if to rescue her, slowing dancing with his daughter. Sharon looked around, smiling when she located David.

"You and your husband sure can move," he said when she came to stand beside him.

"We've been dancing together so long I can't remember what it's like to dance without him. Let's pray we have at least another twenty years of us dancing," she smiled.

Trying not to be so obvious, he asked. "Why aren't you out there with him now?"

"Well, as you can imagine, there are quite a few men attracted to her," she answered, watching her husband and daughter move around the floor. "At this stage in her life, she is not interested in dating and doesn't feel comfortable dancing that close with anyone. So Michael decided he would be her dance partner anytime a slow song plays."

"Wouldn't you like to dance with your husband too?"

She smiled, getting emotional, and rubbed David's shoulder lovingly. "I'm just thankful that she's still with us and is able to dance with her father."

David knew she was referring to the accident and asked no more questions.

"Did you eat enough?" Sharon checked.

Dave rolled his eyes, licking his lips. "Yes. It was fantastic. Eric and Lana are such excellent chefs."

"What about that dessert?"

"Which one, the chocolate or the cake?" he laughed.

"I had both too!" She smiled at the delicious memory, and they spent the next several minutes talking about their love of food. David enjoyed how his conversations with both Sharon and Michael were so natural. He'd never felt this close to any family, especially not his own.

The song ended, and David noticed while Michael came their way, Katherine went in the opposite direction.

"Why didn't you come out and cut up the rug with us?" Michael said, showing David some of his dance moves.

Beaming brightly, David joked, "I didn't want to show you up. I mean, come on, I'm already putting you to shame with my outfit."

Sharon was tickled, grabbing David's arm affectionately. "You are so funny!" She was glad he felt relaxed. She knew David had been nervous and uncomfortable upon arriving. Not to mention she felt responsible for his attire, believing she should have discussed it with him in advance.

David stayed a little longer, talking with Michael and Sharon, eventually leaving for the evening. He said goodbye to everyone, including Katherine, who was standing by Eric. He could tell Katherine was embarrassed. She hadn't gone back on the dance floor the rest of the evening.

Chapter 14

The Invitation

It was July, only a couple of weeks away from official training camp and about six weeks away from the preseason home opener. It was a big day in the Cleveland area, anticipation building. The Pro Football Hall of Fame was located right around the corner in the Akron/Canton area, and the inductee ceremony was that weekend. The team was at the stadium having a light practice. Many well-known faces from around the league were part of the festivities, mingling with the players.

Tim Thompson, a New York quarterback, rolled into town, drawing an enormous crowd. Tim was a good looking yet controversial figure for various reasons. He was a quarterback who won games mainly using his legs, not quite having the best arm in the game. His frame was exceptionally well built, similar to a running back, but he was taller as they preferred quarterbacks to be. Because he was so muscular, he could take the hits when he ran out of the pocket, running to a first down instead of passing. However, that style seemed better suited for college, not translating well into a professional game, so he'd been benched and was now sitting behind the starting quarterback.

But that wasn't the reason for his polarization. He was an outspoken Christian. People either hated or loved him because of it. Most loved his values. He didn't fall prey to temptations, vowing to remain a virgin until marriage. Of course, the media mocked him incessantly, but he took it in great stride, understanding that no matter what they said about him, God's name was proclaimed around the world because of his popularity. And that's all that mattered to him.

David greeted Tim from afar. He didn't know him personally and thought he was weird. He wondered if Tim was using the Christian thing as a way of getting attention. He wasn't too sure if the guy was real, and didn't care either way. As David was warming up, throwing the football, he noticed Michael walk on the field, hugging Tim hello. David didn't realize Michael knew Thompson.

He watched from a distance as they interacted, laughing and even moving closer for a more in-depth conversation. David knew Michael reasonably well by this time. He had spent the last four months with him at least five days a week, working out, talking finances and stocks, but also having those deeper conversations. He could tell by Michael's demeanor when he was serious, loving, or funny. He could read him so well now.

As others approached Tim, Michael shook his hand goodbye. When he turned to look around, he spotted David and trotted over to him "Busy weekend around here," he greeted, hugging him.

"I didn't know you knew Thompson," David said while passing the football to his throwing partner twenty yards away.

"Yes, it's been a long time. We've known him since he was a little tot," Michael said, holding his hand at waist level, indicating when Tim had met the family.

"Is he for real?"

"What? The way he talks about God?" Michael questioned.

"Yep. Is it for show or popularity? You know, to make money," David asked.

"No, he's been like that as long as I can remember. His parents are church planters…went all across America, home-schooled the kids, raised them to know nothing else but God." Michael thought a moment, then said, "It's understandable that people think he's fake, but all that matters is what God thinks of him. And just like us, he is accountable for his time on Earth too."

That was enough to shut up David. This was a normal conversation for the two of them. Somehow Michael managed to bring God into most of their conversations, and oddly enough, it did not bother David that much.

"Hey, how about lunch?" Michael asked, watching David throw a wobbly football.

"Are you paying?" David asked.

"Boy, are you cheap!"

"Look who I learned from." David smiled as he caught the ball and examined the laces, adjusting his fingers and grip since the football no longer felt comfortable in his hand.

A typical exchange for them, but in reality, Michael and David fought over who would pay for lunch, coffee, or anything else. They were very generous with one another. David was conscientious of how often he ate with Michael and Sharon, desiring to repay, never wanting them to think he was taking advantage of their wealth.

As they were discussing the restaurant, David continued to warm-up but only seemed to throw flat, wobbly ducks. Again, David examined the football, repositioning his hand, but that new grip seemed to decrease the balls velocity. He next stretched out his arm, mimicking a throw and mentally rehearsing the necessary movements for a perfect spiral. Nothing seemed to be working, and now David feared Michael would critique his throwing inability. He was preparing to mock his deficient performance but then noticed Katherine walk out onto the field. She was looking for someone, and David thought it was her dad until her entire face lit up when she saw a player. David stopped throwing the ball as he watched her attempt to run across the field, but her heels got stuck in the grass, causing her to laugh delightfully at her struggle. David looked to see who she was trying to reach, and his heart fell to his stomach when he realized it was Tim.

Thompson ran up to Katherine, picking her up off her feet and twirling her around as he hugged her. They were so excited to see one another. Even Michael chuckled when Katherine pointed to her shoe that had come off, still stuck in the grass. David turned sour, mostly from watching their interaction. Katherine acted differently with Tim than any other guy he'd seen her around. Even though they were about fifty yards away and he couldn't hear them, David thought she was flirting with him. She seemed relaxed, freely talking, touching his arm often, and laughing nonstop, as was Tim. It was not the normal professional behavior he was accustomed to seeing.

Katherine never ceased to amaze David. Each time he saw her, she did something unexpected. He could read her at certain times, but overall he didn't have a good handle on her, and that's why he didn't feel as comfortable with her as he did the rest of her family.

"I need to let her know that you're joining us for lunch," Michael said.

David wasn't aware that Katherine was part of their lunch plans, and now he worried Tim would join too. The thought of it made him literally feel sick to his stomach. He wasn't too sure why since he believed Katherine and Tim were a perfect match. They looked great together, talked about God, so it would only make sense for them to be a couple.

"Katherine! Hey, Katherine!" Michael yelled, not able to get her attention. "She's probably talking to him about their dinner plans tonight," he said to David. She was too far away and too engrossed in her conversation to hear her father calling her name. And since her back was to them, he couldn't wave her down either. "I'll call her," Michael said, grabbing his phone from his pocket.

David tapped him with the football, saying, "I'll get her attention for you." With that, he threw a perfect spiral fifty yards deep, hitting Katherine right in the back of her knees, causing her to fall forward into the arms of Tim, who caught her and made sure she was okay.

Instantly Katherine laughed, ensuring Tim she was fine, and turned to see who'd thrown the ball. She saw David pointing to her father, yelling, "He wants to talk to you!"

Katherine quickly grew irritated that David had intentionally hit her with the football and couldn't hide her facial expression.

Michael raised his eyebrows, asking, "Were you aiming for the back of her knees?"

David tried so hard not to laugh, since he knew he'd upset Katherine, but failed miserably keeping it back. "Yeah, I thought it would be funny."

Michael grinned and patted him on the back. "Right into the arms of another man I see." He turned to leave. "I'll see you in about a half hour."

Michael walked away, leaving David puzzled by the comment and the unusual aspect of Katherine joining them for lunch, but blocked it out of his mind to continue practicing. Soon his mood took another downward turn when he spotted Sharon greeting Tim in the same manner she did him, hugging and kissing the man. Now why would that bother him? It was standard for Sharon to hug and kiss almost everyone she knew. David realized he was feeling somewhat territorial with this family.

The Plan

As soon as Michael, Sharon, and Katherine were alone, making their way to the restaurant, Michael said, "Katherine, I asked David to join us for lunch but I want to talk to you about something before we meet up with him."

Still irritated, Katherine was in no mood to be near David. She wasn't thrilled that he'd hit her with the football. It was disrespectful.

She felt she had been nothing but kind, and practically anytime she had been around him, he annoyed her.

"What is it, Dad?"

"As you know, David's contract is about to expire and I want to take him on as a client. I've already talked with your mother, and we agree he would be a wonderful addition to our company."

"What?! You want to ask him today—at lunch—to be our client and you are just telling me about this now? Are you kidding me?"

All of them stopped walking. Her parents had not expected this reaction.

"What's the matter, honey? Why are you so upset?" Sharon asked.

"Why haven't you talked to me about this? Why would you make this decision without me? Don't I own the majority of the company?" Katherine could hardly believe the words coming out of her mouth. She was hardly ever disrespectful to her parents. In the five years of owning the company, she never once reminded them she had controlling ownership. Of course, she felt ashamed but was too angry to apologize at that moment.

"Honey," her father gently touched her arm, "I had no idea you would be this upset. I'm sorry. I won't ask him at all. We will just have lunch and not discuss business."

"Have you already talked to him about this? What did he say? How are you going to get out of this if you've already decided with him?"

"Honey, David has no idea," Sharon said. "This was something your father and I discussed, and we thought now would be a good time before he renewed his contract. Just like your father said, we will not proceed with this. Honestly, we didn't think it would upset you at all and thought you were ready for a new challenge since this is Reggie's last year."

"Well, why didn't you ask me what I thought about bringing him aboard?"

"This is how we handled it with Reggie, and I assumed there would be no problem following the same pattern," Michael said. "I'm sorry this is so upsetting to you. I don't want you to think I'm disregarding you at all. I saw an opportunity as I did with Reggie, and I wanted to seize it before it got away."

"But Dad, Reggie was different…he is different. When he was in jail, he got saved and repented. This guy is rude and disrespectful, and I don't get why the two of you like him so much."

After all the months of keeping her mouth shut, she just broke open. Katherine couldn't stop the flow. She had kept her opinions bottled up inside since the Memorial Day party. What was it with this guy that her parents fussed over him? Was she jealous she now had to share their attention? She knew she had no attraction to him. In the few interactions she'd had, he was cocky, condescending, and goofy. She almost felt betrayed by her family. She felt left out when he was around. They were her parents, and she was protective of them, and she didn't trust David.

"Katherine, we had no idea our relationship with David bothered you. Why haven't you told us how you've felt?"

She felt childish for opening her big mouth yet she couldn't keep it shut. "I don't trust him. I think he's bipolar or something. He acts totally different with you two. I think maybe he's trying to weasel into our family so you'll give him some money."

"Katherine, honey, I have gone over his portfolio and he has done extremely well at managing his wealth. Actually, a lot of what we talk about is the stock market and his investments." With a slight grin, he said, "He's been able to give me some excellent stock picks too."

"See, honey, David is a lot like your father," Sharon helped. "And he has taken him somewhat under his wing since your father knows how it feels to lose a job. Your father had no one to guide him during that time. So far, we haven't spoken to David at all about his career. We want to be his friend and build a relationship with him. We want him to trust us."

Of course, Katherine had seen this many times.

"We've been praying for him and watching God work in his heart," Sharon said. "He doesn't need to be a client. We were only looking to deepen the foundation and help him with his career. We weren't trying to offend you by not discussing this with you. Of course we know it's your company. We're sorry if you feel like we have shown any disrespect toward you."

Shaking her head, tears wet her eyes. "I'm sorry for saying I was controlling owner. Gosh, if it wasn't for you, this company wouldn't even exist. I love this company, and I'm sorry but I don't think David would be a good fit for it. I think he would defile its reputation."

And as if God himself was speaking through her mother, she said, "What reputation? That we are a small company that works with those who no one else wants because they aren't marketable or profitable? Are we trying to have others look at us and think we are do-gooders? I don't want to be a hypocrite doing something for show. I want to honestly, from my heart, help those who are lost and hurting. Now, we may have overstepped our positions within the company and, again, I'm truly sorry for that, but if this company is about showing face and not being true to what we believe in our hearts, then we need to have an honest talk about our company's direction."

Sharon's words convicted Katherine. "You are right, and I'm sorry to you both and God. But I am truly confused by your relationship with him, and, for some reason, I feel like I'm being shoved aside."

Both hugged her lovingly, asking, "Why, honey?"

"I guess since you have been spending so much time with him," she said, wiping away her tears.

"We spent the same amount of time with Reggie. He lived with us for a while," her Dad reminded her.

"Yes, but I was involved in that relationship. I'm not involved with this one."

"I really had no idea you felt this way," Sharon said. "Now I understand why you feel so awkward around him. Our intentions were not to make you feel unwanted or unloved, they were to make him feel comfortable and confident with us so we can help him see God's love." Her mother always had a way of clearing up misunderstandings.

"Are you okay, Katherine?" Michael asked.

"Yes," she said, trying to hold back her tears. "You can extend him an offer. I will be okay with it."

"No," they both said firmly.

"Listen, I wasn't looking at this the right way. I was being jealous and childish…and judgmental. I wasn't expecting he would be a potential client, so this entire conversation has thrown me off. I didn't have a chance to digest or process it correctly," Katherine stated. "What are your thoughts on how to bring him aboard?"

"Look, I think we all need to take a step back and take this topic off the table for a couple weeks," Michael said.

"Dad, we don't operate like that as a family or company. Now, I've been holding my feelings from you and you have been withholding some potential business decisions from me, and it really hasn't been healthy for our relationship or our company. Since we started working together, thankfully, this type of miscommunication has been far and few between. It's out there now, so let's talk about it and decide."

Smiling, Michael said, "You are truly your mother."

Katherine had learned to quickly reason on her feet and turn off her emotions when making business decisions. Her mother was a powerful, godly influence who had taught her to forego unnecessary feelings.

Michael shared his thinking. "I would like to bring him aboard, working on his business skills and his career. I see another five good years left in him. He's just mentally off-course. Your mother will continue to provide for his well-being as she's doing now. Katherine, I would like you to teach him the importance of interacting with people, specifically the media, handling those tough questions and absurd comments."

Katherine took a step back. This was way more than she could handle. She could see her father's excitement, but he wasn't aware of the deep roots of bitterness, depression, and anger lodged in David's heart. She didn't want to work that closely with him. This wasn't like Reggie, who had been eager to learn and wanted to change. David was a guy who punished others verbally when he felt slighted or threatened.

"Dad, he hates Cleveland. He doesn't even want to be here. He has made so many enemies. I'm not sure you understand that he has no interest in looking at himself."

"Well, if we believe God is running this company and your father and I felt led to bring this young man into our home and establish a relationship with him, let's just see what happens," Sharon said.

This was her mother's typical reasoning when situations made little sense and seemed incomprehensible, that God saw differently.

"I'm not so sure I want to do this. I'm not sure I can do this. I think Mom is much better suited at this than I am. Don't you think?"

"First, do you even want to talk business with him?" Michael asked.

"Only if you two believe this is right. You are the ones who know him better than I do."

Michael turned to Sharon. "Then if that's the case, honey, would you work with him, helping him with the media?"

"Yes, of course," Sharon answered.

"Dad, why did you want me to work with him in the first place? Why not, Mom?"

"It's a better fit. Of course your mother can take care of him, but you are already established with the team working with Reggie. It makes better business sense. More efficient and effective with our resources. No need to send two people to the same location. It's not cost effective, Michael explained.

"How about this?" Katherine said professionally. "Why don't we just meet with him for lunch and make the offer? We don't need to decide today who will work with him, whether it would be Mom or me. We can figure that out at a later time. Does that sound like a good plan?"

They agreed and once again apologized to each other, hugging closely. The family had little tension and did whatever it took to repair their relationship as quickly as possible.

Chapter 15

The Offer

Michael checked the time, hoping they weren't too far behind schedule and keeping David waiting. It turned out not to be a concern; David just was entering the restaurant as well. All quickly exchanged hugs and kisses except for Katherine, who only shook hands. It was evident to David by the feel of her hand and the look in her eyes that she was tense. He probably went a little overboard when he hit her with the football.

They sat at the table with Katherine seated next to David. Not her choice, but how it worked out. She still felt very uncomfortable, remaining silent as her father made small talk. He and David started up their usual bantering and laughter. It was so odd to her.

After placing their order, Michael broached the subject. "It's been a genuine pleasure knowing you these past several months, David. I've enjoyed our workouts, even shed a couple pounds."

Katherine grew tense.

"Since we are in the business, we know your current contract is about to expire, and we want to extend an option for you to sign on with us. You know we are a small company, but we have been able to establish a solid reputation. We believe we can offer you the same agreement but much better business relations than your current management company."

Up to this point, there had been hardly any conversation about David's game or management team. And that's why he felt so comfortable with them. Now that was all removed. David felt used. He was correct when he told Katherine he didn't want her selling him a contract, but he didn't expect her parents to be the salesmen.

"So this is why you have been taking an interest in me and being nice, because you want a contract with me? Are you serious? You want to make money off of me? Don't you have enough money as it is?"

The family sat stunned.

As David stood to leave, Michael grabbed his shoulder to prevent him, making direct eye contact as he spoke. "Son, I don't want your money. I love you and want to be involved in every aspect of your life."

Upon hearing those words, David couldn't stop the flood of tears. He didn't know where they came from. He rushed to the restroom and Michael quickly followed, leaving Katherine and Sharon looking at one another in disbelief.

Katherine's mind raced through the conversations she'd had with her parents about David, also thinking through her first interaction with the man, finally understanding. "He's been feeling unloved and unwanted for who knows how long?" she whispered. Her emotions overcame her. "For the first time, I felt that from you two…unknowingly. I can't imagine living with those thoughts for as long as he has. I can't imagine having parents who weren't caring, not ever understanding how it felt until you and Dad began spending time with him and I felt excluded." And then she realized, confessing, "Mom, I haven't forgiven him for how he treated me when we first met. Even though he apologized, I have been holding it against him ever since. I couldn't understand why I so adamantly rejected him, especially when I've been treated worse by others."

Analyzing her daughter's statement, Sharon asked, "Could it be because he scarred a wonderful memory you had with James? You both watched him play often."

Tears felt warm on her cheeks, but Katherine centered herself. James loved to watch David play. She had some fantastic memories with her husband around the game of football, as it should be since they'd spent many years watching together. Her mother remembered well, referencing past games she'd shared with James.

The Bond

Michael caught up to David, who was still making a beeline for the restroom. It was clear he was quite emotional.

"Is everything alright?" the maître d' asked.

"Yes, he just ate something very hot and he's having a reaction to it."

That caused David to laugh.

"Should I call for help, sir?" the maître d' replied.

"Oh, no. Is there some place private we can use?"

"Follow me." He led them to a small, intimate lounge for their use. Michael thanked him with a tip, then shut the door.

He sat next to David, allowing him to cry. David couldn't remember the last time he'd cried. Had he ever done so so hard? He couldn't talk. He didn't know what words to use to form a sentence because he didn't know what he was feeling, other than his own dad had never said "I love you" nor wanted to be involved in any part of his life.

Michael remained silent, only moving when he noticed David's nose dripping, handing him some tissues, which stopped the tears since Michael's presence became conscious. David blew his nose, trying to contain himself. Yet each time he attempted to say even one word, he sobbed anew. Michael knew from experience to remain in prayer and allow David's tears to flow naturally instead of forcing him to talk. After about fifteen minutes, David stopped crying. He sat there quietly for several more minutes, gathering his thoughts.

Looking at Michael with red eyes, he whispered. "I'm sorry I said all those things to you."

Michael put his arm on David's shoulder. "Thank you. I'm sorry if I made you feel like I was using you or had ulterior motives."

David reclined in his chair, wiping his nose. "You and your family have been nothing but kind to me. You have made me feel like part of your family." Teardrops welled up in his eyes once more. "I have really enjoyed spending time with you. That's not normal for me. I don't like many people, but for some reason, I have felt very close to you."

"Same here."

"I don't understand why you would be so nice to me. I was so rude to your daughter when I first met her. I mean, I was a downright asshole. When I saw you coming at me the next day, you were pissed and I was afraid of you, even though you are small."

They both chuckled.

"And after you threatened my life," he grinned, but tears once again found their way, "when you realized that I apologized to her, you changed. You were so kind to me. Why?"

Michael thought for a bit, finally saying, "About, I don't know, twenty years ago maybe…I guess it doesn't really matter how long ago it was…I lost my job and a business I invested in went bankrupt. I found out my partner at the time had been stealing, not paying bills, and obviously lying to me. I had to contact all our vendors and negotiate pay offs. I sold off that business and found a job almost an hour away from home."

David listened.

"I knew the job was beneath my abilities, and felt my earnings weren't reflective of my true talents. I was a snob."

David chuckled.

"I believed those in higher-level positions didn't deserve their titles or salaries. And I seethed with anger and hatred, making sure those around me knew what I thought of the executives of the company. I touted my skills, citing I was better suited for their positions."

Nodding, David listened.

"The company was on the verge of bankruptcy, so there were no promotions or ladder climbing. If a person quit, the job was disbanded and reorganized." Michael's eyes twinkled, recalling, "I can't tell you how many interviews I had. I was constantly looking for another job, but God blocked it."

David grinned, thinking it was funny that Michael believed God wanted him to remain in a stalemate position.

"So one day I returned to my office from a meeting and I listened to a voice mail from a higher level manager requesting some information. This was the fourth time she had asked for it." He chuckled, "I can't remember what she needed, but I didn't like anyone telling me what to do. I knew how to do my job. So I got mad, walked right in her office, interrupted her meeting, and yelled in her face that I knew how to do my job. I told her I was waiting on someone else to get me the information she wanted, but if she needed it today, I could get a gun and point it at his head and make him give it to me immediately."

"Seriously?" David asked.

Michael placed up his hand like a sworn witness would do, saying, "Ask Sharon."

"What happened?

"Well," Michael said, "As you probably can imagine, that didn't go over too well. They pulled me into so many managers' offices to talk about my attitude that my head swirled. I had to go to numerous training sessions on effective communication and professionalism. It was by the grace of God that I didn't lose my job. Of course, Sharon was pretty adamant I apologize to the manager, which I reluctantly did. The manager's husband worked at the company too, and he never said a word about how I treated his wife." Michael thought out loud, "Maybe he didn't because I apologized to her? Maybe he forgave me? He was also a Christian. Or maybe he was afraid of me?"

David chuckled since he understood why the husband would be afraid of him.

"They were a Christian couple, and I was also a Christian, but I was still pretty wild and had to sit on 'God's shelf' while He worked on my heart and attitude."

David tilted his head and scrunched up his face.

"I had to sit on the bench and I hated it."

The story hit too close to home, so David turned away from Michael.

"This is exactly why I haven't talked to you about your career or how you are playing. You get tense and pull away when someone even mentions the subject. I wanted to get to know you and not 'preach' to you."

David softened.

"I hated when Sharon tried to help my career, attitude, or anything related to what I was going through at that time of my life. And I made sure she paid for bringing up those topics. I pretty much verbally abused her. I was a prick back then."

David was shocked to hear Michael admit to this behavior.

Tears flooded Michael's eyes. "But as you can see, I didn't marry a timid woman, and, in her own way, she didn't allow me to intimidate or abuse her. And God did some pretty amazing things to work it all out for our good and His glory. Believe me, it wasn't instant roses; it was difficult, but desperately needed. We didn't have another couple to talk through the sins and problems within our marriage or hearts. We went to counseling for help. So really what I'm saying is that I see myself in you, and I believe that God will use you in a big way if you allow Him."

David again felt uncomfortable; it was too much talk about God. He'd never seen God do anything in his life but give him horrible parents and take away his one, genuine love, which was football.

Understanding him, Michael said. "We are very passionate men. We show it in different ways. I'm loud and outspoken, and often I put my foot in my mouth, needing to apologize."

David laughed, for it was true.

"You are a time bomb waiting to explode if you don't like what someone says to you. I was the same way. But when you were on your game, no one could touch you and all your passion went into football. It was like you were flawless."

Upon hearing that, David sobbed once more. He felt like such a loser and hated it. He hated his life, hated sitting on the bench, hated Cleveland, and he now realized, after all the talk about God, he hated God too. Michael again allowed him to cry it out.

After composing himself, David's anger flared up. "What frigging game? I can't connect the ball with the players, the defense is coming at me too fast, the receivers can't get down the field quick enough, the coaches are screaming plays at me and they don't make any sense and…." He broke down again, not wanting to admit his thoughts, but what did it matter if he told the truth. He whispered, "I'm afraid. I'm actually glad that I'm riding the bench because, when I get out there, I'm afraid to play the game. I'm so afraid."

Tears were dripping off his chin, so he wiped his nose with his sleeve before yelling, "And what's really messed up is that even though I'm afraid, I won't quit and I don't understand why! Why would I stay in this game, sitting on the bench, which I hate, and hope I don't get put in to play? There must be something mentally wrong with me!"

Michael silently thanked God for the young man's confession, seeing a tenderness in his heart after all the hardness it showed.

David demeaned himself, shocked and frustrated by his behavior. "Holy shit, I'm a girl! Don't tell anyone I have been sobbing like a two-year-old. And please don't tell anyone what I just told you."

"I won't even tell Sharon."

Blowing his nose yet again, he said. "I don't mind if you tell her. She's like a mother to me. I just don't want anyone else to know outside the two of you."

"I won't tell anyone. Thank you for trusting me enough to let go of your emotions and really tell me how you're feeling." Michael then fathered, "Listen, let's just forget our discussion today and continue with our relationship. You and I can debate the stock market all day and I feel like I'm getting a much better workout since you've come along. You have saved me from paying a personal trainer."

David grinned since Michael always made him feel loved and knew when to add humor. "Well, I'm not sure I can say the same about you. I've had to decrease the intensity of my workouts to accommodate your age."

In the spark of the moment, they burst out laughing, drawing closer in bond.

"Hey, I'm sorry for swearing," David said. "I know that's something you normally don't do and I don't want to offend you."

"Oh, thanks for reminding me. I have to apologize to the maître d' for lying to him."

"What made you think of saying that anyway?"

"What, that you were reacting to something hot?"

"Yeah," David replied.

"It actually happened to me. Years ago, I was at a Chinese restaurant, saw some mustard on the table, put some on a teaspoon, and tasted it. I didn't know it would be hot and I started gagging. I couldn't stop coughing and my eyes wouldn't stop tearing up, so I just thought of that when he asked me if you were okay. I didn't want to bring anymore unnecessary attention to you."

David was tickled since he could picture the story in his mind and would have liked to have been there with Michael.

Without saying anything, Michael's thoughts turned to Katherine, knowing she would no longer desire to conduct business after David's emotional distress. "How about we get the meal to go and just relax for the rest of the day. We can catch a baseball game. Does that sound like a good plan?"

"I think that would make this whole lunch even more awkward than it's already been," said David "Why don't you just give me your sales pitch and let me think about what I want to do? Maybe I will use it as a negotiation tool with my current company."

"Okay, you have yourself a deal." Although not feeling any better about Katherine, Michael put it out of his mind as they stood up to leave, saying, "Let me make you feel like a real girl now." He embraced David in a warm hug. "I'm so glad you are part of my life."

Holding the bridge of his nose to prevent tears, David said. "Dude, you are killing me."

Smiling, Michael patted him on the back. "Why don't you go get washed up in the restroom while I find the maître d'."

In moments, Michael found the maître d', and pulled him aside. "Thank you for taking care of us. My son....um, well, he's not actually my son, but I feel like he is...anyway, he was not having a reaction to anything hot. I just wanted to diffuse the situation as quickly as possible. I'm sorry for misleading you."

The maitre d' threw back his head, shocked that someone would apologize for something irrelevant. "It's not a problem, sir. Is there anything else I can do for you?" he replied.

Michael assured him there was not and the two made quiet small talk until David was ready.

Chapter 16

The Pitch

Michael's heart raced as he and David walked back to the table. There was no way to talk with Katherine regarding his previous proposal, and he wasn't sure if he should still proceed with their plan. He hadn't expected either his daughter or David's reaction today. His mind wandered to fear and anxiety, which was not typical of his behavior. Michael needed wisdom and did what was as normal as breathing, praying silently from his heart. "God, I believe you have led us to extend him an offer, and I obviously handled this all wrong, but I pray Your plan and Your will be done."

Even before they reached the table, Michael could see Katherine and Sharon were in a deep conversation, and even though the casual onlooker wouldn't notice, he knew his daughter and could read her emotions. Now Michael's nerves were at an all-time high.

When the women saw the two men, they smiled warmly, placing Michael at ease.

"We asked the server to hold off on serving the salad until you were both ready. Should I ask him to bring it now?" Sharon asked, slightly raising an eyebrow to Michael to know if they were remaining for lunch.

"I'm pretty hungry, so if everyone else is ready, I'm ready to eat now," David said.

"I'm ready too, Mom."

"Honey?" Sharon asked Michael.

"You know I'm always ready to eat," he grinned.

Sharon passed the bread and butter while asking for their salads, making light conversation that the bread was the best around town. She wanted all to be comfortable and moved to make things light-hearted.

"I'm sorry for my reaction earlier," David said, not offering anything specific.

"That's okay, sweetie," Sharon said. "It's kind of you for apologizing."

Katherine slightly grinned at David, not knowing what to say.

Turning to face Michael, David asked, "What do you want to offer me?"

Michael looked directly at Katherine. She wasn't too sure what she was feeling or how to interact with David, but she trusted her parents and nodded to her father, encouraging him to continue.

Michael thought about sugar coating the topic, but David had been man enough to place it on the table, so he would speak in the same manner. "Well, we need to review your current contract, verifying we have the correct financial comparatives, but the area we know your management company lacks in is their commitment to serve you and improve your personal image. Our proven track record shows that's where we excel."

"Not to offend you, but you only have what, eight clients? And you are losing Reggie at the end of the season. So I'm not sure how you can prove your track record with only eight athletes. Not to mention you are unknown nationally, so I would think any major endorsement company would eat you alive when negotiating. Your current clients aren't household names, so it limits your experience when dealing with league contracts. All your clients are local and only have area endorsements."

Michael smiled. "You've been doing your homework on our company."

"Well, I wanted to be prepared in case we were to ever have this conversation." Placing his head down, David said, "I just didn't expect I would have had that sort of reaction."

Michael put a hand on his arm. "You have valid concerns, and I'm even more impressed with you as an entrepreneur."

Removing Michael's hand, David teased, "Cut out the flattery, it's not becoming of you."

Katherine was again surprised by her father's interactions with David. She didn't understand it. She'd seen her dad with James, Eric, and Reggie, but this was so different. There was mutual respect between these two men; her father loved David.

"Tell me what your current company has done for your career lately?" Michael asked. "If not your current one, has any other company worked with you in such a way that demonstrated they personally took an interest in you and your needs?"

David felt again like he had these past several months—angry and defensive. But instead of lashing out, he took a deep breath, asking. "What are you proposing?"

"Your image has taken a pretty dramatic hit. I've done my homework on you too, and I know you have some lofty goals for retirement. I know you want to coach and establish yourself as a businessman," Michael said.

David nodded, feeling grateful that Michael took an interest in his life, but he was still defensive because he didn't trust anyone with pretty much any part of his life.

"With your current state, I'm convinced no professional or collegiate teams would want you as part of their coaching staff," Michael stated.

David tensed up, almost lashing out, wanting to leave the restaurant and the Luka's lives for good. Anyone could see he didn't like what he was hearing. It was the truth, though, and sometimes the truth hurts.

"You are skilled financially. I'm very impressed by your investments and the financial decisions you have made, even at a young age. Many athletes are broke five years after retirement. You can retire today and not work another day in your life, living comfortably. But knowing you, I believe you enjoy the challenge of working," Michael said.

David relaxed, but only until he heard, "But again, in your current state, the business executives I connect with would not give you the time of day. I'm concerned you would enter a partnership with individuals who would cause you financial sacrifice."

Insulted, David said. "Do you really think I'm an idiot who would get into business with someone and end up losing my savings?"

"Maybe not. But I know from experience that you need to select a business partner the same way you would select your marriage partner—there needs to be open communication and trust." Michael looked at Sharon, then Katherine. "My first company fell apart because I was unevenly yolked with my partner. But even though I lost the company and some money, I learned a valuable lesson, which has never returned void."

"But again, what are you proposing, that I go into some sort of business with you? What is it that you are offering me?"

"I'm not proposing any business deals at all. What I want to do is work with you in a way that helps your mental state, your outlook on life, and introduce you to my business contacts. You have built yourself a reputation that's not pleasing to many people. You come across as arrogant, condescending, and a true snob. People don't like you. Now, we like you," Michael said, pointing to both Sharon and himself. "You have shown us a side of you that is very loving and caring. Thankfully, you have let down your guard and been real with us."

David was regretting meeting this family and was trying to control himself when he said, "Do you really believe I give a shit what other people think about me? When I was at the top of my game, the media still bashed me for whatever would give them ratings. I don't care that I'm a prick. They are a bunch of idiots, asking the same stupid questions, trying to look so smart. They are really nothing but wannabes. I look at them as roaches."

"You are a brand and your image is everything," Katherine spoke up.

Everyone looked over at her in disbelief because they hadn't expect her to say a word. David was so engaged in his conversation with Michael he had forgotten she was sitting there.

"I'm not a brand! And I don't want to be a brand!" David shot back.

"Whether you like it or not, you are a brand and you are selling yourself; it's just part of the business. You may not believe you are a role model as some other athletes believe, but you are. One reason Jordan is still so popular is because he knew his image was his brand and he capitalized on it."

David turned towards her. "Jordan is still popular because he is one of the greatest players of all time."

"Look at the top earning athletes this year. Yes, they are elite athletes, but most have likable personalities with even a few playing to their audience. Their fans are devoted to their cause. Knowing your image is everything, and it will pay you back in dividends," Katherine stated.

He couldn't argue with her, knowing it was the truth, but it irritated him nonetheless. He turned his back on her, purposely addressing Michael. "Again, no one is answering my question. What are you proposing?"

"To put it simply, to clean you up," Michael said.

"How?"

"Well, we like to do it from the inside out. Like I said before, I want to work with you on your business skills, which just need a little polishing. I will introduce you to my colleagues, reviewing their business models with you so you can start adapting them to your lifestyle, dreams, and goals. We'll also give you finesse in negotiating terms and conditions on your own."

"But I already know how to do that. You just said yourself I'm a good businessman," David protested.

"I said good, not fierce. The way you communicate with your condescending comments and snobbish body style is only setting you up to fail. Being fierce is not about being cruel or mean spirited, it's about being intensely focused and knowing how to leave nothing on the table, building lasting and profitable business relationships."

Passion for what her father was saying took over Katherine. "I will teach you how to deal with the media. Yes, I agree some of their question are ridiculous, but you are antagonizing them. You make it easy for them to lead you on and aggravate you, taking their bait every time only to end up being quoted for saying something that makes you look like a fool."

David blew her off. She just hammered the last nail in the coffin for him. Looking at Michael, he asked. "Why would you do all of this? What are you getting out of it?"

Michael responded, verbalizing what Katherine was thinking. "Great question. This is one reason I like you so much. You aren't a fool. You want to get to the heart of things too, but you need some hand holding."

David wasn't feeling any better.

"Look, when I was a young punk like you," Michael joked, "I made so many mistakes I am surprised I didn't bankrupt several companies. I had to learn the hard way by sitting in some job I hated and wrestling with God over my career. I finally gave up the wrestling match. Then I prayed. A tiny but earnest prayer to let His…" Michael pointed to heaven. "…will be done with my career."

David shifted uncomfortably. Here Michael goes talking about God again, he thought.

"Well, over the course of a couple months, somehow, and still to this day, though I don't remember the reason, I got interested in the stock market. I started buying stocks in my retirement account, then out-of-pocket. Then I invested in technical charting courses, which led me to some individuals like myself who wanted to provide for their families independent of working for a company that might end up laying them off when they got to a certain rung on the ladder. I didn't want to be put in a situation where I had to solely rely on a company to financially support my family. I hoped to provide for them independently."

Katherine leaned into the table eager to take on this challenge.

"By the grace of God, I became very profitable with my investments. And again by the grace of God, I met some Godly men and formed a tiny company. My only requirement: we would serve no one just because of their wealth. We wanted to serve our clients as if they were potential business partners, which meant we would not partner with those who made money in a way that did not align with our beliefs. Nothing that would profit on objectifying women or children, companies that weren't promoting family values and so on."

David listened.

"We wanted only team players, no one who had the potential to infest our team. Now, most of the time we made significant decisions, but sometimes we were blind-sided. Oddly, it brought us together, making us a stronger unit. Eventually, I felt led to mentor young men who had no opportunity to go to college or even graduate from high school. I had to look past their actions, looking at their hearts to see if they were moldable and teachable."

Katherine nodded, recalling some of those her dad had helped.

"See, their actions would reflect anger, bitterness, and hostility—all survival skills for them," Michael said, moving in closer to David. "I could look past that and see their potential, and God honored that work. And to this day, no matter how much money I have made, it doesn't compare to having watched these young men become successful in their own right."

Sharon grinned at her husband.

"About seven years ago, I began feeling restless…as if I needed a new challenge. I couldn't pinpoint what needed to change, but I kept my eyes open for another opportunity." Michael took a breath and his eyes watered. "When the accident happened…"

Katherine swallowed but maintained composure.

"…I took a leave of absence from my job to hold up James's company. It was rapidly falling apart. Clients were leaving left and right because of a clause in the contract tying them directly to Katherine's husband, James. Our entire life was reeling out of control, but I knew I was to be planted with James's company. The only thing I could do to prevent us from filing bankruptcy was to pour a sizable amount of money into it. And I thought if I was going to do that, then I had to sell most of my shares in my firm, step down, and work solely for Cleveland Management Institute Sports Agency."

David understood Michael's decision.

"We decided as a family that this company would perform the same way as our investment company and not take on any clients who weren't aligned with our principals. As you already know, the sporting world is made up of young athletes who often get a hold of some big money and fame, and may travel down a path that places them in the news unfavorably, sending management into damage control. Some end up in jail, tried for sexual assault, drugs, or alcohol-related incidents. We don't want those types of individuals," Michael said.

"We purposefully have put ourselves in a situation where we can remain small and be selective. We have turned away several athletes who would have been a management nightmare. We aren't looking to make so much money that we have to spend more money on public relations. My goal is to make a name with the college athletes, harness some younger, impressionable talent and teach them finance fundamentals, not how to sell your soul and character."

"That's admirable what you have done with the company and where you want to take it," David said, "but you just told me in not so many words that I would be a public relations nightmare, so I'm confused why you are approaching me."

"Well, we've been getting to know you these past several months. I've looked passed the media reports. I know you. I know you are a great guy who has lost direction. I'm eager to work with you to help get you back on the right path. We did it with Reggie."

"So, I'm a charity case?" David asked.

"I'm not trying to offend you. I just want you to know what I see differs completely from what is being reported," Michael said.

"Look, thank you, but I really am not interested in what you are offering me. To be blunt, until I am leading a team again, any management company is a moot point. It's really up to me to get my career back on track, and no management company can do that for me," David said.

"But no other teams will want you with your attitude! They think you are a head case. And your contract with Cleveland is only until the end of this season," Katherine said, again surprising everyone.

David, annoyed, turned towards her, leaning far into the table. "So what are you saying, that Cleveland won't want to re-sign me either?"

"What I am saying is if you work with us and allow us to help develop your image, I guarantee you will sign on with another team and be able to move away from this city you hate so much!" Katherine fired back.

David backed up, smiled, and looked right at Michael. "How can I argue with that?"

"I thought she was only like her mother, but in this business, I can see myself in her too." Michael winked at Katherine.

"Let me think about what I'm going to do. The motivation would be to get out of this city."

"David, to be fair, inquire with your current company. Make sure you fully understand their services for public relations and personal image mentoring. Then honestly ask yourself if you would be open to their teachings compared to ours. I think you will find your answer," Michael said.

When the entrees came, there was no more mention of business. The talk turned to the Hall of Fame event, the media frenzy over Tim Thompson being in town, and Katherine's dinner plans with the quarterback.

David had a poor attitude through the meal, which he hid. He didn't like Tim, and it bothered him that Katherine was having dinner later that evening with him. David couldn't understand his feelings since her comments on his attitude and demeanor had annoyed him greatly. He wanted to work with Michael and was motivated by the prospect of getting out of this town, but he in no way felt comfortable working with Katherine.

Chapter 17

The Talk

It had been a week since David had gone to lunch with the family and discussed business. David and Michael had kept their usual workouts, however, Michael didn't ask him for a decision nor did David mention the offer. Despite this, David felt disconnected from their relationship. He hated being put in the situation he was now in and didn't want to decide. If he didn't sign on with the family, he believed his friendship would end with Michael. If he became a client, he would have to work with Katherine and he wasn't comfortable with her.

As they jogged, Michael asked, "I'm going to the baseball game tonight, do you want to come with me?"

David slowed his pace, feeling depressed. "No, I don't feel like doing much of anything today." He came to a walk. "You know, I don't feel like working out today. I'm going to head home."

"Are you feeling okay, son?" Michael asked.

"I'm fine. I just want to be left alone!" David snapped, walking away. He felt like he was reeling out of control, too many thoughts were going through his mind. He felt paralyzed. He felt like he couldn't go back to their prior relationship, but he didn't want to move forward with the family either. He seethed with anger. He was so sick of being like this, living like this. David hated his attitude, but he didn't want to change. He felt like crying but wasn't sure why. He loved being around Michael, but now he felt awkward and out of place.

Upon getting into his car, even before he started it, tears poured down his face. Why? And for whatever reason, from his heart, he prayed, something he hardly ever gave a thought to do. "God, if you really do exist, please help me."

David didn't know what else to say. He wasn't sure how to pray or what he was praying for, but he knew he couldn't take much more. He started his car, ready to pull away, when he noticed Michael walking toward his direction, looking upset, wiping away tears.

They made eye contact, but Michael wasn't sure what to do. So he decided to treat David as any family member and approached the car, asking him to roll down the window. "Do you want to come in for some breakfast?"

"No, I just want to go home. I'm not feeling too good."

"Son, how about you tell me what's on your mind? You haven't been yourself since we met for lunch. Let's talk about what you are feeling."

"I don't want to talk. I just want to be left alone," David insisted, grabbing the steering wheel tightly.

"Okay, we don't have to talk. Let's just get something to eat. I don't want you going home being upset."

Wanting the truth, David asked. "Why do you care?"

"Why wouldn't I care? I love you as if you were my own son," Michael said.

David wasn't sure what that meant. "Why?"

"Can I get into the car with you?"

David nodded, shutting if off.

Michael took a deep breath and walked over to the passenger side. Once situated, he went to the heart. "Can you tell me about your dad, please?"

"Why?" David questioned, agitated to talk about that nonsense.

"I want to understand a little more about him," Michael replied.

"I've already told you about him."

"You've told me that your parents are married, but don't live together. You said your dad doesn't work and is on disability. You said he only came around for money." Michael continued, "But, I also remember you saying you've had no contact with him in years. Why?"

"Listen, I don't want you to preach to me about my parents. I don't have a relationship with them like you have with your daughters," David warned.

Michael turned his whole body toward David, loving this young man. "Look at me in the eyes. Have I ever preached to you? Have you ever heard me tell you what to do?"

Quietly David said, "No."

"I think you may be afraid you will turn out like your dad, and that just isn't the case," Michael said.

"I know I'm not like my dad!"

"Well, you won't tell me about him, so let's just look at the facts you've told me. Your dad doesn't work. You haven't technically worked in several years. Your dad is on disability. You were disabled for a season and it took you down to second string. Is it because of your dad's disability that he has so much anger?"

David hesitated a while, then said, "No. My mom got pregnant before they were married. My dad was obsessed with her. Completely and utterly obsessed. When they finally married, I guess that's when everything changed. My mom didn't like having me or being married, and they'd only married because she was pregnant. She thought she could do better than my dad, telling him that often. He tried to please her in every way, but she ran around with other men. He wouldn't divorce her…" Looking out the window, he evaluated, "I don't know, maybe as punishment, who knows? But he became severely depressed and couldn't work because of his mental condition. Eventually, he was diagnosed as clinically depressed, put on medication, and then on disability."

Hanging his head in shame, David attempted to shield himself, crossing his arms in front of his chest. "My mom ran off to live with some guy. There was no way I was going to live with my dad alone, so I moved in with my grandma and stayed until I went to college. After they drafted me, my dad came around looking for money." Shaking his head, he grumbled, "He wasn't getting a dime from me."

"What about your mom?" Michael asked.

"I haven't talked to her since the day she left."

Michael nodded. "Do you feel that it's your fault? Do you think it's your fault your dad's depressed and your mom left?"

Making eye contact, David asked, "Why would it be my fault?"

"Well," Michael said tenderly, "it sounds like from the story they wouldn't have married if you weren't born."

Looking back out the window, David said. "Actually, you would think I would feel that way, but I don't. If anything, it really bothers me that my dad wasn't man enough to control my mom. He was weak and couldn't stand up to her, and I honestly couldn't take watching him being beat down by her."

"Sounds like he did to you what your mother did to him," Michael whispered.

"What do you mean?" he said, turning back to Michael.

"Well, and this is only from the little you told me, sounds like your mom married your dad not out of love but because she was pregnant. Your mom wanted out of the marriage, but your dad wouldn't grant her a divorce, so she verbally abused him and then cheated. You also said that you didn't think your dad was a man. Well, I'm sure he didn't feel like a man. How could he? He loved your mother but she didn't return his love."

David felt bad for his dad since being around this loving family had softened his exterior shell slightly.

"Isn't it possible your father was taking his anger out on you since you were younger and weaker? Maybe he couldn't or didn't know how to standup to your mother. It sounds like she dominated him," Michael said.

David sat numb, not wanting to think of his past.

Next, Michael very lovingly asked, "Did your dad abuse you in any other way?"

"You mean did he beat me?"

Michael nodded.

"No. Not really. Maybe once or twice he spanked me, but neither one of my parents disciplined me."

Again Michael lovingly asked, "Any other form of abuse?"

"Sexual?" David questioned.

"Yes," Michael said.

He shook his head quickly. "Oh, no. Not at all!" He understood Michael worked with children who were abused by adults and his heart went out to them.

"Thank God," Michael replied, then asked, "What did you do when your dad took his anger out on you?"

At this point, David wanted to get this conversation out of the way, so he answered, "When I was a kid, I hid in my room, dreaming about running away." His eyes twinkled and a slight grin came over his face. "I always wanted to be a football player, so my thoughts eventually centered around that, on becoming the best." His grin disappeared. "But as I got older, I argued back, calling him a loser for holding onto a wife who didn't want to be married." Shame gripped his heart as he admitted this. "I even told him I was embarrassed that he was my father and a weak man."

Michael patted his hand, whispering. "How did your dad respond?"

"Same. He told me I would never make it as a quarterback and I wouldn't amount to anything."

"How did you respond to him then?"

Looking out the window again, David shared, "You know it's odd, I didn't respond. I said nothing. I would leave and go play football. It's like I worked ten times as hard to prove him wrong."

"It sounds as if God gave you the gift of football to take you away from the pain in your house."

David stared at Michael to explain.

"It was your way of escaping from reality. Your focus was on football so you didn't have to deal with your parents' dysfunction. That to me is a gift."

David grew angry. "So then why did He take it away from me?"

"Oh, I don't think for a second God took it away from you. I think God is trying to teach you something through it," Michael gently responded.

"What? Teach me what?"

"Well, you love football more than anything, don't you?"

David's nod was instantaneous.

"Let's just say after your injury, it knocked you off course a bit and it's been difficult to deal with. Wouldn't you agree that you are somewhat depressed or angry?" Michael asked softly.

"Yeah."

"Do you feel like a man, David?" Michael asked. "Be honest with yourself."

He thought about what he felt, then answered, "I can't say I do feel like a man, but honestly, I can't say I don't feel like a man either. I just don't feel like myself."

"Why is that? What does feeling like yourself mean?" Michael questioned.

Again, David had to think about precisely what he wanted to say, finally understanding. "I was a winner. There wasn't an area in my life where I wasn't winning. I couldn't care less about my childhood. I loved being around my team. I was happy." And with a sexy grin, he added, "And I could have any woman I wanted."

"It sounds like life was effortless," Michael said.

"It felt like it," David replied.

"Now how does it feel?"

"It feels like it's hard to get out of bed. I have to push myself to do anything. I don't feel happy. I definitely don't feel like a winner, and I feel like I'm always angry."

"Sounds like your dad."

Eyes filled with hostility, David got defensive. "Are you telling me I'm my dad?"

"No. I think you are in a situation you can relate to your dad. Your father loved a woman who didn't return his love and he didn't know how to handle those feelings of hurt and rejection. He became depressed and angry. You lost your game. And in your words, your one, genuine love. You have been depressed and angry too. Who wouldn't be?" Michael helped. "But maybe since you've been going through this, you can understand your father a bit more. He was truly hurt and didn't know how to deal with it, and, just like you, he took his anger out on those around him, which happened to be you."

Placing his hand on the steering wheel, thinking through Michael's words, David understood his father's actions.

"I think God is being gracious to help you see your dad in a different light so you can forgive him and actually be able to love him," Michael said.

For the first time, David felt sad for his father and his heart went out to him. Then he asked Michael a heartfelt question. "Why would I need to forgive my dad? He's the one who treated me with hatred."

Michael was pleased David was willing to dig in to the topic. Reaching to pat the young man's hand affectionately, he said "You always ask such good questions. You know we live in a world that seductively teaches revenge. You've heard the phrase 'the best revenge is a successful life'? Well, you have been very successful; did you get any revenge on your dad? Or a better question would be did it change your dad or change your relationship with your dad?"

"No," David answered.

"God tells us to forgive. Many people think of this as a weakness, but they are so mistaken. It's a true strength." Michael touched his heart. "This is not lip service forgiveness—it's from your heart. Think of this like the penalty for holding. You are illegally restraining or holding another player who doesn't even have the football. So why is it even a penalty?" Michael asked.

"Well, it's not allowing fair play." David paused, then added. "It could also risk injury."

"Right. Your dad restrained you. He didn't want you to advance and you weren't even the one holding the football. It wasn't fair. But now you need to examine your heart and find out if you are restraining your dad. Are you holding onto thoughts of hatred, bitterness, resentment, maybe some type of revenge or hostility? Because if you are, it will always penalize you and not your father. And you risk injuring your relationships with those around you. Hasn't that happened already?" Michael pointed out softly.

"Yeah," David said, realizing he had treated Gretchen the same way. When she became successful, reaching her career goals and he was benched, David took out his anger on her. He knew he would need to apologize to her one day.

Michael believed the time was now right to say, "I'm sure you heard of Jesus dying on the cross for our sins."

David nodded instantly.

"Well, when He was on the cross, people hurled insults at Him, mocking Him, saying, 'If you are really God, then save yourself, come down from the cross.'" Michael went on. "Since, of course, He was God, He could've saved himself or wiped those people from the Earth right there and then. But God had a bigger plan for Jesus's crucifixion. And Jesus from the cross said, 'Father, forgive them for they do not know what they are doing.'"

David turned toward Michael, interested in the man's story.

"If you ask God, I believe He will not only help you to forgive your dad but He will actually show you that your dad did not know what he was doing. I'm not in any way saying that what he did was right, but I believe your dad didn't know how to handle those feelings of hurt and rejection, and he took it out on you."

David understood, grinned, and asked, "Is this the personal attention you are talking about giving me if I become your client?"

Michael smiled with tears in his eyes, saying. "You don't need to be a client of mine for me to give you this type of personal attention. You are a part of our family, and this is how you love when you are part of the family."

Relieved there was no more tension, and since they were on the topic, David said, "I'm not sure I feel comfortable around your daughter. I don't understand why she needs to be the one to address my interaction with the media." This admission made him feel weak, like he wasn't a man, so he attempted to back step his words. "I mean, of course, I can handle working with her, and I didn't mean to say she makes me feel uncomfortable, but it's just…well, why can't I work solely with you?"

Michael understood. "Thank you for confessing, telling me how you feel. That's a unique strength you will come to realize will be very valuable to you." Michael didn't think now was the time to ask him questions about Katherine, so he said, "I can work with you, but it makes better business sense for Katherine to work with you. She's there with Reggie and has established solid relationships with most in the organization and the media."

David's mind raced back to their initial meeting, remembering how so many greeted her warmly.

Michael laughed, saying, "She's so much better at it than me. I can be a hot head and she just has her mother's way of diffusing a potential problem, although she's not afraid to speak the truth either."

Even though David didn't want to work with her, he avoided continuing the line of thought, saying instead, "Let's do it."

"Do what?" Michael questioned.

"Let's write up a contract with your company. Let's stick with the original plan. I'll work with you and your daughter."

"Why? What made you come to this decision?"

"How I'm dealing with things now hasn't helped. And you are right, I would not be this open to anyone else or any other company. Let's just say my goal is to work on my image so I can move to a sunny state," David said.

"Maybe Florida?" Michael smiled.

"Maybe," David smiled back.

"Okay, let's get breakfast and then we will get something over to you to sign later this week."

"No, let's finish our jog first, unless you are too old to keep up with me," David joked.

Michael chuckled. "Maybe we can pick up the pace a little. Come, let's go!"

And off they started on their run again, feeling energetic and laughing as usual. While his feet pounded the path, Michael thanked God for His goodness and for speaking through him to allow David to open up.

Chapter 18

The Contract

The family always celebrated life together and signing David as a client was no exception. A favored high-end steakhouse was the welcomed tradition. Lana and Eric joined the festivities with her parents, sister, and the man of the hour.

After popping open champagne, Michael raised his glass to toast, praying, "Lord, thank you for bringing David into our lives. We pray for wisdom with this transition and for much success in his career. And, of course, we thank you for Your goodness."

Toasting glasses, agreeing, the table responded, "Amen!"

There were smiles all around as they ordered, then everyone shifted focus to talk about the coming season. Katherine and Sharon wanted to wash their hands before eating, so they excused themselves to the ladies' room. "It's been quite a busy week of negotiations, hasn't it, sweetie?" said Sharon.

"Yes, but that's okay, I love it," Katherine said brightly.

Gently stroking her daughter's hair, Sharon said, "I know you do, honey. You are so much like your father. I'm proud of you."

"Thanks, Mom."

Taking a deep breath while she washed her hands, Sharon offered, "Now, I can work with David if you don't feel comfortable. You know that, don't you?"

"Yes, I know, you've told me all week," Katherine chuckled. Making eye contact, she said, "I don't feel one hundred percent comfortable like I did with Reggie but that's okay. David is only my second client, so I should have some reservations. I've prayed and thought about this all week, though, and I have concluded that if I didn't work with him, it would be strictly out of fear of failure. I would rather try and fail then to never try at all. I know we have a long road ahead of us, and I'm pretty much convinced that he doesn't want to change his attitude, but that would be his choice. I'd rather know in my heart that I gave it my all than sit back and do nothing and have regrets."

"That sounds like my girl. I only want you to know I'm here for you," Sharon replied.

"I already know that…and I'm glad." Katherine grinned, taking her mother's arm, leading her back to the table.

But she was afraid. She'd worked with many difficult people but never as clients, and she wasn't sure how David and her would interact. Her mind raced back to challenging individuals she'd crossed paths with, realizing there was plenty of time in between conversations to buffer emotions. However, Katherine would work with David several times a week, which wasn't a lot of time to recover from any confrontations. David hadn't even been in Cleveland for six months and he'd made plenty of enemies. Katherine was overwhelmed.

After an amazing meal, they left saying goodbye in the parking lot. It was a beautiful evening, with a nice warm, cozy breeze and fresh-smelling air. Katherine loved these kinds of starry nights.

Approaching David, she said, "I'm not sure what your plans are for tomorrow but I would like to get together and start working."

"What do you have in mind?" he asked.

Lana and Eric honked their horn as they drove away, and both waved to them.

"Well, for starters, I would like to get to know you a little better. Your background, your past…." Katherine watched his body slump over as he looked down at the ground, kicking a stone. "Some simple things like likes, dislikes, favorite color."

That caught his attention.

She smiled warmly, light-heartedly saying, "We are going to have a business relationship, and I like to have fun while I'm working. I hope you do too."

"Yes, of course," David said, watching Michael and Sharon drive off, feeling tense to be alone with Katherine.

"Are you working out with my dad in the morning?"

"That's the plan," he replied.

"Okay. Well, I have your training schedule and it looks to be pretty light this week," she said, looking at her phone to confirm his schedule. "You have another camp with the kids next weekend, but nothing more than that. I think we can get started tomorrow after your workout. Is that okay with you?"

"Yeah, that's fine," he said, kicking another stone, not really caring about any meeting.

"We can meet at our office, which is somewhat busy, or we can meet at my parents' house. I'm sure you want to take a shower after you work out, so I'm looking to see what works best for you," she said in an effort to make him feel comfortable since the conversation was strained and tense.

David's mind started reeling. If they met at her parents' home, they would be all alone. If they met at the office, he would need to deal with other people, which wasn't sitting well with him either. He now regretted making this decision and wanted to lash out so she wouldn't want to work with him.

"Isn't that one of the most beautiful moons you have ever seen?" Katherine said, surprising him.

The moon peered out from a cloud, so big you felt like you could almost touch it. It was orange-yellow tinted, hanging beautifully among the background of trees.

"It's just amazing how perfect it is. No artist or photographer can ever capture that look. And even though they try, it cannot compare with the real thing." She looked at all the stars, continuing, "I love the sky. It's different every day. Sometimes it dramatic; sometimes it glows with red, orange, and blue hues; and sometimes it's gray. But it's never boring, and it's never the same. Just like Lake Erie."

David was captivated by her description of nature, and he couldn't take his eyes off her as she romanticized it. She was like her mom, and he recognized there was no reason to feel uncomfortable with her.

"Let's meet at your parents' house. I usually take a shower there anyway. Is 8:00 a.m. too early for you?"

That brought her back to reality. "Uh, no, that's not too early at all. I'll see you then." She left with a smile, walking to her car, looking at the moon one more time before she drove away.

David stayed awhile, walking around the area, looking at the different stores and watching people. It indeed was a beautiful evening, and he wasn't ready to go home. It reminded him of a Florida night, one of his favorites too.

Chapter 19

The Morning

David tossed and turned most of the night. He was anxious about meeting with Katherine. Of course, she would be pleasant, but he wasn't sure why they had to interact so much. It was 4:00 a.m. and he was wide awake, so he got up, and even though it was dark, he went for a walk.

David lived in a beautiful, exclusive condo right on the lake. It had a great view that he never seemed to enjoy. After all, it was Lake Erie. How nice could it be? He had been to some of the most beautiful beaches in the world. There were plenty of them in his backyard when he lived in Florida.

Granted, he enjoyed jogging by Lake Erie with Michael, but he spent no time sitting out on his balcony enjoying his view. As he sat by the pier, he noticed the football stadium lit up in the near distance. He knew it was close, but he hadn't realize it was one of his many views. He didn't remember seeing the lake from the stadium.

The stadium looked mighty and grand. David always thought it was second rate, but perhaps he was wrong. It was well kept. Gosh, he loved football. What was it about the game that he loved so much? Of course, he loved to play, but it was beyond that. Even though he sat on the bench, the game still gave him a thrill, a sensation that really couldn't compare to anything else he'd experienced. He loved the teamwork. What other profession allows grown men to act like little children jumping for joy when they won a hard-fought game? What job would let a grown man yell out in passion when a pass completed as if it was threading a needle? And what other profession could provide the same level of adrenaline as when taking the ball down the field the last two minutes of the game to come from behind and win?

The morning was peaceful, silent and serene. Just the sound of the waves hitting the shore was all David heard as he thought about football. What a beautiful morning. How many other people might be up? He thought of Michael and Sharon and the nights he'd spent at their home and he knew they were up reading the Bible. He once asked Michael why he got up so early and the man explained that there were no distractions or interruptions so early in the morning. It allowed for complete focus to read and comprehend the Word of God and to pray. He remembered Michael told him he prayed for his family, even for David, and to help his decision-making throughout the day as well as to thank God for all he'd been and would be given.

So on this day's early morning, as the sun was showing its first rays of light, David looked at the stadium, thinking of all football had given him over the years. He bowed his head and, from his heart, thanked God for the game. He didn't pray for a better game. He didn't ask God for anything. Somehow he just wanted God to know that he was thankful for his career. And David felt peace. He sat there a little longer, watching the sunrise until it was time to meet Michael for their workout. After this moment, it became a habit for David to get up early and enjoy his view.

The Meeting

David finished his jog with Michael, ate breakfast with Sharon, and was just getting out of the shower when Katherine arrived. His nerves were at an all-time high as he got dressed, brushed his teeth, and fussed with his hair. Looking in the mirror, he thought he'd need to trim his bread soon; it was pretty grizzly-looking.

Walking into the kitchen, saying good morning to Katherine, he thought she looked pretty. Dressed for success as usual—a beautiful, professional summer dress, tailored to fit her exquisitely. It was white with big poppy flowers all over it and on it rested a white patent leather belt at the waist. Of course, she was wearing high heels, pink patent leather, that tied the whole look together. David wondered how many shoes she owned.

He sat with the family, sipping a cup of coffee, talking until it was time for Michael and Sharon to leave. That's when David's nerves took over again. Maybe they should have met at Katherine's office, but he didn't want anyone else seeing him with her. The staff would know it would be for public relations and he didn't want to bring any more attention to himself.

"Would you like another cup of coffee?" Katherine asked.

"No," he replied.

"We can go into the home office or sit here." She tapped the kitchen table. "Do you have a preference?"

"Anywhere is fine with me."

"Let's just stay here then. The views are pretty incredible. I never get tired of looking outside." A warm smile spread across her face.

She walked to her briefcase, pulling out her laptop and a notebook. She said while setting up shop, "I can be somewhat of a tech junkie. I worked in IT for several years. I used to test the most current devices. That kept me from running out and buying the next best thing since the upgrades weren't always that significant. But I still like to keep up on the latest. Are you into technology?"

"Not really," David replied.

"What about social media? Are you into that at all?"

Feeling out of touch, embarrassed by his choice, he said, "No."

"Great. I'm really happy to hear that." She smiled. "I'm not either. I don't have any social media. Some of my friends called me a loser for forgoing the whole social media thing," she said. "They think it's a great way to reach out to those we haven't seen since high school. And yes, I do agree, but genuine friendships don't need the internet to keep people connected. I am still friends with my girlfriend from kindergarten."

David sat quietly, evaluating Katherine since this was their first real conversation.

"I've seen more athletes get in trouble with social media than I care to see. It's like a popularity contest. Kind of childish, I think. I'm glad you aren't part of that trend."

He sort of grinned at that.

"What about texting? Do you text a lot?"

David realized Katherine was talking business, but she did it in such a way that anyone could miss her approach. She had conquered the art of conversation.

"Not much," David answered, thinking he didn't have many friends anyway.

"Great," she replied again. "It makes this so much easier. I think texting is good for a quick update, but to me I think many use it to avoid conversation and human interaction."

He nodded. He'd certainly employed that technique more than once.

"Plus, there are one too many stories of an athlete texting their girlfriend while sitting next to his wife. It always causes problems, especially when somehow those texts get published."

He relaxed, seeing she wasn't going to attack his personality or demeanor.

Folding her hands, sitting across from him at the table, she grinned. "This is pretty much what you and I will be doing. We will look at what works in this business and what doesn't. You can present yourself anyway you want, but I would caution you to be yourself."

"Are you telling me to be true to myself?"

Sort of chuckling, she said. "I never liked that saying, and I'm not sure why. What I'm saying is there are many people who try to portray an image and it's not becoming of them so it comes across as fake and not likable. Be genuine and you'll never go wrong."

Crossing his arms, ready to prove her wrong, he said. "Well, isn't that what I've been doing and you guys want me to change that?"

"That's not the real you." She smiled pleasantly. "The real you is when you interact with my dad."

David couldn't help but smile because she was right. He felt the most relaxed and like himself when he was with Michael.

"Okay, so I think you see where we are headed." She looked at David for confirmation. "But I still would like to go back in history with you."

He immediately grew tense. He didn't enjoy talking about himself, especially about his past.

Pulling out a small stack of papers, getting a pencil, she asked. "Would you mind if I asked you some questions? They are personal and may be sensitive, but I want to understand what I may need to deal with in the future and plan how to effectively handle it."

"That's fine," David answered as his heart pounded.

"We can sort of dance around these questions or be direct. I will go at whatever pace you are comfortable with but I only ask that you be honest with me. If you lie and I'm covering up a lie unknowingly, it will cause so much more pain in the long run."

"Let's just get to the questions," he replied.

Katherine felt some tension radiating off of David but disregarded it. She looked over her list, ready to document her findings, but she wanted to start with something easy. Although personal in nature, she blushed asking, "Do you have any kids?"

"No."

"Is there a chance you might have kids you may not be aware of having?"

"Do you want to know if I've had unprotected sex?" he asked.

Looking up at him, she said, "Yes, that's what I'm asking."

"You don't need to dance around the questions, you can be direct," David said. "And no, I don't remember ever having unprotected sex that would cause a woman to become pregnant."

He noticed she blushed again while making notes, but she continued. "Would any women come out of the woodwork to accuse you of sexual assault?"

Pointing to her list, he said. "Let me answer probably a bunch of those questions for you by telling you straight. I'm not the type of guy to have one-night stands. I have never been with a woman outside of some sort of exclusive relationship. So that should answer any questions about sexual diseases. Does this take care of those types of questions?"

"Pretty much," she grinned, looking through her list and checking any answered-off. Katherine didn't enjoy prying but she had to know what she was dealing with. "Just one last one. How about ending a relationship? Would there be any horror stories from a break-up? Oh, and were you ever married?"

David knew the break-up with Gretchen wasn't the best, but she wouldn't be the type to broadcast it, so he said, "No. And I haven't been married either."

"Drugs. How about any drugs? Can you give me an overview on that?"

Maybe because he wasn't completely honest about Gretchen, David told all on this subject. "I tried some drugs in high school, but I didn't like the hangover and how it negatively affected my performance, so I stopped immediately."

Katherine wrote notes.

"As far as steroids, I was around those who did them regularly. I knew anything that would strengthen me, making me a better athlete, I'd most likely get addicted to. So for whatever reason, I decided I would never try them, not even once." David realized he was thankful for that decision.

"You already know I don't drink much. I take protein and muscle building supplements, which I can show you. And other than vitamins, I take nothing else."

Nodding as she looked through her list, she found one to ask. "Any run-ins with the law that I need to know about?"

"Just a couple speeding tickets."

Looking up from her documentation, she said. "You are making this very easy." She understood why her parents liked him. He appeared to be a clean-cut guy who'd just lost his way. "Okay, onto the next subject. What about your parents? Where do they live? Do you visit them often?"

David did not want to go there. However, his trust in Michael and Sharon grew immensely since he could tell from Katherine's expression that she didn't know about his childhood. Michael and Sharon hadn't shared it with her.

"Why do you need to know about my parents?"

Katherine caught the change in his attitude. "Um, well, I just want to know your family history—brothers, sisters, relationship with parents—but we don't need to discuss that today."

"I'm an only child. Don't talk to either of my parents."

"Okay. Let's just move onto something else," Katherine whispered, looking back at her paperwork.

David tensed in his seat. "What is it with you people and wanting to know about my family? It's really none of your business, " he said, putting up his wall, not wanting to be pushed.

Making eye contact, she offered. "Well, as you know in this business, things tend to come out of the woodwork, people make up stories, and I like to be prepared in case I need to address this topic. It's really not something we need to discuss today however."

"I've already been all over the media when they drafted me, and those clown reporters asked nothing about my family. And in case you haven't noticed, I'm on the bench, so why in the world would anything come out now?"

Placing her pencil down, she said, "I will work with you as if you are the starting quarterback and constantly in the spotlight. That's just how I do things. I have many plans for you to interact with the public, including the media. I'm not sure if you realize this or not but just your presence alone being in Cleveland has already placed you on the networks daily. You have been a very polarizing figure in the past, and Cleveland was very excited when you were traded to come here. That may have wavered a bit and now we need to build it back up."

He crossed his arms, leaning back in his chair.

As tender as possible, Katherine kept going. "Now, you have made enemies here in Cleveland and with the networks, and they will try to find anything to make you more of a villain than you have already made yourself. So again, we don't need to talk about this today, but we need to eventually have this conversation."

Rolling his eyes, he asked, "What do you want to know?"

"I'm more interested in your mom right now. That is usually the most critical area to the fans. What can you tell me? Can you tell me why you don't talk to her?"

"I don't know where she is," David said, telling the truth.

Katherine knew to tread lightly. "When was the last time you spoke to her?"

Taking a deep breath, he told her, "I don't know, maybe fifteen."

"Fifteen years old?" she clarified and he nodded. "Can I ask what happened?"

It was sounding like a broken record, first Michael and now Katherine inquiring. His leg shook as he retold the same story he told her father. "After she left to move in with some guy and I went to college, I lost track of her. When my grandmother died, I saw her at the funeral. She tried to talk to me but I made it quite clear I wanted nothing to do with her."

Katherine understood from her limited interactions with David that his mother wouldn't have been able to have any type of conversation with him unless he wanted one. He could be downright nasty and rude with little effort. "I'm really sorry to hear that," she said.

Her words agitated David even more. "Look, I don't want a pity party. It's done and over with. It's not that big of a deal."

"Of course it is! You are lying to yourself if you think that not talking to your mom or dad isn't a big deal."

"What, are you a shrink now?" he yelled, shoving out his chair, standing up, and deciding if he should leave or not. "Don't tell me what is or isn't a big deal in my life. You don't know me. You don't know what I'm feeling. You have no idea what you are talking about and now you are calling me a liar? Look, I didn't want to work with you in the first place, and now I regret signing a contract with this company."

With this he stood, staring at Katherine. All she did was push back from her computer, lean back in her chair, rest her hands in her lap, and look at him, not saying a word.

David's breathing was erratic; he was furious. His mind whirled. What just happened? Why was he reacting this way? As he looked down at Katherine, he realized she had laid some truth on him, and he hadn't liked it. Here was a live picture of him standing up to a woman, opposite what his dad did with his mom. It struck him clear as a bell that that's what he had been doing ever since being benched. He'd treated the media the same way because, in his mind, they were less than him. Those actions proved to himself that he wouldn't allow anyone to treat him the way his mother treated his father.

David sank in his chair, suffering flashbacks from his childhood. His mom stood over his dad, criticizing him. David hated that, and now that his eyes had been opened to the fact he was repeating her behavior, he hated what he was doing worse. It was a vicious cycle. His mom dominated his dad. His dad did the same to him, and now if he didn't even like a look from someone, he criticized them harshly too. He didn't know what to say. Part of him wanted to cry, but he would never do that in front of Katherine. How could he be so mean to her when she was only kind to him.

"I'm sorry. I shouldn't have accused you of lying to yourself. You're right, I'm not a shrink and I don't know you," Katherine said quietly. "Listen, I don't want you to have any regrets with us. My mom or dad would be more than happy to work with you. It would probably make more sense anyway since you spend so much time with them. We just thought this would be more cost effective since I am already involved with the team, but sometimes saving money isn't always the best answer."

She closed her laptop, put away her notebook, placed her phone in her purse, and then put her cup in the sink. After getting her briefcase, Katherine stuck out her hand to shake his, saying, "I'm sorry to be rude and leave but I would like to get to the office and meet with my parents to work this out so you are happy with your decision to be our client."

He dismissed her hand, asking, "Why do you say that?"

Confused, she pulled her hand away. "Say what?"

"Why do you say 'I don't mean to be rude'?" he asked.

She didn't understand his question but answered. "Well, I am being rude because I want to end our meeting early."

David reclined in his chair and rested his hands in his lap. "I want to really know why you say that."

125

Tense but remaining poised, she said, "I'm sorry. I don't understand what you mean."

"You said it to me the first time we met. You said it to Trino when he was going off on me. And you said it to some guy who could clearly hear your sister calling you out onto the dance floor at the fundraiser. And now, when I was the one being rude to you, you said it again. You were never rude in any of those situations. In fact, it was just the opposite; the other person was being rude. Why do you put it on yourself?" David asked.

She was embarrassed but didn't know why. Yet she was intrigued that he'd pressed for an answer. "Well," she said, still standing, "I think partially I feel rude when I need to exit a conversation when the person may not be finished talking. Also when I interrupt someone, I honestly think it's rude."

"But I was rude to you both times. Why would you use it on me?"

Feeling the heat, knowing he wouldn't stop until she confessed, she said, "I wanted to diffuse a tense situation, and the best possible way to do that, no matter who it is, is to place it on myself instead of on the other person."

Burrowing his eyebrows to make sense of her answer, he asked, "How in the world did you think of doing something like that?"

Her face felt hot, her neck red. She didn't want to answer him because she feared an argument. But her conviction would reign supreme if she didn't speak the truth. "A proverb."

Puzzled, he questioned, "The Bible?"

"Yes."

"What does the proverb say?" he asked, seriously interested.

She inhaled deeply, exhaled slowly. "A fool's talk brings a rod to his back, but the lips of the wise protect them."

David laughed, and she grew irritated but maintained composure. She wasn't interested in him making fun of the Bible and annoyed her parents didn't see this side of him.

"That's so true, isn't it?" David said, smiling. "Isn't that what you've been trying to tell me?"

Katherine again thought he was bipolar. "Yes, I guess I just didn't go about it the best way. Will you please lock up after you leave? And please close the garage door if you wouldn't mind."

As she grabbed her belongings, another picture rose in David's mind. Katherine stood over him as his mother had with his dad, but Katherine wasn't interested in arguing. If anything, she disarmed the situation. David realized he didn't know how to interact with women. He never had to think about it before. Women naturally came on to him. Gretchen was the closest he'd ever come to asking a woman on a date, but since she was a "go-getter" by nature, he hadn't needed to do that either.

His closeness with Sharon had similarities to his relationship with his grandma. Not that Sharon was old like his grandma, but his mother was young, only twenty years older than David, so she never had that motherly look or nurturing touch. David never once worked for a woman's attention, and now he had to do more than that. He had to work for Katherine's friendship, and it was all new to him.

"Katherine."

She'd never heard him say her name and it threw her off a bit. She stopped what she was doing and looked at him. "Yes?"

"Look, I'm sorry. I don't like talking about my family, and clearly I have issues I need to deal with and I obviously don't want to admit to them. I think you are superb at your job. I honestly mean that. There's not a person in this business who would dispute that either."

Her large, brown eyes softened.

"It makes sense if I were to work with you rather than your mom or dad. Would that be okay with you?" he asked.

Katherine didn't want to be around this guy. Not that she was afraid of him, but she never knew what she was going to get when she talked to him. He was a real challenge. She wanted to tell him to work with her mom but she felt God was nudging her to remain on with him. She knew that feeling so well and knew she could either ignore it or submit to it.

She sat down and leaned into the table, making direct eye contact. "David, I really think it would be more beneficial to you if you worked with my mom. I think you would feel more comfortable with her. For some reason, when we talk, I offend you and, believe me, that's not my intention at all. I like to get to the heart of things, and today I probably overstepped."

Feeling terrible, and not trying to put anything on him whatsoever, she said further, "I'm sorry, I really don't know how to proceed from here. I do not want you to have any regrets about our company and I want to make sure you get the best service possible. I don't think I'm the best fit for this, and that's okay. Both my mom and dad taught me everything I know anyway."

"Katherine," David sat forward. "I know I've been a prick to you and I'm sorry. I actually can see that I've been pretty much a prick to most people, and in order for me to overcome that image, I need someone who is closely tied to this organization. While your parents are respected, they don't have the network you have built over the years. If I truly want to get out of Cleveland by the end of the season, then I need to work with you. I promise I will try my best to not be so defensive. Will you work with me?"

Katherine took a deep breath. "Anything to get you out of Cleveland!" At that, they both started laughing. "Okay, maybe we should just call it a day? I have your schedule, so we can meet again in two days. Would that work for you?" she asked, wanting to leave.

David needed a break himself and agreed. "Do we want to meet here again at 8 a.m.?"

"Yes, that'll work," Katherine said, holding out her hand once more to say goodbye. This time David shook her hand, but he could tell she was tense. Who could blame her?

"I'll let my parents know that you've locked up. See you in a couple days," she said, waving goodbye.

Chapter 20

The Office

Katherine went straight to the office, which was only ten minutes from her parents' and like another home to her. In the heart of downtown overlooking the stadium and Lake Erie, the office was on the nineteenth floor and had incredible views. Michael had moved the business from the east side of Cleveland to downtown once he became a managing partner. They agreed it was more convenient to the teams' venues, but Katherine was happy to be out of the old office building since it reminded her too much of James.

It was odd that the first office held his memory more so than their home. But she and James had spent plenty of time building his dream together, equating to plenty of evenings and weekends at the office. However, Katherine had created a warm and inviting home to rest. She enjoyed interior design, like her mother, but James wasn't as interested, so their home reflected her taste and décor.

The current office was brand new and gorgeous. Katherine, along with her parents, had decked it out with the latest technology and ergonomic furnishings. There was an office for each family member, two conference rooms holding at least twenty people each, and room to expand if needed. Although they could do with one less assistant, keeping an assistant for each along with a receptionist allowed Sharon to plan their fundraising events.

Katherine made the rounds, greeting everyone and asking about their weekend plans. She retrieved her messages and then went to her father's office. He wasn't there, so she tried her mother's, knocking lightly before Sharon waved her in.

"Hi, honey. How did things go this morning with David?"

"I think he's bipolar," Katherine said, sitting down.

Her mom stopped working, catching her laugh. "Why?"

"I'm serious," Katherine replied.

"Okay," Sharon said. "What happened?"

"Well, I was asking questions, background questions, and everything was going well. He gave me way more information than I requested, and I was starting to understand the draw you and Dad have to him. Then I asked him about his family. The usual questions about his relationships with his mom and dad and siblings."

Sharon closed her eyes and placed down her head, shaking it.

"What's wrong, Mom?"

"That's a very tense subject for him," Sharon replied.

"Well, really, which subject isn't tense for him?" Katherine asked. "I'm serious, I think he's bipolar. I mean, think about it. When we first met, he was rude, no different from lunch when dad offered him a contract. He was rude to me at that lunch too. Then today, when I brought up his family, his entire attitude changed. I think there's seriously something wrong with him. What do you think, Mom? Do you think he's bipolar? I'm being serious."

"Well, honey, I'm not a doctor, but no, I don't think he's bipolar," Sharon said. "Tell me exactly what happened."

Katherine iterated the morning events to the moment when she insisted her parents work with him. Then she told of his apology and ability to convince her she was the most connected in the business, which would be his best ticket out of Cleveland.

"Are you afraid of him? Do you feel threatened? Should we get your father involved?" Sharon asked.

"Gosh, no, I am not afraid of him at all. I don't feel like he's threatening me, and, no, we don't need Dad to go after him again." Katherine chuckled. "I just don't know what side I'm going to get with him each time I see him. David seems to treat you and Dad differently. I don't understand why he has to be so difficult. I don't enjoy being around him."

"I will take over and work with him. I don't want you to be uncomfortable in any way." Sharon looked through her schedule to figure out a meeting time.

"Mom, he's right. I head up this department; it's how we set it up. How would it come across if I can't work with him, like I couldn't do my job? Besides, it would take so much longer to get him out of Cleveland, and right now that's the motivation."

Thinking, she nodded. "Okay, honey."

"What can you tell me about his family that will help me understand what emotions I'll be dealing with?" Katherine asked.

"It's a very sensitive subject with him," Sharon said again.

"Obviously," Katherine responded with wide eyes. "Why didn't you or Dad tell me about his history with his parents and what I might encounter?"

"Well, he asked us not to tell anyone and we didn't want to betray his trust."

"So you just threw me out there to deal with the ramifications from asking him questions?" she stressed.

"No, honey, that's not it at all. If we were to tell you about his history, what good would that have done?"

"Well, I could have been better prepared," she whined.

"How so?" Sharon asked.

"Well, I wouldn't have accused him of lying to himself," Katherine mumbled.

"You did what?" Sharon asked.

"I told him I was sorry to hear about his childhood, and I really was sad for him. Then he told me it wasn't a big deal. That's when I told him he was lying to himself if he thought it wasn't a big deal or it didn't have some sort of effect on him. That's when he got mad at me," Katherine confessed.

Sharon laughed. "No, you did not say that to him!"

"Yes, I did," Katherine said. "Why are you laughing, Mom?"

"Because YOU! You blurted out the truth. Your Dad and I have been trying to help him understand in the most delicate way that he needs to deal with his past and you just spoke the truth."

"Yeah, but Mom, you put me in an awkward situation. I wouldn't have said that to him if I had known he was so sensitive about it."

"Really, Katherine? Really? I don't believe that for one second. I know you well enough to know you would drive to the heart. You want to get to the truth. Look, even if the subject was about drugs or his attitude, you would have held his feet to the fire. That's why you are so good at your job. That's how you have established these well-connected relationships with this franchise. But you do it in a way that's adaptable to each person, and you just adapted to his personality," Sharon said.

"Actually, I didn't adapt at all. I was just being myself with him," Katherine said, then thought, speaking her emotion, "Why do I feel like you are constantly protecting him?"

"What do you mean?" Sharon looked to her.

"I just don't understand why you didn't tell me about his family, regardless of what I would or wouldn't have said to him."

"Are you upset that we didn't tell you even though he asked us to keep it private?"

Foolishly, Katherine nodded.

"Well, I can understand that would be upsetting, and maybe this is the challenge we face as a family-owned business. But when you ask me to keep something confidential, I don't share it with your sister or your father. If I did, how would that make you feel?"

"I guess betrayed," Katherine said.

"Also maybe like I was gossiping about you?" Sharon asked.

"Yes. Okay, I understand why you didn't tell me, but I'm still bothered...like you love him more than me."

"Why?" Sharon asked.

Placing her hand on her forehead, looking around the room, Katherine moaned. "What is my problem with this guy? I feel so much like he is trying to take you and Dad away from me. Why am I feeling this way?"

"Maybe think of it as sibling rivalry," Sharon said.

"What do you mean?"

"Well, when you and Lana were growing up, you both fought for my attention. And what would I say?"

Katherine rolled her eyes, smiled, and said, "God gave me two hands and two legs, one for each of you. I can hold both of your hands and you both can sit on my lap at the same time."

Sharon smiled. "Right. Lana doesn't need my attention as much anymore. It's just been you, your father, and me these past several years, and now you have to share us again. But honestly, you haven't needed us this past year. You have made your own life. Since we have some spare time, God has given us somewhat of another child to care for."

Tears came to Katherine's eyes.

"Sweetie, you've always hated to share us with anyone, even your sister. We will always put you two first, outside of God of course. We love you and nothing could ever change that."

Getting up, she hugged her mother. "I love you, Mom."

"I love you too, sweetie," Sharon said.

The conversation moved on. "Now, we need to talk about David, and we need to talk about this type of situation in the future," Sharon said.

"I will be fine working with him. And you guys were right not to tell me anything since that's what he requested. After all, he is our client, and he's your friend or whatever he is to you two."

"Are you sure? This is the second time we are having this conversation. I want to make sure you are good with all of this," Sharon said.

"This is nothing compared to the conversations we had around Trino when I had to interact with him for the first six months. This should be a piece of cake." Katherine smiled.

"Okay, what else is on your mind?"

"Nothing. I'm good," Katherine said. "Do you need anything from me?"

"No, just let me know when you are ready for lunch," her mom said.

"Okay. Thanks. And I'm sorry if I was being disrespectful to you."

"No, sweetie, I'm glad you felt comfortable talking with me. I don't want you feeling as if I'm trying to keep anything from you," Sharon said.

Mother and daughter exchanged more pleasantries, and Katherine left feeling confident and loved. She thought of David and how he probably never had that type of relationship with either of his parents. Her heart went out to him.

Chapter 21

The Call

David was feeling pretty bad about the way he'd treated Katherine. He had thought a lot about what she said, and he knew it was the truth. He reacted poorly. Even though he apologized, he thought of Michael. He knew Michael loved his daughters, and he had not forgotten how Michael confronted him the first time he was rude to her. He didn't want Michael upset, so he called him.

Smiling when he saw David's number display on his phone, Michael picked up. "Is the stock market taking a tumble? You hardly ever call me."

David laughed, saying, "No, the S&P is up fifteen points right now."

"Well, good, it's due for a correction," Michael said. "What do you need, son? Is everything fine?"

"Yes, it is. I just wanted to talk to you. Do you have a couple minutes now?" David asked.

"Do you want to meet for lunch?"

"I don't want to bother you."

"It's not a bother at all. Where do you want to meet? Do you want to meet at the house or go to a restaurant?"

"I can pick us up something to eat and we can meet at your house. How about that turkey artichoke Greek salad?"

"Yeah, that's good. In about a half hour?" Michael asked.

"Yes, I'll see you then."

David had had no intentions of seeing Michael. It was to be a quick call to tell him what happened and apologize. But since Michael offered, David decided to eat with him. He enjoyed his time with the older man and wanted nothing to jeopardize the relationship.

They met at the house, choosing to eat on the covered patio. It was a beautiful day, one that was too good to enjoy from inside. When they finished their meal, having discussed the stock market and Michael's plans with David over the next several weeks, he said, "I wanted to tell you what happened this morning when I met with Katherine."

"Okay," Michael said.

"She's very gifted at her line of work. It's almost an art form how good she is with conversation. She can get to the core in a way that a person cannot hide or run away from," David said.

"What happened? I know her and I know you and I'm sure that was a toxic formula," Michael said.

David flashed a big smile. "First, I want to thank you for not sharing my past with her. She clearly had no idea. I'm thankful you didn't betray my confidence in you and Sharon."

"Boy, are you are really kissing up to me," Michael joked. "Whatever happened this morning must be pretty serious."

David laughed and thought that this was why he liked Michael so much. Michael could always put David at ease immediately.

"Well, I'm sure you know the drill. She asks all sorts of questions about the past. And I get it. She needs to know who I am and what she is dealing with. She asked about my family and I pretty much told her exactly what I told you," David said.

"All right," Michael listened.

David recounted the events of the morning, including his anger and Katherine's accusing him of lying. Michael busted out laughing.

Not expecting this type of reaction, he asked. "Why are you laughing?"

"Because that's my daughter; she gets right to the heart of things! She usually does it in such a way that you don't realize she's taken you down the road that far, but she didn't pull punches with you. She just went for it." Michael smiled.

"Well, I'm not sure I think it's funny," David said but then he couldn't help but laugh either. The two of them had a good chuckle over Katherine's ways.

"So how mad did you get?" Michael asked.

"Well, I guess the worst thing I said was I hadn't wanted to work with her in the first place and I regretted signing on with the company."

"Well, that is true. You told me that too. How did she react?"

David recapped the conversation with Katherine, her offering Sharon as his manager, and how she diffused the tense situation, attempting to recall the Bible verse.

Michael was confused, asking "What did she say?"

"She quoted something about a fool's mouth gets beat and wise lips save them?" David questioned if he was saying it correctly.

"Wait a minute, she said 'A fool's talk brings a rod to his back, but the lips of the wise protect them'?" Michael asked.

Pointing excitedly, David exclaimed, "Yes, that's it!"

Michael broke out laughing again, holding his stomach while delighting in the story. Smiling brightly, he composed himself. "Okay, sorry, continue."

David didn't understand what was so funny, but continued. "So I realized how good she is at her job and told her I was sorry. Then I asked her to stay on with me because it makes sense since she's already involved with the organization."

"What did she say?" Michael asked.

"Well, she doesn't want to, but I think I convinced her to stay with me to help me move on from Cleveland." He smiled victoriously. "I just wanted you to know about everything since you were so upset with me the first time I was rude to her and I didn't want anything to interfere with our friendship."

"Alright, let me get this straight," Michael said, pulling his chair closer into the table. "Katherine asked you a heart-wrenching question and you got mad at her that she laid some truth on you. She then called you a fool and agreed to work with you only after you begged her and promised it would get you out of Cleveland sooner. That's classic. I couldn't be more proud of my daughter right now."

"I didn't beg her to work with me," David protested.

"How many times did you ask her to work with you? Was it more than once?"

"Yeah, but I didn't beg," David said.

Michael tried to hold in his laughter but it was no use.

"I'm glad to see that my honesty amuses you so much," David said flatly.

"I do appreciate your honesty. Thank you for apologizing to her yet again." Michael's eyes twinkled and his smile grinning brightly, but his expression quickly changed as he asked, "Are you okay working with her?"

"Yes. She's actually helped me realize what I'm doing with the media... how I interact with people."

"It's taken her years to learn what she's going to teach you in hopefully six weeks," Michael said. "Once preseason starts, the news outlets will be all over you."

"I know and I'm not looking forward to that," David confessed.

"You told me the other day you don't feel comfortable around her. Do you know why?" Michael asked tenderly.

"I'm not sure exactly what it is. I mean, obviously she'll ask questions that drive to the heart. But she doesn't come across as vindictive or as if she's trying to prove her point. I've seen her lead a person to think so deeply that they have no idea what's she's doing. With me she just lays it out, she doesn't dance around any topic. I like that because there's no game playing. I mean, she's professional. I've never been around someone her age who holds themselves with such dignity and confidence."

"Are you intimidated by her?" Michael pressed him to understand.

"Come on, there's no way I'm going to be intimidated by a woman."

"No, I don't mean like your dad was with your mom. I guess what I'm asking is what are you feeling? Are you feeling dumb, insecure, threatened?"

"I've never been around a woman like her before. She acts completely different from any other woman I've known her age," David said, trying to give Michael a hint.

"Are you attracted to her?" Michael asked pointedly.

"I'm trying to tell you I've never been around a woman who wasn't attracted to me or hitting on me in some way," David blurted out.

Michael burst out laughing again.

"Truly, I'm glad my honesty is giving you a good laugh today," David said dryly.

"I'm so sorry. I really am." Michael still failed miserably to contain his laughter.

David placed his hand on his cheek, tapping the fingers of his other hand on the table before saying, "Go ahead, laugh it up. Just let me know when you're finished so that we can continue this conversation as adults."

"Okay, okay, I'm sorry. I see this is serious to you. Let me see if I can help you through it. Tell me about your past relationships with women."

"What do you mean? What do you want to know?" David asked.

"Well, you told me back in the day you could have any woman you wanted. What did you mean by that? Did you play the field a lot? Were you a ladies' man?" Michael asked.

"I could have been both. I could have played the field and been a ladies' man easy," David said, threading his hands on the back of his head and leaning back in his chair with a smile that lit up his entire face.

Squinting his eyes, Michael said. "Well, why weren't you?"

"I'm not sure. Maybe because so many women would throw themselves at me and I wasn't interested in having a one-night stand," David said, smiling wider.

"How come?" Michael questioned.

"I don't know, maybe it was too easy. There was no challenge. Maybe because I've seen so many guys get women pregnant and I didn't want to end up in that situation. But believe me, I enjoyed the attention."

"What type of woman were you attracted to?"

"Usually someone who had their own career, who had a plan for her own life. I didn't want a woman to depend on me. I wanted someone who could take care of herself," David said.

"How many relationships have you had?" Michael asked.

"One was really short, but if I counted that it would be four relationships."

Leaning his elbow on the table, placing his hand on his chin for support, Michael said. "Same type of women?"

"What, do you mean in looks?" David questioned.

"Yes, and also their personality."

"Mainly blondes, tall and skinny. Somewhat aggressive."

"Tell me what you mean by aggressive."

"Well, I never had to ask any of them out. They asked me out," David stated, feeling confident and rather manly.

Pointing, Michael said, "Sounds similar to your mom."

"What?"

"Let me ask you this, what color hair does your mom have?"

"That's sick, man! You think I was trying to date my mom?" David said, grin gone.

"No, I think you were trying to prove to yourself that you wouldn't allow a woman to treat you the way she treated you and your dad," Michael said lovingly.

"Okay, I think I'm going to be sick to my stomach," David said, bending over to try to block out the image.

"Just relax. I'm not saying you were trying to date your mom. Look, you said you didn't need to work for a woman's attention and women asked you out. You liked the attention, as would anyone, and maybe in some way it proved to you that you were worthy of being loved, you know since your mom didn't show you love. Have you ever had any type of friendship with a woman?" Michael asked.

"Does my grandma count?" David chuckled.

"No," Michael laughed with him. "I think you may see women as objects or as trophies and not as a potential helpmate. And being in your line of work, it would be very easy to see a woman from that view."

David moved his chair closer to the table eager to listen to Michael's teachings.

"Tell me why you are attracted to career-minded women? Why women who wouldn't depend on you?" Michael asked.

"I just don't want a needy woman."

"Are you trying to prevent yourself from getting hurt?"

"I definitely don't get that close to women," David said.

Michael asked, "Do you want to get married and have kids one day?"

"Really, I'm not sure. I don't see that for myself, nor do I think I would want something like that. And please don't tell me I haven't met the right woman. That's such a cliché," David said leaning back in his chair not wanting to hear that nonsense.

"Oh, I don't think that's the case at all. And I'm not into clichés either," Michael responded.

"Then what do you think?" David asked bright-eyed.

"I don't think marriage is for everybody. In fact, marriage can have many seasons of hard work. I think there are certain people who should remain single. TV, movies, the internet paint a picture that once you find the person you want to marry then it's happily ever after. That's not true at all."

"I know that," David said, rolling his eyes.

"I believe God has designed a person for those He intends to marry. That person becomes a helpmate or a helper to their spouse. The Bible is quite clear that we are to leave our mother and father and cleave to one another. The two shall become one," Michael said.

David was interested since he'd never heard anyone speak of marriage this way.

"It seems that everything is based on a sexual feeling rather than understanding a person's heart, actions, and beliefs. Sex is often so rushed that the pleasure of actually getting to know someone is taken out of the whole equation. And more times than not, once you get to know the person, you realize you aren't compatible. But now things are much more complicated by sex and it makes ending things quite more difficult and prolonged," Michael said.

David agreed with the older man, nodding his approval.

Michael continued the train of thought. "Take a look at some of your old relationships. Have they been more complicated because you have rushed into something you shouldn't have?"

"I'm not trying to be conceited when I say this but the women I dated wanted to get me in bed," David said, embarrassed.

"Well, I think you may have been attracted to the wrong type of woman. David, I know you well enough to say you are pretty manly. You like to be a leader, you're not afraid to speak your mind, you are aggressive in your own nature. Maybe you have gone about it the wrong way recently, but I think you would agree with my assessment of you."

"I think I understand what you mean."

"Here's a better example. You desired to be a quarterback and aggressively pursued that goal. You've no fear of driving the ball down the field in the last two minutes of the game. That takes a mental courage not many have. A lot of people shy away from this because they fear failing since they may be publicly humiliated if they don't stand the test."

"Right," David agreed.

"Now the women you have chosen in the past may have not been that great for you. I'm not saying they were bad choices because you realize you like a strong, confident, career-minded woman. But what I am saying is you couldn't be the man in the relationship."

Sitting on the edge of his chair, David pointed to his own chest, offended. "Are you calling me a woman? Are you saying that they had the upper hand?"

"No. I'm saying that you didn't need to be the man. You didn't need to court them. They did it for you. I don't think you know how to interact with a woman who doesn't throw herself at you. And Katherine is bringing that out in you. I think it's a good lesson to learn. It will teach you how to honor a woman the right way," Michael said.

David's shoulders relaxed and he reclined back knowing Michael was speaking truth.

"It seems to me as if you took the lazy way out with women," Michael said.

"What? Now, I'm lazy?" He sat straight up.

"Well, I understand you may think that you are desirable or irresistible since women pursued you," Michael said smiling, "but, since you are a man who works hard to achieve your dreams, I don't believe you put in the effort to maintain those relationships or work through any problems that arose."

"So I need to have a drama filled relationship to prove that I'm a man?" David asked, confused.

"No. It's completely the opposite," Michael said. "I would think those four relationships you had were somewhat filled with drama because you didn't put in the effort."

"You're probably right, except maybe for the last relationship I had," David said.

"Well, tell me about that one," Michael said curiously.

"Do you know Gretchen Parks?"

"The journalist?"

"Yes."

"Did you date her?" Michael asked.

"For a couple years. She was the closet I got to any woman, and I still held her at an arm's length," David admitted.

"Why did it end?"

David took a moment, sadly looking at the distance. "I got benched and, well, you know my attitude. I took things out on her and she left."

"Have you talked with her since?"

"No. Once in a while I see her when she's interviewing one of the guys, but I haven't spoken to her."

"Why not?"

"I'm not too sure. It's done and over with, why relive the past?" David said, unsure.

"Do you think you may owe her an apology?" Michael suggested.

"Probably."

"Why haven't you apologized to her?"

"I'm not too sure. Maybe the timing was never right," David said.

"Why haven't you picked up the phone?" Michael asked. "Are you afraid to admit you were wrong?"

Thinking very deeply, David said, "I don't know, maybe?"

"Let me ask you this. Why did you apologize to Katherine—and twice?" Michael focused intently on David.

David looked at Michael, stunned. He didn't answer right away to understand it himself. "Maybe because I respect her?" he finally said.

Michael probed further. "Why?"

David got down deep, analyzing himself when he answered, "Because she wants nothing from me."

"What do you mean by that?" Michael probed.

"She could have easily enjoyed Trino railing on me but she knew how to handle him and diffused the situation. And again this morning, she wanted to make sure I was comfortable being a client. She wasn't thinking about herself," David said.

"Are you saying that Gretchen wanted something from you?" Michael asked.

"She was sweet, really nice. She's not that different from what you see on TV. She sets goals and achieves them. Any man would be lucky to have her," David admitted, feeling wrong about the past.

"Sounds like you have some regrets."

"I guess I do," came his sad words.

"I'm sure she would forgive you if you apologized," Michael said.

"I'm sure she would. That's the type of person she is." David felt dejected and he didn't know why.

"Did you love her or do you still love her?"

"I'm not sure. I'm sure there were some feelings of love, but I didn't want a serious relationship. I just wanted a companion at times, if you know what I mean?" David said, making eye contact.

"Yes, I understand," Michael confirmed. "Let me ask you this. Were you bothered that maybe she didn't want more from you?"

"What do you mean exactly?"

"You apologized to Katherine because she wanted nothing from you. But did it bother you that Gretchen didn't want more than an occasional companion too, if you know what I mean," Michael asked, trying to speak the same language.

"Hmm, I never thought about it. But I didn't want that either, so why would it matter?"

Michael pressed him to think. "Maybe in part you felt used. Maybe in part you felt you weren't worthy of marriage. Again, maybe you didn't put in the time or effort to work through the problems because you weren't the one who pursued her."

"Come on, I'm a guy, and in this business I don't think I'd really have any trouble finding a woman to marry me," David said.

"I'm sure you are right. But there's a difference between finding the one that God has designed for you and choosing just any woman," Michael said. "You obviously had your pick and probably could have had your fill, but thankfully you didn't go down that road. Maybe, David, you truly want more, but you're afraid. I'm not saying that it's wrong for a woman to ask a man out on a date, but it almost sounds like you lose some respect for that type of women."

"But I wouldn't have asked them out if they didn't ask me," David said plainly.

"That's my point. You haven't dated a woman you've pursued. The pursuit of a woman is a beautiful dance. I still pursue my wife," Michael said passionately.

"What do you mean? You are married."

"Oh, marriage is another chapter in pursuing romance. When two people become one and they share their dreams and fears and confess their sins to one another, that level of intimacy cannot be matched by anything else. It's not something you can buy, fake, or rush. It's something that needs to be achieved together, and when God is put in the mix, it's called a strand of three—unbreakable."

David felt Michael's words.

"There are only a few things in life that make me feel like a real man and one of them is pursuing my wife. You have never experienced that. It may be due to fear or it may be because you are in the public eye, but you are missing one of the greatest gifts to a man. The Bible talks about the woman being a weaker vessel, that doesn't mean she's weak or can't be successful," Michael said.

David knew Gretchen would hate that description.

"But when a woman gives herself to a man when she is loved, protected, and knows she is being honored, then it's a pleasure for both husband and wife to submit to one another," Michael explained. "I think you will enjoy a relationship as it was meant to be one day."

David knew he was witnessing what Michael was saying firsthand with his and Sharon's marriage, and he enjoyed their relationship. "So, just so I'm clear, you've said I'm dating my mom, I'm the woman in the relationship, and I'm lazy. I wonder who Katherine takes after, you or Sharon?" David laughed.

Michael chuckled. "That's my girl. Just like her old man!"

The pair talked some more, always laughing, enjoying each other. They cleaned up, and before leaving, Michael said, "Hey, hold on a minute, I want to give you something."

"Okay," David said while placing the dishes in the dishwasher.

Michael returned with some items. "Here, I want to give you this." He handed him a brand new Bible still in its wrapper. "This is a NIV, the New International Version, which is the same one Sharon and I use. There are many versions of the Bible, like King James or English Standard Version. I have most of them but think this is the easiest to understand. No pressure to read it, but a good place to start would be in the book of Psalms and the book of Proverbs, then the New Testament gospels. Also, Genesis is good to learn about creation."

David was uncomfortable but still said, "Thank you."

Michael then handed him a piece of paper and a couple of keys. "Katherine told us you locked up this morning. Since you will both be working here, I thought it would be easier for you to have the gate and garage codes. These are to lock the bolts."

David held back tears at being so welcomed, joking, "Aren't you worried I'm going to steal something?"

"Of course I am, but Sharon told me I had nothing to worry about."

They laughed once more. Michael showed David which key went to which door and how to enter using the security codes. David felt overwhelmed. Michael and Sharon had completely opened their home, proving they trusted him unconditionally.

Chapter 22

The Media

Katherine and David were meeting again, and his nerves had been at an all-time high all morning. He hadn't spoken with her since their first meeting and wasn't sure what to expect today.

It was almost 8:00 a.m. when she arrived wearing another summer, lady-like, pink dress that complimented her skin tone. Her high heels were spectacular, neutral with jewel-colored beads. In his opinion, her shoes always made such a statement. And so did her lipstick. Today it was a pretty bright pink, which showcased her plump lips and highlighted her rosy cheeks. Each time David saw her, he noticed something new.

Michael and Sharon remained in the kitchen, enjoying another cup of coffee, chatting up a storm, while David watched the minutes tick down as his heart pounded in rhythm. His nerves were difficult to manage, raising exponentially when Michael and Sharon went to the office, leaving him and Katherine all alone.

"How have you been?" she asked. "How's training?"

"Good. I enjoy working with Reggie. I think we connect very well," David said, sort of surprising himself for giving her that much information.

"He's a great guy, isn't he?" she asked, setting up her laptop and grabbing her notebook.

"Yes, he's pretty passionate." He regretted the word as soon as it came out of his mouth. Why would he say something like that? Why use passionate instead of focused. David would need to think before speaking his heart.

"Oh, there's no doubt he's passionate about football."

David grinned, relieved she didn't ask him a question regarding his choice of words.

"Is here okay with you?" she asked, pointing to the table.

"Yes, this is good."

"Are you ready to start or do you need to get something else to drink?"

"No, I'm good," he replied, taking a deep breath, looking to steady his nerves.

"Okay, I'm going to go over some very basic, trivial types of media today. You will know most of it and it will either be boring or you'll think I'm being too simplistic, but just stick with me and I will tie it all together in the end. "

"Okay," he said, hating this type of teaching.

Katherine looked over her notes. "So last time we met, we covered most of your background. I'm sure there are other topics we will need to discuss, but I think I have most of what I need."

David felt ashamed when he remembered how he'd reacted toward her at that meeting, although Katherine didn't mention it.

"I've done this a couple times, but it's been at my office, so I have to figure out the best way to view this," Katherine said, adjusting her laptop. They were sitting across from one another, making it difficult to work on the computer. "I think I need to sit next to you so you can see my screen."

"That's fine." David's heart raced. He could feel his body temperature rising and tried to recall if he had put on deodorant. He remembered he had, but did his breath stink? She sat down so close to him that their arms were almost touching. They had never been this close, and he tried to move away to give himself some extra space.

"I want to show you some interviews of players and how they portray themselves. Here's someone you'll know," she said, playing a video of an old teammate.

David watched, but Katherine's scent was distracting. It wasn't perfume. Was it her hair? Maybe some type of body lotion? Possibly her natural scent? It didn't matter; it smelled clean and like a breath of fresh air. He couldn't concentrate, worried his deodorant was failing since he had begun to sweat. He was highly self-conscious sitting so close to her, yet she didn't seem uncomfortable at all.

"This guy is absolutely full of himself. He only talks about how great he is, doesn't give any credit to his teammates or coaches, or acknowledges the fans," Katherine said as the video ended.

Even though David hadn't been paying attention, he knew the guy and already knew he was full of himself.

She began his lesson. "Don't throw roses on yourself, let someone else do that. Bring attention to a teammate. Be excited for them. This is a team sport and the only way to win a game is as a unit. Honor the coach's play calling and ability to read the defense. And let the fans know you appreciate their dedication and how they motivate the team."

He barely listened. It was so basic, something he'd known for years. Instead, he fixated on her eyes. Enormous, beautifully deep, dark chocolate brown eyes. Actually, so dark brown he could barely see her pupils. Her eyes revealed innocence, joy, excitement. There was no fear or discomfort when she looked into his eyes. She seemed to look past him too, as if she didn't notice him at all. David had never experienced being so close to a woman and having no effect on them.

It bothered him tremendously. He knew if he were back on the top, Katherine would never look past him. She would be eating out of his hand. David's mind wandered to his conversation with Michael regarding his mother. Was it possible that Katherine's reaction reminded David of his mother's lack of love and attention?

Katherine interrupted David's thoughts, looking across the room while she was speaking. "You know, would you mind if we moved into the living room?" she said standing up. "I feel like I'm a little too close to you and I'm getting in your personal space. I would rather sit across from you than turn my head to face you since I'm sitting right next to you," she chuckled, describing the awkwardness of communicating her points when her head and body were in two different positions.

Since she left the table, David didn't have an opportunity to convey his preference. She turned on the TV, saying, "I just remembered that we have internet on our TV, so we can watch these here."

It blew him away. Katherine wanted to be further away from him. Wow! It was a first, and now his attitude took a downward turn. He dragged himself to the recliner.

After she set up, another video played. An athlete was using words he could barely pronounce and not in the correct context.

"He is attempting to sound intelligent, but unfortunately it's having the adverse effect and he sounds uneducated. Even if you have a high IQ, don't broadcast it. The public better relates to someone who speaks confidently and gracefully than someone who uses large words to prove they're smart."

He rolled his eyes. This was so fundamental. What a waste of time. But he said little, trying instead to remain focused and listen.

Then a video of Gretchen interviewing a player rolled. This particular athlete often dated celebrities and models. He was flirting so much with Gretchen that she had difficulty keeping the interview on track.

"Now, this is an extreme case, and I'm sure you have seen this clip before, but here's the bottom line, never flirt with a woman when she's interviewing you."

Of course, he'd seen the video. Not only had it gone viral, but he had also talked to Gretchen about it. Then he realized Katherine wasn't aware he had dated Gretchen. Now he felt convicted to tell her about their breakup.

The next video played was of an athlete having an awful season, blaming his teammates, coaches, and anyone and everyone except himself.

"Don't say you aren't getting any play time, the coaches aren't reading the calls correctly, or the team is young. Just go out there and play your game," Katherine said.

David felt tense. He hadn't been playing his game and that was the problem. Twenty minutes into their meeting and he was already irritated since her lessons were belittling.

"Okay, here's another video. The moral of these videos is to just be yourself," she said.

Tim Thompson's fantastic smile flashed on the large screen as he interviewed flawlessly, giving God praise. That just about did it for David. Now he was completely angry. He didn't like Tim and here Katherine was comparing the two of them. "I already know all this! This is so basic!"

"I know it is, and I don't mean to insult your intelligence. I just want to make sure we hit the very basic media images so you have a picture in your mind of what doesn't work and, in these cases, how it works," Katherine said.

Turning towards her, making eye contact, he said, "But I already know how it works. You don't need to show me anymore videos."

"Then why haven't you been doing this? If you really know how this works, why have your interviews placed you in the spotlight for saying something you shouldn't have said?" Katherine shot back.

Now they were both heated, staring one another down, their chests heaving to control any further outburst.

Katherine thought, here we go again. Each time she interacted with David it inevitably grew tense. And for some reason, he brought out her true nature, the thoughts and opinions she was usually so good keeping under her professional manner. If they kept going at it this way, Katherine wondered if their plans were going to work and if David was going to find a new home outside of Cleveland.

David lashed out. "Look, I'm not playing that well, okay? All these videos are actively playing athletes. I hardly ever get any play time—that's one hundred percent true! I'm not fond of the calls the coaches make, I see the defense lining up differently, but I can't change the play! And since I don't play that often, it's hard to establish my 'go-to' guys!"

Katherine thought. She knew he was right, and then she did something she hadn't done in years, asking, "Are you a dreamer?"

"What?" he asked, annoyed. How immature. She was being childish.

Disregarding his demeanor, she thought out loud. "You have to be a dreamer to be a quarterback. I would think you've dreamt about playing professionally since you were a little boy." Not even looking at him, convincing herself, she said, "Plus, you want to coach one day, so you are a dreamer."

"Okay, I get your point. So what?"

Looking deeply in his eyes with eyes that seemed to be dancing themselves she said, "Let's dream together. You and I, let's dream."

He rolled his eyes at her.

"Alright, I get it, I'm pathetic, but just humor me. Let's just say you are the starting quarterback, back at the top of your game again. Tell me how you see yourself," she asked.

David took a deep breath. "I have no idea what you are talking about."

"Tell me what being at the top looks like. How was it before? I didn't know you back then, but I watched you play almost every game. What was it like to be you five years ago?"

It was very similar to his conversation with Michael. Why were they bringing him back to that time in his life?

He hesitated, wanting to strike out with his tongue, but whispered, "I was a winner."

"So can I interpret that you feel like a loser today?"

David looked around, not wanting to admit the truth but said, "Yeah."

"So because you feel like a loser you treat people like this?" she questioned, pulling up a video of him arguing with the media.

"They ask the most awful questions," he insisted.

"David, I didn't ask you about them. I asked you about how you treat them," Katherine said pointedly. "When you were at the top of your game, were the questions that much better?"

David understood the truth. "No."

"Here, watch these." She had a montage of old interviews with him. She had done her homework, painting David a picture so he could understand her point. Smiling, eyes twinkling, she said, "You were young, but you had some wit. I want you to keep that wit, add some class and maybe some humor. Right now, you aren't humble or graceful and have absolutely no sense of humor."

He felt bad and embarrassed since she was right. David slumped over in his chair, disappointed in himself that he'd lost that spark.

"Let's take Peyton, for example." Katherine showcased the beloved quarterback expertly mingling with the media's questioning. In this video, he was retiring, tearing up as he gave his farewell speech.

"You are out of your mind if you think I would cry on camera," David said plainly.

"No, I'm not suggesting that. I wanted to show you that video because Peyton is so genuine and so well liked. I'm not saying copy him. I'm saying put yourself back into the spotlight as a winner. You are a winner and you will always be a winner regardless if you play football or not."

David noticed a fire; there was passion flaming in her eyes.

"Do you remember this?" she asked, showing a video of David driving the ball down the field in a blizzard, coming from behind to win a game against Cleveland. Her entire face lit up as she smiled. "We watched that game saying some Florida kid came into our home in a whiteout and took us to task."

David couldn't help but smile.

"Here's another great one," Katherine boasted. This footage showed David covered head to foot in mud playing in a downpour, field soaking. "Again, you took this team to task, playing on their turf and in that mud, winning the game." Katherine smiled brightly.

He remembered.

"People loved you. You were the new kid, the rookie, the next elite one. You were it. You still are it. And you will always be it. Once you have it, it never goes away." Katherine said intensely.

"I lost it," David confessed sadly.

"You feel like you lost it because you've never been in this situation before, but you were known as one of the best comeback quarterbacks around. That's where you live. That's where you play. That's your road and path to victory, no matter how muddy or impossible it may be to see. The rain and blizzard didn't stop you, but right now you are stopping yourself," she said very lovingly.

"I wouldn't even know how to get it back. I don't even know where to start." David was surprised by his confession.

"Start with the networks. Start with what I'm showing you. Just listen to what I'm saying to you and speak like the winner you truly are within your heart. Don't allow the media to get a foothold on you. That's the worst thing you can do. I will teach you how to handle each analyst. We will look at them one by one and study their interview skills. I will break it down question by question, showing you how to respond accordingly. And if you speak from your heart, I guarantee you success."

Katherine's enthusiasm and passion were so contagious that David felt excited, having a desire to learn until doubt set in. "And if it doesn't work?" he asked.

With an unknowingly sexy grin, she whispered, "Well, come on, anything has to be better than what you are doing now."

David had seen that grin many times and loved it, especially when she was directing it at him. "Okay," he said, charged up ready for a change.

"Yes!" She smiled. "Let me get another bottle of water and we'll continue. Do you want one?"

"Yes, please," David answered, now looking forward to what she would teach him. Looking back at the screen at the previously viewed videos, including the one by Gretchen, he felt prompted to say for some unknown reason, "Katherine, I need to tell you something."

Walking back to the living room, he could see her concern. "Okay," she said.

"I wasn't completely honest with you the other day about my past."

"Tell me," she said, sitting down, opening David's water and handing it to him, then taking a swig of hers.

"I had a sort of ugly breakup," he confessed. "The reason I didn't tell you about it is because I don't think this person would come out of the woodwork as you say and bring it to anyone's attention."

"Okay, but how do you know that?" she wondered.

Pointing at her picture, he said, "Well, it's Gretchen."

Katherine's mind raced to recall them as a couple. "I vaguely remember you two dating."

"It was not that publicized," he said.

She believed he was lying, so her guard went up and her professional side took over. "Are there any details that I need to know?"

Looking to add the humor she spoke about, he said. "Well, I think you have already experienced some of my wrath."

She backed up in her chair. "Did you hit her?"

"Oh, no! I'm not like that!" David said, again attempting to bring in some humor. "It's my mouth. It has a way of getting people to walk out the door, never wanting to speak to me again."

Not cracking a smile, Katherine asked with dead eyes, "Do you want to tell me the story?"

He got the message that this topic had no place for laughter so he simply stated facts. "It was so long ago, I'm not sure I remember the details. The bottom line is I said some things that weren't pleasant and she walked out. We never spoke again. I actually talked to your dad about this the other day and realized I probably need to reach out and apologize to her someday."

Katherine wasn't aware of his and her dad's conversations. "Okay, since my dad knows the history, that's good enough for me. And I agree with your assessment that she's not likely to go public with anything since she's not the type to bring that kind of attention to herself."

"No, she isn't," he agreed.

"How long ago did the relationship end?"

"About five years ago," David said, feeling good that Katherine was interested and had asked.

"Well, I'm sorry to hear that. She's beautiful and seems genuine. I'm sure it wasn't an easy ending for either of you." Katherine felt her shoulders ease with his confession. "I appreciate you being honest. Thank you, David. I hope you will always feel this comfortable to tell me the truth."

He grinned being glad they'd made it through the sensitive topic with no eruptions.

"Are you ready for some more videos?" she asked sweetly.

And he was. Even though David had been fighting this sort of teaching, he learned tremendously from Katherine. He had fun with her, enjoying her stories and hearing about the distinct personalities she had encountered over the years. He truly was happy they were working together.

Chapter 23

The Class

Over three weeks, Katherine and David met almost daily They developed great rhythm when communicating and started really having fun, even teasing one another as they were becoming a team. Katherine still held David's feet to the fire by speaking the truth, not sugar-coating her words as she did so often when interacting with others. She delighted in this freedom with him, as did he.

One Friday afternoon, Katherine received an email informing her that her Sunday school partner couldn't help teach. She taught a classroom of fifth graders about the Bible and loved it. Katherine learned much more than she could ever teach and felt very humbled and honored that God was using her in such a way. Eventually, she hoped to move on to an older group of students, but knew she needed to prosper where she was currently planted, which she was doing.

As the family was leaving the office, she said, "I guess it will be just me this Sunday. Jessica has to work. There was a change in her schedule."

"I can fill in since your mother is already helping Lana and Eric's class," Michael said.

"You can't, honey. This is your week to usher," Sharon reminded.

"I think I'll be okay by myself. The children are older and there shouldn't be more than twenty kids," Katherine said.

"Well, I'm sure Brooke will find someone to replace Jessica," Michael said, speaking of the children's ministry coordinator.

They kissed and hugged each other goodbye as they left. Katherine looked forward to relaxing at home. The week had been super busy, with only a couple more weeks until the first preseason game, plus her workload had doubled since David had been added to the mix.

The Suitable Helper

It was a bright and sunny Sunday morning as Michael and David jogged the trail. Their workouts rarely fell on a Sunday, but David had designed a new routine to prepare for preseason, wanting to be in peak condition.

David's focus on his training and conditioning was now more intense than it had been in the past several years. Katherine made sure his diet consisted of the highest quality foods, and he frequently visited Eric and Lana's restaurant, shedding seven pounds. Losing another seven pounds would put him at the ideal weight he was when in his prime.

During the cool down, as they were walking, Michael asked, "Hey, what are you doing today?"

"Not much. Maybe catch the ball game. Why?"

"I have a favor to ask you."

"You want to ask me for a favor?" David smiled. "This has to be good."

Michael chuckled. "I'm not sure if you know that Katherine teaches the Bible to kids. They are older, fifth graders."

"No, I wasn't aware of that."

"Well, she's down a helper this week, so she will be alone and could use an extra person," Michael said.

"I don't know anything about the Bible." David shook his head. "I can't teach those kids anything."

"No, no. You wouldn't be teaching. Katherine will teach," Michael assured. "You would help…um, you know, pass out a snack, help with a craft. The stuff you do with the kids at camp."

"Oh, okay." David understood since he has been part of many football camps for kids. "Does Katherine know I would be helping her?"

"No, I just thought of it. If you feel uncomfortable, you can say no. It's fine. She's led by herself before, but I thought it would easier if she had someone to help."

David wanted to see Katherine, so he said, "I can do it. What time and where am I going?"

Patting him on the back, Michael smiled. "You can come with us. Wear what you wore to the fundraiser and meet us here by 9:00 a.m."

"Okay, can't wait to put those clothes on again," he laughed.

The Lesson

On his way home, David became nervous about going to church. It had been years since he'd stepped inside one. His family had not been religious at all, so he hadn't gone to services. All his teams had a pastor, and there was prayer before each game, but that was about it. Besides, he worked Sunday and couldn't attend church regularly.

But being around the family, he couldn't help but hear about God. It would roll off their tongue as if God was a real, living, breathing human being. Occasionally, David felt uncomfortable, but mostly he didn't mind them talking about their religion. It seemed to help the family through some hard times.

At the designated time, he and the Lukas pulled up to a large white church that had a grand steeple. The massive front double doors were held opened by greeters who shook his hand, welcoming him as a new-comer. As soon as they stepped foot inside, Michael and Sharon were greeted warmly by many of their friends. David even recognized a few faces from their parties and business meetings. Sharon proudly introduced him to anyone she knew. It made David feel loved, and everyone was very pleasant and friendly.

When Sharon showed David the worship center, he asked, "Where are the statues and cross?"

"Oh, this isn't a Catholic Church, honey. This is a non-denominational church. We bring our Bibles and the pastor teaches from Scripture," Sharon said.

David nodded not knowing how to feel since he'd never been in a church that read out of the Bible.

"Michael and I were both raised Catholic and are very thankful for the upbringing, but we wanted a deeper relationship with God. We've attended different churches over the years, and this one seems to best suit our needs," she said, walking him back toward Michael.

"Hey!" Eric greeted David. "What are you doing here?"

Hugging him joyously, David told him, "Michael asked me to help Katherine with her class."

"You?" Eric pointed, smiling warmly. "Have you ever been inside a church?"

"Maybe you shouldn't stand too close, the roof may collapse," David chuckled.

Eric and Lana were just as proud to introduce him to their friends, but Michael had to interrupt the greetings to get him to Katherine's class on time. David felt very warm and welcomed by all he met.

As Katherine was setting up her laptop, she heard "Knock, knock. I bring you a helper!"

"What are you doing here?" Katherine asked when she saw David enter the classroom.

"I asked him to help you out since you were shorthanded," Michael replied.

"Okay…" Katherine nervously said, "but I think Brooke may come to help, so if you want to go to the church service instead, you can. I don't want you to feel you have to do this."

"Hey, as long as you don't make me teach, I'm fine with helping. I do this with the kids' camps all the time," David reassured.

"Okay, well, then come on and I'll show you what we will do today." Katherine smiled but felt awkward.

"I'm going to go downstairs now. Do you want to go out to eat after service?" Michael asked.

"Sure!" David replied.

"Great, see you after the service." Michael waved on his way out.

"How in the world did my dad talk you into doing this?" Katherine wondered out loud.

David smiled. "He didn't have to. He told me you were down a person and asked if I would help and I said okay."

"Why?" Katherine blurted.

Nudging her with his elbow, pointing up, he whispered, "Maybe God will help me out with my game."

She grinned. "Oh, I see you are trying to get brownie points with God. Well, I guess you can use all the help you can get."

David's mouth fell open, causing Katherine to laugh. "Are you allowed to say that in church?" he asked. "Aren't you being rude to me?"

"I'm sorry. Really, I'm sorry. I shouldn't have said that," she teased.

David delighted in her sense of humor. "I can tell you are really sorry."

"No, that was rude. I'm just playing around with you. You are being nice and helping me out. I guess I'm not used to you being so nice to me and it's caught me off guard." She brightly smiled.

"Wait a minute, are you complementing me or kicking me?" he asked. "I really don't think you are allowed to talk to me this way in church."

"You are right. Please forgive me. I'll save my comments for work," she grinned slyly.

As David went to respond, they both looked at the door upon hearing, "I'm here to save the day!"

"Oh, hi, Brooke," Katherine said. "I wasn't sure if you could make it today. My dad asked David to help me with the class and he agreed."

David smiled.

"David, this is Brooke. Brooke, this is David Mann," Katherine said.

"Nice to meet you," David said, shaking the woman's hand.

Barely shaking his hand or acknowledging him, Brooke looked at Katherine. "Well, your dad isn't in charge, and since David hasn't had a background check, I cannot allow him around the children."

"I work with kids all the time in my line of business," David said, agitated that Brooke thought he wasn't a suitable helper.

"I'm sure you do, but I'm ultimately responsible for these children," she stated abruptly.

David went to protest until Katherine gave him a look that said she would handle the situation. Since they worked so closely together now, David knew her facial expressions pretty well and kept quiet.

"Brooke has been in charge of the children's ministry for several years. She spear headed it when no one else would step up to the plate. It's like a full-time job, and one that can easily become a dumping ground. She's done a tremendous job at making sure the children are taught God's Word and has always stepped in to teach at a moment's notice," Katherine explained to David but clearly complimenting Brooke.

Katherine turned toward Brooke. "I'm sorry, I should have let you know my dad asked David to help me. This normally doesn't happen, but in the future, if we run into this again, I will immediately let you know."

"Okay, I will let it slip just this one time, but in the future, you need to let me know about these types of changes," Brooke said, her ego clearly fed properly.

"Thank you. I will," acknowledged Katherine.

"I'll go get today's crafts," Brooke announced. "But I will still stay in here today so you have an extra pair of hands," she said, giving David the once over before leaving.

"What was that all about?" David asked.

Walking back to her computer to set up class, Katherine blew out a breath. "Oh, it's a long story."

"She's a control freak."

Sort of grinning, Katherine said, "I can't believe you didn't go off on her. You must really want some brownie points from God."

"I was more interested in seeing how you would handle her," David said seriously. "Expertly as usual."

Burrowing her eyebrows and placing her hand on her hip, Katherine searched David's face. "Okay, what do you want? You are never nice to me. You agreed to help me out this morning. You weren't rude to Brooke when she shot you down, and now you've given me a compliment. This is so unbecoming of you." Her eyes were sparkling and she was talking out of the side of her mouth. "Not selfish, condescending, or arrogant."

"Honestly, are you giving me a compliment or are you kicking me in the face? I can never quite tell with you," David said as Katherine giggled girlishly.

"And what are you two laughing about?" Brooke asked as she reentered the room with a box full of crafts.

"Oh, nothing. This is how we normally interact when we are working," Katherine said sincerely, quickly looking over shoulder to share a smirk with David.

"You work together?"

"Yes. David is our client," Katherine said proudly.

"Oh, that," Brooke said.

"David is one of the Cleveland quarterbacks," Katherine said.

"That's nice. I really don't like sports, especially when it falls on a Sunday. I think it teaches the kids to worship the almighty dollar rather than the true, almighty God. Most athletes make way too much money and give themselves the praise," Brooke said.

"Sure, I've seen plenty of that," David said. "But I've also witnessed many men give significant portions of their earnings to those in need. It may not be the majority, but most good will gestures unfortunately aren't newsworthy."

Katherine was happy to see a student, welcoming the distraction. "Hi, Jimmy!"

"Hi," Jimmy said, plopping down in his chair and leaning on the desk, not at all interested in being in class.

"There's some activity sheets over there you can begin with," Brooke said, taking over the class.

Katherine wasn't fond of working with the ministry coordinator. Brooke always said she would help but she generally took over and ordered people around. While she was great at organizing the children's ministry, she lacked basic people skills. Many volunteers quit serving since she tightly controlled each classroom. However, there was no one else willing to step up to lead the ministry, something that happens too often in churches. Katherine didn't believe her calling was to head up any ministry, only be part of a five-week teaching rotation. Thankfully, this limited her interaction with Brooke.

As more kids entered the room, Katherine allowed Brooke to control the atmosphere. It didn't matter to her, especially in this type of environment.

David quietly made his way to the back of the room to analyze the interaction between Katherine and Brooke. Over the past weeks, he'd studied her actions, reading her body language, and it never disappointed him. Right now, she was on her game, and David enjoyed the show.

As the women set up the craft and got ready for the lesson, David thought how much his attitude had changed over the last three weeks. There was no way he would have agreed to help Katherine if Michael had asked four weeks ago. But since he was around the family almost daily, he found he missed their company when a day or two went by with no communication. How could he say no to helping when they had taken him in as one of their own?

Plus, David knew now he was smitten with Katherine. He was shocked by how comfortable he felt with her, especially after feeling aloof around her for months. She was motivating, encouraging, and fun. Their conversations were deep and intense since she never held back, but then neither did he. And the more intense the conversation, the more passionate each became. Katherine didn't handle David with white gloves as he saw her doing with Brooke, and he was glad she didn't. He would see right through that cheap facade and lose respect for her.

And what was so odd to him was that after a heated debate or discussion, David felt a closer connection with her. The total opposite of what he'd witnessed with his parents. He ran from confrontation with women because they weren't worth the aggravation, but with Katherine, he had no choice but to stay and work through their different viewpoints if he wanted to change his image. They had a long way to go with his attitude, but there was a visible improvement.

"Brooke, do you want to lead the lesson?" David heard Katherine say.

"No, it's your class. Go ahead," Brooke replied.

"Okay, we are going to get started!" Katherine spoke up. "Since it's the start of a new school year and we have a couple new faces, let's go around the room and introduce ourselves. Tell us your name and something about yourself—maybe something you like or a hobby."

The kids loved sharing and talking about what they liked to do. Katherine did this whenever there was a new student in the classroom to make the child feel comfortable and laugh and connect with the others.

After the kids' introductions, she said, "I'm Miss Katherine. Let's see…I like interior design. I love football, especially Cleveland, and my favorite color is ivory."

"That's not a color!" Jimmy said.

Katherine laughed. "I know it's a strange color to like, but it complements so many other colors. Miss Jessica couldn't make it today, so Miss Brooke and Mr. David will help us out." Turning towards Brooke, she asked, "Miss Brooke, most of the children already know you but can you tell them something interesting about yourself?"

David thought Katherine was cleverly handling Brooke. It almost could be interpreted as brown-nosing but he understood she was reading her defense and playing it brilliantly.

Brooke delighted in talking about herself and did so for almost five minutes. David watched the kids getting bored and restless.

After she completed, Katherine look at him. "Mr. David, will you tell us something about yourself?"

David stood up, and the kids gasped at his size. "Well, as you heard my name is Mr. David." Then he had to think of a hobby. He'd done nothing for pleasure in such a long time since his depression. "I work with plenty of children at football camps. I'm a quarterback and…" looking at Jimmy smiling, "…my favorite color is blue, which is an actual color."

All the kids laughed, except Jimmy who said, "Oh, you are that quarterback that sucks really bad."

"Jimmy!" Katherine scolded.

David chuckled. "That's okay. Yeah, I've been having a couple pretty lousy years. Hopefully it will turn around soon."

"Doubt it," Jimmy said.

"Jimmy, apologize right now. That's not being kind," Katherine said again, sternly.

Knowing the drill, he huffed and puffed, saying, "Sorry."

Brooke surprisingly said nothing.

A little girl raised her hand.

"Yes, Olivia."

Looking at David with her big blue eyes, she asked, "Can you touch the ceiling?"

"Let's see." David smiled, reaching his hand up, touching the ceiling. "I can!"

Everyone laughed, even Brooke. David and Katherine made eye contact, silently sharing the thought that kids are so funny. It was clear they both knew that children rarely hold back the truth and have a way of looking at things that adults wouldn't see.

"Thank you, Mr. David. Let's get started with our lesson, class. Since it's the beginning of the new school year, we will start in the book of Genesis to learn about creation," Katherine said.

Brooke nodded, approving Katherine's teaching.

"For those of you who are new to this class, in order for you to see the slides on the screen, I need to turn off the lights." When the room went dark, the kids squealed delightfully. Katherine made them laugh when she made spooky noises before asking, "Is it too dark?"

"No!" they shouted.

"Okay, here we go," Katherine said, using a projector to present the material. She didn't know of any other way to teach the Bible. "Just quickly, this is what we are going to cover." She pointed to the first slide. "We will learn about creation, take the greatest commandment quiz, and then have chocolate chip cookies."

The kids cheered and clapped upon hearing cookies would be served. Katherine always brought food and they loved it. "Alright, let's get started so we can eat!" Katherine looked around the room. "Does anyone want to pray or would you like me to pray?"

"I'll pray," Bella said. Bella had a servant's heart, always offering to pray. She began in her sweet voice, "Dear God, thank you for this day. Thank you for this class, and thank you for cookies. In your name, Jesus. Amen."

Katherine smiled, saying, "Thank you, Bella."

David enjoyed the little girl thanking God for cookies.

"When I teach, I want you to keep in mind that my desire is for you to understand that Jesus Christ died for your sins. God wants to lead your life in thoughts and actions. And God is loving, adventurous, creative, and fun." She moved to the next slide, reading the Scripture written there. "Genesis Chapters 1 and 2. 'In the beginning God created the heavens and the earth....'"

Katherine went through all of creation, including Adam and Eve and the creation of marriage. She had a picture on almost all the slides and the kids enjoyed each one. They laughed, engaged in the topic, and answered the questions Katherine asked. She was extremely passionate about teaching the Word of God; it just poured out of her. She brought no attention to herself since the room was dark, continually pointing at the slides with their scripture. She inserted her personality into her teaching, making the material fun, entertaining, and teachable.

David didn't remember learning about creation and he was fascinated by what the Bible actually had to say about it. Katherine referenced the New Testament, bringing more life to Scripture. She explained how God had a purpose for everyone and used football as an example. Katherine had pictures of the Cleveland starting quarterback; the receiver, Reggie Johnson; and the kicker.

She asked the children what each job these players had on the team. They answered her question. "Now, it's not that Reggie can't kick a football, but since he was created to catch it, he wouldn't be able to kick the ball with the same distance or accuracy as our punter," Katherine said.

David nodded in agreement from the back of the room.

"So God created you each with a specific purpose in mind. You have many other talents that God will use but there is something specific He has in mind for you each of you to do. He also created you each with your own unique personality, which He will use too. Study hard in school and allow God to lead you in the direction He wants you to go and you will always be content," Katherine finished passionately.

The kids smiled.

"Okay, all that's left is to take the quiz and then we will eat," Katherine said, and the kids started cheering.

Katherine began. "Who knows what Jesus said is the greatest commandment?"

Several kids raised their hands and recited part of the commandment. Katherine then flipped to the slide with the scripture of the greatest commandment so the class could see it complete. "Love the Lord your God with all your heart, with all your soul, and with all your mind. This is the first and greatest commandment, and the second is like it: Love your neighbor as yourself," she read. "Who can give me an example of what that looks like?"

"Give to the poor," Bella said.

"Yes! Very good," Katherine said excitedly, happy they were engaged and learning.

"Being nice to your sister and brother," another child said.

"Great! Listening to your parents too. Obeying and honoring them. What else?" Katherine asked.

"Helping someone with their homework," someone else said.

"Yes, that's right. Serving people. Who are our neighbors?" Katherine asked.

No one answered her.

"Do you remember this sheet from last time?" Katherine asked, showing a Love Your Neighbor worksheet. It listed out who neighbors are—immediate and extended family, actual neighbors, teachers, city officials, the president. It didn't leave anyone out.

"Everyone," Bella said.

"Yes, Bella. Very good! We are to pray for those we know, like teachers, but also pray for those in higher places we don't know, like city officials, the Armed Forces, and even our president, whether or not we agree with him."

She looked around, making sure the kids understood. "We are to be kind and loving even to someone who isn't nice to us. Like sometimes our friends, our siblings or…." Katherine said until she was interrupted.

"Like when Jimmy said Mr. David sucked as a quarterback," little Olivia said cutely, feeling bad for David.

Everyone, including David, laughed.

"Well, he does suck!" Jimmy reasoned.

"Jimmy!" Katherine reprimanded.

"Okay, okay, sorry, but he does."

David couldn't control his laughter at this point. He was enjoying being there and was so glad Michael had asked him to help.

"I think that's enough for the day. I believe you understand what I'm trying to say. Next week you will learn about Noah's Ark, one of my favorite Bible stories," Katherine said, turning on the lights.

"Can we eat in the dark?" someone shouted.

"No, sorry," Katherine laughed. "Mr. David, would you please help me pass out the cookies?"

"Absolutely."

As they were getting the cookies, David and Katherine smiled at each other over how honest and cute the kids were.

"Katherine, can I talk to you?" Brooke said.

"Yes. David, can you pass the cookies out by yourself?"

"Yes, sure," he answered.

David could overhear Brooke say to Katherine something about going off script. She was critiquing her teaching. David couldn't hear all the details but he could tell that Brooke wasn't giving Katherine glowing reviews. His attention was taken away from them as the kids were excited to eat and asked him many football questions.

When her conversation was over, Katherine's head swirled from Brooke's remarks, but only for a short time since seeing how David interacted with the children brought her joy. He was so much fun, making them laugh, asking them questions, and even creating a craft. They loved him and surrounded him.

Then service was over, with parents picking up their children. Brooke was called out of the room by someone needing her attention, leaving David and Katherine to clean up on their own.

"What did Brooke say to you?" David asked, throwing some paper clippings away.

"Oh, nothing," Katherine said, deflated.

Making eye contact, he asked again. "Katherine, what did she say?"

Turning away, she said, "It's not a big deal."

"Katherine, I overheard some of her conversation with you and I know she said something that was not 'Loving your Neighbor as Yourself'." David said with a witty smile.

Katherine chuckled. "Oh, you were paying attention to class, were you?"

"Yes, it was very entertaining."

She lost her smile. "Well, I'm glad you were entertained. I was going for teachable."

"And you were. I absolutely learned. I just had fun while doing so, and I know the kids did too," David replied. "I heard Brooke say something about you going off script. What does that mean?"

Katherine turned red, sort of wanting to cry, but she held back any tears, going into professional mode while putting away her computer. "Oh, it was really nothing. She just wants me to stay on the course material."

David stopped cleaning. "Katherine, look at me."

Surprised, she stopped what she was doing and looked him in the eyes.

"I've gotten to know you very well. Don't give me this side of you. You have always preached to me to be honest with you and now you aren't being honest with me. Please tell me what happened."

"Look, I don't want to talk bad about anyone, and she's probably right anyway," Katherine protested.

"I've never heard you say a bad word about anyone, except me." David grinned. "I know you aren't like that. Please tell me what she said."

She relaxed. "She told me I need to stay on script because all the teachers need to teach the same material."

"What does that mean?" David asked.

Katherine rifled through her bag, pulled out some papers, and handed them to him. "The lesson is written out for me. It gives me step-by-step instructions on what to say when teaching the kids. But I can't teach like this. I just can't be myself if I use someone else's material. She doesn't like that I added the football players and some extra Bible verses. She doesn't like that I go off script, but that's my style and..."

David understood and quickly interrupted her. "That's why you are so passionate when you teach, plus it keeps things fun and interesting. And the kids love it."

"I just feel like I'm shackled if I try to teach someone else's material. And I get it that some people are really good at teaching that way. It just doesn't work for me," Katherine said, feeling a measure of relief from David's supportive words.

"Don't change your style at all. It works. I don't believe the kids would be as interested if you only read from this paper," David said, handing it back to her. "And from your lesson, you said that God created us each differently. Be who God created you to be."

"Wow! Now I'm feeling really uncomfortable around you. You aren't this nice at all. Can you please say something arrogant and condescending?" Katherine joked.

A wicked smile flashed across David's face. "Okay. Is Jimmy Brooke's son?"

"No! That's bad!" Katherine laughed, holding her stomach.

David laughed with her, then they both resumed cleaning.

"Thanks for the encouragement, David, and thank you for helping me with the class today," Katherine said warmly. She honestly was happy David had insisted she tell him the truth. Katherine loved teaching the kids, but Brooke could deflate a person in a second.

"It really was my pleasure. I hope to come back. Where does this go?" David asked, lifting a box full of the day's activities.

"Right out in the hall. Thanks for that."

"Glad to see you are putting him to work, Katherine," Michael said, walking into the classroom.

"Well, he was whining about lifting a heavy box. Does he constantly complain when you two workout?" Katherine winked at her father.

"Non-stop," Michael replied.

"Please! Ask your dad about our jog the other day," David said.

Michael busted up laughing, saying, "Let's just say I had to go to the bathroom pretty bad."

"Enough," Katherine said, placing her hand over her ears and shaking her head. "I've heard one too many stories about my dad's bathroom incidents."

They ignored her plea and told of how, in the middle of their jog, Michael had to knock on a neighbor's door to use his bathroom. The three of them were rolling with laughter as David retold the story.

With David as part of the company, the family went out to lunch and spent most of the afternoon together watching a baseball win. It became a regular event for David. He attended church with the Lukas, joined in lunch, and practically spent the entire day with them. He came to find he enjoyed going to church.

Chapter 24

The Decision

David was a bit nervous during his jog with Michael. He was weighing a decision and planned to discuss it with Michael and Sharon during breakfast. He felt awkward and overwhelmed by his emotions. After they sat down at the kitchen table with their food, David said, "I need to talk with you both about something I've been giving a lot of thought to over the last two months, especially these last couple weeks."

"Sure, honey, what is it?" Sharon asked.

"I'm not even too sure where these thoughts originated, but I can't seem to get them off my mind, especially lately," he said.

"What is it, son?" Michael asked with concern.

David pushed away his food and leaned back in his chair, analyzing what he thought about doing. He knew Michael and Sharon would be supportive but he was afraid of the process he was about to take. Drawing a deep breath, he said, "You know I haven't spoken to my mom in years…many years." He looked around to focus and steady his emotions. "I feel for some odd reason I should reach out to her."

"Okay," Sharon said, moving her food to the side and looking to encourage David.

"I'm not too sure why at this point in my life I would even want to see or speak to her, but I just can't seem to get it off my mind," David confessed. "And if I'm really honest, I don't want to do this at all, and I'm not too sure if she would want to see me."

David teared up, leaning onto the table for support. "I don't understand why I'm thinking about her or why I would even want to contact her." He looked at Sharon. "She wasn't a good mother…it's hard to give her that title. She's been nothing but heartless pretty much my entire life, and now I'm thinking of contacting her to shut me out again? Why would I consider doing this?"

Sharon held his hand, allowing David to pour out his heart.

"Do you think in some sick way I like the abuse? Maybe since I'm trying to clean up my image and haven't been so abusive? Is it possible I need that in my life?"

Sharon squeezed his hand a bit tighter. She wanted to make sure he felt her tenderness.

Wiping his nose with his sleeve, he chuckled. "I know I still have a way to go, but I'm handling myself so much better. But do you think maybe the abuse is normal to me and I miss it? And now I want to contact my mom so the abuse makes me feel normal again?"

"Oh, sweetie, I love you so much! I'm so thankful to have you in our lives," Sharon said, rubbing his hand. "No, I don't believe at all you like the abuse. I think what you are experiencing is God speaking to your heart."

"I agree," Michael said.

"I think you are being submissive to what God is laying on your heart to do," Sharon said softly, not looking to freak David out with this type of godly talk.

"But I'm not sure what I'm supposed to do and why. I'm not even too sure where she lives or if she'll want to see me," David said.

"Well, let's just take one step at a time. Let me locate her and then we can figure out what to do next," Sharon said.

"Don't be overly concerned about her reaction," Michael said. "Let God take care of that part. Do your part and let God take care of the details for you."

Looking at Sharon with his red-rimmed, watery, blue eyes, he said, "I don't want to put this burden on you to locate my mom."

Grinning through her sniffles, Sharon replied, "This is not a burden at all. This will be my pleasure."

"Thank you," David said, taking another deep breath. He thought deeply, then spoke. "I know I will have to visit my dad too, but I can't really think about that right now."

Sharon smiled with tears, silently thanking God.

And then David searched his heart. "Do you think that's okay or do you think God would be mad if I waited to contact my dad?"

Joy poured forth from Sharon as her face radiated gladness. Wiping away her tears, she said, "I know God loves you so much! And I think He is so pleased that you would ask about His feelings. It tells me you are concerned with how God views you, and it tells me you love Him."

"Son, God loves us more than our earthly parents can ever love us. His love is never ending and He is full of patience and grace. Let's just start with your mother. You will know when it's time to contact your father, and we will be there with you every step of the way," Michael said.

"Thank you," David whispered, looking at each of them. "You have been…." He tried to speak but was too choked with emotion. "You both mean so much…." His voice cracked again. "You've helped me…."

Sharon squeezed his hand again. "We love you too!"

David smiled and quietly thanked God for them, something he did almost daily.

"Let me heat up our eggs," Sharon said, taking David's plate. "I don't like eating cold eggs."

"I don't mind," Michael said, eating as Sharon and David laughed at him.

The Turn of Events

Even before she could make it to the stove, Sharon's cell rang. "It's Katherine," she announced.

David's heart raced. They weren't meeting today but he relished their time together and hoped she was calling to schedule a last-minute meeting.

"Hi, honey. How are you?" Sharon answered as she warmed David's food. "Yes, he's here. Let me give him the phone…oh, okay…"

Both men watched Sharon as she listened, seeing her eyes open wide. "What? Really? Okay, I'll tell him. We'll see you later. I love you too, honey. Bye."

Sharon forgot the food, sitting down with her mouth open.

"Sharon, is everything alright?" Michael asked.

"Rick broke his arm and is out for the season. David, you are the starting quarterback."

David's heart fell to his stomach and his face lost all color.

"What happened?" Michael asked.

"I'm not sure. Katherine said they have been trying to contact David all morning and they called her for a comment. She was running out the door to get to the office to field calls."

They sat silently. David was freaking out since he wasn't playing at his peak but he was excited to lead the team at the same time. He knew all too well how Rick was likely feeling, though, and his heart went out to him.

Breaking the silence, Michael asked, "Anything else God may be laying on your heart? This may be God's way of blessing you for listening to Him and submitting, even when you didn't understand."

"But would God injure Rick to bless me? That doesn't seem right. It seems evil," David said.

Retrieving her phone, Sharon searched "Cleveland quarterback", saying after a moment, "It was a consequence."

"What?" both men asked.

"He was not only intoxicated but apparently…or allegedly…high on cocaine and fell down a flight of stairs." Sharon looked up from her phone. "He's lucky he only broke his arm."

Now their home phone rang as did Michael's cell. David had left his in the car but could imagine it had plenty of missed calls. No one answered their phones since they knew it was the press hot on the story.

"So I ask you again, anything else God may be laying on your heart?" Michael said.

All three of them laughed uncontrollably. It was as if they saw the hand of God at work and it was more than apparent He was making Himself real. There was a joy but much fear, for they couldn't comprehend God's holiness. They felt unworthy of His love and grace. God did not harm Rick; instead, He protected him from his folly and only allowed him to suffer minor consequences.

Sharon's phone rang again. "This one is Katherine!" she said. "Hi, honey! Yes, we read the accusations…yes, he's right here." She passed the phone over.

David's heart pounded. "Hello?"

"I'm so sorry my mom told you the news. That wasn't professional of me. I was bombarded with phone calls and reacted instead of talking with you directly," Katherine said nervously. "I obviously haven't handled a situation like this before. I think I got caught up in the moment and drama."

"No problem," David said, knowing she was looking at how her actions may have affected his feelings.

"Well, I guess congratulations are in order. I don't mean any disrespect towards Rick. I'm sure he's full of regret," she said. "More importantly, how are you feeling?"

"I think I'm still in shock. I obviously did not expect this at all."

"No one did," Katherine replied. "There's a press conference at 1:00 p.m. today. The media will be all over the stadium. They are already camping out. Is the TV on? It's all over the networks. This has just become the hottest topic."

"No, the TV is not on. Your mom found the details on the internet," David said as Sharon found the remote and flipped through each sports channel.

"I haven't issued a statement. You and I can discuss it. You know they will be all over you for the next couple days. This will have a three-day shelf life." Katherine then gently said, "Let's figure out the best way to handle this and prevent it from gaining any more momentum, alright?"

"Yes." David understood she meant for him to keep away from the spotlight.

"Obviously, this is sensitive since it involves drugs and alcohol. I have your practice schedule. I'll meet you at the stadium before the press conference."

"Okay," David said, ending their call.

He knew she was in work mode, attempting to figure out the best approach to handle the media. At this point, he trusted her completely as his manager and would listen to her instructions without resistance.

There wasn't much talking as he ate. He was deep in thought, preparing mentally to be the next man up.

Chapter 25

The Leader

David drove to practice and couldn't believe the number of news outlets reporting on the team. He was able to slip out of their eyesight using the private entrance. All eyes locked on him, however, when he entered the locker room. It was packed with staff and players. His nerves attacked him, for he'd just became their leader and had no confidence in his abilities.

Reggie was the first to pat David on the back and confidently touted, "I believe in you."

If only he believed in himself. Right now, Reggie felt like his only friend. David hadn't connected with many other players, but now this situation forced a change.

"Okay, listen up!" The coach rounded them up. "Rick is out for the season. We are hoping his arm heals quickly and that he gets the necessary rehabilitation to address the other issues he needs to overcome."

Players patted their hearts, nodding their heads.

"David, is it. He's our guy. We brought him here because we believe he has what it takes to help us achieve greatness as a team. With veterans such as Reggie, Marshall, and Tyler, we will succeed. Our amazing lines will hail their power and our special teams…" Coach smiled, "…well, you are just special."

The team chuckled, which put David at ease.

"Let's come together as a team," their coach said, looking right at David. "Let's not speak or use social media that will keep the media hanging around us any longer than necessary. Everyone understand?"

The players agreed.

"Okay, let's warm up!" The coach shouted, motioning for the guys to hit the field for practice.

David was nervous and he hated the feeling. He wanted to go back to his days of confidence. Running to take his place on the field, he felt unsure and overwhelmed. He had not expected ever to start again. He only had imagined that he would fill in for a couple of games because of others' injuries.

David tossed the ball, warming up his arm. It felt good to have the ball in his hands again. With each pass, he put a little more distance on the ball. Then some running plays, and his confidence slowly grew. His connection with Reggie established chemistry—they were a talented team.

Reggie's spirit and passion were contagious. He motivated David by making him laugh when he caught the ball, dancing in the end zone. Reggie played out of love, not for fame or fortune. He wasn't showing off his greatness; he still had the wonderment of a little boy and a thankful heart for his occupation. For Reggie, it was pure joy and an honor to play the game.

David then worked with the rookie receiver, Devon Welsh, a California native. He was young, blonde, cocky, and fun. The more they worked together, the more comfortable they felt with the routes.

Eddie Hammond held the top spot for the running back. He was a big lug from Tennessee—a typical 5'9", 250 pounds of solid muscle. Most of the team called him a redneck since he was a true country boy. Chewing tobacco, fishing, and hunting were his hobbies. His legs were massive and he didn't stop running even when pushed back. Eddie could always gain a few more yards. He was known as one of the best backs in the league.

The more David worked with the offense, the more comfortable he felt in the pocket. It was only a light warmup getting everyone familiar with the drills, but that old winning mentality was presenting itself, making him proud of his abilities. Now they were ready to pick up the pace, inserting defense.

Quickly, the intensity level drastically increased. David had little time to stand in the pocket to find his guys, but they were creating a rhythm, something David hadn't had in years. He was feeling and looking confident. David was excited and determined, now running out of the pocket, looking forty yards down the field at an open Reggie. He slung the ball, which Jordan picked off for an interception. It deflated David since it was proof he was still off his game.

"Did that look sexy?" Jordan yelled, running toward David, showing him the ball. "It felt sexy!"

Jordan Sanders strutted, the league's flashiest cornerback and nephew of the greatest showmen ever to enter professional football. He had an inflated ego with the talent to back it. He had quite a reputation with the ladies too. Women swooned over him and he loved the attention. Jordan had been traded to Cleveland just a couple of days ago. Plus, he was an old teammate, one who frequented the bars to dance and compete with David in winning over women back in the day. It had all been in fun since David wasn't the type to have one-night stands. Jordan still dated frequently. Even though he was now older, he hadn't grown out of the bar scene.

"Run it again!" Coach yelled.

They reran it, changing the routes several times until Jordan intercepted the ball again.

"I got you beat!" Jordan yelled, laughing as he pointed the ball at David.

"Let's move! Come on!" the coach shouted, looking over his playbook then toward the third-string quarterback. "Warm up," he said to him.

Back in the pocket, David handed the ball off to Eddie. They were moving down the field. The ball snapped, then was tossed quickly to Reggie for the completion. Things were progressing. David called the next play, ran out of the pocket, throwing on the run, but it was another interception.

"Okay, that's enough! Williams, run some plays!" Coach barked.

They took David out, putting in his back-up. David had his opportunity and he hadn't been able step up. He did his best to fight the depression that swarmed over him. The only saving grace was that this was a closed practice not open to the public or media.

All morning, David and Williams traded positions. Of course, Williams had his eyes on the starting spot, and a profound doubt set in David that he wouldn't get back to peak performance.

Practice over, David had to prepare for the press and shift his mindset. Walking lazily to the locker room, Jordan trotted up to him with a smug smile. "How 'bout you show me the night life?"

Hiding his sense of defeat, looking to blow him off, David said, "I'm too old for that scene."

"Come on, man! You aren't the same cat I remember," Jordan said joking but not joking, patting David's shoulder.

Jordan reminisced about the good old days, even making David laugh a time or two. Recalling it all with Jordan lightened up David's mood and lifted his spirit. He loved that time, the competitive nature and cockiness he had back then. Now he felt like an old man in a young guy's sport.

The Press

Katherine waited as David took a shower and changed into street clothes. He emerged from the locker room wearing his usual sweat pants, hoodie, and hat. Katherine read it well—he looked beat. Wishing to cheer him up, she smiled brightly. "Hi. How are you? Are you excited? I'm so happy for you." She quickly added, "Not that I'm happy Rick is hurt."

Not cracking a smile, he said, "Yeah."

Disregarding his lack of life, Katherine got down to business. "Alright, let's figure out your statement." Reaching in her bag to retrieve a notebook, she said, "I brought you something to eat."

"There's food here," he said.

"Okay," she replied, seeing he'd gone back inside himself. Over the past several weeks of being together, David's attitude had almost completely changed. He had been eager to learn, funny, and analytical. But something had happened this morning she could see and it had caused his personality to run away.

In an empty conference room, the two of them sat alone and it quickly turned into their worse meeting to date. Not that he was rude, but David hardly spoke as Katherine coached him on the questions she knew the media would ask. Even if he gave the perfect answer, authenticity came from within, and right now his body language and dead eyes said he was beaten down again.

Preparation complete, it now was up to David, who stood on the sidelines in the press room as the coach addressed Rick and his accident. Even though the surgery had been a success, Rick's arm needed pins, placing him out indefinitely. There was some hope he would play the last couple games of the season, but it depended on how well he recovered.

Coach stated David was the starter but they would also work with Williams to prepare for preseason. He addressed each player and how they were forming a well-rounded team. After taking some questions, it was time for David to step up to the mic.

His heart felt like it was leaping out of his chest. His face was white as a ghost and his mouth was dry. At least he had trimmed his beard so he looked less grizzly than usual. The room was packed, and David squinted from the bright lights blinding his eyes. He remembered those lights so well and how he used to love them. Now he wanted to run and hide from them.

Katherine, along with her parents, stood in the back of the room. She held her breath and said a prayer as David approached the microphone.

"I want to first start off by saying that I hope Rick has a full and speedy recovery. I know the team feels a loss for him and we are all saddened by the news," David mumbled.

"Are you glad that you came to Cleveland now?" Trino yelled.

"Um, well…um, I'm glad to have the opportunity to start. Um, well, but I'm not glad that Rick is hurt," he replied.

Katherine sighed in relief. He was proceeding fine.

"So are you still less than thrilled to be in Cleveland?" Trino pressed.

"Um, well, um, I just want to do my job and do the best I can. This is a great team and, um, anyone would be proud to lead them," he replied, giving the scripted answer when he really wanted to say he wasn't the best any longer, had no game left, and was flat out afraid to lead.

Another suitable answer, Katherine thought.

"The team only won five games last year. Do you see yourself winning more than that?" someone asked.

"Um, this team is hungry to win. We'll just take each game as it comes."

"You had at least three interceptions in this morning's practice. It doesn't seem like you are very hungry!" Trino said.

David shook, his eyes pierced and ready to attack. Someone had given out inside information and he felt set up. Now his pale face burned red. He placed both his hands on the podium and looked down as his heart pumped rapidly. He wasn't sure what to say but he was the leader and that meant leading with his attitude as well as his play. "Well, um…well, I guess I'm a little rusty and in learning mode."

He did it, Katherine thought. The answers weren't rolling off his tongue and he had to select each word but he could hold back an outburst.

The reporters continued questioning for several minutes more, and each time David searched for the right words to speak. He left the conference spent. His head spun from the emotional roller coaster and yet the day was only half over. He dragged himself to the locker room to shut the world out and catch his breath but Jordan stopped him as soon as he stepped off the stage, walking him away from earshot.

"Dude, who in the hell are you?" Jordan laughed. "What happened to you? What happened to the guy who used to tell the media to go screw themselves?"

He tried to grin, replying, "I guess that wasn't working for me too well."

"It did when you were playing with vengeance," Jordan said. "I miss that fighter."

David missed the fighter within him too.

The team's coordinator called Jordan to the microphone. "Let me show you how it's done," He called back to David.

David found a close-by TV and couldn't help laughing as he watched Jordan bantering with the media. They loved him. David loved him. Who didn't? They'd had some great times together.

After the press conference, Katherine and her parents met with David. They could see defeat weighed on him heavily. He wasn't himself; he looked hazy and his thinking wasn't clear. He almost appeared drugged.

"It went well," Sharon said, trying her best to encourage him with her upbeat tone.

"Yeah," David said, slumping over in his chair in the same conference room he had met Katherine in earlier. She thought for sure he'd perk up since he'd handled himself so much better but his lifeless eyes only looked at the ground.

"How do you feel?" Michael asked.

"Okay." He shrugged his shoulders.

They could see he didn't want to talk. He was emotionless. He wasn't his usual self around them. They weren't too sure what to say either. Outside of saying he'd done a good job, Katherine was silent as well.

"How about coming over for dinner tonight?" Sharon asked.

"Let's see how I feel once I get out of here for the day," David mumbled as he fidgeted with his hands.

With nothing else to say, David headed to the field for afternoon practice. It was neither worse nor better than the morning's drills. Afterward, he went home to be alone. David wasn't interested in being around anybody—not even the family.

The news cycle swapped stories of Rick's drug-related injury and a montage of David's interview. It was the media's opportunity to make fun of him and they did so by counting the times he said "well" and "um," even attaching music to create a rap song. The clip went nationwide; it was that funny. At least the local channels covered only the story, choosing not to poke fun at David.

Katherine was pleased with David's presence. Of course, he'd done so much damage in his past dealings with the media that they would find anything to ruin the little reputation he had left. But she believed he was on track to revise his image. All this was new to him, and he'd handled it better than expected.

The Morning News

A week had gone by since the press conference, and Katherine was right; the story had a three-day shelf life and only because of Rick publicly announcing he would enter rehabilitation for his drinking and drug addiction.

David continued two-a-day practice. Some were opened to the public, and the fans were encouraging. They were die-hard Cleveland fans, coming to Berea to see their beloved team practice. They motivated David, but he still wasn't on his game. The team was a stronger unit, however, coming together well. David enjoyed his old friendship with Jordan and new friendships with Reggie, Eddie, and Devon. But he was still missing a beat that the team could see.

David still jogged with Michael before morning practice, but he wasn't himself. He was quiet, somber, and sluggish. Even during breakfast when David attempted a conversation, it was a struggle. Sharon didn't want to put any more pressure on him than he felt, but she needed to tell him something important.

"David," she began, "I located your mom."

Seated at the head of the table, Michael and Sharon sitting on either side of him, he looked away in pain, but pressed forth asking coldly, "Where is she?"

"She's about thirty minutes away from where your grandmother lived," Sharon said.

Pushing away his food, he asked, "How did you find her?"

"Well, with the internet, it's not too hard to find anything these days."

David rubbed his face while stress flooded his body, flatly saying, "Maybe I should wait until the season is over to visit her."

"Sweetie," Sharon said, "There's something you should know. Your mother had a stroke and she's in a government nursing home. From the little information the nurses would give me, she's not doing too good."

David sat back in his chair. This was the last thing he needed to hear. A lot was coming at him and he didn't know which way to turn. Since they announced he would be the starting quarterback, David's mind had been foggy and his thinking indecisive.

"I'm not sure what to do," he said with wide eyes, shaking his head, trying to manage his stress. "I'm not sure when I will be able to get out to see her. Preseason is in two weeks and I'm still off my game. I feel I should spend all my time practicing or watching tape."

Michael pushed away his food, calmly serious about the matter. "What do you want to do?"

David looked around contemplating, searching his heart. "I don't want to see her, not just now. I think it would throw off my game even more."

"Son, whatever decision you make, we will be here for you," Michael said.

David was confused and couldn't think clearly. Usually with the family his mind was never tangled, but since becoming starting quarterback his thoughts were scrambled and damaging. He'd begun to hide from the world, even the family. He'd pushed people away, especially Katherine.

"What would you do?" David asked, looking directly at Michael, pleading for help.

"I would go see her," Michael replied.

"But I'm not sure how to fit it into my schedule," David said.

"Let's go Saturday after your morning practice," Michael said, sliding his plate back in front of him.

David took a deep breath and agreed. "Okay, I'll get the three of us airline tickets. I'm assuming you will both go with me."

"Of course we will go with you," Sharon said, touching his hand.

"You don't need to get airline tickets. We'll take our jet," Michael said, taking a bite of food.

"You have a jet!" David exclaimed.

Taking another forkful of food, he explained, "Well, I own it with a couple other guys."

David couldn't stop the words, even if he had tried. "How much money do you have?"

"It's really not that big of a deal. It's a small jet." Michael indicated with his hands as he ate.

"Don't let him fool you. Out of everything he owns, that's his favorite toy. He'll use any excuse to fly it somewhere," Sharon said.

David knew the Lukas were wealthy but this took it to another level. They gave so much of their wealth away, and outside of owning a 14,000 square foot home, their "toys" were minimal. They didn't have flashy cars or boats. Despite knowing them for six months, this was the first he'd heard of their jet. Michael and Sharon surely didn't brag about what they had.

They decided they would go to see David's mother on Saturday. David didn't sleep well from that point on, loaded with the anxiety of leading a team, fretting about his under-performance, and worrying over seeing his mother for the first time in years.

Chapter 26

The Mother

On Saturday, David boarded Michael's impressive jet. It wasn't even five years old and, because of Sharon, it was dressed impeccably, reflecting elegance and class. It could accommodate twenty easily, and boasted a top-notch staff.

David's mind was filled with junk. That morning's practice was the worst one to date, and he was beyond frustrated. Sadness and anger from unhealed childhood memories flooded every part of his body, which grew more tense as the plane climbed. Michael and Sharon tried to speak with him, but he had nothing to say. They understood he was likely fearful of his mother's rejection, so they silently prayed. David fell asleep despite himself, which pleased Sharon.

David awoke just before landing, feeling refreshed. He was thankful he'd zoned out for most of the flight and decided to clean up a bit before the final descent. Even though nervous, he was ready to visit his mother.

David insisted on paying for the car service currently taking them to the nursing home to share in the travel expense. Plenty of memories rushed his thoughts as he traveled his old, home-town streets. Sharon asked if he remembered the area, so he pointed out playgrounds, restaurants, and his school. Some good memories there, he admitted, mainly all related to football. But it all looked tired, in need of a facelift. The little town appeared run down. Even his grandmother's old home could have benefitted from a paint job.

Sharon enjoyed listening to David's childhood stories. His eyes twinkled when he recalled his friends and teammates, but that light quickly dissipated as he thought of how his skills had diminished significantly and his playing days might be over.

It wasn't a long ride and they soon pulled up to an old, multi-story, institutional-looking building. It was situated in a place surrounded by boarded-up homes, broken fences, and rusted cars. It wasn't a pleasant neighborhood, and not one of them felt safe. Sharon asked the driver to wait, then remained near David as they entered the building. Disgusting! It was more of a homeless shelter than a nursing home. It was overly crowded with people everywhere, even sitting along the hallways. It smelled of stale urine and body odor.

Sharon's heart filled with sadness that no family was around to care for the sick and disabled men and women. Many looked to be addicts, some were begging for money. She could see David wasn't doing too well, so she hid her feelings and approached the receptionist asking, "Hi. Will you please tell me where we can find Lisa Mann?"

While the receptionist looked up the room number, Sharon prayed for God to give them the strength to endure. She already regretted the trip since the home was a dump and it was apparent the patients weren't cared for properly. Sharon's concern was for David's well-being and emotional needs since no one expected this condemned facility to be anyone's home.

Once they found Lisa's room, Sharon and Michael remained in the hall, planning to wait for as long as David needed to visit. But he hesitated before entering the room, trying to muster up the courage to face a woman he hardly addressed as mother. This meeting was long overdue. With his heart pumping wildly, wondering what they both would say, an odd sense of peace came over his being. It encouraged him to enter the dingy room.

It was dark, dated, and down-right nasty. Two beds were in the small room, but one was empty; a sad, thin curtain hung between them to provide little privacy. No window, no TV, and no phone could be seen. There were holes in the dry wall and the closet door hung by only one hinge. The overhead fluorescent light was not only blinking but seemed to be humming. David could see his mother's legs under graying bedcovers. He took a deep breath, then went to her bedside. Horror seized his heart upon laying eyes on her. He knew she was in her early fifties, but she looked seventy, staring blankly at the wall, never noticing someone had entered her room.

"Hi, Mom," David said softly.

Lisa turned towards David, puzzled by the unfamiliar face.

Moving closer, he teared up. "It's me, David."

As soon as she recognized him, remorseful sobbing overtook her. Her cries were so loud that Sharon and Michael began silently praying. They both understood the sound of regret.

David tried fighting back the tears, but it was no use. Barely able to speak, so high were his emotions, he whispered, "I just felt the need to come and see you. I'm sorry it's been so long."

She could barely move since her left arm was paralyzed and even though her speech was impaired it didn't drown out her wailing. His mother stretched out her right arm as far as possible, trying to heave up her weak body to get to her son, but was only able to motion for him to come closer. She grabbed his hand, kissing it, nonstop, thanking him profusely for visiting. He could not have known her only wish of late was for death. Though she could not tell her son this, she could at the very least attempt to show him her sorrow for running out on him when he was barely a teenager.

Seeing her feeble, worn out, mangled frame, David wept outwardly. He bent down to hug her, not more than a little fearful he would break one of her bones. Once he had her in his arms, he held her tenderly, for he was overcome by love for this woman whom he had never wanted to see again in his lifetime. His hardened heart melted and sadness poured forth, yet he was thankful he had listened to that small, still, persistent voice that had led him here. The sounds of their crying together filled the shabby room. David was glad he'd made the trip.

It took a long while for them to separate. When they did, David kneeled on the floor next to her bed so that he could remain close and looked into her gray, sad eyes while holding her hand. He was unsure of what to say since she was a stranger, so he decided to retrace his life from when they'd last saw one another. He spent almost thirty minutes alone talking about the move to Cleveland, Michael and Sharon's placement in his life, and how they located her. He ended explaining that they had even traveled with him.

Lisa looked around expectantly and David understood she wanted to meet them. Without a second's hesitation he told her he would introduce them. Michael and Sharon were an important part of his life now.

He was visibly emotional when he stepped out of his mother's room, saying to the Lukas, "I'm sorry, I took so long."

"Spend as much time as you need, son. That's why we are here," Michael said.

"How is she? How are you?" Sharon asked.

"She's not doing well. She doesn't look good at all," David said, rubbing his red, puffy eyes.

"We need to talk with someone who can give us an update on her health," Sharon said, agitated there were no visible nurses or other staff.

David agreed. "I told her about you and she wants to meet you. Is that okay?"

"Of course, honey," Sharon said sweetly.

They walked into his mother's room and Sharon was immediately angry about the condition of her environment. It smelled and was dirty. Her heart broke upon seeing David's mother. She had some of David's features but was paralyzed on her left side. She lay there wrinkled, brittle, and thin-haired with sores and bruises running up and down her arms. By the foul odor, Sharon knew no one was changing her diaper or bathing her properly. She could only imagine rashes irritated David's mother's rest, causing many sleepless nights.

Sharon held the woman's hand. "It's so nice to meet you. We love your son. He's a good man."

Lisa cried, nodding her head.

Even though his mother looked different, David could tell her demeanor had changed. She seemed softer and more caring than when she had left. Her eyes were full of sadness but no longer miserable. Of course, she was weak and frail. She must be undernourished too since she was so thin. And it wasn't easy to have a conversation since she could barely talk. They communicated as best as they could, even chuckling as Michael told her funny stories about David.

Finally, a nurse entered the room and Sharon asked, "How long has Mrs. Mann been here?"

"I believe she's been here since March," the nurse answered.

About the same time he had arrived in Cleveland, David thought.

"Does she receive physical therapy daily?" Sharon asked.

"We give her physical therapy as much as we can. As you can see, we are over-crowded and under-staffed," the nurse explained nonchalantly.

"Do you know what happened to Mrs. Mann? When did she have her stroke and how did she end up at this location?"

"I think she had the stroke around the beginning of the year. She was staying at the homeless shelter located in this facility," the nurse said.

David's eyes welled up with tears upon hearing that news.

"Is there a doctor here today that I may speak with?" Sharon asked. "I would like to get the latest update on the condition of her health."

"No, there are no doctors here today," the nurse said.

"Well, how about a head nurse? Who can give me this information?" Sharon asked in a tone that demanded action.

"I can try to locate the head nurse," the woman said, leaving the room.

"I'll be right back," Sharon said, following the nurse with determination.

Both Michael and David looked at each other, deciding to follow Sharon. David hadn't seen Sharon upset and it wasn't like her to display anger.

Sharon followed the nurse, with the men trailing closely behind.

"Hi, I'm Sharon Luka. I would like to know Mrs. Mann health condition," Sharon crisply said.

Peering over her glasses, the head nurse asked, "And how are you related to her?"

"I'm her son," David spoke up.

"Well, I can let you know about her health condition," the head nurse said, looking past Sharon. "Mrs. Mann suffered a stroke at the beginning of the year as you can plainly see. The doctor has given her a couple more weeks to live since her organs are shutting down."

Tears streamed down David's face and his heart fell into the pit of his stomach.

"She's coming with us!" Sharon announced.

The head nurse grew indignant. "Where do you think you are taking her? You can't just come into our facility and take a patient out."

Unperturbed, Sharon looked the nurse in the eye. "I want to see the manager of this hospital right now. Mrs. Mann is not staying in this place one more night."

"Fine, I'll get the manager for you, but you can't just take her out of this hospital," the nurse said, walking away.

"We'll just see about that," Sharon shot back.

"What are you doing? Where do you think you are taking her?" David asked frantically.

"Home. With us." Sharon answered, looking at her husband, saying, "Michael, please tell the driver to go pick up a wheelchair at that medical supply store across the street."

As Michael left, David stopped him, asking, "Where are you going?"

"You want me to say no to her? Do you think I'm a fool? You go stand up to her," Michael said. "Did you notice any medical store across the street? This was her intention from the beginning."

Leaving Michael, David pleaded, "Sharon, please, what are you doing?"

"David, I'm not leaving your mother to die in this facility. I can't do that. I couldn't live with myself knowing that your mother is in this filthy place. She will stay in the home on our property. We will take her to our doctors and get her a full-time nurse."

David wept. He leaned up against the wall, then slid down and wept from his heart. "Thank you," he said between his sobs. Looking up at Sharon, his grateful eyes full of emotion, he continued, "Thank you. I never expected anything like this from you."

Sharon knelt next to David, hugging him tightly. "You have done more for my family than you could ever know."

David was confused and started to ask Sharon to explain when the head nurse interrupted. "Mrs. Luka, this is the facility manager, Ms. Marsh."

"It's nice to meet you. This is David Mann, Lisa's son," Sharon said as David stood to shake her hand. "I understand this is a government run facility and you are overwhelmed with patients, although I know you are doing your very best to meet their needs. But Mrs. Mann is coming home with us—her son—so we can provide an extra bed for you to offer to another patient with needs."

David now saw where Katherine had learned how to diffuse a tense situation and come alongside a person persuasively to meet both needs.

"Mrs. Luka, I would love to honor this request, but she's under government care, both medically and financially. I can't let her go with an expectation that she will continue those services. In order for all her expenses to be paid, she needs to be in an approved nursing home," the manager said.

"I will cover her expenses," David said without hesitation.

"And who are you again?" the manager asked.

"I'm her son."

"Well, removing her from this facility is within your rights. Come with me and I'll get the paperwork ready for you to sign," she said professionally.

David and Sharon followed the manager and several minutes later the paperwork was complete. The manager walked them back to David's mother's room where Sharon thanked her for her time.

"Mrs. Mann, you are coming home with us. Is that okay?" Sharon asked.

Lisa cried, full of shame, shaking her head no. How could she tell them? After all she had done in her life, she felt she deserved to rot in this hole.

"Your son is part of our family, and now so are you," Sharon impressed. "There is no way we are leaving you to stay here."

Lisa again shook her head.

"Mom, you are coming home with us. You aren't staying here any longer, do you understand?" David stated this so firmly it was clear she knew better than to argue against him.

Lisa nodded and touched their hands, trying to thank them.

"I see where he gets his determination," Sharon laughed as she squeezed Lisa's hand.

Lisa smiled even brighter, as best she could, and happy tears ran down her face.

"Is it alright if I pack your belongings?" Sharon asked.

Lisa nodded her approval. Both David and Sharon went through her belongings only to realize there was nothing worth keeping. Sharon found her medication and placed it in her purse, leaving everything else in the dilapidated room with David's approval.

"Mom, is there anything specific you want to take with you? We aren't finding much," David asked.

She pointed to a bedside table. David opened the drawer, finding her identification, medical cards, lipstick, and some photos. He looked through the pictures and tears again stung his eyes but this time they were happy ones. A flood of thankful emotions toward God overwhelmed him.

Sharon held his hand, looking through the pictures. "Is this David?"

Lisa smiled the best she could for she was proud of her son.

"How old was he?" Sharon asked.

"Ten," Lisa said.

"He's so handsome," Sharon said with motherly tears in her eyes. "Look, you are holding a football."

David was tickled by the memory and smiled that he had accomplished his little boy dream.

"Is this your mother?" Sharon asked.

Lisa nodded again.

"She's a beautiful woman, just like you." Sharon smiled, looking at another picture. "Who's this?"

"That's my dad," David said.

"What a handsome man," Sharon said, and for whatever reason, tears pierced her eyes.

Lisa looked off in the distance and Sharon knew she had regrets.

"Mom, anything else we should take?" David asked.

Lisa shook her head. It was clear she was ready to leave it all behind.

"Are we ready?" Michael asked, showing up with a brand new wheelchair.

David turned to Lisa. "Are you ready, Mom?"

His mother nodded, attempting to pull herself up from bed, but was too weak to do so. David came to her side, bent down, asking, "Can you put your arms around my neck?"

She tried but being paralyzed and having no strength made it difficult.

"Mom, I'm going to be as gentle as I can, but I'm going to have to lift you into this chair. Are you ready?"

She agreed, and with hardly any effort, David lifted her, placing her gently in the wheelchair. He removed his coat and wrapped it around her, and she cuddled with it dearly as she quietly cried. Michael pushed her down the hall as David and Sharon protectively flanked her side, ensuring she was okay. Lastly, the trio oversaw her final signature before leaving as one.

After David placed her in the car, Michael broke down the wheelchair. "I see you didn't take on Sharon either." His smile quirked from the corner of his mouth.

David laughed. "I'm no fool either."

Relief swept David's heart once they made it to the jet. He carried his mother safely aboard as she rested her head on his shoulder, realizing this wasn't a typical family. Even before they departed, Sharon contacted a nurse to meet them at the house, providing a list of items and supplies to be purchased before their arrival.

David learned on the flight home that once Sharon located his mother after researching the nursing home, she had placed an on-call nurse on standby with the hopes to bring home Lisa. Sharon didn't even need to walk into the nursing facility to determine they came for a purpose and not a visit; it was a done deal in her mind. Michael knew his wife and her determination and would step out of her way every time when she had her mind set on helping someone in need.

In short time, they took Lisa to the family's doctors, who updated her medication and prescribed daily physical therapy along with a healthy diet. Lisa enjoyed the little home on the Luka's property along with the twenty-four-hour nurse. David visited daily, often morning and evening. Sharon visited as well, turning the radio to a local Christian broadcast with the volume low so Lisa could hear it slightly in the background while she rested.

David was again thankful for this family which God had brought into his life. They had opened their arms to his mother; they were showing him how to love. And even though he loved Sharon dearly, he enjoyed getting to know his mother.

Less than a week later, while eating breakfast with them, David said, "Well, I guess I need to go see my father next."

"I have his address. Just let us know when you are ready," Sharon said, sipping on a cup of coffee.

David looked at Michael, then let out a rousing laugh. He should have known Sharon would already have the ball rolling. He knew they would visit his father as a group in short order.

The Father

With just weeks until the first preseason game, David's play was as flat as his emotions. He hid from Katherine too. Now he was sitting on Michael's jet to journey two and a half hours to visit his father in Florida, a meeting he was clearly dreading.

Again, he wasn't much for words. He was tired physically and emotionally, and his mind reminded him often that reaching out to his parents was a terrible decision since he couldn't get his head back into the game. But that small, still, persistent voice put all reason aside as he took action.

They parked in front of another government-run facility after reaching their destination, although the building's exterior and neighborhood showed its condition was pristine. They walked into the premises, this time David taking the lead.

"Excuse me," David said to the receptionist. "Will you please tell me where Mr. Jack Mann is located?"

Following the nurse's direction, they reached his door, and David indicated he would visit his father alone. It wasn't that much different from seeing his mom. His heart raced fearfully, his hands trembled, and he needed to take several deep breaths to center himself. Since the visit with his mother went better than expected, he had strong hope this would go well.

He entered a clean and well-maintained room. For an assisted living facility, the room had a nice homey feel to it, with an over-sized window that brought in plenty of sunshine. It was a private room with a double bed that was neatly made. The walls were freshly painted (David could still smell the paint) and local photos of the beach, parks, and Florida's sunny skies decorated the room. David was glad his father's home was not in the same condition as his mother's former residence.

His father was sitting in a rocking chair watching the college game of the day. He looked up when he noticed David.

"Hey, Pop," David whispered.

"What are you doing here?" his father asked with his usual cold daggers.

"Well…" David said shamefully, slumping his shoulders and putting his hands in his pockets, "um, I thought it's been too long since I've seen you and I wanted to come for a visit."

"For what?" his father asked harshly and then stood. "You haven't come around in years and now all of a sudden you show up and I'm supposed to be glad to see you?"

"No. You are right, I should have come sooner. I really didn't make time." He hung his head.

"You had enough time. You were benched. What else were you doing? No teams wanted to pick you up. Now you come to see me. What do you want?" His father's eyes pierced with anger, his face a deep red as he placed his hands on his hips.

Backing up submissively, David cowered. Despite all those years of separation, it was like his father hadn't missed a beat. However, now

David didn't object his rhetoric; he finally believed the words his father professed. He sheepishly said, "I don't want anything. I didn't visit before since I wasn't sure you wanted to see me."

Jack backed him up, pointing his finger in David's face, shouting angrily. "Well, I don't want to see you. Get the hell out of here! You've been nothing but a bum. You were a big shot for a couple years, and you turned your back on me. Now you're washed up, sitting on the bench, hanging onto a sport that's passed you up. And only since some guy broke his arm, you're starting again? You won't do anything with that team, in that lousy town. Why don't you just give it up? You're nothing but a loser who will never amount to anything."

Upon hearing Jack's rebuke, even Sharon's wisdom couldn't subdue Michael's rage. He burst through the door, grabbed a hold of the back of Jack's shirt and slammed him into the wall so hard a photo fell down, crashing to the floor. Michael then gripped the front of Jack's shirt collar, lifting the man up off his feet, threatening with no apology. "Listen, buddy, you better shut your mouth or I will do it for you. You got it?"

Both David and Sharon tried to separate Michael from Jack Mann but Michael's eyes were furious. His breathing came heavy and inches from Jack's face.

"Who the hell are you?" David's father yelled. "Get out of here before I have them call the police."

"Michael! Michael! Please! It's okay. Please, let me handle this," David pleaded.

Michael loosened his grip, slowly backing away but never breaking eye contact with the older Mann. Sharon grabbed her husband, looking to calm him down.

"We are leaving, Pop. I just wanted to stop by and to tell you I was sorry for not coming around. And to let you know I saw mom and she isn't doing too well. I won't be bothering you again." David turned to Michael. "Come on, let's go."

"What's wrong with your mother?" Jack asked, his anger evaporating into worry.

Looking back at his father, David said, "She had a stroke and the doctors have given her only a couple more weeks to live."

"Where is she?" Jack asked, following David like a child frightened by the darkness.

Sharon stated the simple fact, not moving. "At our home."

Only addressing David, Jack said, "Take me to her."

David hung down his head, defeated. Again, this was significantly more than he expected. How in the world could this all possibly work out? David felt nuts.

"You will need to pack some of your belongings," Sharon said.

David looked right at Michael, waiting for any sign it was okay. Sharon caressed her husband's arm to help guide his decision. He was upset and not eager to be around David's father. And then he spoke his mind. "If I hear you ever speak to my…your…son in that manner again, you will not be welcomed in our home. Do I make myself clear?"

As if he didn't hear him, Jack said, "I want to see my wife."

Taking a step closer to him, pointing his finger and raising his voice, Michael reiterated, "Do I make myself clear?"

"Yes," Jack replied quietly.

Michael left the room. Sharon helped Jack pack, and David sat on the bed motionless, protecting himself from feeling. He didn't feel the need to cry, but he did feel like he needed to paralyze his emotions.

No one said a word on the flight home. David felt terrible that now his dad was being brought into the family and he wasn't sure what problems would arise. Would his mother be upset with him for bringing his father to Cleveland? He was so embarrassed by his dysfunctional family. Sharon and Michael must think he was pretty low class. The shame further sunk his depressed mind to deeper depths. He regretted contacting his parents.

No one spoke on the ride home. When they arrived at the Luka's, David took control. "Pop, let me tell Mom that you are here."

Jack nodded, remaining by the car while David walked over to the small house.

"Here, let me get your bag for you. Are you hungry? Would you like something to eat?" Sharon asked.

"No," Jack said.

As Sharon took Jack's bag out of the car, Michael came up to help her. She touched him lovingly, feeling his tension.

Upon reaching his mother's house, David knocked lightly, then walked in. The nurse smiled at him. "She just woke up from a nap."

"Hey, Mom," David muttered. He went to her recliner, bending down and kissing her cheek.

She smiled at David.

Sitting close to her, he said, "Mom, I went to visit Pop today because I felt I needed to see him. I hope you aren't mad but I told him you are staying with us…well, the family…and he wanted to see you. He came home with us and he's here. Is it okay if he comes in to see you?"

Lisa's face winced in pain and she looked away. David's heart dropped and he regretted the visit to his father even more. Then his mother looked back at him, grinned slightly, and nodded. David let out the breath he hadn't realized he was holding, feeling a wash of relief. "Thanks, Mom."

David walked back the way he had come, looking for his father. Sharon was the first to spot David waving to bring Jack to the small residence Lisa called home. Michael followed along. David met up with them, leading the way in the dark, warm, summer night. Walking along the path to the sound of footsteps, he desperately tried to still his anguished jitters. He was bringing his father to his mother to be together in the same room for the first time since he was a young boy.

As soon as Jack saw his wife, he doubled over in agony, falling to his knees. Weeping, he crawled to her, wrapping his arms around her when he reached her chair, sobbing like the broken-hearted man he truly was. He was tortured that he had not been there to protect and care for his wife—the woman he long loved, the woman whose love he hoped for in return.

Lisa visibly trembled from the pain of regret and sadness. The decisions she made in her life amounted to wastefulness and selfish urges. Believing her life without Jack would amount to happiness had only lead to utter darkness and misery. Jack always loved her and she not only had abused that love but had neglected their marriage. Her wailing grief was more than anyone could endure. Neither the family, David, or the nurse could hold back tears as they witnessed the reunion.

Finally, David couldn't take anymore and walked outside. Sharon followed, placing her hand on his back. David turned toward her and collapsed into her embrace, bearing his entire weight on her. He could no longer control himself and needed support. Understanding David's emotion, Michael unwrapped him from his wife and took some of David's pain onto himself, weeping with him. David utterly gave up, giving himself over to the family, baring his heart. Michael and Sharon helped shoulder his burden, and a tiny flame of hope was lit within him.

This was an intimacy David had never experienced in his life. It was a real, live moment of David exposing himself—the good, the sin, and the weakness. This was exactly what God intended, he realized—to expose ourselves and rely on Him.

David's father remained with Lisa in the small house, not leaving her side, to care for her as he'd always desired. David visited daily, although he and his father talked little. They mostly sat in silence, but it was fine with David. He was doing the right thing, which was honoring his parents even though they were strangers in reality. Sharon continued her daily visits. Michael tried not to hold any harsh feelings toward Jack and attempted to be as polite as possible whenever he joined them.

David felt such a bond with Sharon and Michael as they did with him. The level of commitment and love between the three of them deepened in a way that David hadn't realized existed. However, he continued to hold Katherine at arm's length during the entire process, one that she felt and understood. Life was throwing too much at him right now and his mental state was clearly in disarray, leaving him unable to handle another voice guiding his steps. He was attempting to understand how to unite with his parents, how to lead and quarterback a team, how to take direction from his coaches, and how to properly address the media. Something had to give and Katherine was the first to go. David's play neither worsened nor improved, but his thankfulness and love toward God grew.

Chapter 27

The Journey

About a week later at breakfast, Michael asked David, "Is there anyone else we need to go and get this week?"

That made David laugh hard, which was something he desperately needed. "No. That's my entire family," he said upon recovering his breath.

"I'm glad they are here. Your mother seems to be doing better," Sharon said.

"Yeah, she doesn't look like she's on her deathbed," David said sadly.

"Are you doing alright, son?" Michael asked.

"This is just a lot to take in," David said, rubbing his face. "I'm trying to get my head back in the game and my parents are living here…neither of which I expected. I almost want things to go back to how they were when I was sitting on the bench and I wasn't thinking about my parents."

"Why?" Michael asked.

"Life seemed less confusing," David answered.

"How so?"

"I didn't need to think about what I would say, how I would act, or really have any emotions or feelings." David smiled. "Ever since I've met you people, I've done pretty much nothing but cry."

They all chuckled.

"Well, prior to meeting us people," Sharon joked, "when was the last time you cried?"

"Gosh," David thought, "Maybe a little when my grandma died, but before that was when I was a kid."

Michael looked at David. "How come?"

"Really, there was no reason."

"You never shed tears when you were benched?" Michael asked.

"Which time?" David joked.

They laughed as a group once more.

"No," David finally answered.

"Have you ever cried about your parents, your childhood, or the lack of family?" Michael questioned, wanting David to dig further within his heart.

"No." David then pushed his thinking and said, "It never bothered me. I guess I didn't know what I was missing. It was all so normal to me, and since I was an only child, I was used to being alone and I didn't mind it."

"Well, why do you think you have been crying so much lately?" Sharon asked tenderly.

"I'm not sure. I guess I just feel so tired."

"Maybe it's your body's way of saying it's tired of being strong and putting up a front," Michael posed.

"What do you mean?" David asked, turning toward Michael for he wanted to hear his thoughts.

"Well, it's possible that you've really never allowed yourself to feel any emotions. You've been so good at being independent, strong, and confident that perhaps you've proved to yourself that you don't need anyone. You've said you have opened up to us more than you have opened yourself up to anyone in your past. Maybe you really crave that," Michael said.

"Maybe. Maybe it's just because I'm so beaten down that I've given up."

"That's what God intends," Michael replied.

Puzzled, David said, "I don't understand."

"Well, we are a people who think we don't need God because of our sinful nature. God allows certain things to happen in our lives to get our attention. He wants us to give up and give ourselves over to Him. We think He is trying to hurt us when in reality He only wants the best for us. You never had a family. It's as if God has given you to us to be part of our family. He knows what you need more than you know."

"Well, why didn't He just give me a good family in the first place?" David asked, honestly.

Michael smiled. "You always ask the best questions."

David grinned.

"I'm sure it grieved God that your parents weren't what they could or should have been. We don't know a lot about your parents. We aren't too sure what happened in their lives," Michael said. "I really believe God is leading you to a better place. Much better than where you were before."

"Well, I hope it's to a better place than where I am right now," David said, slumping over in his chair, fidgeting with his hands.

"If you really think about it, don't you believe in some ways that your life is already better than it was before?" Michael asked.

It took little thought for David to say, "Surprisingly, yes. But not my game."

"That will change in time."

David thought for a moment, then he said, "Maybe it's time for me to quit, I mean after this year. Maybe I just don't want to admit that my life as a quarterback has been over for years. And I'm holding onto something that is gone—that has been gone for quite some time."

"Why do you say that? Is it just because your play is not where it used to be? Or does it have something to do with what your dad said the day we brought him home?" Michael pressed.

"Do you mean the day when you lifted him off his feet and almost knocked him out?" David asked, grinning knowingly.

Michael turned red, placing down his head shamefully. "Yeah, I guess I need to apologize to him for that too."

Smiling, David said, "You were pretty mad."

"I like to think of it as passionate," Michael chuckled.

"I can tell you stories of his so-called passion," Sharon teased, playfully swatting Michael on his arm.

They laughed, but soon David analyzed Michael's question. "I really don't think that what he said bothered me. I used to use his words to prove him wrong. Jordan called it vengeful play. Like there was something I had to prove. Now, it's lethargic, flat, and standard at best."

"Are you describing your game or yourself?" Michael asked.

Sadly, David said, "I really see no difference in either."

"You know, I don't fault your parents for how they raised you. I'm not by any means excusing their behavior or saying what they did was okay. But since I have my own kids, their actions are understandable to me, but not justifiable," Michael said.

David furrowed his eyebrows, scooting his chair closer in to the table to pay attention to what Michael was going to teach him.

"When you are a parent, it's like being a coach of a football team. You need to really understand each one of your children and set them up for success. They need to be disciplined and challenged. It's a hard, analytical, and, more often than not, a very unrewarding game. I can understand why parents check out. It's not all the romance, glam, and glitz that we can sometimes convince ourselves it is supposed to be. It's work beyond anything you can imagine. It's worry that takes on a whole new meaning. It's studying and praying to really understand how God created a particular child. And above all, it's the most selfless job. I believe in order to be an effective, loving, and trustworthy parent, you must completely put yourself aside in order for your children to create their own legacy."

David felt sad that he didn't have the sort of parents Katherine did.

"I look at you as my own child. I don't see a lethargic, flat, and standard at best kind of a guy. I see a man who has all but given up and is still hanging on, fighting. I see a man who is full of love, passion, and guts. I definitely don't see standard. I see exceptional, brave, and courageous. I don't think your game is over. I think your game is just beginning. I see a God who's leading you to a place that will be much better than if you continued down the path you rode in your so-called glory days. I see a God who is using us to help you navigate and stay on course. And I couldn't be more proud or humbled to be part of this journey. I'm so proud of you. I really don't think I could be any prouder if you were my own flesh and blood."

Tears welled in the corner of Michael's eyes, threatening to fall like the ones now streaming down David's face.

"I think the center position resembles a parent. They pass the football to the quarterback and stand up to block the defense. The football is sort of like passing on the family legacy, and then the parent protects their child from the many obstacles that are trying to take that child down. I think your parents weren't strong enough to handle the blocking. And that's okay since God gave you the ability to scramble out of the pocket and throw on the run."

"Yeah, but I can't scramble and throw on the run as I used to do," David said.

"Well, you don't need to do that as much since you have better blocking these days," Michael said, smiling and patting David fatherly on the hand.

"Yes, something I'm very thankful for," David said, smiling back.

They all talked some more in the loving atmosphere of the kitchen before it was time for David to go to practice. Michael had lifted the athlete's spirits, but his play still remained flat.

Chapter 28

The Preseason

A suite located right on the fifty yard line held the family along with several clients and friends. It was a beautiful August Friday evening, and the stadium radiated energy from devoted fans ready for a season of hope. They toasted champagne just in time for the opening kickoff, and the crowd went crazy when Cleveland got to the thirty-yard line. David ran onto the field to cheering fans, though it was mixed with some booing, which was expected because of his tarnished reputation.

Katherine hadn't seen David since they had announced he would be the starting quarterback. With the intensity of practice, watching film, and his spending time with his parents, there hadn't been any time or reason for them to meet. She noticed he looked trim. Maybe not back to his fighting weight, but close. His step was livelier, but still lacked life. Katherine sort of missed him, their conversations, and laughter.

Now they communicated via phone, and he usually was quiet and withdrawn. It was nice that he wasn't condescending or angry any longer, but at least then there had been a spark of life. Now he read detached. She suspected he was purposefully hiding out and avoiding her.

He looked good passing the ball. The entire team looked unified. The play was nothing exciting, but the fans were hungry for anything, cheering wildly each time Cleveland caught the ball or made a tackle.

But, again, it was flat.

Reggie and Jordan were the most exciting to watch. David completed a pass to Reggie, who ran it for a touchdown, dancing in the end zone. The crowd ate it up, making David laugh, relieved to place points on the board.

Jordan played to the crowd. He loved to be the center of attention, entertaining the fans. Any time he knocked down a ball or made a tackle, he would tell the fans to send him some love, which they happily gave. Jordan was glad he had come to Cleveland. He more than sensed he was at the end of his career because so many injuries had sidelined him, so he was happy a team still wanted him with a fanbase that appreciated his passion.

The score was tied at 7 in the second quarter, down to the two-minute warning. David was feeling more comfortable, especially hearing the fans cheer him onto victory. The ball was snapped and he had to quickly scramble out of the pocket, throwing to Devon. But it was picked off and ran in for a touchdown, deflating David.

He sat on the bench with the offensive coordinator trying to understand the interception, but David had little time to review the replay on the tablet since Cleveland's special teams returned the kickoff and he had to take the field. He was heavyhearted, and it was a chore just to take a knee to wind the clock down to halftime.

In the locker room, David sat dazed. They were only down by a touchdown, but it felt like so much more. The coaches reviewed the routes, strategized, and encouraged David, but they could see the look of defeat in his eyes. No matter, it was time to head out to the field. Back out to the roaring crowd.

The fans, crazily dressed in dog masks and faces painted orange and brown, threw energy into their voices, motivating the team. David slowly got into a rhythm until he scrambled out of the pocket, throwing on the run, for it to result in another interception. The opposing defense had discovered a weakness.

This was not good. This was a major weakness that not only caused turnovers but placed points on the board. David knew this losing strategy would cost him the game. The coaches called for the second string quarterback to warm up. Of course, this was normal since it was preseason. They would test all players, evaluate the competition for the various positions, then make the necessary cuts. David knew his role as a starter was in jeopardy.

Out on the field again, David scrambled, throwing the ball out of bounds. No interception but this wasn't a way to win games. Three and out. David wasn't able to gain a first down in the second half, and three downs and out was now common in this game, leaving them punting on the fourth down.

Reggie did his best to encourage David, helping him to get out of his head. David paid little attention to his attempts at motivation since he was busy analyzing his game and figuring out how he used to play. Spending so much time on the bench, he'd forgotten, losing his instincts.

Again back on the field, the defense blitzed, so David passed the ball to Reggie for a completion. Not a perfect throw, though. Reggie had to jump high in the air, grasping it with one hand and trapping it in his armpit, but it ignited momentum, and Cleveland gained a first down.

On the line, the ball snapped. Another blitz. David scrambled only to get sacked. His teammates hurried to help him up. The opposition now had exposed another offensive weakness. David couldn't handle the pressure.

Lining up, counting down, David handed the ball to Eddie this time, who rushed for another first down. Momentum building again, they were in the red zone, only twenty yards left to get a touchdown. Hearts racing, adrenaline pumping, fans deafening, everybody could taste a touchdown.

Play called, the defense rushed, pressuring David and causing him to hand the ball off to Eddie, who was pushed back for a loss of three yards. Second and goal. Ball snapped, again David handed off to Eddie, but he was blocked once more with no gain. Third and goal; one more try. Ball in hand, David dropped back in the pocket, the defense coming for him. He scrambled, looking for Reggie, covered, looked over to Devon open in the end zone, and threw the ball. No luck. The Cleveland crowd deflated at the latest interception.

David was yanked. He hung his head low on the sidelines as Williams finished the game. He should have been happy when Williams brought the team from behind, winning by a field goal, but he just couldn't manage it. At least the fans were excited for a win, even though it was an ugly one.

Press Time

The after-game press conference was up next. Katherine and her parents went to the locker room to visit a visibly upset David. He wasn't talking much, to them or anyone else. Katherine shook his hand, congratulating him on a team victory. David kept his brooding silence even when she gave him words for the press. It was obvious he was pushing her away. Once she finished her job, she went by Reggie, who stood happy with his performance.

David knew he'd withdrawn from the world, even Katherine, but he knew she wasn't sure how to change his mental state. Was it even possible? Sharon and Michael remained by him, although from a distance, providing space, but their presence gave support. He put off showering as long as he could to have extra time before facing the press.

After the coach assessed the team's performance before the reporters, it was David's turn to be in front of the glaring spotlights.

"You are weak out of the pocket. Three inceptions, one returned for a touchdown, and a sack. How do you account for that?" Trino asked.

"Well, um…" David said, then remembered being raked over the coals for those words. "I think I'm still working out the kinks to get into a rhythm."

"Williams completed the job and he's been on the bench longer," Trino pressed.

"As a competitor, I always want to be the one to win the game…but the team needed a change in order to pull this one out," David said, choosing his words carefully.

"You haven't looked much like a competitor," Trino pressed.

Looking around, David cut him off. "Anyone else have questions?"

Katherine didn't move. She made no visible signs betraying her thoughts on his behavior. Some looked to see her reaction, but she stood completely still.

David handled the rest of the reporters' questions reasonably well, not giving much ammunition to dissect his attitude. Now the talk surrounded his weak play. The analysts' talking points were Williams was the obvious starter with David the one to ride the bench.

Chapter 29

The Protector

David dragged himself home, exhausted after the adrenaline-fueled day, and fell asleep almost immediately. He was numb, sore, and weak when he woke the next morning. He had no interest in his usual jog with Michael or in visiting his parents, but he had practice and wanted to warm up, so he went to the house anyway.

During their jog, Michael didn't mention the previous day's game. He spoke about the stock market and the coming of fall. The morning air was crisp, feeling good to them both. Michael could read David so well and knew he should show love through actions instead of prying David open to talk. The young man wasn't ready.

David ate quietly with Michael and Sharon afterwards, making small talk so as not to be rude. He visited his parents before practice with Michael following, thinking it was strange since it wasn't what the older man usually did.

"Hi," David said flatly as he entered the home, seeing his parents along with the nurse watching TV. He didn't want to be there at all, in particular near his father. Jack's normal speech after a poor performance was a montage of critical barrage of unsolicited advice.

Lisa smiled, kissing her son as his father remained silent.

"Hi, Pop," David said, pulling a dining table chair into the living room to sit with them. Michael followed suit.

"Hi," Jack replied monotone, which was normal for his demeanor.

"How did she eat last night?" David asked the nurse.

"Good. She has a good appetite lately. They both have good appetites," the nurse joked.

"Just like their son," Michael said.

Although David grinned, he didn't respond with his usual wit.

The morning news played as background noise and served as a deterrent to the strained conversations happing as of late. David tensed up when the broadcast reported the sports news, cycling through the

Cleveland win, David's weakness, and their analysis of Williams, whom they named the quarterback for the job. David believed in the rhetoric, submitting further to defeat.

"The line's weak, #33 isn't blocking," Jack said. "They can put in that other quarterback but it won't make any difference."

David's mouth fell open. His father had barley spoken and now he was talking about his game. It was hardly a compliment, but his father only ever found fault with David's performance, even as a kid.

"I see it too," Michael said. "No mention of it in the press. David will figure out how to compensate. He's one of the best at reading the line."

Jack nodded, not saying another word.

David stayed a little while longer making small talk, then said his goodbyes, heading off to practice with Michael following him to his car.

"Well, I'm glad my dad didn't say anything that would cause you to attack him again," David said, attempting to grin and reverse his overall discouraged attitude.

"You will not let me live that down, will you?"

"Absolutely not, that's gold." David chuckled. "I know why you came to visit my parents with me. I am glad I didn't have to separate you two."

Michael laughed, then said. "You know your dad is right. There is a weakness on the left side. That's pretty tricky to pick up unless someone knows the game. Your dad must know it. Has he ever played?"

Burrowing his eyebrows, eyes searching for an answer, David tried to recall any mention from his father. "I don't know. He's never mentioned it," he said.

"It sounds like he's followed your career. He knew you moved here and about Rick's broken arm. What took him down to Florida?" Michael asked. "It's interesting that your mother remained in your hometown and your father moved to Florida."

"I'm not sure. I just assumed it was to get money from me."

"When did he move there?" Michael asked.

"I think it was around the time my collarbone got broken," David answered.

Michael nodded, placing his hand on David's shoulder. "I believe your father loves you very much, son. I just think he doesn't know how to show you."

David took this in a moment, then nodded sadly.

"I don't want you to think I'm trying to replace your father. I can never replace his love or fill his shoes. A love for a parent runs deep, and I'm sorry if it may come across as if I'm trying to take his place."

David grabbed a hold of Michael, hugging him tightly. "I love you so much." Pulling back slightly, rubbing his arms lovingly, he assured, "You are showing me how to love him. You are helping me become a better man. You make me think, and you pull the best out in me. I thank God for you daily." With tears in his eyes, he chuckled. "Thank you for confronting me that day."

Relief flooded Michael, and he patted David happily on the back. "Thank you for letting down your guard and coming into our lives. You've done way more for our family than we could ever do for you."

"What can I have possibly done for your family? I've been rude, disrespectful, and, at times, hostile," David said perplexed.

"You've brought a tremendous amount of joy," Michael said.

David scratched his head trying to make sense of Michael's comment.

"Honey?" Sharon yelled. "Telephone. It's Katherine."

"I have to get to practice. I'll see you later tonight," David said hurrying to his car.

"Okay, see you later," Michael replied, running off to take his daughter's call.

As he got in the car, he heard Michael saying hello to Katherine. He really missed her, but he didn't want to be around her right now. There was so much happening in his life that he feared he would be rude, and he had no intentions of heading back in that direction. He narrowly had escaped an outburst with Trino after the game and believed he couldn't afford that with Katherine. They'd made so much progress and he didn't want to ruin their interaction.

But David knew the truth, that their fun working relationship had already taken a hit. It was purely business now. Their phone conversations were brief and to the point. She attempted to joke with him, but he seemed to take the jibes personal. She read his distancing loud and clear, maintaining a professional work mode as a result, and he hated it. Although he had brought it on himself, he wasn't sure how to change things back between them. He knew Katherine would be professional no matter what, but that was the side she showed everyone else. He desired the person he brought out in her, and he couldn't do it any longer.

The Preseason Event

David went to practice, working on the weak side of the offensive line, running out of the pocket and throwing. He was very weak with these plays. He could see the hole. Even so, he needed to work these routes hard. He watched film, making necessary changes to right his game. He pulled old footage of his glory days, realizing he was always weak out of the pocket, but he had a solid line then that had hidden his flaws.

The family traveled to Detroit to watch Cleveland compete in a charity game. What really should have been a joint practice turned into an event for fans and players to give back to the communities, all while evaluating their talent against opponents to make appropriate changes in time for the season opener. David smiled when he saw many Cleveland fans had made the trip too, wearing their home colors. That happiness soon faded, however, when David fumbled the very first snap. It left him even more heavyhearted, and not even ten seconds into the game. At least Jordan and the defense prevented any points on the turnover.

David was back on the field, trying to wipe the fumble from his mind. He could see the weakness on his left. When the opposing defense lined up, he wanted to call an audible, but his hands were tied because the coaches wouldn't allow him the privilege. The ball snapped, and they broke the line. He ran out of the pocket and was sacked within seconds.

Slowly David got up. He could barely hear the play from the offensive coordinator since the Detroit stands were crazy loud. Same formation. Still a hole on the left. The ball snapped, then line broken, but David whipped the ball, connecting with Reggie.

David started clapping, happy for the catch. He knew if he got the ball within three feet of Reggie, he would connect, but his passes had to be more accurate. There wasn't enough time to go through his progressions with a weak offensive line, so David needed to strengthen his own weakness. He needed a quick release, but right now, his timing was off because of the defense's speed.

They ran the ball two more times. It was 3rd and long, and it was obvious he would throw a pass. He saw the hole; Cleveland snapped the ball. The defense came at him, so he went running for his life, throwing to Devon. And it was picked off for a touchdown. It was the second turnover of the game, and this one for points.

David dragged himself off the field and sank on the bench, watching the replay of his interception with the offensive coordinator on the tablet, knowing he was losing the game for his team.

Second quarter and he was back on the field. David told #33 to watch his hole. Tension flared when that teammate told David to watch his turnovers. Anger now impregnated in the team. David knew he wasn't leading effectively. He wasn't motivating; he was creating a hostile environment.

The staff didn't want to chance any more turnovers, so they ran the ball until it was 3rd and long. David could read blitz, but no audible could be called. The defense again broke the line, and David passed while being sacked. The ball was deflected, picked off again, and run in for another touchdown. David yelled out frustratingly, placing his hands on his helmet, then dropped to his knees where he pounded the ground with his fists.

He was yanked and benched. Williams came in for the second time to win the game. Afterward, David knew the press would be merciless. Deep down, he knew they were right. Even with the weakness, he felt so slow. He saw his shortcomings. He really had declined over the years. In his rookie season he had been able to stoke a fire that kept him cunning and sharp. That seemed impossible now. Frailty seemed to define his game, maybe even his manhood.

His own questions were the same questions from the press. His teammates pulled away from him, looking instead to Williams as the leader. It was a long bus ride home, with David sitting in silence, headphones on, pretending to listen. He was numb. It was just a joint practice turned into a fund raiser and he couldn't even deliver in those conditions.

Chapter 30

The Second Preseason Game

Neither the family nor his father mentioned his game. David continued to watch film and practice hard. The coaches called him in mid-week, informing that Williams would start the next game and those thereafter. David was benched again and secretly glad. Now he could hide from the world.

He cut off even more communication from Katherine, allowing her calls to go to voicemail without returning them and not even sending a simple response to texts she sent. He had no room for her in his life any longer. His priority was first to his mother and where he would move her once he fulfilled his contract obligation in just a few short months and got out of Cleveland. Then came his father and how that relationship would work going forward. So trying to fit Katherine anywhere in his life just couldn't be done. Besides, he would have to face her in a couple of weeks because of a photo shoot. But other than that, he remained clear of her, not even discussing Williams taking hold of the team's reins.

His intentions were to stay away from the family too, but since his parents resided at the Luka's home, he had no other choice but to visit. He regretted bringing his parents to Cleveland since he was now tied to them and it left him with so many emotions to work through, more than he could bear. He still trained with Michael, but barely broke a sweat. He forced himself to make small talk both during breakfast and the time spent with his mom and dad.

Of course, the media had a field day singing, "I told you so!" But David was glad he didn't need to deal with their pathetic questions any longer. It made hiding out easier, but where to hide? Where to go? What would he do for a career now? Who was he? He'd tried to change his image, even made progress, but robotically. He'd learned it didn't help to explode, and even with the growing anger building up inside, he could control himself. But he wasn't himself. Who was he?

David decided in his heart this was his last season. He would retire from football. He would move back to Florida. His parents' situation complicated that move, but he would figure out the best location for them all.

For weeks, David silently seethed at the thought of the second preseason game and seeing the guy who had changed the trajectory of his world, sidelining him in a lifeless city. His only saving grace was the bench kept him from facing Tyler Lewis, the guy who broke his collarbone. A rush of bitterness swept over him when they finally made eye contact in the stadium.

Tyler Lewis was aggressive, intimidating, and heartless. On the field, he was known for dirty plays and illegal hits. He led the league in sacks and penalties. There was no denying he desired to weaken his opponents by hitting so hard it was difficult for his opponents to stand back up. He dominated by fear, making sure a player never forgot the pain he could deliver.

From the bench, David watched William's rhythm. The team had found its missing spark. They were having fun, coming together. And the scoreboard reflected this spirit, Cleveland being up by a touchdown.

David sat with hardly an emotion crossing his face. His practice the past week had been light and overall weak. He had no qualms about riding the bench; he wasn't sad. The life he'd planned had taken a significant turn, and his thoughts drifted to trading stocks for a living, leaving the game altogether. Then the crowd's angst pulled his attention to the field. Williams was down. Lewis had sacked him, and now he was slowly getting up, jogging off the field, holding his hand in pain. Coaches shouted orders; David warmed up as they called a timeout.

David's heart raced as he threw the ball on the sidelines, getting his arm ready to take the field. The offensive coordinator instructed his play, David looking at the playbook in between throws. There was not much time to think and get set mentally. He ran onto the field to a mixture of cheers and jeers. His mind was not in the game at all. No focus. Everything had happened too fast, with no time for him to catch his breath.

Cleveland ran the ball several times to protect their lead. It was the beginning of the fourth quarter, and the Cleveland coaches were trying desperately to prevent David from passing. They didn't want to chance a turnover.

David's only thought was to get through this game. Williams had probably just taken a bad hit and certainly would be back later in the week. David believed this was his job, the job of a back-up quarterback, to cover until injuries healed. He should play a maximum of three games this season and then be out. Out of the profession and out of Cleveland.

David protected the lead, but now the ball was in the hands of the other team. On the bench, he reviewed the next set of routes as Philadelphia tied the game. David's mission was to protect the ball by running it, but no matter their efforts, the team wasn't advancing down the field. Three and out became a pattern, nowhere close to attempt a field goal.

The clock was winding down as David stood on the line. The ball snapped. He handed it off to Eddie, but then immediately felt his neck snap back. Lewis had sacked him late with penalty flags thrown everywhere. Slowly, David made it to his knees and took a deep breath, standing briefly before he bent over, dazed. The personal foul for roughing the passer gave Cleveland an extra fifteen yards and a first down, inching them closer to field goal position.

Why was Lewis in the game? The clock was under the two-minute warning in the fourth quarter. No starter should be in the game at this point, so why was Lewis? David couldn't catch his breath, but then came the blitz and the breaking of the line. The charge was coming fast. David handed the ball off to Eddie as planned, but it bobbled in David's hands. A fumble! David jumped on the ball, several players piling on top. Massive chaos ensued. Who had the ball? Officials blew the whistle, shoving players out of the stack. David came up with the ball, barely able to stand.

Second and 15. David handed the ball off to Eddie, gaining eight yards on the completion of the play. Everyone, from the players to the coaches to the fans, knew Cleveland had to pass. David covered his helmet with his hands to hear the play, heart racing as he called the route in the huddle. They lined up and David read the defense. He wanted to call an audible upon what he saw but he didn't have the authority to change the play. When the action began, Lewis leaped over the line, forcing David on the run. Afraid of the impending impact, he looked for Reggie, covered now over to Devon, seeing the slightest opening. He had to be spot-on accurate to make this work. Threading the needle, the throw—intercepted. The opposing crowd roared when their team took the ball in for a touchdown, winning the game.

That was it; this was beyond anything David could ever imagine. There was absolutely no game left in him. He submitted to all the talking points of being a washed-up head case. Everyone's hope was that Williams would heal in time for the last preseason game, or that Cleveland would sign another quarterback.

The Showdown

The family met David in the locker room and feared when they saw him. Katherine's heart dropped to her stomach; she understood that "my life is over" look. Michael, Sharon, and Katherine knew David's career was over. The Lukas could only pray that God would open his heart and David would receive Him as his personal savior, for God always meets us at rock bottom if we look for Him.

David was utterly flabbergasted when he heard William's wrist was broken from the sack by Lewis. This meant he would again be the starting quarterback until a proper replacement was located. It was so unbelievable. He had no desire or passion to play and wanted to quit right on the spot. Now he hoped he would get hurt and be taken out for the rest of the season.

The media was in a feeding frenzy, like sharks drawn to the bait. The coach dodged as best he could, however, he couldn't avoid the many questions on David's inability to play. It was clear that David's career was over and the coach was taking heat on acquiring the obviously substandard athlete. Coach did his best to reiterate they all believed in David's talents, along with the team's younger players, and the coaching staff would address their weaknesses.

Katherine watched David step up to the microphones, looking worse than the first day they met. His beard was severely overgrown. His hat didn't hide his unruly hair, which was almost as long as his beard. His eyes pierced with anger, his skin was pale, and although he was in tiptop shape, he looked bloated which was made worse by his hoodie and sweats. It was clear he was ready to take the media head on since he was in no mood for their interrogation.

Question after question, David gave no suitable answer. Mumbling the same old phrases, he played the same old song and dance. They were in control and he wasn't able to deflect.

"The first two games, you gave up interceptions and fumbles, which translated to points. Both times Williams stepped in to rally a win. Now today you fumble and lose the game to an interception. How do you account for that?" Trino asked.

"Well...um...um, there is no way...um...to account for a loss," David said.

"What adjustments are you going to make to get your head back into the game?" Trino continued.

"Um...well, I still feel...um...rusty and...um, I'm hoping to turn it around soon."

"You've given us the same answer for three weeks. You haven't been the same since your collarbone broke. Is there another injury that hasn't been reported that is affecting your game?"

"Are you calling me a liar?" David stared directly at Trino. His baby blue eyes turned pale icy, cold grey in fact, piercing with hostility and venom. David's penetrating gaze dominated the press room to a silent fear. With seething contempt, he looked directly into Trino's soul, ready to shred it to pieces.

Katherine froze, holding her breath.

Trino, not one to run and hide, took up arms, never breaking eye contact as he charged his target. "Well, are you lying? It seems to me you may not be honest. You now have the most turnovers in preseason, more than all your previous years combined when you lead Miami. It just seems to me that there may be more to your injury that's causing..."

"I've had about enough of your fat-ass mouth!" David lit in. "It's real easy to sit behind a microphone critiquing players' performances when you yourself couldn't make it as a football player in high school! How many times were you able to sack the quarterback? If I read it correctly, you were benched your sophomore year and quit after that season. And now you have a career telling an audience how bad I'm doing? You make money off someone else's performance, or lack thereof. You couldn't last a season and half and you sit there berating me and other players? What a loser. Really, what a loser job you have. You are still sitting on the bench, miserable and desperately trying to make yourself happy on someone else's failure. You weren't man enough to play the game back then, and you could never be man enough to handle this game today. So go ahead and continue asking your pathetic questions, attempting to make yourself feel good, but I will not answer them anymore!"

And with that, David stormed off to the locker room. Katherine didn't even blink as all eyes locked on her for signs of any reaction.

The Art of Persuasion

"Dude, you just called him a fat ass on national television!" Jordan said, laughing so hard he was bending over to catch his breath.

David was furious. He was furious with his play, with Trino, and his entire life.

"Listen, you need to flirt with them out there," Jordan smiled.

David wanted to attack Jordan but he was so comical David couldn't help but listen.

"Come on, man, you are supposed to make love to the camera, not have angry sex with them. You just left them unsatisfied and wanting revenge," Jordan continued. His comment lightened David's mood.

Wrapping his arm around his buddy's shoulder, pulling him close, dead serious, Jordan locked eyes and said "Dude, you need to play a little cat-and-mouse game with them. Flirt! Don't verbally abuse them. You won't be able to get in bed with them if you do."

"Is everything about sex with you?" David asked.

"Baby, isn't it always?" Jordan said winking, taking a step closer and pointing at David's chest, whispering, "The cat I used to know would rock out with women. I wouldn't admit it, but you taught me a thing or two. You had that cool, confident, cocky way about you, which doesn't come easy for a white guy. Now you are just angry. Instead of you enticing the media, they are enticing you right down the path they want you to go in order to give them the headlines and attention they need to get ahead in this game."

David backed up, analyzing this statement.

"Let me show you how it's done," Jordan said.

David hid, watching from a distance as Jordan took the stage.

"Let me start by saying that, Trino, you may have a fat ass, but it's still a mighty fine looking fat ass." David couldn't help but laugh along with the press. Everyone loved Jordan. He knew how to get them eating out of his hand.

After the press conference, Trino found Katherine. "When I get David Mann alone, nothing you can say or do will be able to hold me back this time. Understand?"

She only nodded. Leaving, she pushed her way through the journalists, who were only looking to get a comment from her on David and CMI's decision to take him on as a client. She secretly wished they hadn't. It wasn't a beneficial situation for anybody. It wasn't right for the team, the family, or their company, but it especially wasn't for David. His mouth had opened a media firestorm and everyone wanted to fuel the fire.

Chapter 31

The Apology

The fiasco had more than a three-day shelf life since practice was open and David played worse than ever. Having disregarded everything Katherine had worked on with him, his attitude was out of control. The media captured new damaging footage, swirling it all over the internet. David's head was being called for. "Let him go" became the mantra, and the executives were looking at offloading him to another team or cutting the head case from the roster completely.

David ran with Michael the morning prior to the last preseason game. It was more run/walk since David felt heavy-footed. Michael tried his best to pull David out of his funk, but nothing worked. Afterward, they ate in silence. David placed his dirty dishes in the dishwasher, ready to walk over to see his parents while Sharon prepared to follow to bring them some fresh fruit. "I might as well go too," Michael announced.

Nothing much different happened at his parents' place. Normal greeting, hardly any small talk, TV buffering the silence, only now David's latest outburst was on the highlight reel.

"He has a fire in his belly," Jack said, listening to the pundit's view on his son.

"I call it passion," Michael piped in.

"He used to use it on the field. Now he uses it on people, like I did when I was his age," Jack said, making no eye contact with anyone, only looking at the TV.

"I think we've all said things we've regretted. Wouldn't you agree?" Michael asked Jack directly as if they were the only two in the room.

Jack acknowledged. "Still, he's better than that."

"You're right. He's one of a kind. We are fortunate to have him in this city and as part of our lives," Michael said.

The men let the conversation drop for the moment, and Michael fell deep into thought, knowing it was time to speak from his heart. "I guess I got overly protective of him when....I...um....laid my hands on you in Florida. I'm sorry. I guess I had a hard time controlling myself" he offered, seeking forgiveness.

Jack looked at him, nodded, then his and Michael's attention went back to the news. But not David's, who couldn't believe his dad. It was the second time he'd used Michael as a buffer to convey his feelings for his son. Michael was Jack's avenue to assure David he was a talented football player. It was odd. Why couldn't he say it directly to David?

The Neighborhood

After the visit, Michael followed David to his car. "Let me ride with you to the field today. Sharon will pick me up."

"How come?" David asked.

"I want to show you something," Michael said. "Come on, let's go. We don't have that much time."

David agreed, heading toward the stadium before Michael told him to take a different route.

"Where are we going?" David asked.

"You'll see."

About fifteen minutes away from the stadium, the neighborhood turned shady. In his brand new, high-end, top-of-the-line SUV, David drove through the ghetto getting dirty looks. It was the roughest place in the city, with houses boarded up and gangs dealing drugs on the corner. In this place, even a fight or two broke out early in the morning hours.

"Okay, stop here," Michael said.

"What, are you crazy? We are going to get shot. I'm not stopping here."

"Then don't put it in park. Just stop the truck and look around," Michael said.

For some reason, David did just that.

"Have you ever been in a neighborhood like this back home?" Michael asked.

"No. If I had been, I certainly wouldn't hang out there," David answered.

"That's my point. You should have been part of this type of neighborhood. You should still be there."

David turned toward Michael, desiring to understand what was placed before him.

Then Michael began preaching with love to David. "With your upbringing, you should have been on drugs. Your mother was a drug addict, and now she's reaping the consequences. But God in His mercy used you to rescue your mother from her deathbed. And He's given you time to spend with her."

David closed his eyes, placing the SUV in park.

"Your father's anger issues should have landed him in jail. There is no earthly reason why your dad didn't kill the man your mother left him for. Again, all by the grace of God. God protected your father from doing anything that could have cost him his freedom."

Tears leaked from David's eyes at the thought of God protecting his father.

"God in His grace provided your grandmother as a way out from your father's outbursts. God gave you football to prevent you from ending up on the streets like these kids right now."

David opened his eyes.

"At this time of the morning, it's time to go to school. Do you think these kids go to school?"

He rested back his head, blowing out a deep sigh, understanding that football indeed had kept him off the street.

"God gave you the determination and confidence to succeed in football. Also the drive to study so that your achieved a finance and business degree. God even blessed you with a football scholarship, leaving you debt free. He gave you the insight to fight and learn from your parents' mistakes. You are one of a kind, David. You didn't have anyone to help you, but what you don't understand is that God has been with you every step of the way."

David made eye contact with Michael, feeling the weight of his mentor's words as his heart leap in his chest.

"He led you to football, college, the stock market, and Cleveland. And now with the other quarterbacks out, he's leading you back to the game."

David looked away, wanting to block out his words.

Wiping his eyes, Michael leaned toward David. "I know you can do it! Your dad knows you can do it. You need to believe you can do it!"

David's eyes filled with fear, popping wide open. A couple of teens had come at the truck with bats. "Okay, we have to go! This isn't good! This place isn't safe!" But even before David could put the SUV in drive, Michael opened the door and got out. "Are you nuts? You are going to get us killed!" David yelled, rolling down the window.

"Hey, Willie, how are you? Are you coming by the office tomorrow?" Michael asked.

"Hey, Mr. Luka, I didn't see you in the car," Willie, a teen street gang member, replied, putting down his bat even though the others continued holding up theirs. "Yeah, I'll be there. What are you doing in my neighborhood, huh?"

"I'm checking in on you, kid. I want to make sure you are staying out of trouble. Did you complete those assignments I gave you last week?" Michael asked.

Willie whispered to his friends to lower their bats. "Yes, sir, that very night."

"You're a great kid, Willie. I look forward to working with you tomorrow. Do you have a ride to work or do you need me to come and pick you up?"

"No, I'm good, sir. Thank you for asking."

Michael pointed to the boys standing near. "Okay, who are your friends?"

Willie introduced his friends and Michael shook their hands. He chatted with them for a couple minutes, making them laugh. "Hey, I have some things I need moved around the office. It is heavy lifting and you boys look strong. If you come with Willie first thing in the morning and help us out, I'll give you tickets to tomorrow's game in our suite. It's up to you."

The teens were excited, all agreeing to come with Willie.

"Willie, you are in charge. Make sure they understand the start time, being respectful, and the dress code. You can take them to Mr. Dular. You know the drill—get them some clothes and another outfit for yourself," Michael directed.

"Yes, sir. Thank you, Mr. Luka," Willie said politely smiling brightly.

"My pleasure, son."

Michael got back in the truck and David prepared to drive away. "You are one crazy mother! Dude, you are nuts. Completely crazy. I thought for sure we were going to die."

"So did I. I'm glad I knew that kid!"

And for whatever reason, they laughed uncontrollably. David couldn't remember the last time he'd laughed so hard, but he knew it was with Michael. Since he had been thrust into leading the team and his parents had come to town, life wasn't funny, only filled with serious conversations. He needed the laugh just to feel like he still had breath in his lungs.

David felt much better at practice, although his good mood ended all too soon as he threw several interceptions and fumbled the ball. However, it was a light practice with the afternoon free, and he looked forward to sleeping off the rest of the day. There was a press conference first thing in the morning and the thought of it made him angry.

Chapter 32

The Visit

Once home, after eating, he landed on the couch. He was just about to nod off when he heard a knock on his door. Who in the heck would come to his condo? He'd never had one visitor.

He looked out the peephole, dropping his head when he saw Katherine. He'd forgot about their meeting today regarding a photo shoot. A local magazine would be interviewing David at his condo and she wanted to ensure his place was appropriately staged, even though the shoot was a few weeks out.

David held open the door, not even acknowledging her. "Hi," she said sweetly, walking in. "How are you?"

"Okay," David mumbled.

"Did you forget we were meeting today?" Katherine said, standing in the foyer.

David said nothing, just looked at her. He didn't want to lie but he had forgotten.

"It's alright. You have a lot going on, so it's understandable," she continued. "I can tell you aren't up for this, so let's try to get through it as quickly as possible."

Katherine walked into the living room, placed down her purse, and removed her jacket before walking through the dining room and kitchen, horrified at what she saw. With a little laugh, she attempted to joke, "We have to clean this place up."

David stood silent. He was not up to any meeting since he had been ready for a nap only moments earlier.

"There is a lot of work that needs to be done here. You have boxes that aren't even unpacked. Your furniture is mismatched and there are wires all over the walls." She pointed at the audio cords taped around the room.

She was in work mode, calling David on the mat, and he wasn't in the mood for her comments. It was by far the worst day for their meeting. All he wanted was sleep. His practice had been awful, the press were relentless, and not only did he need to face them tomorrow but he had to play a game he had no desire to play any longer.

"I get that you haven't unpacked. I know you don't want to be here. And the wires on the wall are not a big deal, I can fix that. But what's with the furniture?" she asked. "Are you sleeping on the couch?"

On what looked like a garbage-picked sofa was a sheet trying to mask an assortment of stains and holes, hardly covering the foam poking through the ripped cushion. The sorry-looking pillow and blanket didn't help. Several plates with dried-up food, half-drunk coffee cups, used napkins, and take-out containers lined the coffee table and floor.

"Yeah, I don't have a bed."

"Why?" she asked, confused but agitated all the same.

"I sold it with my place back in Florida," he said.

"Wait a minute. You sold your bed along with your home back in Florida and that was how many years ago?"

"I don't know," he mumbled, "since I got traded to California."

"Are you telling me you never got a bed and you have been sleeping on the couch ever since?"

David didn't say a word but Katherine knew the answer. Now she was getting mad. She didn't know why, but she could feel herself growing furious.

Walking into the kitchen, the scene got worse. "David, this place is a pigsty!"

The sink overflowed with dirty dishes. Stuffed trash bags, splitting open, laid on the floor, needing to be taken out. Katherine didn't want to look in the refrigerator and get anymore disgusted for fear she might throw up.

"Why don't you get a cleaning service?" she asked.

"I have one."

"Well, when do they come to clean?"

"Once a month," David answered, hating the inquisition.

"Are you telling me you don't clean up after yourself for an entire month and then they come in and take care of this mess?"

Again, he was silent.

"This is disgusting!" she said, pushing up her sleeves. "Why? Why are you doing this to yourself? Why are you living in this filth?"

His eyes pierced hers, but he remained silent.

"What is wrong with you? Really, I want to know. Is there more to your injury like Trino asked?"

"Katherine, don't start. I'm not in the mood…" David said, anger rising until she cut him off.

"I don't care what kind of mood you are in, this is ridiculous! Seriously, David, what is going on with you?"

"Look, I've had about enough…"

"Obviously, you haven't had enough or you wouldn't be living like this. Seriously, what is with you? This is not the guy I remember from when you were playing in Florida. Look at you! You don't take care of yourself, you are living as if you are on the streets, and your attitude is almost worse than the day I first met you!" Katherine said, getting in his face.

"I'm warning you, please, stop…" David urged.

Standing in front of him, pointing her finger, she yelled, "Stop? You want me to stop? You need to stop acting like this, living like this, and looking like this. You can't take your garbage out? You're going to leave it here for the cleaning service to throw away? It stinks in here. How could you live in this smell? Why would you do this to yourself? Live life…"

That pushed him over the edge and he now pounced. "Live life? You want me to live life? Well, what the hell about you? How are you living your life?" David shouted. "You hide behind your business, telling everyone else how to live their life when you aren't really living your own! You expertly handle everyone around you, knowing exactly what to say, but you won't lay the truth on yourself!"

Katherine clenched her fists, grinding her teeth. She stood still among the smelly trash and filth trying desperately to control her anger, not wanting to say something she would regret.

David did not let up. "You study and analyze your competition and your clients so you can help them, but you don't help yourself. You give of yourself and serve everyone else, but you excuse your own needs."

She placed her hands on her hips, ready for a brawl.

"You aren't living all your dreams and desires!" he continued, on a roll with his piercing eyes seemingly touching her soul. "Do you even dream anymore? Do you even have any desires? You are just as dead as I am inside, but you hide it better than I do. You are afraid too, and you hide it so well it's hardly detectable. But I can see right through you.

I see your fear. I see your concern and I see your worry. So don't give me your bullshit."

Katherine refused to back down. She stood toe to toe and began yelling at him. "You have no idea what you are talking about. You've been nothing but miserable since you've been benched. You have an opportunity to lead this team and you are still acting like you should be benched. You're the one who gave up! You gave up your hopes, your dreams, and your desires."

She stormed off to the foyer. David didn't like her walking away from him, but now he would make sure she didn't return once she left.

"Oh, that's priceless! I gave up? I gave up? You may have gotten out of that bed physically after your Mom got sick but you are still laying in it mentally. How many guys have asked you out since your husband died?"

Hatred poured forth from her eyes, but David didn't care. Standing so close, only mere inches separating them, he could feel her hot breath steaming from her nostrils. He kept going. "I'm on to your game. I see how you use God as an excuse to stay single. I don't believe that for a moment. You are the one who gave up. You are telling me for the rest of your life you are going to remain single because you lost your husband?"

Closing her eyes, licking her lips, and shaking her head, Katherine worked to center herself. "Be very careful, David. I'm warning you right now. Be very careful with…"

"What, you will never have sex again? Why? Because you are afraid? I think that's exactly what you need. I think you need a real release instead of going home fantasizing about your dead husband and masturbating!"

It came so fast. Katherine slapped David right across the face. She struck him so hard that it actually knocked him back a bit. He hadn't been expecting that, and neither had she, but she'd used all the force in her to shut him up. She didn't say a word as she walked back into the living room, grabbed her jacket and purse, and headed straight for the door.

David instantly panicked as he watched Katherine prepare to storm out. He was doing his best to fight back the tears until after she left. Katherine saw his emotions from the corner of her eye but didn't care. He went to the living room and sat down as she grabbed the door handle.

But, as she opened the door, it was as if she heard God's voice say, "Stay."

Oh, no, she thought. Oh, no! Not today! Not now! She took another step to leave and the word "stay" came to her mind again. She was furious, wanting to scream "no!" with every ounce of her being. With the next step, the word "apologize" entered her heart. You got to be kidding me, she thought "Apologize" came again with insistence. She knew this voice, and this was one of those times she hated to hear it. She didn't want to listen.

Then a Bible verse came to her mind: "Foolish people laugh at making things right when they sin. But honest people try to do the right thing."

Chapter 33

The Obedience

With her hand on the door, ready to walk out, she hung her head in submission. Taking a deep breath, she slowly closed the door, then walked back into the living room. Still holding her purse and jacket, she sat down on the sofa and looked at David sitting in the chair across from her. "I'm sorry," she whispered.

Hearing her apology broke the last of David's self-control. He wept uncontrollably, tears coursing down his cheeks like they were small rivers. Katherine remained silent, not moving. She knew this type of weeping all too well. And she knew from experience that if she drew David's attention to anything else, he would clam up, and he needed to expose himself to his very core.

He did. He wept bitterly as Katherine's heart prayed Romans 8:26: "The Spirit helps us in our weakness. We do not know what we ought to pray for, but the Spirit himself intercedes for us with groans that words cannot express."

Pain and anguish sliced through David's heart. It was intense, scary. He was rocking back and forth to console himself. He seethed with anger, bitterness, and resentment. Many people, many images, and many memories captured his mind, but only one stood out above all. He was mad at God. David couldn't take much more. Complete despair came from his core; his emotions were loud and intensely passionate.

In every instance of tears shed with Sharon and Michael, David had remained in command of himself in those moments. Right now, however, he'd lost all sense of control as such rawness poured out of him. He was unable to stop, to regain order. Whatever this was, it was unleashing itself with a vengeance.

"I can't stand this!" he seethed. "I hate this! I just hate this so much!"

Katherine listened, remaining silent.

Rocking back and forth, looking to stop the tears, he cried out, "What the hell? I mean, really, what the hell is going on with me?"

Tears wet Katherine's eyes, but she didn't move. She didn't offer him comfort. She didn't touch him.

"Maybe there was something more to that collarbone hit than I realize? Maybe, somehow, it just messed me up mentally. Maybe I don't want to admit that something more happened back then." Looking to understand, attempting to control himself, he voiced his confusion. "How in the hell did I go from being one of the best quarterbacks to where I am today?"

She silently prayed David would expose his soul, getting to the heart of the matter. He needed to extract the very root buried so deep within his heart that was causing him not to function any longer and expose the lie that he'd believed since he was benched.

"Is it possible that I was really never that good? Is it possible I just had such a great line that it hid all my flaws?" David thought it through. "I don't get how that could be true. How could I go from winning State, winning the Sugar Bowl, being drafted in the first round, and missing the playoffs by one game within the first couple years of my professional career to being so completely taken out of the game that I can't throw the ball accurately anymore?"

Hyperventilating, he didn't want to speak the next words, but couldn't stop. "I mean, I don't even want to play anymore. I hate this game! I hate who I've become! I am washed up and a head case."

Katherine prayed that David would continue to explore what his heart was revealing—the unnerving rhetorical bondage that had paralyzed his internal discourse and imprisoned his inspirational leadership abilities. David's one time battle cry had been so influential that he could lift the spirits of tired, worn-out, hurting men to overcome their disbelief and rise to remain strong and courageous on the way to victory. Now, the negative effects of his life-changing injury had twisted his heart's true narrative, and he believed the defeatist lies as gospel. The warrior within him had surrendered to the enemy, and David lay consumed by doubt so infectious that it was bleeding division onto his team.

A little more settled, though tears still streamed down his face, David concluded, "I guess this is just how it ends. I'm an old guy in a young man's sport, and I guess I just don't want to admit it." He reclined back in his chair, but closing his eyes did little to stop the shedding of his emotions. "And I can't even quit right now if I wanted to. I have to play."

Katherine understood the desire to quit on life when all seemed futile but God keeps pressing you forward.

Covering his face shamefully, sobbing outright, he confessed, "I actually hope I get hurt so I'm taken out of the game. That's my only refuge right now."

Shutting her eyes, she felt the weight of David's words.

Shaking his head, he continued. "And here's what is really messed up, this is just a game! This is not even that big of a deal, it's just a game! There's no reason I should be this upset over a game. People are dealing with tragedy all over the place and I'm mentally messed up because I can't play anymore. There must be something really wrong with me."

Her head hung low, upset that David didn't value the position God had placed him in as a leader, thus belittling the gift. She prayed he could understand, like she did, that God plants us in certain positions no matter how insignificant and shallow it may appear to us or others, and that we are to prosper where planted for our own growth.

"Maybe I need to get on some type of medication. Maybe there's something off with me. Maybe I'm…"

And that's when Katherine interrupted. "Maybe God is going after your idol," she whispered.

His tears stopped immediately and he looked at her. "What?"

"Maybe God is going after your idol," she calmly repeated.

Agitated, he asked, "What are you talking about?"

"It's been my experience that God will go after anything we put in our lives before Him. He will do anything to make sure He has our complete attention," she said, avoiding David's gaze.

He analyzed her remarks. "Was your husband your idol?"

Katherine closed her eyes but nodded.

"But isn't that cruel? How could you love a God who would take away your husband and child?"

"Well, it would seem like that, wouldn't it?" Katherine asked, looking off in the distance.

David wiped his face with his sleeve, sitting taller.

Katherine slowly spoke. "It would seem as if God was intentionally trying to be mean and ruthless so that I would…I don't know…maybe try to prove how much I love Him, but that's not the case." With a slight chuckle and teary eyes, she said, "Just like Job in the Bible. He was blameless and upright. Feared God and shunned evil and everything was taken from him, yet he still praised God."

It was as if he wasn't present and she was talking to herself. David watched her intently.

"I wasn't like Job. For those first three months, I asked myself that exact same question and then some. Is God cruel and ruthless? It was a time in my life I never want to repeat." She shamefully hung her head.

David wasn't sure what to do. Should he sit next to her? No. He didn't move.

Katherine went on in a voice hardly audible. "I was barely surviving. I was planning on ending my life. And I knew exactly how I would do it. The only thing stopping me was my mom. I couldn't bear for her to live with that pain. I knew firsthand what it was like to lose someone you loved, and I couldn't do that to her. It was a very scary time for me, for my whole family."

David swallowed, practically stopped breathing, and allowed her to share her soul.

"And after I found out Mom was sick, it was like something…I don't know…I don't even think I can put it into words. It all just completely took the breath out of me. I actually hated God." She lifted her head and stared out the glass doors. "And right then and there, I had to make a decision. Would I continue serving this God whom I'd trusted since I was a kid or would I serve myself?"

He understood her hopeless feelings toward God and why she would question her commitment. Wasn't that where he was standing now?

A slight twinkle lit up her eyes. "And this Bible verse kept coming to my mind—Jeremiah 29:11. "'For I know the plans I have for you, declares the Lord, plans to prosper you and not harm you, plans to give you hope and a future.'"

David watched her face soften, softening a portion of his heart since even in the most dire moment God spoke life to her core.

"And anytime I thought about taking my life, I would think about that Bible verse and say to myself God must have something great planned for my life. And it was so…um…enticing to me that I thought if I were to take my own life, when I met God, I would be filled with regret for not fighting my way through this time. You know, because in reality we are only here for a short time anyway."

His heart leaped for joy that she fought her way through the lonely darkness.

With a slight grin, she continued. "And with how God designed me, I thought if I gave up, it would be truly out of fear. And I would rather try and fail than to never try at all."

When she made eye contact with him, he saw life within them. She chuckled, saying, "That's the whole reason I agreed to work with you. My first instinct was that I would fail with you, so I didn't want to try. But I wouldn't be able to live with myself if I didn't try. And I knew I would regret it for the rest of my life."

He grinned for she always had a way of speaking to his heart.

"I also knew from all the time I spent with God that if He was changing the plans I had for my own life, then He would give me something greater. I mean, after all, He is the One who created me and knows what is the absolute best for me, and I wanted that." She relaxed.

"But you lost your husband and your child. Really, how could you think anything would be greater than that?" David asked, honestly.

Placing down her head, she said. "I know. I know. You are absolutely right. But what I know now is that I would have never gotten involved in this business and become the person I am today if my husband were still alive. I'm not in any way saying God intentionally killed them so I can run a business. It's not about the company or money. But I was so fixated on my husband that he was becoming my god. And I can remember clear warnings that I was making him an idol, and I serve a jealous God who does not stand to compete with any other idols. God cannot use us as He intends unless He's our heart's desire."

"So are you saying that if you hadn't made your husband your god he'd still be alive today?" David asked.

"No. I'm saying that God was never first in my heart leading my life. I knew I was going to heaven, but I never made Him Lord of my life," she replied.

"This is too much," he said, shifting uncomfortable in his chair. "I'm sorry, I just don't get it."

"I know it seems like a lot, and it's hard to understand," Katherine said, placing down her purse and jacket and moving some garbage off the sofa to the coffee table that separated her from David. "Let me try explaining it this way. I was making my husband my god, which could never work because he isn't actually God. He couldn't know what's best for me because he didn't design and create me. So when he wasn't actually making me feel the way I expected him to make me feel, I would choke the life out of him and our marriage." Taking a deep breath, she admitted, "James was my helpmate and I didn't like when he would hold me accountable. I guess what I'm trying to convey is that all of us are sinners no matter how much we are devoted to living our life for God. And in our life we have blind spots and sins that God wants to mature and equip so we are lacking in nothing. That is the helpmate part in marriage. A marriage can be so intimate that only the spouse can see this sort of behavior, and I would get frustrated with James when he would hold me accountable."

Burrowing his eyebrows, David begged for clarification. "What?"

Understanding his confusion, she said. "Football for years was giving you everything you needed to make you feel fulfilled. But when you couldn't play anymore, you became depressed, no longer fulfilled. When you picked up that ball again and couldn't perform, you started choking the air out of the ball. You yourself said that you hate the game, that you want to quit or hope to get hurt so you don't have to play anymore."

He nodded in agreement.

"How do you go from loving something so much to hating it in only a couple years? That's exactly what would have happened in my marriage. I am almost certain we would have ended in a divorce with me looking for another man to fulfill my needs when in reality only God can fulfill my needs."

"Yeah, but come on, we are only talking a divorce. This was a death."

"Yes, I agree, but how many divorces would I have gone through to learn that no man could ever completely fulfill me? Where does it stop? Take a person who is an emotional eater. At what point do they push the food aside to realize they are using it to fill a void or to escape some hurt or pain in their life? When they are sixty pounds overweight? One hundred pounds? Two hundred pounds? Where does it end?"

David placed his foot on the coffee table, accidentally knocking over a take-out container.

"God disciplines those He loves, just like a good parent does. I'm not saying the loss of my husband was a discipline, but He had my complete attention." She confessed honestly, "I'm not sure anything else would have gotten my attention."

Now David understood completely.

Chapter 34

Setting the Stage

Even though she could see a measure of comprehension in David, Katherine knew he didn't see the whole picture yet.

"You can't understand how I don't date and say I fantasize about a dead man and masturbate," she began, "but I just don't have a desire to live my life with anyone. It's the same way you no longer have a desire to play football."

"Yeah, but how can you possibly go without having sex or in some way….um….satisfying yourself," he asked.

Katherine thought about how she wanted to answer the question. "My sister makes this great chocolate molten lava cake. Have you ever tried it?"

"No."

"It's beautiful. When you see this cake, you can't wait to taste it. I actually get excited when I see it," she delighted. "It's about this size of a baseball, made with dark chocolate, has a slight chew but the inside is like lava. The interior has this thick, hot, ganache filing that oozes out on the plate. She serves it with real whipped cream and toasted pecans." Katherine wiped the corners of her mouth, recalling the heavenly goodness.

David's mouth watered from just her description of the luscious dessert.

"When the hot filling oozes out, melting the whipped cream, you can't separate the two…it's like they were meant to be together." She used her hands to describe the action. "The crunch of the pecans and the texture of the cake provide just the right amount of bite to keep it interesting and substantial."

David was completely absorbed in her story, hardly breathing from her vivid description.

Looking around, thinking out loud, she continued, "She also makes this low-fat lemon pound cake. It's good, but I only like lemon in my water. Plus, you really can't add anything extra to the pound cake. I just can't think of what tastes good with lemon. Maybe strawberries?"

He watched her intently, fascinated by the way she was describing her reason for remaining pure.

"Anyway, many years ago I was on this low-fat kick and I would eat that lemon pound cake. Now, it tasted good, but what I really wanted was that chocolate molten lava cake. So because I wasn't satisfied by the lemon pound cake, I would eat an extra slice of it, attempting to satisfy my craving. I'd end up eating four or five slices, never being satisfied, only feeling sick to my stomach and guilty for overeating."

Looking at him, she said, "That to me is masturbation. It is never satisfying and leaves plenty of guilt. And to this day, I have never eaten another piece of that lemon pound cake. And when I see it, I am actually completely turned off by it."

Understanding her point and being playful, David asked, "Does that chocolate molten lava cake come with one of those cherries?"

"You mean one of those maraschino cherries?"

"Yeah. They're a bright red color."

"Well, I guess you can ask for one, but I think it would ruin the dessert."

Confused, he asked, "How?"

"Actually, that's what they put on kids sundaes. It's like….um….well, it's like cheap sex," Katherine said, laughing.

It surprised David that she was talking like this, but he was intrigued. "What do you mean?"

"Well," she said, her eyes lighting up, looking around. She almost was talking out of the side of her mouth. "Kids' sundaes are cheap. They are what, maybe a dollar? Are they real ice cream? They don't use real hot fudge or real whip cream, and I'm not sure they come with nuts. But the kids love those cherries. Why? Because they look pretty. I mean, do they even taste good? And are they real cherries?"

David smiled, enjoying her mind. He watched the quirk grow in her smile.

"Again, is that even satisfying? It's a small portion that's too sweet and doesn't hit the spot. I would think that's what having sex outside of marriage is like. You think it's going to be so good when in reality it's just a kid's hot fudge sundae without real hot fudge." Katherine laughed over her analogy.

David instantly popped up with astonishment and scooted to the edge of his seat, his eyebrows almost touching his hat. "Wait, a minute. Are you telling me you didn't have sex before you got married?"

Instantly, Katherine realized she'd unknowingly backed herself into a corner and she didn't know how to escape. Her face was bright red and she was stammering for words.

"Katherine, is that what you are telling me?" he pressed.

"Wow, I didn't mean for the conversation to go in this direction," she replied.

Leaning forward in his chair, he asked, "How is it possible that you knew your husband all those years and you didn't have sex together before you were married? Are you a prude?" Thinking out loud, he answered his question, accusing. "You must be a prude!"

"Oh, please, I'm not a prude." Katherine said, looking directly at him in a way that David knew she was serious.

"Well then, you tell me how you didn't have sex until you married. Who does that anymore? And why would you do that?"

"My parents, Lana and Eric, same way!" Katherine announced, defending herself.

"What? Are you guys in some kind of cult?" he asked, humorously astonished.

A fearful embarrassment took over Katherine, then she pleaded, "Oh, please don't tell them I told you! That wasn't right of me. It sounds like I'm gossiping behind their back. That's their business and not for me to tell anyone else."

"Hey, don't worry, I won't say anything," he promised.

Katherine believed him, feeling relieved.

"But you have to tell me how that's possible? I mean, you are basically telling me you were a virgin."

"Well, in the Bible there's this…"

"You people and your Bible! Are you in a cult? Seriously, are you trying to pull me into the cult?"

Laughing hysterically, she said. "No, we aren't in a cult!" When David chuckled she asked, "Do you want me to answer your question or not?"

"Yes, please, this ought to be good," he grinned.

"Anyway, in the Bible, " she said with an unknowingly sexy grin, "there's a book called the Song of Songs. It's about…well…um…I guess it's God's instruction book on lovemaking." Blushing, she explained, "It warns us not to rush…um…sex. That timing is everything."

"Okay, but you aren't telling me how it's possible for you to date your husband and not want to test drive the car, if you know what I mean."

"How many cars did you test drive before you bought your SUV?" she asked.

Confused, David questioned, "Are we actually talking about cars or are you asking me how many women I had sex with?"

"Nope, we are actually talking about cars. I don't want to know the number of women you have been with." Katherine closed her eyes, disgusted.

"Two other SUVs. And about the same number of women," David said, winking at her.

She ignored his latter remark.

"Did you purchase the vehicle because you compared it with the other SUVs?"

"No, not really. I pretty much knew I wanted that model."

"So regardless of how it drove, you were going to buy it," Katherine said, hoping to change the subject.

"Well, this current one, yes, but in the past I've made my decision about a purchase from test driving a particular vehicle," he said, looking all proud.

Katherine knew she had to continue with this subject and thought how to answer his question best, landing on "How did you know you wanted to be a quarterback?"

"Because I loved the game of football," he answered.

"But what was it about that particular position?" she asked.

David thought about his answer, then blushed. "Alright, don't make fun of me when I say this."

Making deep eye contact, she assured, "Of course, I won't."

Feeling hot, sort of perspiring, he said, "I felt like my hand was specifically created and designed to hold a football."

Katherine smiled. She loved David's answer but understood it embarrassed him, so she continued, "Did you ever try kicking the ball? You know, to be a punter?"

"No, I never had a desire to play any other position but quarterback."

"And you did whatever it took to achieve that goal?" Katherine asked.

"Yes."

"Including putting aside any other desires you had that would interfere with your game?"

David stumbled in following her argument. "What do you mean?"

Shrugging her shoulders, she said, "Well, you told me you didn't drink because it affected your game…."

"Oh, I get what you are saying. You are basically telling me I would work through my injuries and weaknesses and turn from any desires or emotions that would prevent me from achieving my goal."

"Yes, exactly! When you hold up the goal, continually keeping it in focus, you can speak the truth to yourself. Then the obstacles that are trying to take you down only become hurdles you can jump over," Katherine said passionately. "Or in your case, you are able to see the hands of your teammate through all the opposition, connecting the ball. And that's so satisfying, isn't it?"

"Yeah," David said with a far-off, sad look, confessing, "I will never be able to feel that again."

Chapter 35

Proverbs 27:19:

"As water reflects the face, so one's life reflects the heart."

"Of course you will!" Katherine passionately countered without a moment's hesitation. There was no way she was going to let David wallow in his train of thought.

Reclining back, placing his hand up to his lips, David revealed, "No, I'm done. I just didn't want to admit it to myself. I'm going to quit after this season. This is my last year."

Katherine studied his face as tears stung his eyes. He used his hand to prevent them from leaking out. Shaking his head, he felt he couldn't stop telling the truth. "I knew I shouldn't have come here. I knew I shouldn't have signed on with this team. But there was just something pulling me here. I was trying to fight it. I was thinking of quitting when no one else wanted to pick me up."

She nodded to encourage him.

"I'm like one of those guys where everyone else knows his career is over but him and he still hangs on and can't let go. That's me!" Taking a deep breath, rubbing his face, he went on. "I'm so pathetic. And now I will go down in history as probably one of the worst quarterbacks. I'll be an example of a guy who didn't quit when he should have."

Katherine listened, her heart aching for him.

Slamming his fists on his legs, David cried out, "Gosh, I hate this so much! And I can't do anything about it! I'm completely stuck. Who would have ever thought in a million years that both quarterbacks would be taken out and I'm put in and can't deliver?"

"God," Katherine answered.

"Please, Katherine, please!" David warned. "I really don't want to hear about it. Seriously, can't you talk about anything else? I can see how you turn off these guys who hit on you. It's very clever for you to use God to weed them out."

Katherine couldn't help but laugh. She thought he was pretty funny, but David was in no mood for comedy.

"This is not funny! This is not a joke!"

"I'm not laughing at you. Really, as much as I joke around with you, or attempt to joke with you, I would never laugh at you."

He took a breath. "Really, it's actually fine if you do laugh at me. That's what I should be doing because this is almost comical.".

She didn't laugh.

"Here I am, thirty, staying in a game that has passed me by. No other teams want me except for a cold, depressing, hostile, loser of a city that no one else in the NFL or any other sport wants to come to."

"Well, that's your perception," Katherine said flatly.

"Well, isn't perception reality?" David shot back.

She thought for a moment and then came up with an idea. "Do you have a full-length mirror?"

"What?" He always seemed to be taken back by her comments. Now he was thinking something was wrong with her, like her brain wasn't wired properly.

"You know, a full-length mirror. Do you have a full-length mirror?" Katherine asked again.

"There's one on my closet door in the master bedroom," David said, blowing her off.

"Come on, let's go!" Katherine said, standing up, sort of tip toeing through used food containers, soiled napkins, and half-filled coffee cups that littered practically every surface.

"Where?"

"To the mirror."

"Why?"

"I want to show you something," she said energized by her idea.

"Come on, seriously! I don't feel like it. Please, just leave me alone so I can take a nap," David said, agitated.

"What, on the couch?" she pointed. "That should be relaxing."

"Why do you have to start again?" David warned.

"Here, just come with me," Katherine said, sticking out her hand so she could help him up.

David took a deep breath, taking hold of her hand as she helped pull him out of his chair. It was the first time he'd touched her outside of handshaking, and she wasn't tense. She was excited and full of life. Her eyes dazzled, making him very intrigued in what she had to show him.

"Am I going to get grossed out from the mess in your room?" she asked teasingly.

"Probably."

David walked her to his bedroom and she gasped at the clothes strewn all over the room. There wasn't any furniture and her heart felt sad that he lived as a nomad. He brought her to the entryway of a fabulous walk-in closet. Each nine foot door had a full-length mirror, and they looked at their reflections.

"What did you say about Cleveland?" she asked.

Not hiding his agitation, he barked, "What?"

"How did you describe Cleveland?"

"Come on, please, Katherine. Can't you just leave me alone?" he begged.

"I think your exact words were 'cold, depressing, hostile, loser city that no one wanted,'" Katherine repeated. "Take a look at yourself. Tell me what you see."

David put his head down, trying to remain calm.

Katherine gently lifted his head, forcing him look in the mirror. He did.

She touched his dark gray, ripped, beanie hat, saying, "Cold."

She touched the side of his baggy, coffee-stained, light gray sweatpants. "Depressing."

She touched his faded, dark blue, torn hoodie, asking, "Doesn't this represent hostility? Isn't this what some gang members wear?"

Pointing at him from head to toes, she instructed, "Look at yourself. Really take a good, overall look at yourself."

He couldn't help but look at himself, standing next to Katherine, and he compared himself to her. Again, she was dressed impeccably, wearing a lightweight, rose-colored, tweed skirted suit. A crisp, snow-white blouse with ruffles peeked out from her collar and sleeves. Her shoes were dynamite, the best to David's memory. They were nude leather, matching the color of her legs perfectly, with a shiny gold stiletto heel. Her hair was pulled up and only a few strands fell somewhat sexy on her face.

"What are you saying about yourself?" Katherine asked lovingly.

David didn't say a word.

Katherine pressed him ever so gently. "Aren't you saying you are a loser who no one wants?"

David put his head down and said, "Are you telling me that if I dress differently I will play better."

"No, I'm saying that perception is reality. And you are living what you perceive to be true," Katherine said.

He took a deep breath as tears stung his eyes.

"Did you dress like this…" Katherine said, pointing at him up and down, "live like this…" she pointed to his room, "and act like this when you were winning?"

"No, but it didn't matter, I was winning," he said.

Katherine faced him, reaching out and placing her hands on both his elbows, and looked deeply into his eyes. With confidence, she believed, delivered even. "You are still a winner and you will always be a winner. Even if you never play another game in your life, you need to look at yourself and realize that football is not your savior. You are dead, before you are even dead. I know from experience."

David looked away from her. Lovingly, she said, "Look at me."

He didn't listen. The thought of never playing another game in his life terrified him to death. He would prefer a career-ending injury taking him out permanently rather than living in this torment, benched on the sidelines because of a paralyzing mental state that overshadowed his entire existence.

She touched his chin, turning his face back toward her. "Look at me."

And when he did, he saw something in her eyes for the first time. Her eyes dazzled with a fiery passion for life, excitement for truth and courage rooted in faith. He knew she possessed all those things, but she was giving herself over to him in a way she hadn't in the past. She was exposing her soul. Never once breaking eye contact, she convicted his heart, preaching. "I have no doubt you can do this. God has put you in this position, and He will give you the strength and ability to do this. I believe God was the one pulling you here."

"And what if I can't do it?" he feared.

Batting her eyelashes, speaking out of the side of her mouth, she said. "Well, then at least you know you've tried and you can live with no regrets."

David couldn't help but buy into her fervor. He knew she lived what she believed. He knew she understood exactly where he was in his life, and if she could pick herself up, then so could he. "Alright, let's do this,"

David said with firm commitment. He pulled away from her and looked at himself in the mirror.

"Okay, but what are we doing?" she asked, laughing.

"Let's get me out of these clothes!"

Backing up, she said, "What?"

"Let's get me a new wardrobe."

"But what about all these clothes?" Katherine pointed to the clothes lying on the floor.

"Do you really think there is anything that is worthy of keeping?" David smiled, eyes twinkling, almost flirting.

"No," she smiled back.

"Okay, so come on, let's go!" David said enthusiastically.

"You mean now? Like right now?" Katherine said, not expecting his sudden change at all.

"Yes, right now, before I change my mind," he said, winking at her.

"O…K…" she hesitated.

David grew warm to his plans. "And I want to get my haircut. Your dad has nice hair, take me to his guy."

Katherine hadn't expected this and worked to devise a plan on the fly. "Hold on a minute. I need to make some calls and see if they have any available appointments."

"Just tell them there will be a good tip in it for them," he chuckled, leaving her side to clean up his room.

"Alright, I'll do this with you on one condition," Katherine warned.

"Name it!"

"Please take out your garbage. It stinks in here!" she said, not cracking a smile.

"You got it," he agreed, following her as she walked out of his bedroom. Now feeling high and somewhat cocky, he said, "I can't wait to tell the guys I actually got you in my bedroom. The entire team will be high fiving me."

"Yeah and make sure you tell them the truth, that I was actually using words like cold, depressing…you know, words describing how much you were turning me off," Katherine said playfully, not looking at him.

David stopped dead in his tracks and his mouth fell open, warning, "You better not have that grin on your face."

Katherine turned around and showed him that smirk he loved so much as they both laughed.

Chapter 36

The Renewal

As Katherine retrieved her phone, David quickly cleaned up, throwing out old containers and used plates, napkins, and cups. He even tackled the refrigerator, tossing out moldy cheese, expired milk, and leftovers he hadn't eaten in weeks. Katherine shook her head at the sight of the waste.

He smiled, listening to her sweet talk her way into an appointment as he emptied his dishwasher, filling it with dirty dishes. He was amazed it only took less than fifteen minutes to clean up. He knew he would not allow himself to live in filth any longer.

As they were ready to walk out the door, David remembered something. "I'll be right back."

Running to his bedroom, opening the closet doors and moving clothes to locate it, he searched, trying to remember where he'd placed it. He stopped momentarily, thinking, then he looked up, remembering where he'd put the Bible Michael had given him. Reaching up, he grabbed the Bible from the top shelf, ripped off the wrapper, and flipped through the pages desperately searching. When he couldn't locate it, he found the Table of Contents, using his finger to scan down the list until he found the book he wanted. Finding it, he opened to the Song of Songs. David used the Bible's ribbon bookmark to mark his place, then closed it and placed it back on the top shelf to read later that night.

He left excited, looking forward to shopping. He felt renewed and refreshed, ready for this change, no matter what happened with his game. As he followed Katherine, he called the cleaning service, asking them to swing by today and give his home a deep clean. He apologized for the mess they'd dealt with, guaranteeing they wouldn't experience it again. David also set up a schedule for routine, once-a-week cleaning.

The Model

Katherine took David to an upscale shopping center. After parking, as they walked into a clothing store, she explained, "I've known Kenneth for years. He dresses my whole family, including my dad and Eric. Even Reggie is a client."

Holding open the door for her, they walked to the men's section. David whispered in her ear, "I hope he's not gay."

As if on cue, a flamboyant, skinny guy threw open his arms, squealing in delight. "Katherine! Girl, look at you! I knew those shoes were meant for you."

David watched as they kissed one another on both cheeks, chatting up a storm and getting caught up on each other's lives. Then Katherine turned toward David, proudly introducing him. "Kenneth this is David. He's one of our clients and the starting Cleveland quarterback."

Licking his lips as he checked out David from head to toe, Kenneth shook his hand, saying, "My pleasure to meet you."

David was visibly uncomfortable, feeling naked after being sized up. He couldn't understand how Katherine and her family were friends with an obviously gay man.

"Yeah, nice to meet you," David said flatly.

"Easy, Kenneth, you are scaring him," Katherine warned with her laugh.

"Katherine!" Kenneth hit her teasingly. "Okay, what are we doing today?"

"A whole new wardrobe?" Katherine asking, looking to David. At his nod, she excitedly instructed Kenneth, "Let's get him the works!"

The stylist grabbed her arm, strolling to a private section, leaving David behind to quickly catch up. He shook his head, watching them interact. They sounded like high school girls, giggling nonstop over trivial topics. Impatience was taking a toll, though he started feeling at ease when Katherine finally said, "David has a press conference tomorrow and he usually wears that."

"Oh, no, no, no!" Kenneth gasped, taking in David's hat, hoodie, and sweatpants.

"Now, I'm not sure if he would wear a suit, but maybe we can get him in a nice shirt or sweater." Katherine spoke to Kenneth, completely ignoring David.

"Maybe we can do a blazer?" Kenneth thought. "You know one of those velvet, peacock blue blazers?"

"Oh yes, I love those," she said. "But I'm not sure he can pull it off."

"What?" David said, but both ignored him.

"Well, maybe we can get him into one of these sweaters?" Kenneth said pointing. David thought it looked nerdy.

Katherine considered the expensive, argyle, cashmere garment, trendy because of some athletes' popularity. "Yeah, I know Brady wears these, but I'm not sure David has the right attitude to pull off this look either."

"What?" David said, again ignored as the two looked through racks of clothes trying to determine a suitable outfit.

David wasn't agitated by their treatment of him. He was getting competitive instead. For the first time in years, the little flame lit within grew into a fire. How dare Katherine think he wasn't able to pull off a look? Who did she think he was?

"Well, we can play it safe and go with a sweater vest," Katherine said.

"I want a suit," David announced boldly.

They were shocked, then looked at each other excitedly before running over to the suits, again leaving David out of the decision process.

"I say we start with the tie," Katherine said.

"Yes!" Kenneth replied. "A tie to a man is like a pair of shoes to a woman. It either makes or breaks the outfit."

Browsing through a table of ties, she held up a striped one similar to the one David had worn at the fundraiser. "This can be tricky because he's somewhat goofy, so we want to make sure we get the right mix for him."

Now even more bothered that she thought he was goofy, he looked at the same tie he already owned. He hated that tie! Then he realized Katherine couldn't see past his exterior. He absolutely believed she thought he was a winner, and he knew she spoke her heart, but she always looked past him—until today in his bedroom, for just a couple minutes she had opened her eyes, truly seeing him. And he knew she didn't see him as a man. No, she saw a broken person, a guy going through a difficult time, a charity case. She had no idea what he was made of, and he couldn't wait to show her. He felt strongly motivated by her words describing him as goofy, safe, and having no style. There was no turning back now.

Kenneth and Katherine were so preoccupied comparing ties, they didn't notice David browsing the rack next to them. She held up another tie, saying, "This is the tie that my dad wears, I think it will…"

"I want this tie!" David said, sticking it in their faces.

They stopped and looked at it. It was a beautiful, deep dark cherry-colored satin tie with complementing colored thick stripes. It spoke of class, elegance, and richness. Only the most upscale suit would do as its partner.

"Are you sure?" Katherine asked, shocked, even though she loved the tie. It's exactly what she would have selected.

"Yes." His tone tolerated no exceptions.

Kenneth looked at David with a new eye. "Tell me, what look do you like?" he asked.

"I like the way she looks," David said, pointing to Katherine. "She looks…I don't know…put together."

"Classy," Kenneth said.

"Yes, classy. But it's not stuffy."

"Stylish," Kenneth said.

"And it's not, like, in your face."

"Lady-like," Kenneth replied.

"And it looks expensive."

"Elegant and sophisticated," Kenneth said.

Katherine stood shyly as they used her to outline David's style. He touched the ruffles by her neck, causing goosebumps, saying, "She always has something like this that stands out. I don't know, it's…"

"Flirty," Kenneth said, finishing the thought.

"No, it's…it's sassy!" David said, describing Katherine's personality to a tee.

"Yes, it is sassy!" Kenneth said, shouting with glee.

"I want that whole look, without being lady-like," David laughed.

"Are we done using me as the model for your tastes?" Katherine asked, smiling.

Flirting, David said, "Yes, your services aren't required any longer."

"Oh, please! You wouldn't be here if it wasn't for me," she laughed.

David laughed too, knowing the full truth of her statement.

Chapter 37

The Reveal

All three went their separate ways to round up clothes, each bringing a pile to David's assigned dressing room. Kenneth was good at eyeballing David's measurements, but he needed to make sure they were accurate, so he asked David to take off his hoodie. Kenneth blushed when he saw just a hint of David's muscles stick out of his T-shirt. Katherine laughed at the sight. David didn't like her laughing, even though Kenneth's reaction was funny; it bothered him that Katherine didn't enjoy the view. It was the first time he was out of his uniform and sweats yet she wasn't interested in looking at him. He'd never experienced this with a woman. Katherine wasn't trying to seduce him by hiding her feelings. She simply wasn't attracted to him, and David knew it.

Then he caught his reflection, understanding why. As he stood in the upscale, dark mahogany wood-clad walls, with elegant chandlers and complementing scones lighting the dressing area beautifully, he clearly didn't fit within his surroundings. David was perched on a small round pedestal so Kenneth could tailor his clothes. The massive floor-to-ceiling trifold mirrors before him didn't hide his baggy, yellowing, stained, wrinkly T-shirt. Since he'd lost over fifteen pounds, being back to his prime weight, the stretched out T-shirt hung shapeless on his torso. He looked like a sloppy mess.

"Go make yourself useful and get me one of those fitted T-shirts," David asked Katherine with a smile.

"What size do you wear?"

"XX-Large. He may even take a XXX-Large," Kenneth said while he measured David's chest. He gave her the brand name and location as Katherine smiled knowingly at the scene.

David found it amusing too but again instructed, "Go on, get me the shirt. That's the least you can do for me."

Placing her hand on her hip, she readied for a fight until she realized he was joking. "Yes, sir," she answered instead with a mock salute.

"That's exactly what I want to hear out of you," David replied.

"Did you say those shirts were in the boys' section. Kenneth?"

"Please, I'm all man, baby," David joked.

"Okay, if you say so," she snickered.

Kneeling down in front of David, measuring his inseam, Kenneth said, "He is!"

They all laughed as Katherine retrieved the T-shirts, returning with several colors and sizes. "Here, Kenneth."

He opened a package, handing David a satin-like, crisp, white fitted shirt. When David took off his old one, Katherine turned around to avoid seeing his naked upper body. Still, she heard Kenneth gasp, "Oh, my!"

David noticed Katherine's shoulders shaking and knew she was laughing at Kenneth's expression. Again, it bothered David that she wasn't the least bit curious to see his chest, so he threw his old T-shirt at her, which landed on her head.

"Yuck!" she yelped, using only a couple of fingers to remove it as quickly as possible since she wasn't too sure the last time he'd washed it.

"Okay, you can look now, I'm dressed." David announced.

Katherine slowly turned around, looking out of the corner of her eye to make sure he was clothed. When she got a full look at him, her mouth dropped open. She stumbled back, swallowing hard.

Her reaction tickled David; it was the most priceless sight he had seen from her. David was built. He had muscles all over and it was completely natural. His diet had taken his body fat down to 10 percent. The T-shirt was so tight and form-fitting that it showed how defined and lean he was.

Katherine found it difficult to look at him since it only made her want to see more, so instead she attempted to concentrate on socks, ties, or anything other than his physic, even though it was hard to block out the vision of him.

And he loved it. He had never experienced this with Katherine, seeing her blush nervously. She couldn't be herself around him in this moment, and it delighted him.

"I've been meaning to get some of those fitted boxer shorts," David announced. "Katherine, can you go get those for me?"

"You know...I'm going...over there...getting some more casual clothing for you, okay?" Katherine avoided looking at him, not wanting to make her stammering worse.

"I'll get them for you," Kenneth said, running to find the boxers. David and Katherine chuckled over his excitement.

Katherine wandered away to see what else she could find David to wear, enjoying the shopping immensely. She had done this often for James, although she always couldn't get him to wear the latest styles. Peaking up at David every so often, she chuckled when she saw Kenneth eagerly return with plenty of selections and colors and smiled happily when she overheard David say, "I'll just take these with me. No need to try them on."

The Suit

Kenneth worked thoughtfully, considering what would look best on his new client, and placed several shirts and suits in the dressing room. While changing, David asked, "How long have you known Katherine?"

"Gosh, years. Before she was married. I actually knew her mom first," Kenneth said as David walked out of his dressing room and stepping back up on the small pedestal. Kenneth examined the dress shirt, deciding another size would be the perfect fit. Exchanging the garment, the stylist folded the oversized one neatly as David buttoned then tucked the more tailored version into the black suit pants. "I was working here, but not as a personal stylist. Sharon was working with the guy who previously held this position. She's such a pleasant and beautiful woman, isn't she?"

Looking for Katherine, which didn't take long since he always knew her whereabouts, David hummed, "Yes, she certainly is."

"What was his name?" Kenneth wondered, placing his finger to his lips. "Richie. That's it, Richie! Well, now he goes by Rich. Anyway, Richie's boyfriend got sick and was dying of AIDS. Sharon was a very good client of Richie...I mean Rich...and went to the hospital to sit with him. Obviously, Rich was going through a tough time, but Sharon sat with him, holding his hand. I guess she really didn't say much, just made her presence known."

David understood since Sharon often did the same with him.

"Anyway, after his boyfriend died, Sharon went to Rich's house, bringing him meals, checking in on his mental condition," Kenneth continued. "His parents didn't talk to him because of his lifestyle."

David nodded, trying on another shirt Kenneth handed to him.

"I'm sure you know they are Bible thumpers," Kenneth added.

"What do you mean?" David asked, having never heard that term.

"You know, they read the Bible all the time and talk about God."

"Yeah, okay," David replied.

Kenneth continued his story, turning David toward the mirrors, once again examining the outfit and then grabbing some pins. "Well, somehow...I don't know, maybe because of the pain of losing his boyfriend...Rich started asking Sharon questions about her faith and he got saved and completely changed his lifestyle."

"Get out of here!"

"I'm serious. He now heads up some type of ministry preaching to those who live our lifestyle, telling them there is hope to change." Kenneth pinned David's dress shirt, adjusting the fit. "Of course, in our community, we believe he was never really gay. So that's how I got this job. He left and moved out West."

"Wow, that's amazing."

"Yeah, it's something alright," Kenneth said. "That was maybe ten years ago, and I've been dressing Katherine ever since. She's one of my favorite clients."

"I really can't believe this is a sustainable business," David said.

"You would be surprised how much people spend on clothing. This is a multi-billion dollar industry."

"Yeah, I know it is, but I'm shocked there is such a market for your services," David said.

"Well, if you do it right, it's really so much easier for you to have my services," Kenneth said. "Take Katherine, for instance, she doesn't purchase unless it's on sale. Since I know her size, I'll hold pieces that are marked down on clearance, whether its shoes, outerwear, or gowns."

"That's smart," David said, impressed.

"But there are others who want to be trendsetters and they'll pay any amount to be the first to sport that look. Of course, I'll give them a discount if I'm able."

"Well, I need a whole new wardrobe, but once I update, will you take care of me the same way as Katherine?"

"Absolutely and I'll even give you my discount today."

David smiled in appreciation. "Thank you. So how did you get interested in this business?"

"Well, I've always liked fashion," Kenneth said while he tailored David's pants length. "My dad had a hard time with my interest. I think he was embarrassed of my choice."

David wasn't sure if Kenneth was talking about his lifestyle or career choice.

"He couldn't understand I was good at what I did. I can bring out the best features in every person. I love it!"

"What do you mean?"

Standing up, Kenneth looked towards the clothing floor, pointing. "Well, take Katherine, for example."

They turned toward her as she looked through a rack of blazers.

"As you said, she embodies class, style, and elegance. That's my doing, but with her flair. She allows me to take her out of her comfort zone, taking risks even though she knows what makes her still look graceful."

David nodded agreeing that her wardrobe choices elevate her way beyond her colleagues. Her style selections were timeless classics, looking far more expensive than what she paid.

"See that woman over there?" Kenneth said, "The one wearing a red dress that's too tight, too short, and too low cut?"

David was used to that sort of dress and it did little for him.

"A lot of men love that look. They think she's sexy, alluring, and would probably be funky in the bedroom. I see a girl who's desperate for attention, that's high maintenance, and insecure. She will attract a guy who will always look at other women, fueling a drama-filled relationship. She is actually attracting a man who will do nothing but feed her insecurities."

David was impressed by his insight.

"Now, take Katherine." They both looked back toward her. "Start with her shoes. They are the sexiest thing she wears. You will never see her showing an excessive amount of skin. Her heels tell a story about her. They usually sparkle or shine, just like her personality. They are just a little edgy, which says she's adventurous. And they make a statement, which speaks of her uniqueness. Even these particular shoes she's wearing today, at first glance they look simple and boring, but that gold stiletto heel just shows you how really intriguing she is."

David switched his eyes over to Kenneth. He was romanticizing his job of dressing people for a living. He could see why Katherine and Kenneth got along so well.

"They are the perfect height too. Not so high that she can't walk in them, but high enough to show off her sculpted calves. As you continue up her leg, you are stopped by her skirt, or dress, which is always tailored to the perfect length. She doesn't need to go with a miniskirt to show off her legs. You can tell by her calf muscles that she's got a magnificent pair of stems."

David was enjoying this accurate description of Katherine.

"Then from the way her clothes hug her body, it shows off her bottom in a way that can take your breath away," Kenneth said, now looking at David. "Tailoring is everything. Her curves would never be so crisp and clean if she didn't have the right fit. Just look at her tiny waist. I wonder if my hands would touch if I wrapped them around her waist."

David chuckled.

"Then you go up to her chest, which is not large by any means, and in today's world would be considered small. But I give her some embellishments on her blouses and dresses, providing an optical illusion, creating an hour-glass figure. Many people, especially women, think it's all about the chest. They are mistaken. I can spot implants from any distance."

David listened intently.

"Most women believe to attract a guy they need to have a perfect cup size. But Katherine would never buy into that myth. And it actually shows her true confidence, which just maybe her sexiest quality. She doesn't care to try to impress others by changing herself," Kenneth said.

David liked Kenneth and was glad Katherine had brought him here.

"And then you continue up to her neck, which, in itself, is a piece of artwork. Her full lips draw you in up to those big, brown eyes, which would melt any hard heart. And then, when she smiles, you can't help but fall in love with her," Kenneth completed his poetry, never having taking his eyes off her.

Just then, Katherine, who was nearby, looked over at them and smiled as Kenneth hummed peacefully.

"Are you sure you're gay?" David asked.

Peering over at him, he said, "You want me to prove it to you?"

Backing up a bit, David raised his voice, calling, "Katherine, Kenneth is hitting on me!"

"Well, stop flirting with him!"

The men looked at one another, announcing "sassy!" at the same moment and laughing as they bonded.

"Okay, what do you think?" Kenneth asked, pointing David to the mirror, showing him the outfit he'd dressed him in.

"Katherine, come here and tell me what you think," David yelled.

She approached them as David turned in her direction, showcasing a three-piece black suit with a lace vest; crisp, white dress shirt; and the dark cherry tie. A fabulous pair of shoes completed the look.

"Wow! I mean, wow!" Katherine couldn't contain her reaction. David looked dynamite. Addressing Kenneth, she said, "You are truly a master at your craft."

"Hey, I'm the one bringing the clothes to life!" David protested.

"Yeah but one slip of that tongue of yours and you'll ruin the whole look," Katherine said, never taking her eyes off his attire.

David smiled. "See, I told you, sassy!"

Chapter 38

Anew Eyes

David enjoyed how much Katherine admired his physique in the sophisticated suit. She wasn't even looking at his eyes, however, she wasn't seeing him as a sex object either. She never did. He knew Katherine enjoyed fashion, taking much joy in the outcome, knowing how to dress for success. Then he noticed a far off look cross her face. She was analyzing something, coming up with an idea he could tell.

"Kenneth, I think he can pull off the peacock blue velvet blazer. I think it would bring out his big blue eyes, making them look dynamite."

David hadn't realized she knew the color of his eyes.

"With a great pair of fitted jeans and these shoes," Katherine said running away as the men looked at each other confusingly, wondering where she had gone. She was back in in a flash, though, with a pair of camel-colored loafers. Then she excitedly pointed. "Oh, and what about that checkered shirt?" They followed her direction to a white, button-down dress shirt with a faint but large blue-checkered pattern.

"Oh, yes!" Kenneth said.

And they were off again, finding many outfits for him. David took real pleasure in watching Katherine pick out pieces that would accentuate his features, and he loved her taste. He tried on every outfit she brought to him.

He was feeling much better than his old self. Admittedly, he had never taken care of his appearance properly. Occasionally, he dressed nice, but only wore jeans, which suited him fine. However, this type of style took him to a different level, giving him confidence differently. Now he believed he found his suitable attire outside of his football jersey. He was surprised how comfortable and natural he felt in a three-piece suit, how it translated he was more than just a quarterback.

When they were done, David had at least thirty different outfits, ranging from a tux all the way down to workout wear. Everything was new. There were several suits for his press conferences. There were shoes, undergarments, socks, lounging clothes, bathrobes, pajamas, and accessories. Nothing was left out.

When Katherine saw the amount of clothing, she pulled David aside. "This will cost you a lot of money. You don't need to get all these outfits today. Kenneth can hold whatever you want to purchase later."

Showcasing the hoodie and sweatpants he'd placed back on, he said, "Thank you for your concern, but I have been wearing this type of outfit for over five years. I would have spent this amount of money over that period if I had taken care of myself as I should have."

She understood, happy he made the purchase.

The plan was for everything to be tailored to David's precise measurements and Kenneth would deliver the items while David was getting his hair cut. David provided his address and contacted security to grant Kenneth entrance. He wouldn't need to do a thing since Kenneth would take care of his needs. David shook Kenneth's hand, thanking him for his services, happily leaving a rather large tip.

Such Love

It was time to move on for David's hair appointment. Walking through the shopping center, Katherine could already see a change in him. Even though David wore his old clothes, he stood taller, more confident than she remembered seeing.

"Thanks for taking me to Kenneth. He's a good guy. And he really likes you."

"I really had fun!" Katherine smiled. "And he is a good guy."

"He told me about what your mom did for that Richie...I mean Rich...guy."

"How in the heck did you get on that conversation?"

"I asked Kenneth how he knew you and your family, and he told me the story," he replied.

"Yes, that's quite a story." Looking over at him, she said, "You know my mom took a lot of heat for being a friend to him."

"Why?" David asked.

"Well, in the so-called Christian community there is a lot of, well, I wouldn't call it hatred, but there's a lot of, well, there's not always love toward the gay community."

That he knew.

"My mom showed him love without saying a word. She did it with her actions, so much so that Rich actually asked her about God. Some of her friends chastised her for hanging around him. They said she wasn't a true Christian and all gay people are going to hell."

"What do you believe?" David asked.

Katherine didn't want to get into this conversation. It was a deep, analytical one that would involve Scripture heavily. Yet she felt that conviction to speak the truth, and she had to do it fast because they were nearing the hair salon.

"I think the easiest way to say this is," she stopped walking to look at David, "if you believe in Jesus Christ, that you are born into sin, and that Jesus Christ is the only atoning sacrifice for sin, then you are covered by His blood. We are all sinners, but when God sees us, He sees His Son's blood covering our sin. We are commanded to love one another as Christ loved us. My mom truly demonstrated that love and it spoke to Rich's heart so much that he accepted Jesus Christ and completely changed his lifestyle."

He listened as he was beginning to understand that sort of love.

"I actually love Kenneth and pray for him weekly. We both understand our beliefs. I've talked to him about God several times, and he allows me that freedom even though he doesn't accept it as truth. At times, I listen to his heartbreaks just as I would listen to another woman's heartbreak. But there's a clear understanding that I don't want to hear any graphic details. But that's with anyone and not because he's gay," Katherine said passionately.

He nodded understanding Katherine was a respectable lady.

"There are certain people that I connect with, and he's one of them. Sometimes I think I connect better with non-believers than with those who professes to be believers. If I thought that Kenneth was in some way interfering in my relationship with God, then I would sever ties with him. But I don't see that as being the case at all. I have no idea what God is going to do in someone's life or heart. As you said earlier, never in a million years would you have thought you would end up in Cleveland."

Katherine had made her point and they began walking again. David smiled for his heart was beginning to feel love for her.

Chapter 39

The Concern

Upon recognizing this new feeling of love, it quickly changed to fear. "Hey, what's going on with you and Timmy?" David said, mocking Thompson with the juvenile nickname.

"What? Where in the world is that coming from?" Katherine asked slightly smirking.

"He just seems like the perfect guy for you. What's the story with you two?" David asked bluntly.

"Wow! You don't beat around the bush." Katherine said, impressed by his interest in her relationship with Tim.

"Come on, are you secretly seeing each other? Don't worry I won't leak it to the press."

"Oh, I'm not worried about you leaking anything to the press."

"Then you are seeing him," he worried.

Rolling her eyes, she said, "I never said I was seeing him."

"Oh, I'm sorry, I now understand. He's not attracted to you then."

She stopped, turned towards him, placed her hand on her hip with that unknowingly sexy grin, and pointed her finger at his face. "Let me tell you a thing or two…"

Her speech was interrupted by a voice coming from behind her shoulder. "Hello, Katherine," Brooke said. It was the children's ministry coordinator coming out of the hair salon.

David's ear-to-ear grin disappeared, Brooke having ruined the moment. He loved getting Katherine fired up and was waiting anxiously for her to give it to him, but Brooke doused her flame. David didn't care for this woman at all.

"Hi, Brooke," Katherine said politely.

"Are you getting your hair done? It looks like it needs to be restyled since it's falling in your face," she said while adjusting several locks for Katherine.

David let Katherine catch his eye roll. Brooke didn't understand sexy, he thought, even when it was staring her right in the face. She was very dowdy and dressed accordingly, even though she was similar in age to Katherine.

"No, I'm not getting my hair done," Katherine replied, fixing her hair back to the way she liked it. "This is the latest style. I'm surprised they wouldn't have shown it to you."

"Oh, yes, they did. It just looks different on you," Brooke replied. Bored with the conversation, she turned toward David. "Who's this?"

"Brooke, this is David. You remember, from Sunday school?"

"Oh, yes. You look different. Did you lose weight?" she asked.

David hid his agitation. "Yes, I did. Thank you for noticing."

Brooke talked non-stop for almost ten minutes, not asking them questions or caring about their lives. She was more interested in bragging about herself. David had difficulty recapturing Katherine's attention since she was being polite, not wanting to hurt Brooke's feelings.

"I'm so sorry to be rude and interrupt," David said, causing Katherine to hide her big smile, "but we have an appointment and we don't want to be late since that would be rude to…who, Katherine…Philip?"

"Yes, it is Philip."

"Oh, I didn't realize you had an appointment. You should have said something to me Katherine," Brooke chastised.

"Well, Brooke, you know Katherine. She didn't want to be rude and interrupt your story," David said professionally. "But here's an idea. Next time you can ask her if she has time to talk instead of assuming she isn't busy."

Katherine smiled until Brooke said, "How could she possibly be busy? She doesn't have a husband or any children to go home to."

Katherine's feelings were hurt, but it was typical behavior from Brooke. But Katherine tensed since David was controlling the conversation and Brooke had just set him off. Katherine quickly gave him a look that she would handle it but he disregarded her.

"Oh, you must have a husband and children then, Brooke, I would presume?"

"Of course I do!" she exclaimed, rolling her eyes that David would be so oblivious to the obvious.

"It's really nice you can get out and get your hair done," David continued. "What a great family you must have. You are probably very busy yourself. We don't want to keep you any longer since you probably want to head back and spend as much time as possible with them."

"Yes, but…"

Grabbing Katherine's arm and walking away, David called cheerily but dismissively, "Well, it was nice seeing you. I'm sure we will catch you at church soon."

The Core

"David, that was amazing. You handled her amazingly. I'm really proud of you! You didn't get upset at all." Katherine's heart was bursting with joy.

"Oh, I was pissed. I just hid it," he replied. "Katherine, I don't like her at all. She's sneaky, like a snake. I don't trust her for a second."

"I know, David, I know," she said, checking in for his appointment with the receptionist.

Waiting until she came back, he said, "Seriously, there is something almost evil about her."

"She's just probably been through a lot in her life and is really insecure as a result."

"I know insecurity and that isn't it. She's jealous. But there's something else there too, I just can't figure it out right now." David had to drop his conversation since they both looked in the direction of Katherine's name being called out.

"Katherine! So good to see you!" Philip said, hugging and kissing her. He was the image David expected—a trendy, perfectly-styled man flaunting a highlighted coif and an impeccably manicured beard with a flashy wardrobe to match. David grinned in satisfaction, knowing this was the man for the job.

"Hello," she smiled brightly.

"Love your hair! You did it exactly the right way. It looks like you just had fabulous sex." Philip clasped his hands together. Looking at David, he asked. "It does, doesn't it?"

"I personally wouldn't know," David smiled, a bit of a boyish grin directed at Katherine.

"No, you wouldn't, not looking like that," Philip confirmed.

Laughter bubbled forth from Katherine as David's mouth fell open.

"Philip, this is David," Katherine said. "David, this is Philip."

"I'm not so sure I want to shake your hand after that remark," David teased.

Placing one hand on his hip, talking with his other, Philip replied, "Oh, come on. If I can make her look like that, imagine what I can do for you."

"Sold!" David shook his hand.

"Wonderful! Now, follow me and let's talk about what we are going to do with you." Philip led them away.

"Where do you find these people?" David whispered in Katherine's ear, giving her goosebumps again.

"They are the best at their trades."

Entering the stylist's private salon, David sat as Philip placed a cape over his shoulders, covering his clothes. "Okay, let's start with what we are going to do here. Can you please remove your hat?"

David took it off, throwing it on Katherine's head, causing her to scream as the men laughed. She quickly picked it off her head, holding the grungy, filthy, ragged beanie by two fingers. "Will you please throw this away for me?"

"No! I want to keep that as a souvenir." David grabbed it back lest she decide to throw it away herself.

"Well, at least make sure you wash it." Katherine wrinkled her nose though she smiled.

Philip ran this fingers through David's thick mane, saying, "You have a fabulous head of hair."

Katherine agreed immediately. "I know! Can you believe he's been covering it up with that hat?"

"Really? Katherine, how could you allow him to wear that hat?" Philip asked.

"Believe me, I've wanted to yank it off his head ever since I first met him," she confessed with serious humor.

David enjoyed their conversation. Just like with Kenneth, Katherine was talking about David as if he wasn't present.

"So, what do you think about his hair? What style? I love that longer, fuller look, but he's lazy and I don't think he would keep up on the maintenance." She looked in the mirror at his hair, thinking over the possibilities.

David couldn't believe she'd just called him lazy. Then he thought about his messy condo and attire, quickly understanding her reasoning.

"Well, it really depends about the beard," Philip answered.

"Oh, yeah, that makes sense," she said. "I think the beard takes away from his blue eyes. So I think the beard should be as short as possible."

It was the second time today Katherine had talked about David's eyes and he loved it.

"Well, what about the maintenance on that?" Philip asked as he picked up a comb and began untangling the overgrown monstrosity. "We can get that sexy, 5 o'clock shadow but no matter what we do today, if he will not maintain it, he'll just end up looking like this again in four weeks."

David spoke up before Katherine could answer. "I want the beard completely gone. Shave it off. You can leave my hair somewhat longer, I like that look too." Then he went further. "I would like you to clean up my eyebrows and any unnecessary hair as well. Also, I'd like a massage today. Can you help me out with that?"

Katherine and Philip clapped excitedly, thrilled they'd been given permission to transform his grizzly looks into something more civilized. They began talking again as if David wasn't around.

"Okay, but here's my concern, Philip. He's had this beard for so long, I'm worried that his skin tone won't match, like he'll have a farmer's tan on his face. Plus, won't he have some bumps or underground hair to contend with?" she asked.

"Katherine, you come to me because I'm the best. I'll take care of all that. You'll never know that he had a beard when I get done with him. I'll give him a facial and even out his skin tone," Philip reassured.

"Then let's do it," she said, clasping her hands together in anticipation of the finished product.

"Yeah, it's okay with me too," David laughed, and Philip and Katherine joined in too, realizing they'd kind of taken over.

"I need to get everything lined up for you. Give me a couple minutes and I'll be right back." Philip left the room.

"Now that things are settled here, time for me to go," Katherine said.

"What? You aren't going to stay with me during this whole process?" David whined, sitting in the chair with the cape wrapped around him, kicking his legs childishly, not wanting her to leave.

"No, you are a big boy, you can handle it all by yourself," she grinned.

Again she referred to him as a boy. It made him determined to change her image of him.

260

"Listen, I've seen your attitude completely change from this morning. I have the utmost confidence in your ability in handling the press tomorrow morning. You handled Brooke superbly and she's challenging. I know that you can do this. Just speak from your heart." Upon seeing his look, she said, "Look, the eyes always tell the truth, so if you are lying, they will see right through you and go into attack mode. And if you absolutely can't take it, you better be a great actor, because they will do anything right now to get their headline."

"What do you mean 'the eyes tell the truth?'" David asked, knowing the answer but wanting to keep her around longer.

"Well, they're like the window to your heart, to your soul. It's an easy read."

"How do you mean easy to read?"

"Um, you can tell a person's emotions by looking into their eyes," she replied, looking around at the salon's customers "Take that guy on the phone over there. You can see that he is happy. Of course, he's smiling, but his eyes are bright."

David nodded.

Katherine spotted someone else. "Over there, see that girl? She's smiling, but not her eyes. And look, that woman is complaining but she's doing her best to be polite; you'll see her eyes are not as bright as that guy's on the phone."

"What about her?" David pointed to a woman sitting under a hairdryer wearing a distant look.

"She looks worried or concerned to me. Don't you think?" she asked, silently praying for the woman.

"Yeah, she does. You know, there's something about Brooke's eyes that I've seen before but I don't remember where or what it is," he said.

"Well, I guess we all have some type of look in our eyes that we translate to others," Katherine offered, looking for the best in Brooke.

"What do my eyes say to you?" David asked.

"Anger," she replied, not even looking at him but laughing.

"No really, what do you see? Do you just see anger?"

"Yep, that's what I see."

"Katherine, I'm serious. What do my eyes say to you? Look at me and tell me. I want to know the truth."

Katherine looked directly into his eyes, which caused her heart to race. She usually saw hurt, pain, and despair, but now she saw a freshness—rejuvenation, hope, and intensity—which startled her. She quickly looked away.

Reading her so well, David saw her fear and didn't want to lose her, desiring her thoughts instead. "You know, as I've come to know you, I've actually grown to like you, and I really feel bad that Timmy doesn't find you attractive. You aren't my type either, but you can rest knowing there are other masses that would like to date you."

That set her off as he knew it would. He understood how to get her fired up and this was one of many ways he could do so.

Katherine placed both her hands on either side of his chair to capture him, leaned in so close that only inches separated their faces, and stared deeply in his eyes, taking him on. Feeling self-conscious, David backed up, but she leaned in further, aggressive, almost controlling him. He swallowed, holding his breath.

Her passionate, almost sultry voice filled the little space between them. "I see a guy who's on the verge of complete success. I see a look of determination, an intense fire and a fierceness that's unstoppable. I don't see that little boy who was afraid, depressed, and full of anger, bitterness, and resentment. I see freshness, hope, and courage. I see such passion that it almost takes my breath away and causes my very core to tremble with fear. I see that killer instinct, a fighter with such strength that it's unbeatable."

David's mouth dropped open.

She pulled back from his face, slapped his chin, and said, "Close your mouth or a fly will fly into it. That's how you act. Got it?"

And with that, she grabbed her purse and jacket, walking out the door and waving goodbye as he yelled, "You better not have that sexy grin on your face!" Kicking his legs like a child in distress, he asked of those near him, "Anybody see if she had that sexy grin on her face?"

Chapter 40

The Comparison

His eyes twinkled delightfully. He just loved her. He absolutely loved how she had just played him. And there was nothing he could do either since she had made the most clever exit. Now he understood she no longer viewed him as a boy but as a guy. Still, it bothered him that she didn't think of him as a man.

"Hey, Katherine wanted me to tell you not to be late tomorrow. The interview starts at 9:00 a.m.," Philip said, entering the room David was tucked into.

"You know she slapped me in the face this morning!" David smiled. It was a memory he wanted to keep fresh, and Philip seemed like a guy he could share with.

"Oh, do tell! I've never seen her mad. What did you do?" Philip said, excited to hear some gossip.

But David only shared that his words had been less than respectful, not giving much detail since it was none of Philip's business. David didn't like to gossip because he hated how the press did that to him. Philip told David that Kenneth referred Katherine's family to him and that's how he met her. He shared some old stores of how he enjoyed her as a client, and the two men bonded over pleasantries of Katherine.

David spent hours at the salon and spa, having his hair cut and beard shaved and getting a full facial and massage, and even a mani/pedi. He pampered himself lavishly. He wanted to spoil himself, so whatever services and products they offered, he gladly purchased.

He could tell he was back to his glory days in both attitude and looks. As the beard came off, several women stylists hung around in case Philip needed help. After his massage, more females approached him, offering coffee, tea, and other beverages. Eventually, the room was too small to hold all the women vying for his attention. David enjoyed them flirting with him. It had been a long while.

"It's amazing what a good shave and haircut can do, isn't it?" Philip asked.

"Yes, I agree," David said, admiring the man's work.

"Funny how all these women looked past you when you first came in, don't you think?" Philip added as David nodded, seeing the reflection in the mirror produce a better version of himself.

Not many women noticed David while he was depressed, but that was not Katherine. She was there every step of the way, except when he pushed her out. But this morning she wasn't standing for him shutting her out any longer. She went toe-to-toe with him, never backing down for a moment. He was utterly thankful for her, and all these women failed in comparison.

The Home

David went home relaxed, feeling like a million dollars. As he entered his condo, he noticed for the first time the lack of warmth and comfort. Though the place was spotless and even smelled clean, it lacked that feeling of home, like Michael's home. Perhaps that was a reason he enjoyed being with the Lukas.

As he continued to look around, his eyes were opened to what a spectacular place he lived in. His kitchen was decked out with top-of-the-line stainless steel appliances, solid stone surfaces, and exquisite cabinetry. An amazing dark, hardwood floor complimented the gorgeous stone in the two-story foyer, which hosted an elegant chandelier. His condo was a true masterpiece and he had lived in it like it was a shack.

His mind raced to that morning when Michael took him to the ghetto and was stunned that even though physically he wasn't living on the streets, mentally, he'd created an environment that translated ghetto. It was a picture he couldn't shake.

He saw the beat up, outdated, cheap couch that had been his bed for years and cringed becoming disgusted. How could he not see this before? How could he sleep on a couch? Why would he do this to himself? David was horrified.

Walking into the master suite to change, he saw Kenneth had placed all his old clothes neatly in a garbage bag. Attached was a note: "I hope you don't mind but I packed up these clothes to donate. I think you trust my decisions and know that I would only keep anything that had value and style- Kenneth." At the bottom it read: "P.S. For some reason I didn't think you would have quality bath linens, so I brought some bath and hand towels for your pleasure as a little gift from me."

David smiled at Kenneth's kindness while he lovingly looked at his master closet with its nine foot double-mirrored doors as the true showpiece it was. He'd never realized how beautiful his master bedroom was with its crown moldings and thick trim. The ceiling height was ten feet with a fantastic tent ceiling, and another exquisite, somewhat sexy, chandelier hung in the center of the place that should host a bed. That spot was empty, dead, and lonely.

He entered his closet, taken aback by the beauty of how Kenneth had laid it out for him. It looked like a high-end store. His closet even hosted another chandelier in the middle aisle to highlight the clothes, something he hadn't noticed until now.

Kenneth tailored everything. All his new clothes were present and accounted for, not a piece missing. Everything was placed perfectly in the closet drawers. The shoes were placed in order from casual to dress, lighter color to darkest shade, as were his suits, shirts, and casual clothing. His closet was full, but since it was a massive size, it could hold plenty more outfits, which David knew he would purchase over time.

At the end of the closet was a suit hanging on a wardrobe set apart. It would become a pattern of how Kenneth would display outfits for his viewing. A note attached read: "Wear this tomorrow for your press conference." The look was complete with the undergarments, socks, belt, tie, and shirt. David didn't need to put any thought into his attire for tomorrow.

Gladly taking off his old hoodie and sweats, he put on a new lounging set. Since he'd spent several hours at the spa, no shower was needed. He'd already taken a steam bath after his invigorating massage which had exfoliated his entire body. David threw out every piece of clothing he'd worn today, not considering them good enough to donate.

Viewing himself in the mirror, David stepped back. He was radiant. Shamefully, he lowered his head, sad he'd allowed himself to disappear. And it was as if God spoke to his heart as he thought about his condo. He hadn't been able to see and appreciate its beauty and stately presence since he'd cluttered it up with filth. Only after the help of others, who not only cleaned up his appearance and his environment but, more importantly, his thoughts, could he see what God created within him. That flame, which had grown into a fire today, was now roaring wildly, and it would take much more than a fire hose to extinguish. David looked up in gratitude and thankfulness to God.

Viewing the bags full of products he'd purchased from Philip, he now desired to take care of himself. He had bought a full line of hair, facial, and body products. Just this morning, hardly a bottle of shampoo or bar of soap sat in his shower and he couldn't care. Now that was changed. Regardless of his future, his need right now was to properly care for the body given unto him, treating it as a temple.

As he placed the products in his master en suite, he relished how the beautiful neutral-yet-warm palette contrasted against the dark walnut cabinetry. The two-person shower was fitted with body sprayers, a double shower head, and a massive rain shower hung in the middle. It doubled as a steam room, which David had never used it as. There was even a his-and-hers digital temperature control programmed to suit his desires. All fixtures were high-polished, sparkling nickel, and he was thankful for such an exquisite retreat. He felt called to care for his living accommodations better and furnish his home with only the best pieces. He would ask Katherine for help with the decor, and the thought excited him.

He thought about Katherine, the family, even Kenneth and Philip, each with their unique gifts and talents to bring out the best in a person expertly. It was the reason David wanted to coach football one day. He remembered how his previous stature brought out the best in his teammates. Now he couldn't wait to lead them tomorrow.

Before calling it a night, David contacted Philip and Kenneth, thanking them for their services and asking them to meet with him tomorrow. They agreed. Looking around one last time, he thanked God for the day, insight, and help he needed even though he hadn't desired it.

He slept peacefully for the night.

The Old Cleaned

David rose earlier than usual, probably because he was no longer comfortable sleeping on the sofa. He made a shake with plenty of time left before going to the stadium, so he decided to head down to the pier to enjoy the sunrise. As he found his keys, he noticed the Bible on the coffee table and grabbed it to take along.

As soon as he walked on the pier and sat down looking at the expansive lake and amazing sky, he relaxed, breathing in the fresh air, feeling close to God. Opening the Bible, he tried to figure out what to read. Last night, he'd read the Song of Songs and understood the overall meaning, but it wasn't very straightforward.

Deciding the beginning would be best, he located Genesis, remembering the first two Chapters from Katherine's Bible class. Still, as he got deeper into the book, he was amazed by the story of lies, murders, and polygamy. He couldn't pronounce many names, and a lot didn't make sense, but one thing he understood, God loved those who didn't want to follow His rules.

Afterward, he felt like praying but wasn't sure what to say, so he asked God to help him with his game and the media. For a split second, terror of failing struck his heart until a picture of his condo and all its beautiful, clean glory came to his mind, as if God had said, "Imagine what your condo will look like after it's filled with the best furnishings."

David recalled the beauty of his closet after being cleaned and outfitted with his new clothing. David's heart has been cleaned out but, as Katherine described yesterday, it would be an on-going cleaning for nothing in life is maintenance-free. And like his condo, even though it was clean and smelling fresh, it was still empty, though properly ready to be filled with the best furnishings.

A peace filled his heart and mind with determination, for truly his life had been filled with rich treasure since being in Cleveland. Now his heart was ready to be filled properly too, for he knew God always looked upon him as kinship, having placed him in positions to lead, encourage, and conquer ever since he was a little boy.

The Commotion

Katherine arrived at the stadium early, a nervous wreck. She knew the media would mock David incessantly if he opened his mouth in any wrong way since he was sporting a new look. It was his first time addressing the press since he'd shouted at Trino, storming off. Fear enveloped her heart, something she hadn't felt in years, and the only way to shake those emotions was to give it over to the Lord.

Quietly, to herself, she prayed, "Lord, I've done everything I could do to help him. This is now completely in your hands, just like it always has been." And then she confessed, "I believe I am fearful because I know this will be a reflection on me and our company. I'm sorry for that. I pray you give me the words to help him get back up after this is all over."

Even before she could properly finish her prayer, she heard, "Hey, Katherine!"

"Hi!" she said to her sister, hugging her and removing a tray of pastries she was balancing with one hand. "Do you need help bringing in the food?" Today Lana and Eric were catering breakfast and lunch, something they occasionally did for fun involvement with the family.

"No, Eric is getting it now. I wanted to set out some coffee and breakfast treats to soften them up a bit," Lana chuckled.

Even though she thought it would take more than food to quell their anger, Katherine grinned. Being with her sister lifted her mood, and she joined in helping set out the pastries and drinks.

When their parents arrived, Katherine's nerves re-emerged since David hadn't shown up yet. There was plenty of time before the conference started, so he was in no way late, but there was always a chance. It was difficult settling down in the face of this worry. Last week, she'd took a lot of heat for his action and she wasn't looking forward to going through that again.

While her parent's visited Reggie, Lana, holding a tray of goodies, whispered to Katherine, "I'm going to serve them..." she pointed to the reporters, "like a peace offering." Katherine looked over at the hungry wolves, but knew food wasn't what they desired, it was David. Fear once again made a home in her heart and Katherine backed up, retreating to the waiting room where the players and coaches gathered before being called to the podium.

Katherine chuckled and touched her sister fondly for trying to help soften the blow for David, then grabbed a stack of napkins to give her, when Lana dropped the entire tray of food right on the floor.

"Oh, my gosh!" Katherine called out and immediately fell to her knees, picking up the tray, cleaning the floor, and placing everything on the table, but her sister stood eerily still, mouth opened. Scared, Katherine asked, "Are you okay? What's wrong?"

Lana didn't answer, only stared at the crowd. Katherine looked in the same direction, noticing Kenneth and Philip, whose being there confused her, then seeing Eric laughing and smiling, talking with someone who resembled David. Feeling someone tug her arm, she switched her attention as her dad said, "You cleaned him up pretty good."

Turning back to locate David, her mouth fell open as he approached them, hugging. "Lana, so nice to see you!" he greeted.

"Awesome!" she squealed, bouncing happily. "You look so awesome!"

Blushing, David said, "Thank you."

Making eye contact with Katherine, who hadn't spoken, he gently tapped her chin. "Close your mouth before a fly flies into it."

Swallowing, smiling, jumping up and down just like a little girl, she reached out and grabbed Kenneth, then Philip, hugging and kissing both. "You guys are absolutely the best! You did such a wonderful job!"

"What about me? How come everyone else gets a hug and a kiss except for me?" David whined with arms wide open waiting for a hug only to be denied again.

"I'll hug you!" Lana squealed.

"And I'll kiss you!" Kenneth said, waiting his turn.

Everyone laughed when David said, "No, thank you, I'm fine, really I'm good!"

Michael and Sharon fussed over David as did his teammates. So many crowded him, pushing Katherine aside, making it impossible for her to get him alone to prep for the press. As she watched him, her heart raced. He was handsome. The beard had hid the beauty of his eyes; they looked completely different now. Instead of gray, they were a vivid blue, bright and light, resembling gorgeous Tahitian waters. Alive with joy.

The beard had also hidden the apples of his rosy-colored cheeks, grown over his luscious, red lips, and obscured his pearly white teeth.

All his features, and he had plenty of great ones, had disappeared because of the overgrown, grizzly beard that allowed him to hide from the world.

David seemed larger than life and interacted as such. He was in command as a group gathered around him. It was the authentic person, the one she knew and had come to enjoy—the person who interacted with her dad, Eric, Reggie, and even her. Then a touch of sadness filled her heart, recognizing that she would now need to share that real person with others. It had been special holding him to herself.

And then she repeated in a whisper, "One and done. One and done," reminding herself only one season with him and then she was done. She was halfway through her part of helping him out of Cleveland and that knowledge kept her from the full sadness of losing a relationship that had become special to her.

The Fear

After the initial masses cleared, David found Katherine. "So what do you think?" he said, modeling his new look.

Katherine thought, considering whether to joke or be truthful, choosing honesty in the end. "Handsome. You look handsome," she blushed.

He blushed too.

"Okay." She pulled herself into work mode. "How are you feeling? Do you know what you are going to say? Please try not to yell at Trino again…"

"I got this," he interrupted.

"And try to avoid the path that will cause…"

"I got this," he said again.

"And don't forget to…"

David grabbed both her arms, pulling her toward him, feeling her tense up but disregarding it. Looking intensely in her eyes, he said calmly, "Katherine, I got this."

Fear struck her heart and David read it in her eyes, bothered she was afraid of him, hating she was tense upon his touch. It hurt him.

Unwrapping from his grip, she said. "Okay, I'm sorry." Wishing him well, she walked to the back of the room.

He was confused because yesterday she had been open. Now, today, the look of fear. Why? Why was she so afraid of him today?

His mind whirled. Maybe she felt comfortable when only touching him on her terms? He was her closest male companion, so it wasn't like any other guy touched her the way he did. Maybe she didn't like men touching her?

Then a new thought entered his mind. Thompson! Tim Thompson touched her and she never flinched. It made sense for them to be a couple he reasoned. They really were a perfect match.

The Cat

"Look at what the cat just brought home to daddy!" Jordan growled, pulling David aside, away from the crowds that were vying for his attention.

David laughed, breaking his mood that was beginning to sour over the thought of Katherine and Tim Thompson.

"My man is back! You are one sexy cat!" Jordan fussed. "You are going to kill the ladies. I thought you had it before, but you are screaming sex! It's written all over you and you can't do anything to hide it."

"Shhh, I get it. I clean up nice," David said.

"No, you don't get it, and that's why the ladies will fall even harder," Jordan corrected.

"What in the world are you talking about?"

"Come here, man." Jordan pulled him to a full-length mirror. "Dude, look at you. Look!"

David did, smiling but confused.

"Man, you don't see it, do you?" Jordan asked.

David lowered his head, laughing. He really liked Jordan and understood his popularity. He made a big deal out of other people.

"You have on a three-piece suit, dress shirt, and a satin, baby blue tie with hints of turquoise to show off those big baby blues of yours. Plus, you got rid of that growth that was on your face and the hat, now showing off your true lion's mane," Jordan said, causing David to laugh anew.

"And here's the kicker, you have no idea how incredible you look." Jordan whispered seriously, "Don't change that. The instant you become full of yourself is the instant you turn into a fool. Understand?"

Understanding Jordan's language, David nodded, trusting his long-time friend.

"Now, who's the woman that did this all for you?" Jordan asked excitedly, clasping his hands and rubbing them together like he was waiting for a scrumptious meal. "Who are you trying to impress? Who's the one that has put the love and romance in my man?"

"No, no, no. I just needed to clean up a little," David defended, but blushed.

"Alright, I understand. Papa doesn't want to spill the beans just yet. That's okay. I can take a hint." He winked. "So who dressed you? Who helped pick out your clothes? Where is she?" Jordan said, looking around.

"Well, that guy over there put my outfit together." David pointed to Kenneth.

Jordan looked over at him, then back at David, asking, "You didn't go gay on me, did you?"

"Hey, come on now, you know you would be the first one to know," David winked.

Both men laughed. Clapping, yelling, pumping his fist in the air, Jordan danced away over the excitement of his friend reemerging, shouting, "My man is back!"

Chapter 42

The Pit

More teammates patted David on the back, commenting on his new appearance until it was time. The coach was the first one up, giving the everyday speech, but the media wanted David and were in attack mode. Their passion to strike was like an undercurrent in the room.

A collective gasp sounded when he stepped up to the microphones in front of the camera.

"I know, I know, you are wondering who I am. But I can assure you it's really me. I'm David Mann. It's nice to meet you." He smiled warmly, eyes bright, meeting the gazes of the journalists caught off guard.

Katherine chuckled, thinking how perfect. One point for David!

Nevertheless, Trino was ready for a fight. "Do you expect your game to improve since you got rid of the bread and got new clothes?"

"Good morning, Trino. I owe you an apology," David said, serious. "I'm sorry for what I said to you last week. That was not only completely childish, but it was…" he searched for the exact word, making heartfelt eye contact when he found it, finally announcing "…foolish. It was a completely foolish thing for me to say to you. I know you have a job to do and obviously are great at it or you wouldn't still be in the business. I know how much you love football and I'm sure it devastated you to be benched. I obviously would know that feeling since it's happened to me now…what…four times?"

David chuckled along with the journalists.

"But you were able to pick yourself up and create a whole new career out of something that was perceived as a failure. I have a tremendous respect for that, and I hope to do the same," David said.

Trino didn't flinch. "So now you are looking for a new career?"

"No! No, I'm still here to lead this team. I just thought I needed to clean myself up before I tried to lead anyone else," David confessed.

"What are you hoping to achieve?" another reporter asked.

"Well, like any athlete, I hope to win. I want to win," David responded, not mocking the redundant question.

"How do you see yourself doing that?" a reporter asked from the other side of the row.

"I need to go out and give it my all…" David said.

A reporter interrupted him. "Do you mean you haven't given it your all?"

David didn't mind the question at all, and it didn't bother him being interrupted. "No, I can't say that I haven't given it my all. I have but I just wasn't doing it in the right frame of mind."

"What's your frame of mind like now?" The question came from another.

David thought, finally saying, "Hopeful."

"Will hopeful win you any games?" a reporter mocked.

With boyish charm and a grin that lit up his eyes, David said, "Well, anything is better than my frame of mind before, don't you think?"

But they weren't convinced, looking to argue, trap, and create hostility. David didn't take the bait. He was in control and they were clueless of it.

"Can you explain how that just yesterday morning after practice you were argumentative and today you seem…I don't know…nice," a reporter asked.

Everyone, including David, laughed.

The reporter clarified his question. "No, really, was it something someone said…a revelation? What was it?".

"That's a good question." David leaned into the podium with his hand to his chin, thinking, searching how to describe the new behavior. "Let me see if I can explain it this way," he opened. "It's like I fell into a pit that wasn't that deep but deep enough that I couldn't climb out of by myself. Anytime I tried, I fell back down. And I was furious for falling because up to that point I was never in a pit before. As teammates, coaches, and friends would lend a helping hand…it's like I would bite them in an attempt to prove I could get out by myself. Eventually they stopping coming around to help me."

David softly chuckled to himself, shaking his head. "And then I thought I could dig my way out of the pit to prove I didn't need anyone's help. So I started digging and digging and digging. And really, the only thing I was doing was digging myself into a deeper hole." His eyes lit up with the truth. "That pit was so dark I couldn't see anything, and I didn't realize how helpless I was until one day someone threw me a rope. But out of my ignorance, I didn't understand how to use it. So a slew of people came down to sit with me and show me how to use the rope to climb out."

Looking at Michael, he said, "And I realized that if you have a strong, encouraging father…"

Looking over to Sharon, "And a loving, supportive wife…"

Locating Reggie, "And a friend who is so full of passion that it can't help but be contagious…"

Smiling at Jordan, "And an old, dear friend who speaks in a language that's only understandable between the two of you…" he grinned, "then you are truly blessed."

Scanning the crowd, searching for the perfect words to continue, he said, "But even with all that, I'm not sure if I would have gotten out of that pit unless I had that truth slayer, that one person who would speak the truth no matter how much I hated to hear it, the friend who would put it all on the line." He smiled and touched his chin. "You know, to slap me upside the head to get my attention and shove me in front of a mirror to make me take a real good look at myself—the real me—show me what I was really made of." Directly speaking to Katherine, David said, "Well, that's beyond anything I can ever ask for or imagine."

Katherine became misty.

"Once I got out of the pit and I realized that it wasn't my home anymore, I could see my filth. So I cleaned up, shaved, and put on some new clothes," he laughed.

Katherine's professional side kicked in and she straightened up. She had to pull it together since she knew David would no longer need her guidance. He had them eating out of his hand now and they were falling in love with him.

Chapter 43

The Rebirth

The press conference wasn't over yet. A young reporter cleared his throat and asked, "David, assuming you will coach one day, what would you say to a player going through a rough time like you?"

"Great question, kid! What's your name?" He looked at the straitlaced, neatly cut innocent, young man, whose face boasted a few freckles and green eyes.

"Tommy. Tommy Duncan," he replied.

"And how old are you, Tommy Duncan?"

"I'm twenty-one, sir."

"Recently graduated from college, Tommy?"

"Yes, sir. Cleveland State," Tommy replied.

"And where do you work Tommy Duncan?"

"I work over at Station 8."

Katherine thought it was brilliant. David was rewarding this reporter for asking such a great question, shining the spotlight on him in the perfect way.

"Where's the other guy who normally reports, Tommy Duncan?"

"He's sick. I got called last night."

"When did you do your research on me?" David asked.

Tommy blushed, feeling foolish, believing the others would make fun of him. "Once I was assigned as his back-up."

"You are going to be very successful, kid. Here is your chance to get the ball and run with it, and you were prepared. Great job!" David said. "I'll tell you what, Tommy Duncan. I'll answer your question right after I give you some instructions. Is that okay?"

"Yes, sir," he stated eagerly.

"You see the pretty lady standing in the back?" David pointed at Katherine, who outwardly appeared calm even though she was freaking out inwardly.

"Yes, sir," Tommy said.

"She's my manager and a mighty fine one at that. Actually, her entire family is pretty amazing over at Cleveland Management Institute. And what you have been eating this morning is from Lana and Eric's restaurant," David advertised.

Katherine was tickled that David was completely in charge, oozing confidence. Her heart was joyful for she could see David would prosper no matter what team he went to next year. And that's what she wanted for all of her clients, only the best.

"After we are done, introduce yourself to her."

"Sure," Tommy replied.

"Her family does a tremendous amount of charity work. I would like to work with you to put a spotlight on it. They do a lot to help the community and it would benefit the city if you were to report on it firsthand. Does that sound like something you would be interested in doing with me?"

"Yes, sir!" Tommy said excitedly.

"Perfect, kid. Now, I want to warn you, treat her with respect. She's got a mean right hook, plus you'll have to contend with her father."

Everyone laughed except Tommy, who was serious, promising, "Oh, I will be respectful to her, sir."

"I know you will, kid. And you can call me David."

"Thank you…David." A blush crept over his face over being given such an opportunity.

The Leader

David switched gears, refocusing the room. "Now that that's settled, let's get back to Tommy Duncan's question. He wants to know when I coach one day what would I say to someone who is in a mental state of mind that's undermining his own play. Well, I would say what most of these coaches have been saying: that they believe in me and my abilities and that's the whole reason they brought me to their team."

His boyish grin appeared as David went on. "I would tell that player in no uncertain terms that I understand where they were in their thinking. I mean, just as Trino said, wasn't I one of the greatest rookies out there only now to be known as the worst quarterback in preseason history? I'd let it be known that, just like these coaches, I wouldn't bring someone my team that I didn't believe in or would think would infect others. And I would repeat that to him over and over again until I could tell by the look in his eyes that he believed me."

Leaning into the podium, David's passion made an appearance. "Then I would remind him of why he loves football. I mean, really, what an incredible game it is. In my opinion, it's the best sport out there. The Super Bowl is really another national holiday."

A determined spirit colored his next words. "I would remind him he was absolutely designed and created to play this game. That he is in a very elite position few can withstand. And that he stood the test by obtaining this level, and his current mental state is just another test he'll pass. That he made it through high school, college, and finally to a group of less than one hundred men to play this position in the professional league—a whole new level. And now, he's down to just thirty-two men who have passed the test to start while the others stand on the sidelines hoping to get the ball." David said it all fiercely, speaking his true heart.

"And within those thirty-two men are only a few who stand out; we know them by name. There may be just a handful of them who are considered truly elite. Then, finally, there's only one man standing in the final game. That one man, who through all the injuries, the slander, the defeat, and the hits, who can stand back up and win that coveted trophy and that signature ring. Because really, isn't it when you are down and out that you discover what you are truly made of?" David asked intently.

Thinking about how he wanted to explain this next part, he paused momentarily. "I would then remind him that this game represents life. It is never boring, always exciting, and a wild adventure. That just when you think you are going to get a touchdown, the ball is fumbled. When you are driving down the field, it's intercepted. And when you think you are going to lose, somehow you are able to overcome doubt, fear, and the pressure to come from behind to win."

Talking out of the side of his mouth with an intriguing smile, David romanced as he held up his hand, looking at it. "I would tell him his very hand was designed and created specifically to hold a football. I would make him feel that ball, reminding him how even the football feels different given the situation. Sometimes it's hard and cold from the snow. Other times, soft and supple from the perfect temperature, and then my absolute favorite feeling of it being hot and sweaty from the intensity of the game. And as with anything, I'd remind him that timing is everything in this game, and when you see a small opportunity, you take it. You throw that ball effortlessly to your teammate who's fifty yards away, running, looking up for that ball to catch, and you stop breathing just long enough until you hit that target. When it lands perfectly in his hands for a touchdown, nothing can stop you from exploding with sounds of passion that words can never describe. Wouldn't you agree?"

"Oh, yes!" a woman reporter yelled.

Everyone laughed as David said, "Well, I guess Angela agrees with me."

Katherine's knees went weak and she felt faint. She had never heard David describe his love for football. He had done so vividly, with no embarrassment.

"Sounds like you have to prove something," Trino remarked.

"Hmm, I haven't thought about that," David replied. "But to whom? Me? The coaches? The team? You guys?"

"Maybe," Trino said.

"I'm not sure. Ask me that question again one day," David offered.

Then his cocky, fun-loving attitude showed brightly, and he laughed. "And what do I need to prove to you guys, anyway? You'll get your headline regardless of how well I play or don't play. Let's see, what will be the headline? 'David Mann Cleans Up, But Can He Clean Up the Field?'"

The room of reporters laughed heartedly.

"How's that? Is that a good line?" David asked, enjoying the banter for the first time.

Katherine smiled as he played with them, watching them take the bait. He was brilliant.

"No!" a reporter shouted. "New Look. New Attitude. New Game?"

David nodded with a smile. "That's a good one!"

"No. 'Mann Cleans Up His Act, But Is It Only An Act?'" another shouted.

"Oh, yeah, that's a good one. That will get people reading for sure," David said.

"Well, is it an act?" Trino asked point blankly.

"Well, tune in, it's to be continued." David shyly smiled, causing them to laugh again. "Okay, okay." He settled them down. "Now I know you all have been dying to ask and you want to know, so I will tell you."

Katherine loved how he was teasing them, getting their full attention.

"Who dressed me and cleaned up my face?" He smiled.

They roared with laughter, mesmerized by him.

"Come up here, guys," David asked as his pros walked next to him. "This is Kenneth, and as you can see, he has absolutely exquisite taste. He put together this and many other outfits for me."

Kenneth smiled, happily waving to the cameras as the journalists chuckled.

"And this is Philip. He is the one who chiseled that growth off my face." David laughed, then went about advertising their services and where to locate them. After, he called out, "Tommy Duncan!"

All went silent to listen.

"You may want to interview Kenneth and Philip. I'm sure they can give you a nice story, an article to publish or to use on your website. Do you have a website, kid?"

"Yes!" Tommy said proudly, shouting out his social media page.

"Alright, I have to wrap it up here," David said. "I'll see you all after tonight's game."

David looked directly at Katherine before walking off and she threw him an Italian kiss she was so excited. He winked at her before making his way to the locker room.

Chapter 44

The Respect

The press room was a buzz. The journalists were in a frenzy to get out the news as quickly as possible. As soon as David entered the locker room, he was surrounded by his teammates, coaches, and now Michael and Sharon. Katherine couldn't get to him since Tommy was giving her his credentials.

"Here's my card, ma'am. My email, work, and cell numbers are listed, and let me give you my home number too." He blushed as she placed his card in her purse.

"This is wonderful, Tommy." Katherine grinned. "I'll make sure I contact you so that you can be part of our family...I mean our team."

"Anytime. You can call me anytime, day or night," Tommy said.

She could understand why David had singled out this kid. He was eager and sincere, full of life and hope. "Here's my card," she offered in return. "If for some reason you don't hear from me in a week, just call. But I can assure you by mid-week you will hear from me."

"Thank you! Thank you, ma'am," Tommy said excitedly. "And don't worry, I'll treat you with respect."

Katherine loved it because she knew David warned of consequences if he didn't. "Oh, I know you will," she replied. "And you can call me Katherine, Tommy."

"Yes, Katherine," he said glowing that he would be part of the team.

She excused herself, attempting to greet Philip and Kenneth, who were standing off to the side, mobbed by reporters who were each looking to get any tidbit of gossip. Talking with both Kenneth and Philip briefly, she had to fight the crowd again to make her way to the locker room and congratulate David on his triumph. It was no easy task since many stopped to congratulate her on his transformation, asking if it would translate to the field.

Finally making it to the locker room, she located David from a distance and it took her breath away. She was so accustomed to his beard and hoodies that he was nearly unrecognizable. All of a sudden she felt self-conscious and shy. Work, she told herself. If she talked shop, it would guarantee her professional demeanor and she'd be able to see him better as a client.

The Man

Pushing people out of the way, Jordan made his way to David's locker. "My man, hittin' it with them out there!" Jordan said, giving David a high five.

"Hey, Jordan, I want to introduce you to Michael. He's more than a friend to me and one of the owners of my management company," he said.

Michael shook Jordan's hand. "Glad to have you a part of Cleveland. We've always enjoyed watching you play."

"And over there," David pointed, "is his lovely wife, Sharon. And over there...."

Jordan followed David's finger until he landed on a young lady wearing a great fitted latte-colored skirted-suit which hinted at her shapely body. Licking his lips, he said, "Wow, I'm going to tap on that."

Michael's eyes filled with anger, but even before he could speak a word, David shoved Jordan up against the wall, lifting him by his suit. "If I ever hear you say another disrespectful word about her, I will literally throw you out a window! I don't want you looking or thinking about her in any sexual way! I don't want you licking your lips when you talk to her, I don't want you checking her out from head to toe, and I don't want you hitting on her. Do I make myself clear?"

"Dude...dude...David!" Jordan yelled, finally getting his attention. "I will treat her like she's your little sister. I promise! You know me. You know I'm serious."

David released his friend, thinking then mumbling. "That's probably all she'll ever be to me, anyway."

"What?" Jordan said before being interrupted by an angelic voice.

"Hello, I'm Katherine. You must be Jordan Sanders. It's so nice to meet you. We are thrilled you came to our town. You play the game with such electricity and fire! I've enjoyed watching you for years and I'm so happy to be able to watch you in person every week." She shook his hand.

"Um…um…yeah…nice to meet you too," Jordan stumbled, melted by her charm and beauty.

Michael stepped in to hug his daughter, congratulating her on the success as David whispered to Jordan, "First time I've ever seen a woman leave you speechless."

"That's because you threw me off, man! I was trying to treat her like she's your baby sister, only she's all woman."

Staring him down, David warned ,"Easy."

Blowing him off, Jordan addressed Katherine. "It was truly my pleasure to meet you." Then, bowing slightly and taking hold of her hand, he kissed it, leaving her blushing.

Michael excused himself, following Jordan. David chuckled under his breath, knowing Michael would be reiterating to Jordan that his daughters should be treated respectfully or else.

"Congratulations! You were so wonderful. Truly, you were dynamic, interesting, and even funny." Katherine couldn't contain her enthusiasm for David's success.

Holding open his arms, he asked, "So do I get a hug?"

She furrowed her brow and stepped back, fearful she wouldn't be able to maintain her professional boundary.

Understanding her, David played to lessen her worries. "Hey, how come you didn't greet me the same way you just greeted Jordan when we first met?"

"What? Are you kidding me…" she started until she realized David was joking, making her laugh and having fun with him. Then she remembered her purpose. "Kenneth wanted me to ask you if he could get back into your condo. He has another outfit that would be perfect for tonight's press conference."

"Sure," he replied. "Hey, are you doing anything today?"

"Just coming to the game tonight, why? Do you need something?"

"Well, yes," he said, handing her his set of house keys. "Can you just let him in, if you don't mind."

"Sure, I can do that for you," she said, then quietly asked, "Is your condo clean?"

"It's sparkling. And, I'm glad you brought that up. I almost forgot. Will you please go with me tomorrow and help me purchase furniture?"

"Great! I'm so glad you've decided to get a bed. You will get such a better rest at night."

"Actually, I want to furnish my entire condo. So if you aren't too busy, I would appreciate you helping me select some great pieces. You have wonderful taste, just like your mom, and I would love your help."

Hesitating, Katherine asked, "Are you sure you want to furnish the whole condo? What if...your play...aren't you concerned?"

David could read her like a book. "Oh, I know what you are saying. You are concerned that my game will continue to be off and I will be released mid-season or sooner, so why would I spend the money to furnish some place when I may not be here more than a month anyway."

Ashamed, avoiding eye contact, Katherine only said, "Yeah."

David flirted, looking to promote some easy bantering. "What about all those speeches of how much you believe in me?"

Katherine touched him gently, looked lovingly in his eyes, and said, "Oh, there's no doubt I do believe you have what it takes. I'm just not sure..."

David completed her sentence. "That I believe I have what it takes."

Katherine put her head down in shame. She honestly didn't want to hurt his feelings.

Gently lifting her chin, he said into her eyes, "I believe!"

David's passion sent chills down her spine. Fear overcame her spirit once more, for she was having a difficult time seeing him as a down and out client any more.

He hated her fear, so he added, "Besides, I can just take it with me to my next location, right?"

"Right!" Katherine responded brightly, relieved by his save.

One of David's teammates called over, breaking their conversation. "Hey, you two match. Did Kenneth lay out both your outfits?"

Realizing they were wearing complementing colors, David walked over to the mirror, pulling Katherine along, saying, "Look at us! We totally match."

Admiring their reflection, they delighted in how well they looked next to one another.

"What a difference from yesterday's sight. Now I actually look like a human being. Standing next to you yesterday, I looked like a caveman. Now I actually look like...um...um..."

"A man," Katherine prided.

That got David fired up,. "Okay, so you will go with me tomorrow to shop for furniture?" he asked walking back to his locker.

"Yes, I will help you," she promised, following him. "What are you thinking about getting? A couch, a couple of chairs, and a bed?"

"No, everything!" David said as his eyes twinkled with excitement from visualizing his condo looking like a home.

"Everything?"

"I don't want one room empty. That means the living and dining rooms, both bedrooms, and the office needs furniture too."

"Wow! Alright then. I'll need to take some measurements. Do you mind if I stay at your place for a couple hours while I get those?"

"Of course, stay as long as you like. There's nothing in it to steal anyway," David joked, happy to know she would be at his home. Getting ready for practice, he took off his suit jacket but continued planning his new furnishings. "I need a table to put my mail and keys on when I get home…something in the foyer."

Tilting her head, she watched him hang up his suit jacket, saying, "okay."

Loosening his tie and removing it, he said. "I want a formal but practical table. Something I can eat on since I've been eating on my couch."

Her eyes popped open wide as he unbuttoned his dress shirt and took it off, his white fitted undershirt revealing a hint of his lean build.

Kicking off his shoes, David rambled on. "Of course, I want the living room decked out, but what I'm really looking forward to getting is a king size bed and filling up my master bedroom. It's such a stunning room with the ceiling height and massive trim."

"Okay, okay, I got it! Keep your pants on. We'll get everything you need. I'll see you after the game," she said, putting her hand over her eyes, then walking quickly away.

David was in the middle of taking off his belt when he realized he had been undressing in front of her. He laughed hysterically. Sitting down in front of his locker, taking off his socks, he thought of how much he loved making her nervous. He wanted to do it more often.

Looking up, seeing Katherine's parents over by Reggie's locker, he watched Michael hold Sharon's hands, bringing them up slowly to his lips and kissing each lovingly, making Sharon blush. It was just the same way Katherine had blushed when Jordan kissed her hand.

David had witnessed Michael kissing his wife's hand countless times but never thought much of it until now. Michael was romantic. Even though Jordan wasn't interested in settling down, he was still romantic at heart. It inspired him.

Chapter 45

The Challenge

It was time, the last preseason game. David's most recent practice had been his best in years. The team was coming together and feeling much more confident. There were still rusty spots but they'd made a big improvement. David, Reggie, and Jordan had bonded naturally.

The crowd cheered as they took the field, and the internet lit up since David's new look was plastered all over the place. But he didn't care about his image; all he wanted was one thing—the ball. David couldn't wait to get his hands on the ball.

The team's play was so much better than the last three games. But there was still a hole. Collins, #33, wasn't blocking, and David analyzed it while he played. Was he not strong enough? Possibly didn't care? Did he want David to get hurt? What was it?

On the sideline, David pulled Collins aside. "Hey, man, the game is getting better, don't you think?"

"Yeah, but we'll see what happens," Collins replied. "They've got their secondary players, no real starters out there."

Yes, that was true but David saw something else, that look of defeat.

"How long have you been on this team?" David asked.

"About four years."

"Right out of college?"

"Yep, first-round," Collins said.

"How disappointed you must be," David said, knowing how difficult it was to remain motivated playing through injuries while being part of a losing team year after year.

Collins made eye contact. He hadn't been expecting that comment.

"You obviously worked hard to be drafted first round. I know personally what that takes and it's difficult."

"Yeah, it wasn't easy," Collins replied.

David grinned. "I'm sure you came here thinking you would make a difference and nothing's really happened. Then this season, Rick gets knocked out along with Williams and you are stuck with me since they are having contract problems lining up another quarterback."

Collins chuckled, but he didn't think it was funny.

"Look, I know you love this game, I know you do. But I also know that you aren't blocking. Maybe you don't want to get hurt or maybe you lost interest since we probably won't win anyway. I get it."

Upset, Collins asked, "Are you telling me I'm not doing my job?"

"Are you telling me the guy you're blocking is tougher than you?" David pointed to Collins's opponent stalking the other sidelines.

Collins stood his ground.

"I've watched film of you, both college and pro, and I know you can do better. And you do too. Now, you may have only lost your fire like I did. And I get that. But if you want off this team and traded elsewhere, then get fired up because no one else will want you. I know that from experience," David said, staring into Collins's soul.

The younger man disregarded him.

"I'll tell you what. Go out there for this second quarter and give it your all. And if you think it's a waste, then stop. Okay?" David challenged.

Collins remained silent, looking out over the field, still wondering if giving his all would make any difference.

The Men

It was time to get back out there. Taking the field, David read the defense, wanting to call an audible, but his hands were tied. This time, Collins held the line, giving David time in the pocket to throw the pass. Cleveland moved the ball thirty yards.

David patted Collins's helmet as they regrouped. "You the man! You the man!"

Now the team was fired up. Again, David read the line and couldn't change the call. The defense was coming at him fast, but not from Collins's end. David ran out of the pocket, throwing a duck, but Devon reached out and grabbed it for another first down.

Momentum was building amongst the players; they were getting into a groove.

The next play it was Eddie's turn to break through, another ten yards gained. The crowd was crazy, pumping up their hometown heroes. Now able to stand in the pocket because of Collins, David had much more time to think through his progressions. He was still rusty, but only he knew it.

This was it, the call David wanted, and he was determined. The ball was snapped and he loved the feel of it in his hands. The men held the line. Reggie ran downfield, looking up as David threw the ball easily, landing it perfectly in his hands. He ran right to the end zone, dancing victoriously to the delight of the fans. A rush of passion took over David's entire body as he shouted out in joy, body slamming his teammates.

The Still Small Voice

The locker room was pumped up, alive and energized. It was halftime with the score tied. Coaches reviewed plays and David collaborated with them, precisely the camaraderie that had been missing from David's career for years. No mention of the secondary team. Right now, the core group was defined.

Ready to charge, the team was back out for second half. Play was intense, with both teams scoring, making the game tied at 14. Now in the fourth quarter, their opponent kicked a field goal, advancing by three points with four minutes on the clock. David needed a touchdown to win.

On the line, David read the defense, wishing to call an audible but he still had to submit to the calls transmitted through the radio in his helmet. The ball was snapped to David but the defense rushed him—a blitz—and he was on the run, looking for Reggie. Man-on-man coverage, David couldn't throw to Reggie. He looked for Devon only to find him heavily covered too. David looked back over to Reggie. On the run, hesitating, not wanting to pass but did—intercepted! At least Cleveland was able to tackle them at Cleveland's thirty yard line preventing their opponent from getting a touchdown.

Beyond frustrated, moving to the sidelines, David yelled out furiously, slamming his helmet on the bench over and over until it ricocheted off, landing several feet away. No coach or teammate could tame his anger since he knew he shouldn't have thrown the ball. Now he wanted to be left alone. Sitting on the bench, he fell to thinking, "I'm weak out of the pocket. I can't do this. I just can't do this anymore."

And it was as if he heard God's voice say, "But I can."

Taken back, he couldn't breathe. It was the familiar voice. Or was it? Thinking he was crazy, he asked, "What?"

The small, still voice replied, "I can."

Confused, David said, "I'm not even sure what that means."

"Trust me."

"How?" David asked.

And then the question came, "Do you trust ME?"

He thought, hardly breathing, analyzing the question. This was the same voice that led him to contact his parents. The voice that led him to open up to Michael, Sharon, and Katherine. And the same voice that led him to Cleveland. "Yes, I trust you. But I'm not sure what that means and I'm not sure…"

The crowd's wild roar adverted David's attention to the field. Jordan had intercepted the ball and was now running toward David, who quickly found his helmet, for the change to offensive play.

"I know what your problem is!" Jordan said, slowing him down.

David ignored him, putting on his helmet, taking the field.

Grabbing his arm, Jordan stopped him. "You are like a high school boy that's looking to get laid."

"What?" David yelled, trying to loosen his friend's grasp.

Not letting go, he said, "You are so desperate to get laid that they can read it a mile away. You need to dance with them a little bit."

David had no time to respond as Jordan patted his backside. He reviewed the play with the offensive coordinator, working to clear his mind and understand the play call but still gripped by Jordan's words.

Rushing on the field, David was still lost in Jordan's words as he tried to fasten his helmet. Something was poking his ear. Since the play clock was winding down quickly, David reached inside and pulled out the transmitter hanging by its wire, throwing it over to the sidelines, indicating to the coaching staff he was without their voices.

In his heart, he heard, "Go off script."

He was in the huddle with no play to call, no transmitter, no timeouts, and time running out.

"Go off script," he heard again.

He shook his head slightly to clear it. What does that mean? Then he remembered Katherine teaching her Bible class and talking about being who God created her to be.

"Who wants the ball?" David asked.

"What?" many responded.

"Look, we have about twenty seconds before the snap. My radio is broken. Who wants the ball?"

"I want it!" Reggie called.

"I'll take it," Devon said on top of him.

"Reggie called it first."

"But he's an old man," Devon said, jesting him.

"Prove him wrong, Reggie." Then David refocused the huddle. "We have less than two minutes, no timeouts, and eighty yards to go. Let's get to the end zone. I believe we can do this!"

"You'll get the ball next," Reggie said to Devon as they took their positions.

Fired up, David called the play. On the line, he saw the defense, but this time it didn't matter since his hands weren't shackled and he was able to call an audible. He was free!

David counted down, the ball snapped, and the defense broke the line. David scrambled, remembering two words from Jordan: desperation and dancing. David immediately understood the defense had been reading his eyes. It was an easy read. Now that Collins was holding the line, it gave him more time in the pocket, but David showed all his cards. He was desperate and wasn't dancing with them the way he had in the past.

David looked over at Reggie, who was open, then to Devon, pump faking before whipping it across midfield to Reggie, who gained thirty yards but couldn't get out of bounds to stop the clock.

A quick huddle this time. "Devon, you're up!" David said, calling the play.

"It will look sweeter than Reggie's," Devon said, firing up the competition.

David felt like a kid again once the ball was snapped, enjoying taunting the defense. He was light on his toes, completing a pass to Devon for a twenty-five yard gain.

David huddled them up once more.

"You only got twenty-five yards," Reggie said, teasing Devon.

Devon patted Reggie on his helmet. "Yeah, but I got out of bounds and stopped the clock."

"Give me that ball!" Reggie said.

"No, they'll see it coming. Let's give the big lug a chance." David smiled mischievously.

As replacement players joined the field, David thought for sure the coaches would change his game plan, so David asked, "What do they want me to run?"

"Nothing. You are doing well on your own."

"Let's go!" David shouted.

On line, the ball snapped, and David pump-faked, handing it off to Eddie, who gained another first down. The sold-out stadium was on their feet, screaming and barking. Fifteen seconds remained to get a touchdown.

David had only one thing to say in this huddle. "End zone! Get open in the end zone! I want in that end zone!"

David couldn't remember the last time he'd thrown a touchdown pass in the end zone. It had to be years and he determined he was going to do so. He waved his hands up, firing up the crowd even more. It was deafening now, completely deafening.

Ball snapped, line held, with plenty of time to throw but no one open. It was man-on-man coverage in the end zone. Tackles were broken and David had to scramble out of the pocket, freeing up Reggie ever so slightly, and David knew now was the time. He threw a beautiful spiral as Reggie jumped in the air with all his glory, catching a perfectly thrown ball for a winning touchdown.

Everyone—fans, players, coaches—screamed for joy as David silently thanked God. He didn't understand but somehow knew God had taken care of the win.

Immediately, music played as Reggie and Devon danced in the end zone. David jumped into the adoring fans, then went over to his teammates, dancing with them. It was so captivating that Jordan danced on the sidelines with the cameras capturing the party in Cleveland.

Leaving the field, David tapped the kicker, shouting. "Go do what you were created to do!"

Even though a field goal wasn't needed, Cleveland's kicker made the extra point, doing what he was indeed created to do.

Chapter 46

The Ultimate Flame

The locker room celebration seemed more like a playoff victory than a last preseason win. But this happy family knew the missing elements were all accounted for, including their fierce leader who seemed much more equipped to shepherd his team than when David was the starting quarterback in Florida.

Congratulating, Collins said, "Great game, man!"

"Hey, I couldn't have done it without you!" David replied.

The coaches gave praise all around. They privately spoke with David, allowing freedom to call audibles whenever he wanted.

In the shower, alone with this thoughts, David, in his own way, spoke to God. "Thank you. I don't understand You, but I want to get to know You better. I'm afraid but if you will go slowly with me, I will learn."

He heard words reassuring to his heart "I know, that's how I created you."

His eyes filled with tears and a flame was lit for God.

The Celebration

David stepped up to the cameras, wearing a dark blue suit, baby blue dress shirt, and a beautiful, sophisticated silver tie. He'd arrived.

"How did you feel out there today?" a reporter asked.

"Incredible! What an incredible feeling! These fans are awesome!"

"You were upset after the interception, throwing your helmet. Then you were messing with it on the field. What happened to it?" another reporter asked.

"I broke the radio." He blushed. "I had to rip it out."

"You seemed confident calling plays," a reporter called from another section of the room.

"You know, I didn't feel as shackled, but we are a team. I will lead this team working with the coaches. And I'm thankful for that."

Another question came. "This is your first win, if you want to call it that since it's the final preseason game using secondary unit and third string guys. Do you think you will continue winning?"

"I just want to enjoy today's victory," David stated. "Tomorrow I will concentrate on the home opener. But I will tell you this, I think each of us was designed specifically for this team and I think together we can achieve greatness."

"Define greatness," a reporter asked.

"Let it define us," David responded.

"What did Jordan tell you after he intercepted the ball?" a reporter shouted out.

Turning red, grinning brightly, David put down his head, saying, "There are just some things that need to remain between friends."

Seeing his reaction, they pressed him but David wouldn't budge. That was between him and Jordan. No one would understand their communication, and David wasn't even too sure he understood it either.

The media asked many questions and he answered them brilliantly. David realized this group, these journalists, were created to do their jobs. Some did it flawlessly. Others went the cheap route to get noticed, but he was fine with them, almost feeling a bond since he was guilty of foolishly argumentative and provoking behaviors himself. All he wanted was to concentrate on making amends and creating a better working relationship with the press.

"What was with the dance?" another reporter asked.

With his boyish charm, he smiled. "I just felt like dancing."

They laughed as David exited the podium to hugs and kisses from his teammates and the family. Katherine was the only one to give a quick hug but he gladly accepted it. It was their first hug, and she felt like she was created to fit perfectly in his arms.

Along with Jordan, the family celebrated with David and Reggie's family. Remaining so long they closed the restaurant, the group toasted with champagne, ate the best steaks, and savored the to-die-for desserts. It was a beautiful night, one David didn't want to come to an end. But still, the time came for everyone to say goodbye.

David went home too excited for bed. Besides, he'd forgotten his custodial team had removed all the furniture from his condo. He had absolutely nothing to sleep on but it didn't matter. He wanted to go to one place tonight and that was down by the pier. Grabbing his Bible, a blanket, and pillow, he went down to the place he felt closest to God. There he wept out of joy and thankfulness.

The Book

David woke to a gentle breeze and the sound of lazy waves hitting the shore. He loved the sound, lying for some time enjoying the moment. Surprisingly, he wasn't sore from sleeping on a bench all night. His rest had been deep and refreshing, and he rose with a thankful spirit.

Desiring to prolong his enjoyment of the peaceful morning on the pier, he opened his Bible to continue reading since he had plenty of time before he had to attend the day's light training session. He couldn't get enough of the book. There was much he didn't understand, but nonetheless it was mesmerizing.

Practice went well, the players continuing to bond as a team. David ate lunch with the coaches, going through film for the home opener. Next, it was time to get ready for his shopping trip with Katherine, and his heart raced with excitement. He slipped the peacock blue velvet blazer onto his broad shoulders, loving that Katherine had hand selected it for him. Getting a glimpse of himself in the mirror, he admired his reflection, not conceited, but pleased that Katherine knew how to bring the best out in him. Strolling to the valet, he thanked the staff for bringing his dark cherry Corvette to his feet.

He was always fond of his Vett. It was the first thing he'd purchased once drafted, a gift to himself. He had wanted a Corvette since he had learned how to drive. Recently, he'd hardly ever drove it, but today he had the urge, loving the powerful feel of the machine. Considering where he was going to, it was going to be more than a great ride.

The House

Pulling up to Katherine's home, its appearance surprised him. For sure, David thought her home would be a smaller version of her parent's mansion but it was far cry from that. It wasn't dated or dumpy but it wasn't the type of house he pictured her living in. It didn't seem to resemble her personality, or at least what he thought was her true self. Lightly taking the steps, he smiled after ringing the doorbell, hearing her high heels as she walked to the door. His heart raced upon seeing her again when she opened it wide.

"Hello!" Katherine greeted. "Oh, I love your outfit! I'm so glad you got it. Do you like it?"

"Yes, very much. Thanks for picking it out for me."

Smiling, she said, "Come on in, I just need to grab my purse and then we can go."

David walked in, looked around, exclaiming, "Now this is you."

Confused, Katherine asked, "What do you mean?"

"The exterior is nice, but it doesn't seem to reflect your tastes. This is exactly what I expected. It has your personality, that timeless, classic, and fresh look, like how you dress. Your office has this same feel," David explained.

"Well," Katherine looked away, taking a deep breath, "this was James's home before we got married."

David feared he may have said something wrong. "Oh, I'm sorry. I didn't know," he said contritely.

"That's okay, how would you know? " she said without concern. "Come on. Let me show you around."

Katherine took him through each room of the 2,400 square foot colonial which was impeccably dressed. It had the best furnishings, drapery, and lighting, and the rear views overlooked a beautifully landscaped pond. That was the highlight feature.

The last room they entered was the master bedroom and it didn't match the rest of the house. There was a mattress with no headboard, a single bedside table, no dresser or TV, and no drapes. It felt devoid of warmth and life. It couldn't be finished.

"Looks like you are in the process of redesigning this room. What are you thinking about doing with it?" David asked.

"Oh, no, I'm not redesigning. When I came back home after living with my parents, I just couldn't bear sleeping in our shared bed, so that was the first thing to go. As you probably can understand, I just wanted something to sleep on, so I only got a bed frame."

Blushing, he said, "Boy, aren't you glad I came over here today? First, I ripped on the outside of the house and now the bedroom. Again, I'm sorry."

"Really, it's okay. I have been thinking about updating this room for a while, but I've finally decided that it's time to move."

"Really? Where are you looking at moving?"

"I'm not too sure yet." She looked around the master, taking a breath, then said, "I'm going to wait until after the season and then begin that whole process."

Seeing her ever-present grin slip to worry and a slight fear cloud her usual bright eyes, he asked, "Are you sure you are ready to move? You seem unsure."

Katherine forced a slight chuckle to help ease her sadness. "I've known for some time, but I guess I just don't want to let go. This is the last thing we had together." Shaking her head, she said. "Wow, this is a pretty deep conversation. You must be really looking forward to spending time with me today to still be standing here."

"Hey, you don't have to do that."

"Do what?" she asked with her enormous, dark brown, innocent eyes.

"Laugh off your feelings. This has to be a very difficult decision for you to make," David said with heartfelt emotion.

Feeling sad, she nodded.

"That must be James," he pointed, walking over to the photos sitting on the one bedside table.

"Yes. Obviously both from our wedding day. They are my favorite."

"He was a handsome man. You can see you really loved one another," he said, looking at a picture of the two gazing deeply into each other's eyes.

"Yeah," she said sadly, then blew on the photo, wiping the dust from the frame.

"Do you have any other pictures?" he asked.

"Not here. I put everything in storage and just kept those out. I thought they best reflected us," she said as they looked at another picture of James and her dancing and smiling.

David looked at her lovingly, saying, "I'm sure you miss him."

She grinned, having no desire to talk about James ever again, asking, "Do you want to see my closet?"

He could see the sadness in her eyes and her need to change the subject. "Absolutely," he said with enthusiasm.

She led him to the master walk-in closet, complete with an island and stunning dressing area. The whole space was decked out superbly, nothing out of place. It was like he was standing in the finest upscale boutique. A crystal chandelier, matching scones, thick crown molding, specialty glazed painted ceiling and wall coverings combined to highlight the magnificent cabinetry and floor-to-ceiling LED-lit shoe towers. "Kenneth must have done this for you."

"Actually, no. He had his input but it was my vision," she replied with satisfaction, then quickly thanked God for giving her the ability to have creativity.

"I want an island in my closet," he announced, touring hers and admiring her clothes.

"Well, we can do that. You would even get the money back after you sell."

"That's you, always looking at the bottom line. You are just like your dad," David laughed.

"I know." She laughed with him.

Picking up a black velvet high heel, he said with sincere admiration, "You have the most magnificent shoes."

"I know, I have too many, but they just make such a statement," she said, looking at the camel loafers David was wearing that she'd picked out.

"You definitely have good taste." He looked at her lovingly for he enjoyed how much she cared for what she was given.

She smiled, feeling a little uncomfortable, then asked. "Are you ready to go?"

"Yep, looking forward to it."

As they walked out of the house and she saw his car in the driveway, Katherine lit up. "A Corvette! I love it. I didn't know you had this car."

"I hardly ever drive it." He blushed before saying, "I love it too. It has a special place in my heart. I got it as a gift to myself when I signed on with Miami. It has special memories."

"I can imagine," she replied.

Now it was David's turn to watch her blush as he opened her door, enjoying treating her like a lady. "Okay, where are we headed?"

"Well, the furniture store I'd like to take you to is about thirty minutes away. Is that okay?"

"Yes, of course," he replied, knowing her concern about other people's feelings. He didn't want her to feel that way ever with him.

Chapter 48

The Experience

They rode with some light music on in the background, talking endlessly about his press conferences and the win. They laughed often, and before they knew it, they were at the furniture store. This wasn't a big box, national chain shop. Even with the little time David had been in Cleveland, he'd heard this particular store was the only place for those with distinguishing taste. It offered custom pieces and exceptional quality, serving mainly the high-end client.

"This must be a nice place. They have valet parking," David said.

"Oh, yeah, I guess they do. I've never noticed," she replied as the valet opened her door.

Walking over to her side, he asked. "You've never used the valet before?"

"Not here, there's no real reason. The parking lot is right over there."

"Interesting. I guess I'm used to valet since all the teams have it. It must be one of those little luxuries in life that I enjoy," David said.

Katherine nodded, silently agreeing. She enjoyed someone opening her door, helping her out. It was classy.

Katherine greeted the receptionist. "Hi Tina. Is Mr. Payne in?"

"No, he is scheduled to arrive in just a bit," she replied kindly.

"Thank you. We'll look around a bit. Will you please let him know I'm here when he arrives?"

"Certainly," Tina said.

Walking into the expansive showroom, David joked. "I'm surprised Mr. Payne is not here yet. Didn't you call and let him know we were coming today?

"Of course I did." She smiled since she enjoyed his playfulness. "This is a different type of experience than Kenneth and Philip. Kenneth brings items that best suit his clients and Philip figures out the most flattering hair style. With furniture, it's all about the look and feel. I need to walk around and figure out what best suits me, or in this case you. Mr. Payne knows that about me, so I told him approximately what time we would arrive and not to rush in to meet us."

Leaning in close, he whispered, "Is Mr. Payne gay?"

"No," she said with a little smile. "I think you will like him. He's from England."

"Sounds good. Let's go pick out a bed!" he said, clasping his hands together.

"We can, but I think we should start right here first." She pointed at foyer tables.

"What? How boring."

"We could go right to the bedroom furniture, but as you can see, this is a large showroom. It's clever how they designed the floor, beginning with the entrance of the home. The bedroom sets are located all the way in the back of the store."

"But that doesn't make any sense. You spend most of your time in the bedroom....ah, sleeping…you know…getting eight hours of sleep a night," David said, keeping things from the gutter.

"Okay, first off, you have been sleeping on your couch for how many years? And second, not everyone gets that much sleep," she said.

"You don't sleep eight hours a night?"

They were interrupted before Katherine could shoot back a response. "Can I help you find anything?" Debbie, a blond bombshell of a saleswoman asked David, leaning in closely to him and ignoring Katherine.

"No. We will be working with Mr. Payne," he replied flushed since she was invading his personal space.

"Well, since he's not here, let me know if I can help you with anything. I'll be hanging around, just in case you need me." Debbie said, licking her big, pouty lips before walking away.

Katherine chuckled, watching her hit on him so obviously.

"What are you laughing about?" David asked.

"Nothing. Okay, here's what I'm thinking," Katherine said.

"I'm listening," he snickered.

"As you walk into your home, the first thing you see is the foyer. It's the first impression. Then the formal dining room, living room, and the office before even making it to the bedroom. If you want, we can start off there, but since it's the last room in the house, it makes more sense to start here first."

David, feeling cocky since Debbie had flirted with him said, "But all this other stuff is boring. The master bedroom is truly where you want to be anyway."

"Fine, let's start there," she sighed. "It's just I believe you are setting up your place with the anticipation of seeing the master. Think about it, when you saw my house, you seemed genuinely interested in my choices and asked me about several pieces of furniture and artwork. When we finally got to my bedroom, you had a certain expectation but were disappointed. You actually thought I was redesigning my bedroom. The first part of the home sets up the bedroom experience."

David smiled since he wasn't sure if she was being her typical analytical self or being somewhat suggestive.

Realizing she may have gotten off track, she blushed. "Well, I guess in my opinion it does."

"I see your point," he understood.

"On second thought, it probably makes sense for us to start in that direction," she said, pointing to the bedroom section.

"Okay, okay, I get it. Come on, let's just start here," he replied.

"Are you sure? We can go to the back of the store. I feel like I'm being too pushy."

"No. You're right." He rolled his eyes. "Let's look at these tables."

The Entry

Given the go ahead, Katherine warmed up to the job. First step was to give David an education on furniture basics. "Okay, quickly, these are traditional pieces that will never go out of style. Then you have antiques. Some more modern pieces are displayed over there and some transitional ones are back there." Katherine pointed at each section, directing David's view.

"Well, I definitely don't like these or those over there." David pointed to the antiques and modern tables. "I sort of like these, but they seem a little boring," he said, examining the traditional ones. "But this is really nice," he said, viewing a gold leaf table with drawers. " He turned to a solid exotic wood piece. "And I like this one too."

"They really are both nice," she agreed, looking at each one, opening the drawers and doors. "This is the first statement you will make when someone walks into your condo, so you have to ask yourself what you want to say," Katherine said, romanticizing the furniture.

David considered her comment, wondering what he wanted to convey regarding his home. Even in Florida he hadn't put any thought in his waterfront house since he mainly spent all his time at practice and training.

She pointed to the gold leaf table. "This one is classy, elegant, and timeless. The exotic wood one is edgy and stylish but still timeless."

David analyzed the tables, saying, "Too bad we can't combine both of them."

"Actually…." Katherine grabbed her phone, flipping through the photos, then showed one to David. "Your foyer is spectacular. I love the height of the ceiling and the chandelier is so classy."

David smiled and was delighted she had prepared, taking photos of his home to help them find the perfect furnishings. He would have never thought of doing that.

Wondering why he was looking at her with a smile, she asked, "What?"

"It's just so you to do this."

Returning her attention to the pictures, she said. "I know, I'm pathetic."

"No, it's smart," he replied.

She grinned, then pointed. "The chandelier has polished and matte gold and silver tones. It's absolutely exquisite."

"I know," he replied, touching her arm. He felt her tense up slightly but not as much as in the past. "So I say we go with gold leaf table."

"We can, but I'm thinking this wood piece may be the one."

"How come?" David asked.

"Well, you have these fabulous travertine ivory tiles. I think it would blend too much. You need a contrast. That's why black and white looks so good together."

"I see what you are saying. I think the gold leaf table would be too formal, then, maybe stuffy," he said.

"Well, for the foyer, yes, but maybe not for somewhere else in your condo. It is a great-looking piece." Katherine admired it. "You have enough room to flank both sides of your front door. We can get some pretty large scale mirrors to hang above them and reflect the chandelier."

David watched her excitement, treasuring how no matter what she did, she did it from her heart and enjoyed life.

"And these lamps would be perfect to place on either ends of the two tables. And we may want to think about getting a rug, but let's just keep looking for now. We've just set the tone of the home!" she announced, not even attempting to hide her enthusiasm for the high-end, elegant setting that somehow had this edgy, sexy, romantic feel that seemed to capture David perfectly.

David smiled, thoroughly enjoying her vision. His heart raced at the thought of creating the rest of his home with Katherine since she had the ability to make him feel no less than royalty.

Suddenly, her bright-eyed personality turned sullen. "I'm sorry. This is your home. Please control me." She hung her head in an effort to curb her enthusiasm.

"No, this is perfect! Now I understand why you don't need a salesperson to help you," he replied.

Together they looked at lamps and mirrors to ensure they were on the same track.

"Katherine, I love both of these mirrors. What do you think?"

"Well, I like them both too. This beveled mirror has such clean lines. I love that look." She pointed to the mirror hung next to it. "But this one has the look of the gold leaf table and would match the chandelier."

"It's like I need to see it all together to decide," he said.

"Well, we can do that. We can have both pieces delivered. You know, put it all together and bring back whichever you don't want," she replied.

"Have you done that before?"

"All the time," she smiled. "It used to drive James crazy."

"How come?"

"He didn't understand why I brought home so much stuff and returned most of it. He thought it was a waste of my time," she said. "But eventually he understood it was my hobby."

Falling in love with her design ascetic, he said, "I can see how someone can enjoy this. You are creating an environment and want to create a certain mood."

"Exactly! Now do you understand why I wanted to start here?" she teased.

"Yes, yes. Can we move on?" he joked.

"Absolutely. What's next?" she asked, pointing to the living and dining furniture. "You decide."

"I say the dining room."

"Sounds great," she replied, leaving him to follow as she walked around the enormous formal dining selections.

The Setting

"Here's my thing," David said after about fifteen minutes of examining dining room pieces, "All these tables look alike. They are either dark wood that's too stuffy or so light they look country. The fabric too is pretty much ivory and boring."

"Well, you can put a pool table in the dining room. I've seen that before," Katherine replied.

"What?" David asked, surprised.

"Seriously, it's not a bad look. I've seen it. And if you pick out the right table, it looks really stylish."

"I'm not sure about that," David replied.

"Well, think of it this way. What goes in your dining room is what you are saying about yourself. So far you told me you aren't stuffy or boring. You can have that whole cool bachelor pad going on with the pool table," Katherine said.

"I'm not sure I'm that type of guy," he said.

"Oh, I thought with the Corvette, you might want to go down that road."

"What?" David said, thrown back by her comment.

"No, I didn't mean that. It's just that usually a person with a car like that is looking for attention."

"Wait a minute, what?" David asked smiling ear-to-ear with his eyes dancing since he loved their conversations.

"I'm sorry, I didn't mean that either. I actually really love Corvettes, but it does translate bachelor. And that's okay. You are a bachelor and we can make your place reflect that lifestyle." She grinned, stating the obvious.

Enjoying her company and the way she looked at life, he pulled her along, saying, "Let's just keeping looking around."

They continued through a maze of quite a few tables with nothing standing out until David spotted something. "What about this?" He tapped on a magnificent, handcrafted table that looked to be created by a skilled craftsman that was taught by many generations. Regal, elegant, fit for a king, it would look stately sitting in his gorgeous formal dining room underneath the grand chandelier, beckoning guests to linger in the comfort of the oversized, upholstered chairs.

She tilted her head and said inquisitively, "Really? I would have never picked this out for you."

"How come?" he asked confused. He thought it would be perfect in his dining room.

"Well, for one it seats fourteen people," she stated plainly.

"You think it's too big for the room? It looks like it comes with removable things. What are they called?" he asked.

"Leaves," she replied.

"Leaves. Look, it comes with two, so taking them out will make it smaller to fit in the room."

"Well, don't you think something like that over there is a little more fitting for your place?" She pointed to a smaller scale, intimate table suited for romantic meals.

Questioning her choice, he asked. "How come you don't think this one would work in my place?"

"I mean the color is just beautiful, it's actually quite remarkable, but this is something I can see in my parents' home," she said.

David understood. She didn't see him as a family man and, truth be told, he really didn't know if he was one himself.

"I see your point. Well, I can get that over there you are suggesting, which is nice, but to me a table isn't something that you buy very often. So I look at this as an investment. It has that classic design you always talk about, so I don't see it going out of style. And it would fit into any home environment, don't you think?" David asked.

"Yes." She chuckled. "You sound like my dad."

Laughing too, he said, "Don't tell him that." Getting back to business, David sat down at the table of his choice, making certain he was comfortable. "I don't like the material on the chairs."

"That's okay, we can get whatever you like." Katherine showed him several books of swatches. "And if you don't like these, we can go look for something at a fabric store."

Hearing her say "we," David was thrilled that she was thinking about spending time with him in the future.

Flipping through one of the books, he said, "I don't even know where to start."

"Well, let's get the living room colors picked out first and then we can determine these colors."

"Great idea, Katherine. You don't know what it means to have a partner like you."

Chapter 49

The Fake

With a new mission, David and Katherine trekked to another section of the floor. As they walked toward the living room furniture, Debbie approached David again, ignoring Katherine as before. "See anything you like? Anything I can help you with?" she crooned.

"No, I'm good. She's helping me," David said, pointing to Katherine.

"Well, if you need a different opinion, I'll be waiting over there," Debbie cooed. Her words were laced with suggestion, and with that she turned and walked away seductively, looking back over her shoulder to make sure David understood her intent.

Katherine was looking at living room furniture, her back to Debbie, although she didn't need to be facing her to know that Debbie was making her attraction apparent to David. In fact, anyone could clearly see this woman desired David. It made Katherine chuckle as she looked at sofas.

Coming up behind her, David asked. "What are you laughing about?"

"You are going to need to beat her off with a bat."

David smiled. "You should talk. Men constantly hit on you."

"Well, you better get used to it. It's going to be happening all the time."

David eyes popped wide. "Wow, you are pretty confident in yourself."

"I was talking about you. Plenty of women will be throwing themselves at you."

"Oh, yeah. I know," he thought out loud.

She flashed a clever smile. "Now who's confident?"

"I actually didn't mean it like that. It happened all the time when I started. It's just been a long time since women have given me that type of attention, so I'm thrown off a bit," he confessed.

Katherine noticed a nearby nice-looking sofa. Sitting down, she asked. "What about this one?"

He sat down next to her.

"So how did you feel now getting all this attention?" she asked shyly.

"I don't like it," David said.

"The sofa or the attention?" Katherine asked, looking at him for clarification.

"The sofa." David laughed. "The attention is okay. I'm mean, who wouldn't enjoy getting attention?"

"It depends upon the attention," Katherine said, sitting on another sofa, then asking, "Do you like this one?"

She was working while they talked, looking for the perfect sofa, but David was more interested in their conversation, following her around, sitting on any couches she sat on.

"Well, really, what kind of attention is bad attention?" he asked, though he answered the question before Katherine. "I know, I know. I'm not talking about the type of attention I got from the media before."

"Well, I don't like when a guy hits on me even before he knows me. I think it's telling of his personality," she said, not looking at David while moving to the next sofa.

"How so?" At this point he couldn't care less about furniture, although he continued to sit with her as she couch hopped.

"It tells me he's shallow. He doesn't know my character or personality. He only cares about the exterior," she replied.

"Well, how is he supposed to get to know your character and personality if you don't go on a date with him?" David asked.

"I don't know, those things just tend to work themselves out. I think if you can study a person from a distance, you start to understand who they really are. In a formal date setting, you can make up anything."

"Fake. Someone can be fake on a date, you mean" David said, sitting on another sofa as he watched Katherine look through fabric samples. She was multi-tasking, not even looking at him. And he was really interested in the conversation.

"Yes, that's a good word for it," she agreed.

"Yeah, but what about if you met some guy in this place right now and you found him attractive. Wouldn't you want to go out with him?"

"No."

"Hold on, wait a minute. I know you aren't dating, but let's say you are. Why wouldn't you want to go out with him?" David asked seriously.

"Because if he's asking me out, then he's done it before, and he'll ask out other women in the same manner. It means I'm not special," she said matter-of-fact.

"What?" David said louder than intended, completely immersed into their conversation and somewhat forgetting their surroundings.

Looking at him, smiling, Katherine said, "How in the world do we always get into these types of conversations?"

"Because you set the precedence to always be honest and I know if I ask you a question, you will be honest with me." He smiled.

"Oh, so you're blaming me?" Katherine replied with her unknowingly sexy grin.

"Yes, it's all your fault." Sitting at the edge of the sofa, he returned to the earlier part of their conversation. "So tell me what you mean by that?"

"Do you like this couch?" she asked as if she hadn't heard him.

"It's okay."

She got up and walked around while David followed. "I'm sure you have been in plenty of bars, right?"

Proudly, he replied, "Yes!"

"Well, I've gone in some too…because I like to dance," she added.

David remembered her dancing, knowing it was true.

"Well, guys would ask for my number and I'd say no. Some would give me their number and I would see these same guys hit on other women a little later. So I knew if they were asking for my phone number and then were asking for any woman's number, well, I would be just another notch in their belt. It turned me off."

"Yeah, but this is a furniture store." He swung his arm wide.

Katherine stopped what she was doing and made direct eye contact. "I know I'm weird, but it just doesn't make me feel special."

"Yeah, but what if you are passing up the person you are supposed to spend the rest of your life with?" he pressed.

"I think if God had a person in mind for me, He would move heaven and hell to ensure that I would know him before I went on a date with him."

Thinking out loud, David mused, "Oh, so that's what's going on with you and Timmy."

Katherine buried her eyebrows wondering what he was talking about.

"You are getting to know him first so that you can determine if you two should be dating," David said flatly.

"What is with you and Timmy…I mean Tim?"

"Nothing," David said defensively.

"Then why do you keep asking me about him?" she said point-blank.

"Because you've never answered the question," he reminded.

Katherine flashed her unknowingly sexy grin, then walked away.

"See, you still won't answer the question," David said, fired up, following her.

Katherine wouldn't answer him.

"You are not being honest," he teased.

Smiling, talking out of the side of her mouth, she called back, "How can I not be honest when I haven't said anything at all? You are guessing."

Not hiding his curiosity, David kept at it. "Come on, tell me about you two! What is going on?"

Katherine walked away again, still looking for the perfect sofa. "Nothing is going on. I think I may have already told you that."

"I don't believe it," he said. "You two make the perfect couple."

Katherine shook her head at their conversation.

"I mean, you both talk about God. He's good looking and so are you. You actually match quite well together. It would only make sense for the two of you to be a couple."

"What about this one?" she asked, sitting down.

"It's okay," he replied somewhat bummed.

"Yeah, I'm not too thrilled with it either."

"That's it! He's boring!" David proclaimed happily.

"What are you talking about now?" Katherine smiled brightly, getting a kick out of David's antics.

His smile of pride reached all the way to his eyes. "Timmy! Timmy is boring!"

"Oh, my gosh. What is with you? He's extremely nice and quite a gentleman."

"Okay, so you admit you have been out on a date with him. And nice equals boring," he said.

"I'm nice and I can assure you I'm not boring," she replied.

Pondering, David said, "Then he's fake. That's it, he's fake!"

"What? He's not fake," she chuckled.

"Then you are fake. You are faking it with him," David announced, happily.

"What? What are you talking about?"

"You are leading him on," he declared.

Katherine laughed over David's comical remarks. "Are you on something?"

"No, I just figure you out!"

"Alright, easy, tiger. Relax." Katherine soothed. But her next words immediately captured his attention. "I'm not leading Tim on. And I'm not fake. And I'm not faking anything with him. Okay?" she said, looking David directly in the eyes to still him.

He was so captivated by her calling him a tiger that he no longer wanted to talk about Tim.

The Intimacy

Katherine and David moved from couch to couch, the realm of possibilities seemingly endless. Thinking while they shopped, he said, "You know, I never understood why anyone would be fake anyway."

"I don't know either," Katherine replied, surprising David with her agreement.

"I know I was a prick to the media, and even to you," he admitted ashamedly, "but one thing you can never say about me is that I was fake. I was real to the core."

"Yes, that, without a doubt, is true about you," Katherine said, looking intently at a beautiful, dark blue and gray velvet sectional. It screamed class.

"You've never been fake with me either," David realized.

"No, not once," Katherine said, checking her measurements to see if the couch would fit in his living room.

"I've always really appreciated that about you."

"Well, that's because you've allowed me that freedom. You allow me to be real with you," she said, testing to see if the couch cushions felt as luxurious as they looked.

"What do you mean?" David asked, watching her on the couch.

Katherine answered without looking at him, lifting the cushions, checking out their construction and durability. "You didn't like when I was professional with you. It's like you would get, I don't know, bored or restless, or maybe even resentful."

"Yeah, but that's because you basically laid the truth on me the second day we met, you know, with Trino there. And I knew that was the real you," David said, now looking at the sofa and seeing its potential.

Pausing long enough to recall the memory, Katherine chuckled, saying, "Yeah, I guess I was pretty bold with you."

"Please don't ever change that," he said.

"Change what?" Katherine asked, placing a cushion back in place.

"Always be real and never fake with me," he asked.

Not looking at him, sitting back on the couch, she said, "Oh, I can assure you I would never fake it with you."

David's mouth dropped open and he wondered if Katherine understood where their conversation had gone. He could clearly see she was in work mode, determining if the sofa would suit his home. Pressing her a bit, he asked "I wonder why someone would do that?"

Standing up, she said, "Something is missing."

Since she wasn't looking at him, he wasn't sure if Katherine was talking about the sofa or if she was answering his initial question. He went back to that topic. "Maybe it is insecurity. Maybe they believe that no one would love their true selves without faking it, which is sad," David said, standing in front of the sectional, looking at it, loving the exquisite velvety texture.

"Maybe," Katherine said while walking to another sectional.

"Maybe they want it to be over as quickly as possible because it's more of an obligation," David said as he sat on the blue-gray couch Katherine had just left, getting comfortable.

"Could be," she said, looking at a price tag on the new sectional she was viewing.

And then David got deep in his thinking. Leaning back, placing his arm over the back of the sofa, he said, "Maybe they are truly afraid of the intimacy and would rather run away from it than face their fear."

"That's exactly it!" Katherine announced excitedly, seeing him sitting on the couch.

David smiled, pleased with her approval, but again not completely sure if it was over the conversation or the furniture.

"That's exactly what was missing!" Katherine announced. "Oh, I've got to get Mr. Payne, " she said, hurrying out of the section of couches. Then she stopped midway, turning around embarrassed. "I'm sorry, David, I didn't ask you. Do you like the sofa?"

He delightfully chuckled at her concern. "Yes, it's completely me." As Katherine left, he couldn't help but think of how much he adored her. He loved their conversations and how well they worked together.

The Common

"You look great on that couch. You make it look real sexy," Debbie said, her purr as thick as a cat's.

"Oh, yeah? We like it too," David said, caught off guard by Debbie having inserted herself next to him while he wasn't looking.

"What else are you looking for?" she asked, sitting close beside him. "I'm sure I can help you with what you need."

Instantly on his feet, flustered, David said, "Just considering a bunch of furniture today. Um, I don't mean to be rude, but I need to follow her."

Leaving to look for Katherine, David realized just how uncomfortable he felt with Debbie throwing herself at him. Katherine had opened his eyes yet again just by being herself.

Chapter 50

The Expectation

Finally, when they caught up to one another, Katherine apologized. "Sorry, I took so long. It's a big store and a long walk. Mr. Payne's still not here. I didn't mean for our shopping to take up so much of your day."

Relieved to see her, David said, "Not a problem at all. I'm in no hurry. I'm enjoying this whole process."

Together, they found magnificent pieces for the living room and office, including a console for the TV and his audio electronics. David wanted the fireplace to be the focal point of the living room and to build a warm, manly, sort of sexy palette. He wanted inviting and classy.

"Okay, last stop. Here you go. Go select your bed," Katherine said, happy David would finally be sleeping on an actual bed.

They stood in front of two smaller showrooms, one filled with only mattresses and another with bedroom furniture. Katherine found it interesting that David went to the mattress section first. She followed as he walked around the aisles of white beds.

He lay on a king size mattress that caught his attention. "This one is nice. What do you think?"

"Um, I'm sure it's nice. As long as you like it, that is what's important," she said, guarded.

He noticed she had stiffed her posture. "Well, come on and try it," David encouraged, patting the white mattress.

"It really doesn't matter to me how it feels. You're the one who's going to be sleeping on it, not me."

"Come on, don't you want to get into bed with me?" David asked, winking at her.

Closing her eyes, a look of disgust took over. "No."

David didn't like the look and took it on as a challenge. "Well, would it help if I took off my jacket?" he asked, removing it.

Raising her eyebrows, then closing her eyes again, Katherine shook her head.

"I can take off my shirt. I'm sure that would work," he teased as he unbuttoned a button, revealing a portion of his chest.

She stated dead serious, "Nasty."

Now he was agitated. "What is with you? It's only a mattress."

Sort of chuckling, she said. "I would rather not."

Burrowing his eyebrows in conquest, he asked. "Why not?"

Attempting to laugh to lighten the mood, she said, "I just don't feel comfortable."

Annoyed, he demanded, "Why?"

"It's really not that big of a deal. I just don't want to." She said stone faced, not budging from her decision.

That upset him. "I know it's not that big of deal, that's why I'm asking you to get into bed with me!"

"This is turning into a big deal when it shouldn't, so let me try to explain it this way. We work together. I'm your manager. I just don't feel comfortable. It would make me feel uncomfortable. I'm sorry, I don't know of any other way how to explain that to you."

"I think you are acting childish."

Katherine shrugged it off.

Looking around, he spotted the blonde, pointing. "I bet she'll get into bed with me. You better hop in here before I ask her."

"Here, I'll do one better for you," Katherine said, walking away to get David exactly what he was asking for.

David watched, confused, as Katherine called the saleswoman over for help. "Hi, Debbie is it?" she asked politely.

"Yes, it's Debbie," she replied, looking at David.

"Debbie, David could use your help. You see, I work with him and I don't feel comfortable getting on that mattress with him. I know it sounds ridiculous, but it just makes me feel a little…"

Ignoring Katherine, Debbie crawled onto the bed next to David almost before she said, "It would be my pleasure."

"Thank you, Debbie. I knew you would be accommodating," Katherine said sweetly, making her point. She looked at David, whose mouth was open. "I will be over there. I saw a lamp that may work nicely in my office."

He watched her walk away.

"What position would you like to try?" Debbie asked.

David immediately stood up, seeing Katherine study a lamp, not remotely caring about him.

"Don't you want to get into bed with me?" Debbie suggested.

David looked at her laying on the white mattress with her cleavage pouring out of her dress, which was so short you practically could see all the way up. Her eyes oozed sexual intent, a look he had seen thousands of times but had long forgotten during his dark days. Now cleaned up, that look was all he'd been seeing, but never from Katherine.

He understood Katherine's disgust in an instant. Walking away from Debbie on the bed, he called, "Katherine."

Not looking at him, she answered. "Yes? Did you find what you were looking for?"

"Yes, and it wasn't that," David replied.

"Okay, well, there are plenty of mattresses. I'm sure you will find one," she replied flatly.

"Katherine, look at me."

Surprised by his request, she did. "Yes."

"I'm so sorry. I shouldn't have treated you like that." Taking hold of her hands, looking intensely in her eyes, he said, "I know I hurt your feelings. You clearly were telling me the truth. You didn't feel comfortable and I disregarded how you felt. I'm sorry."

Never breaking eye contact, she said, "Look, David, you're right. It was childish. I can't explain it, I just didn't feel comfortable testing that mattress with you."

"No, you weren't being childish. I was. I was taking a joke and going too far with it and I'm sorry."

"You don't need to apologize anymore. I forgive you. It's alright," she said. "Listen, our conversations tend to get on the deeper, more intense side. Maybe I'm…we shouldn't…"

Interrupting, David said, "Please, I won't even consider that. If we stop having those deep conversations, then we'll stop being us." Feeling her tense, he slowly let go of her hands. "I've never had a working relationship with a woman, so I'm not sure how this all works."

"I understand." In truth, she didn't want them to stop having their deep talks either and she also had never worked this closely to a man and wasn't sure what was normal.

Debbie approached them, holding out a card. "David, here is my card with my home and cell number on it. Feel free to call anytime."

"I'm not interested. We are waiting for Mr. Payne," David replied, never taking his eyes off Katherine.

Katherine blushed as Debbie had no choice but to walk away.

"Please, don't you ever do that again, " he said.

"Do what?" Katherine asked.

"Go and get some woman to take your place."

"Then don't ever again joke about any woman taking my place," she warned.

David breathed. "Not a problem at all."

"Okay," Katherine breathed as well. "So what's left to get?"

Hesitating slightly, he said, "I still need a mattress and bedroom furniture."

At the look on her face, he hurried, "Honestly, I want your opinion. I want to know what you think about the mattress."

Not understanding, she asked, "Why?"

"What's that word you use all the time? Um, something with your brain—oh, brainstorming! I like to brainstorm with you. I want to make sure I've thought about every aspect of my decision, and you are great with helping think through things."

"Well, why didn't you say that in the first place?" she asked.

Excited, he asked his own question. "Would you have gotten into bed with me?"

She shook her head. "No!"

"Come on, am I that disgusting?" he asked, laughing.

Kathrine smiled. "When you talk like that, you are."

Chapter 51

The Cost

Instead of continuing in the mattress section, David decided to find his master furnishings. Walking toward the endless bedroom sets, Katherine said, "So, again, you have antique, traditional, modern…"

"Actually, I think I will know it when I see it," he said.

Helping still, she pointed out, "There's a sleigh bed. That's always a safe choice. It will never go out of style."

"It is nice, but I feel like I would be confined in it. It almost looks like a crib."

Katherine was thrown back a bit. "Wow, I never looked at it that way. That was my old bed."

"Really? That's the bed that you and James had together?"

"Yes."

"You never felt confined ?" David asked.

"Not really," Katherine said, wondering if she had. She saw another bed. "There's a four-poster bed over there."

"Yeah, but it's all you would notice in the room and I think it would hide the chandelier. Plus, I think I would be afraid of the posts falling on top of me."

Impressed, she said, "Wow, you really are thinking through this, aren't you?"

"Well, my last bed looked pretty spectacular. It was similar to that one over there." He pointed to a platform bed.

"Well, then why don't you get that one?" she asked.

"Mine sat on another platform and you had to climb about three steps to get into it. It was made for the room," David said.

"Now I completely understand why you sold the bed with the house. That makes perfect sense. But you can hire a contractor to build a platform in your room."

David shook his head. "No way, not in this room. It would look so cheap and out of place. That room was designed to hold an elegant bed."

319

"Well, there's an upholstered headboard you could consider." She pointed to a plain fabric headboard with no attached footboard set.

"Now that's a little closer to what I'm thinking," David said, sitting on the bed and leaning against the headboard. "It's not quite right, though."

Katherine thought the bed was pretty nice. When David got up to look at other possibilities, she decided to try it out, settling in and leaning against the headboard.

"See, you don't look comfortable to me," David said, looking at Katherine. She had one foot on the floor and was sort of crouching down so she could relax the back of her head on the headboard. "And it's not high enough for the room's ceiling height."

"I'm sorry. I'm having a difficult time finding furniture for my own room, so it's not that easy to brainstorm with you about yours," she confessed.

Making eye contact, he said warmly, "You are helping me more than you realize. It's okay, I understand." He knew it was a sensitive topic that was giving her this mental block. "I'll tell you what. Let's see if Mr. Payne is here. I'm sure he will be more than willing to help us."

Agreeing, and feeling greatly relieved, she picked up the courtesy phone to page him.

Within minutes appeared a polished English gentlemen with thinning grey-hair and spectacles. David instantly liked something about the mature man. "Katherine, you're truly a vision. Extraordinary as always," Mr. Payne said, hugging and kissing her.

"You are such a gentleman." She blushed and proudly introduced, "This is David Mann. David, this is Mr. Payne."

Shaking David's hand and patting him on the back, Mr. Payne enthused, "Brilliant game yesterday. It was thrilling to watch."

"Thank you, sir. It was thrilling to play."

"Have you found everything you need?" Mr. Payne asked Katherine.

David took control. "Mr. Payne, I'm having a hard time locating what I envision for my master suite. What I see here just isn't…well, elegant enough to suit my tastes."

"I understand. Does anything here resemble what you envision?" Mr. Payne asked politely.

"I sort of like this upholstered headboard but it doesn't have the look to fit into my suite."

Katherine still saw nothing wrong with it and sat on the bed again to figure out what he was seeing.

"That's great, Katherine, thanks!" David said, looking at her. He turned to the professional. "Mr. Payne, Katherine looks ordinary on that bed and you said yourself that she's a true vision. Does that sort of give you a picture of what I'm after?"

Mr. Payne smiled. "Yes, I most certainly can see your vision."

"Katherine, did you take any photos of the suite?" David asked.

"Yes. Here," she said, handing him the phone.

"See, Mr. Payne, see this chandelier? This photo doesn't do it justice but I want to highlight that chandelier. And then there's a fireplace directly across from the bed, so I would like the headboard high enough so that I can lean back and enjoy it," David said excitedly.

"Are you planning on putting a TV over the fireplace?" Mr. Payne asked.

"Well, I wouldn't mind one but I don't want to ruin the feel of the room," David replied.

"We can put a two-way mirror over the TV so that when it's off you won't even know it's there," Mr. Payne said.

"Great, then the chandelier will reflect in the mirror. That will look stunning," David said.

"David, what you are after is not on the sales floor. We need to make a custom piece. Would that be something of interest?" Mr. Payne asked.

"Absolutely!"

Mr. Payne cautioned, "Now, so you know, the cost will be greater and it will take quite a bit of time to create."

"Sir, anything extraordinary is worth its weight in gold, and I'm a pretty patient man," David replied excitedly.

"Wonderful, then we shall begin with the drawings. I need to excuse myself so that I can get my portfolio," Mr. Payne said.

"Take your time, sir. And that bed Katherine is in right now, I'd like that set for my guest bedroom, and let's get Katherine one for her bedroom too," David announced.

Anxiously, she spoke. "Oh, no! No, but thank you. But really, no."

"I'll let the two of you discuss that while I get my things," Mr. Payne said, leaving them.

Once they were alone, David pleaded with her. "Katherine, please let me do this for you. You have been so helpful to me with so many things. Just take it as a gift"

"No, please, no, David. Look, I want what you are describing. I want a suite like that too."

David's heart raced, hoping her words meant she would finally see him.

"I mean, I want to find a new home and then create a retreat," she said bashfully.

Feeling defeated, he said, "Okay, then I want to go with you when you start looking for a place to live."

Smiling, sort of tickled, she said, "David, you will be long gone, the season will be over."

Chapter 52

The Invitation

When it was all said and done, David had furnished his entire condo. Their time with Mr. Payne was exceptional, the man using his years of design expertise to create an entire master suite ensemble. Using the measurements Katherine had brought, the three of them walked through the look, feel, and functionality of each piece. Together they selected fabric, pillows, bed linens, and additional furnishings for the suite. Their tastes complemented one another. The store was set to deliver everything, except for the custom pieces, the next day. It was VIP service at its best.

However, David didn't believe he could have done any of it without Katherine's input. "Thank you so much for doing this with me. I could have never made those decisions without your help," David said with heartfelt appreciation on their drive home.

"It was really my pleasure," she said.

"I'm starving, aren't you?" he asked, driving through the charming town with its inviting storefronts, boutiques, and alfresco cafes.

"Yes, I'm pretty hungry too."

"Let's get something to eat."

"Sure, where do you want to go? We can stop at Lana's or I'm sure my mom has something cooking," Katherine said.

"No, I mean a restaurant."

"Oh, well, there are a ton of restaurants over here. Just take your pick. What are you in the mood for?" she asked.

"I'm in the mood to put on one of my new suits and go to the Top of the Town. I've heard rave reviews about the food and the view. Then I want to walk around by the waterfront. I haven't been there, so I would like to see it. Let's go together!" David said excitedly. He could sense her reservation, seeing her squirm in her seat. "Look, you've helped me so much. I would like to treat you to something nice."

"Well, it's my job, plus you took us all out last night," she replied.

"I know it's your job but it means a lot more to me than you just doing your job."

Katherine didn't respond.

"I'm going regardless if you go or not," David said, even though he truly wanted her to go.

Nervously chuckling, she asked, "All by yourself?"

"Yes. My parents will be sleeping soon. Your parents are out tonight. I'm going to spend the night at their house since I don't have anything to sleep on. I'm in the mood for a nice dinner and glass of wine, so if I have to go alone, I'm fine with that."

Thinking for a moment, she said reluctantly, "Okay, I'll go with you."

"Great!" David said, not hiding his excitement at all.

They drove the rest of the way home, talking about the pieces of furniture David had purchased and where everything would be placed. He asked if she would help him tomorrow once it was delivered, to which she excitedly agreed. David dropped her off at her house, letting her know when he would return.

The Truth

David almost ran to his condo from where he parked, showering and placing on his stunning three-piece black suit with the dark cherry tie in record time. He loved the look and was excited for a night out with Katherine. It would be something different than a normal working session. Instead of taking the Corvette, he decided his high-end sedan would be the right fit for the evening.

As he drove to her home, he was nervous. Prayer seemed the remedy. "Lord, I really like Katherine's company and I enjoy my time with her. I pray the evening goes well." David didn't know why he prayed, but he somehow felt it was in his heart to do so. As of late, he was more sensitive to those feelings.

David pulled into Katherine's driveway as the sun was setting, appreciating its beauty while walking to her door. Taking deep, calculated breaths, he rang the doorbell. It wasn't a date but for some reason he felt nervous. That was until he heard the familiar sound of her heels walking toward the door. He loved that sound because it told him she was wearing something spectacular.

"Hello again!" Katherine smiled, opening the door.

David's mouth dropped open and he couldn't stop himself from saying, "You look absolutely beautiful."

Katherine blushed nervously. "Thank you."

Knowing her pretty well, he said, "Kenneth really knows his trade, doesn't he?"

Katherine wore a nude, long-sleeved sheath dress that had a black lace overlay. The illusion was as if she was only wearing black lace, and it looked stunning on her. The dress showed off her shape. She wasn't intentionally drawing attention—anyone would be noticed in the dress—but Katherine was so shapely, she couldn't hide her figure. The sheerest black hose and the black velvet high heels David had admired earlier pulled it all together.

"Yes, he does," she laughed, relaxing. "Let me grab my purse and we can go."

And as she walked away, David got a glance of her shapely behind, which was just as impressive. He felt really out of place with her, though didn't understand why. He'd been around hundreds of women in excellent shape, but something about Katherine made him breathless.

"Nice purse," he said, surprising himself that he could tear his eyes away to notice it.

It was a nude, satin, rectangular purse with a matching jewel closure. It was her only accessory and it completed the look.

"Thank you," she replied, locking her front door as they made their way out.

"I notice you don't wear a lot of jewelry. No earrings. Why not?" David asked as they walked to the car.

Katherine smiled, looking up delightedly. "Lana and I used to climb trees when we were little kids and Mom was afraid the earrings would somehow get tangled in the branches and rip out of our ears, so we didn't have them pierced. As we got older, she said we couldn't get them pierced until we were eighteen. She was trying her best to create us—in her words—unique instead of clones of everyone else. For some reason, neither us ever got our ears pierced."

"Wise woman," David said, thankful for Katherine's uniqueness.

She smiled up at him until she saw his car. A top-of-the-line, shiny, jet black, luxury sedan with a tan leather interior. "Wow, where did you get this?"

He opened her door, winking when he closed it, then walked over to his side. Her heart raced and she suddenly felt shy.

"It's mine," he said, now settled and backing out of the driveway.

"How many cars do you own?"

Laughing, David said, "This is it. Just three."

"How long have you had this one?"

"Got it right before I broke my collarbone," he replied.

"What made you choose a sedan like this? It seems so...I'm not sure. It just doesn't seem like something you would own."

"What does that mean?" he asked, delighted.

Smiling, Katherine said, "It's a car my parents would own."

"Okay, that's the second time today you've said that. First with the table and now with the car. You need to explain yourself."

"Well, it's just so family-ish," she said.

"It's just a car and just a table. It's no big deal," he replied with a gentle smile.

"You're right. I'm sorry. I have a tendency to analyze things too deeply," she said, feeling foolish.

David started laughing. "I was joking around with you!" he assured. "I love how analytical you are. Don't change that about yourself, especially with me."

"Yes, but it unnerves most people. It's so refreshing to be myself around you."

"Well, why can't you be yourself around other people?" he asked.

"Because I have a tendency to get to the heart of the matter and that makes people feel uncomfortable, so I've learned to go at their pace and allow them to open up if they feel comfortable doing so," she said.

David looked over at her with a raised eyebrow. "Which I notice happens rather quickly with you."

"Well, I think it's because I allow them the freedom to talk about themselves."

"I know you do," he said, "from experience."

Katherine smiled warmly at those words.

"Now, I know my response made you feel uncomfortable when you called my table and car family-ish." They both chuckled before David continued. "You deflected by putting the blame on yourself, changing the subject. It's a brilliant tactic that most people wouldn't understand. And I know you well enough to know that you will keep the conversation on yourself long enough until a person feels comfortable to start talking about themselves again. It's so clever of you. I'm not even too sure if you realize what you are actually doing."

"What? How in the world…" she gasped until he interrupted.

"I read defense and analyze people for a living too." David smiled.

She felt butterflies in her stomach.

"Anyway, back to the 'family' car," he snickered. "There is a story behind this car. One of the Miami owners was astute, kind-hearted, and, I don't know…um, of a certain class. He had a great family and wife. He owned one of these vehicles. And we made a connection. It wasn't quite on the same level as with your father, but we enjoyed each other's company. At that time, he was a mentor to me."

She listened, mesmerized by his story.

"One day, I was driving in my Vette," he smiled at the memory, "and I passed a dealership, and this car just stood out to me. So I turned around and went back to look at it. I'm not sure why. I couldn't picture myself in the car. It was, as you said, too family-ish."

They laughed together again, each secretly loving the combined sound of it.

"I didn't, or couldn't, see myself as a family man. The idea was just too stuffy. This car seemed too stuffy. But when I looked at both my Corvette and this car side by side, it was able to stand on its own. Then I was intrigued. So I took it for a test ride, and I completely fell in love with the ride and the interior beauty," David said, romanticizing his love of the car.

Katherine grinned, enjoying the depth of his heart and mind.

"But I couldn't get over the stigma of it being a family car, so I didn't buy it," he chuckled. "And you know what was interesting, even comical? Every time I saw this vehicle, there was always a family inside. I never saw a couple or anyone under thirty driving the car."

Katherine gave him a "see, I told you so" look.

"So after months of driving by the dealership, one day, out of impulse, I pulled in and bought the car right on the spot before I changed my mind."

"What? Why?" Katherine burst out.

"I don't know. I just had that nagging feeling I needed to purchase it. I'm not even sure if I can describe it," David said, understanding now it was probably God. "This was the last thing I bought before my collarbone was broken."

"That's interesting," she said.

"Now, I didn't want to tell you that story because it had the potential to make me look foolish. So to divert it, I blamed you, saying you were over thinking a table and car, which caused you to stop talking, as would anyone. You usually call me on the mat, saying I'm deflecting, but you didn't today."

"Now that's pretty deep. I would need to think about it because you are exactly right."

Helping, he suggested, "Maybe this feels to you like a date and not a job?"

"And I guess because we aren't in a work environment, I probably feel a little guarded with myself," she agreed.

"That makes sense. We are both dressed very nice, riding in a classy vehicle lit as if by candlelight," he pointed to the dashboard lights, "and with soft music playing in the background. It's quite romantic. Don't you think?" David asked softly.

"If you think this is romantic, wait until you see the restaurant," Katherine replied nervously.

David could immediately sense her misgivings. "Just think of this as two old friends going out to celebrate a renewed life. I promise I will be nothing but a gentleman," he assured.

Katherine smiled, relaxing, enjoying the smooth ride and the soft music. Then her mind traveled. She narrowed her gaze out the windshield, thinking deeply.

"What are you thinking about?" David asked.

"Am I that obvious?"

"I can always tell when you are evaluating something," he smiled.

Katherine opened up. "I was thinking it's a shame that some people deflect, like you did, even though I believe you were joking with me." She felt unsure, so she asked, "You were, weren't you?"

"Yes, of course I was joking with you!" he replied. "But what do you mean?"

"Well, you told me a very interesting story about this car, and we could have taken that conversation in many directions, talking nonstop. But maybe people stop the conversation because they fear what you just said—feeling foolish, maybe odd, maybe being laughed at—instead of allowing the conversation to take its own course."

"Yes, I agree, but I could have made up the entire story about the family thing in order to gain something from you later, you know, to benefit myself." He hoped he'd made his point clear.

"So you mean you could have been lying and I wouldn't have ever known?" she asked, grinning.

"Yes."

That unknowingly sexy grin featured prominently on her face when she looked directly at David and said, "That's exactly why I would never go out on a date with a guy I didn't know. I knew you were telling me the truth."

David roared with laughter. "I'm glad you are feeling comfortable to be yourself again."

Chapter 53

The Restaurant

They both laughed, talking nonstop until they arrived. When they pulled up to the valet, David asked the attendant to allow him to open Katherine's door. Helping her out, again, his breath was taken away upon the full view of her stunning dress and shape.

Walking into the building, they smiled at each other since they were eager to spend the night out on the town. Getting on the elevator, the ride to the thirtieth floor was long, and they didn't talk for whatever reason. David had a hard time trying not to look at her curves, so he focused on the floor numbers increasing.

Even before the elevator doors opened, the sounds of a violin and piano surrounded them with romance. David announced their arrival at the hostess stand, and, being a gentleman, he allowed Katherine to lead the way to their table, catching another glimpse of her perfect hourglass figure. He didn't want to view her sexually, so he looked around the restaurant; he noticed several men admiring her.

Katherine always drew attention but tonight it had risen to a whole new level. It intrigued him since both men and women noticed her, except a few who were focused on their spouse. It reminded him of Michael's attention to Sharon and David wanted to talk with him how he had built such a marriage. Mr. Payne's words describing Katherine as being a true vision were so accurate. But David knew Katherine wasn't dressing to get attention; she couldn't help but draw attention. It was how she was created. She didn't even realize she had this sort of effect on people.

Their table was located by an open terrace which showcased the city's stunning glory. The view was truly radiant. He indicated to the maitre d' that he would pull out Katherine's chair to seat her, which he did to her rosy blush. He knew she loved being treated like a lady and he equally enjoyed treating her so. It was effortless because he saw the benefits of being a gentleman and how it fostered respect and a bonding trust.

"Isn't this beautiful?" Katherine gushed, viewing Cleveland.

"Yes, beautiful," he said, but looking solely at her.

"I love it here. It's been years since I've been here."

"Really?" he questioned.

"Katherine! I'm so happy to see you." A beautiful, mature woman held out her arms. Katherine stood, engaging in a hug as David stood too, noticing the emotions between the women.

"Yes, it's been too long," Katherine said, wiping her tears. "I almost forgot how beautiful your restaurant is."

"I'm so glad you decided to finally come back. We'll make something extra special for you. Do you still love lobster?" she asked, releasing Katherine from their hug, but still holding her.

"Yes. I've missed yours, that is for sure." Katherine smiled, again wiping her tears. "Rose, this is David…"

Interrupting, Rose began, "Is he your…"

Katherine smiled at David. "Oh, no, we work together. Actually, he's more like family these days."

David's heart felt close to her. He loved that description.

"Oh, you are our new quarterback! You had such a fabulous game the other day. I wish you much success here," Rose said, shaking his hand, practically hugging him.

"Thank you. I feel like I've already had much success here," he replied, looking lovingly at Katherine.

Because Rose made such a big deal of David, several patrons approached them, shaking his hand, asking for autographs, even taking pictures with him. Katherine relished in it, offering to take photos. It lasted a good twenty minutes before things settle down and people returned to their tables.

"You better get used to that. It will happen more often," she said, smiling.

"You know, it's different from when I was with Miami."

"How so?"

"I'm not sure. I need time to understand it, but it just feels so different now."

Their server introduced himself, asking for a picture with David with a slightly embarrassed smile, then handed him the wine list. "I know you like champagne, Katherine. I'm going to order a bottle of wine for myself. Do you mind if I order a bottle of champagne for you? I know you prefer a dry version. I think you said it reminds you of ginger ale when it's too sweet."

Katherine blushed. "Yes. Thank you."

What a beautiful blush! It was a side she only showed him, which made him feel so special. David ordered the bottles and within minutes they were brought, opened, and poured. David tasted and approved. Katherine followed suit.

Addressing their server, David said, "She won't tell you if she doesn't like it. Let me try it."

Katherine blushed.

"You know, it's still a little too sweet," David said, "What else do you have that is a little dryer? I'm sorry I'm used to wine, but I'll learn how to select the champagnes too."

The server educated David on the varieties and David made his selection, thanking the man as he left to retrieve the new bottle.

"Alright, what in the world are you doing?" Katherine asked.

"I know you well enough that you won't send something back you don't like. Truthfully, did you like the champagne?" he asked.

"It was okay," she replied.

"Okay isn't good enough," he said, "which means you don't like it."

She nodded that he was right.

"Well, why didn't you just send it back?" he asked.

"Because I don't want to waste it," she replied in her typical way of being grateful for what she was given.

"Do you know how much profit they make from these bottles?" he reasoned.

"Do you know that this is just a luxury and there are plenty who don't know where their next meal is coming from?" she said. "Believe me, I can drink something that I don't like, it's fine."

"I see your point, but you aren't purposefully wasting it."

The server brought the new bottle and while he opened it David said, "Katherine is concerned the other bottle will go to waste."

"No, sir, we'll serve it by the glass. It's not a waste at all." The server offered Katherine a reassuring smile.

David tasted the champagne, announcing happily, "That's exactly it."

Katherine grinned, blushing once more as she tasted the bubbly, agreeing. After the server left, she whispered, "Thank you."

"For what?" he asked.

"For bringing me here and making me get what I really wanted," she said.

David raised his glass. "Well, here's to new beginnings."

"Yes," she agreed nervously, bringing the rim of her delicate glass to toast the side of his with a tiny chime.

"So tell me how you know Rose," David asked, pushing his menu slightly aside. There was no need to rush the evening.

"Well," Katherine teared up, "we...James and I...would come here quite often."

"Oh, I'm sorry, I didn't know," David said sincerely with love.

"How could you know? I didn't tell you."

"Why didn't you?"

"I'm not sure," she replied. "I've wanted to come back for quite some time. My parents suggested it several times, but I always shied away. You don't know the background, so I thought it was the perfect opportunity to get it over with."

"Wow, you are using me to get over a fear? Thanks! Really nice!" David chuckled, taking a sip of his wine.

Laughing herself, Katherine countered, "No, it's not like that at all!"

"I'll hurry and eat so we can get this over." He smiled.

Pleading with her eyes, she said, "No, really. I'm having a good time. I knew I would, so that's why I decided this was the time."

He couldn't resist her look in this moment. Her big, chocolate-brown eyes were almost begging for him, but he knew she was a true lady and this was how she was designed. It was a new look and he loved it, which caused him to blush. "Okay, I believe you."

She smiled.

"So I assume Rose knew you and James pretty well," David asked.

Katherine looked far off. He noticed her eyes misting. "There's something deeper to the story isn't there?" he asked.

"Wow, I really had no idea we would be talking about this tonight."

Raising his eyebrows and shaking his head in a friendly way, David said, "I now understand why you won't go on a date with someone you don't know. Too many things might come out. I can read you and there is no hiding with me."

She grinned peacefully that he understood what some would perceive as an oddity.

"Your mother probably instilled that in you and Lana. It only makes perfect sense. That's why neither of you dated a lot growing up. You both could weed out men from a distance. That's absolutely brilliant of your mother. Now, how would she have known that all by herself?" he wondered.

"Do you want me to be part of this conversation or would you like to continue to talk to yourself?" Katherine chuckled.

"No, I'd rather talk to myself." He adored their natural humorous interludes.

She laughed delightfully. "You are so funny. You remind me so much of my dad."

"Please enlighten me," he said.

"Yes, my mother taught us that…technique. I guess that's a suitable word for it. And you are right, it's absolutely brilliant. It's never failed me. It works with friends, business associates, and men alike. My mom was always gifted with understanding people; I believe it is a gift from God. My dad says he would never be as successful as he is today if it wasn't for her. And I personally agree with that because she's done the same for Lana and me."

David was caught off guard as his heart filled with love for her parents. He agreed with Katherine so much he felt his eyes misting. "She is a wonderful person. I have the utmost respect for both your parents."

"I know you do."

"Do you want to tell me the story about Rose? Are you ready to talk about it?" he asked.

Taking a sip of her champagne, Katherine said, "Yes, but first let me give you a compliment."

Lighting up like a Christmas tree, David said, "Oh, no, this is not going to be one of your famous kiss and kicks?"

Smiling brightly, chuckling, she asked, "What?"

"You know, when you say something so sweet and it's like you're giving me a kiss and then you end it with a cutting remark, like you are kicking me right in the face."

Katherine busted up laughing. "No, no! This is truly a compliment. Well, at least I think it's a compliment. Besides, I only slap you in the face."

"Yeah, and it was well deserved, I must add. I'm not sure I ever apologized for that remark. I'm sorry for treating you disrespectfully."

"Thank you for apologizing," she said, taking another sip of her champagne. Her eyes traveled away from their tables and she fell into staring off in the distance.

"What are you thinking about?" David asked, gently calling her attention back.

Katherine looked at him and turned red, feeling busted. "It's odd, if you hadn't said that to me and I hadn't slapped you, do you think we would be sitting here right now?"

Sitting back, he said, "That's a lot to think about." He tapped his fingers gently on the table wondering what would have happened if Katherine hadn't returned and apologized for striking him in the face. If it would have led to a moment different than this, he didn't want to imagine it.

Chapter 54

The Prayer

They sat back in their chairs, startled by the gift, as the server appeared with a massive seafood tower and placed it on the table with a small flourish. "This is from Rose."

"Yummy," Katherine said. "Thank you!" She examined the two-tiered, silver tower that was adorned with fresh colossal shrimp, iced Alaskan King crab legs, already shelled, and Maine lobster with hungry eyes.

Watching her select a piece of shrimp, finding the perfect bite, David said, "You love food, don't you?"

"Yes, but only of the highest quality."

As they enjoyed the appetizer, David and Katherine exchanged memories of their favorite restaurants. Sharing the funny moments and celebrations of life enjoyed in those places kept them laughing and talking over one another in happiness.

After the server refilled their glasses and removed the seafood tray, David settled back, sipping his wine. "Wait, we have several unfinished conversations. We still need to talk about Rose, you wanted to give me a compliment or a kick—I still haven't quite figured it out yet—and I think there's something else…."

"Was it something about my mom and what she taught us or did we finish that conversation?" Katherine wondered aloud helpfully.

"I don't think we completely dissected that, but I'm sure we'll come back to it."

Smiling, she agreed. "Okay then, let's go with the kick or kiss or whatever you call it."

Rubbing his hands together, leaning into the table, David said, "This should be good!"

"You are great at what you just did," Katherine told him.

Tilting his head, he asked, "What did I do?"

"We start a conversation but don't finish before we begin another one, and before I know it, we have three or four different conversations going on at once, but you always make sure we come back and finish each topic. That's an outstanding quality to have. It makes it seem like you are genuinely interested in me and what I'm thinking." Katherine smiled into David's eyes lovingly yet with her mischievous grin.

Gesturing to an imaginary crowd with his hand, showing her off he announced, "And there it is—the kiss and kick!"

Her big eyes popped open. "What are you talking about? How in the world did I kick you that time?"

"Come on, don't be coy with me," David said with a witty smile.

"I'm not!" Katherine shook her head emphatically. "Seriously!"

He realized then she genuinely did not know she was complimenting him and then ending the praise with a remark that could translate as condescending, and that it was coming across as flirtation. It simply was her natural personality.

Begging with her brown beauties, Katherine insisted, "Please, you have to tell me!"

His heart melted. "Okay, okay." Blushing, he looked away since her expression was that captivating. "You have a way of sucking a person in with your words and just when they get close enough you literally kick them away."

Pleading for the answer, she said. "I got that part, but apparently I'm missing how I just did that to you."

Her sensual eyes aroused him, making it difficult for him to maintain eye contact. This was how she was designed, and he was created to bring it out of her, for he'd never seen her look at anyone else with those same eyes. Taking a breath, he said, "You told me that I am good at making sure we complete our three or four open conversations and that it makes it seem as if I'm genuinely interested."

She struggled to follow. "Okay, and…."

"I am genuinely interested or I would never go back to those other conversations." David laughed.

Then she got it. "Oh, I'm sorry! I didn't realize I was doing that. I'll think before I speak so that I can better select my words."

David leaned forward, his vivid blue eyes determined that she understand. "Don't you dare ever change. I love you just the way you are."

Fear struck Katherine seconds after his words. Her face went pale and her eyes popped open. She couldn't turn away from him and wasn't able to escape the intimacy growing around them. She was feeling queasy and lightheaded until she heard a voice that rescued her.

"I'm sorry to bother you, but can I have your autograph?" a young woman asked.

Katherine jumped up. "I'm going to use the ladies' room. I'll be right back."

David was freaking out, holding on to his composure only a little better than Katherine. Why did he say that? Where was that coming from? He didn't mean it. Did he? They were having such a fabulous time. How in the world would they be able to continue with dinner now? Full of fear, he had no idea what to do.

Maybe flirting with the girl who wanted his autograph was an option, but he remembered the consequences of that decision this morning. He could blow his declaration off, pretending it hadn't happened. He had been down that road and the play didn't work with Katherine. David started to panic, unable to think of anything to say when she inevitably returned, so he did something unusual—he prayed. "Lord, I have no idea why I said that, and I'm not ready to understand it, but would you somehow give me the words to get us back on track with our evening."

The Answer

Katherine felt trapped. She wanted to go home. She almost laughed at her situation—hiding out in a bathroom stall in the finest establishment in Cleveland, deep breathing to prevent herself from hyperventilating or desperately running out the door. She had just wanted to have a nice dinner with David. How had it turned into this? What even was this? How would their working relationship be now?

Her anxiousness kept growing until the word "pray" came to her mind, then it came out of obligation. She groaned. She didn't really desire God's voice on how to handle the situation since she only wanted to leave. All she could honestly pray was "Help me to somehow end this night quickly so that I can go home."

Leaving the restroom, returning slowly to their table, her heart raced when she saw David sitting alone, no one else wanting his autograph or photo. She slipped into her chair, picked up her menu, and looked to order to hurry dinner along so she could leave.

David was sad with the obvious change in her personality. The word "truth" was instilled in his heart. "Katherine," David whispered sadly.

Not looking up from her menu, she said, "Yes."

"Please look at me."

Full of fear, she made eye contact. "Yes?"

"I'm not sure why I chose those exact words. I think it's like how you give me the kiss and kick. Are you able to explain why you do that?"

"No. I don't mean to be mean. I'm not trying to hurt your feelings. Truthfully, I'm not." Her eyes were full of desperation and sorrowful regret.

"Can I have your autograph?" Another fan had approached after seeing their moment of quiet.

Addressing the woman, David said, "I'm sorry. I'm right in the middle of a conversation. Will you please give me ten minutes? Then I'll be happy to do so."

Katherine was utterly shocked he had asked the woman to wait. It pulled her out of her fears and worried thoughts. What David had just done in preserving their time was so romantic. She felt very loved, and so she relaxed.

Returning his attention to Katherine, David continued. "I know you aren't trying to hurt my feelings; you are just being yourself. And I can't help but love that about you. I'm not saying I'm in love with you. I don't even know what that means. I'm just saying that I love the person you are. You are absolutely right, we would never be sitting here if you hadn't slapped me in the face. And we both know that."

She grinned, relaxing her shoulders, finally able to recline back in her chair.

"You expect respect. You almost demand it. I wasn't respecting you and you made sure that I would never speak to you in that manner again. But it wasn't your slap that changed me. It was the fact that you didn't walk out and you apologized to me. That hit me more than the slap could have ever affected me."

Tears moistened her eyes. God laid it upon her heart to stay, and she listened.

"I do love you, but I love your whole family too. I'm sorry if that makes you afraid, but it's who I am. You've always told me to speak from my heart, and that's exactly what I do, and I can't change that even if I wanted too." David leaned deeper into the table, never breaking eye contact with her. "My hands were so shackled when I wasn't allowed to call any audibles. And my play was off because I couldn't be myself and I had to follow someone else's rules. You don't like that either. I know you. If being who I really am makes you feel uncomfortable, I'm sorry. I don't want to change, and I also don't want you to feel uncomfortable."

She swallowed nervously since he was speaking to her heart which was now pounding with passion.

"I can take you home right now if you would like, and I promise I won't be upset at all. I would prefer to finish our evening but I don't want in any way to make you feel uncomfortable."

Turning red, Katherine said, "I'm sorry. I'm sure I misinterpreted what you said…"

"Don't do that," David insisted. "Don't do that with me!"

She nodded, looking away for she knew she couldn't deflect. He knew her too well.

"Don't treat me like you treat everyone else. Don't blame yourself or even belittle yourself like that with me. I would have interpreted what I said for its true meaning as well. Katherine, I'm being completely honest. I'm not sure why it came out that way. I can only think it's because I just feel so much love for everything you and your family have done for me and my family."

She took a deep breath knowing David would hold her accountable for attempting to mask the truth.

"If you think about what you all have done, it's absolutely amazing. Your dad has been almost more than a father to me, if that even makes any sense at all. Your mother…"

A quick motion caught Katherine by the corner of her eye. Seeing another woman approach, she held up her index finger, saying, "Just one moment, we're in the middle of a conversation. Just ten more minutes, if you don't mind."

"Your mother," David said without missing a beat, "my God that woman is amazing. And I mean no disrespect by calling on God's name, but it was her complete doing bringing my parents here. I mean, that story in itself is beyond anything I can comprehend."

Tears filled both of their eyes.

"I've lost over fifteen pounds from Lana and Eric feeding me such healthy and delicious food." David chuckled.

Katherine laughed too feeling at ease.

"And all I need to do is look in the mirror to see what you've done for me. It goes beyond the clothes and the beard. It comes from the inside, and that's what you taught me. How could I not love that? Seriously, I'm not trying to make you afraid. I'm not trying to get you in bed. I'm just being me and telling you the truth. I want nothing more. I'm sorry if that makes you nervous or afraid, but I just enjoy us. And I have no idea what that is, but whatever it is, it works." He smiled. "And you know what's interesting? I don't want to analyze it. I just want to live it."

With joyful eyes, Katherine said, "I think you are telling me thank you in your own way."

He grinned. "I think that's a fabulous way of putting it. So thank you for everything you have done for me."

"It has truly been my pleasure," she replied, happy and comfortable with David and their dinner once more. "Okay, these women are salivating over there. Let me call them to get your autograph and picture."

David didn't take his eyes off her while she stood and waved a slew of women over to the table.

"You are really confident, aren't you?" David asked.

Looking back at him, she said, "What do you mean?"

Placing his elbow on the table, resting his chin on his hand, thinking out loud, he said, "Your mother and sister possess that same radiant confidence. What is that? Where does it come from?"

"Do you really want to start up, what, a fifth conversation?"

Snapping back into reality, he chuckled. "You're right. We'll leave that for another day."

Chapter 55

The Worth

With lighter hearts, and a more honest connection, David and Katherine worked as a team, he signing autographs while she took the photos. Of course, the women were giddy, flirtatious, one even outright hitting on him as she placed her card on the table.

"Excuse me, ma'am, you forgot your card," David called out when she left.

"Oh!" The woman was dumbfounded. "That's in case you ever need to contact me...business related."

"This is my manager," David said, still holding the card. "She handles all my business affairs, but I'm sure you didn't know that." He looked at the card, asking Katherine, "Are we in the market for acrylic nails?"

"No," Katherine replied plainly, trying not to laugh and hurt the lady's feelings.

Handing the card back, he said, "Thank you, but we aren't in the market for your services."

Katherine covered her face with her hands when the woman left. "Oh, David!"

Pouring himself another glass of wine and refilling Katherine's champagne, he asked confused, "What?"

"Oh, that poor girl!" Katherine said feeling the woman's humiliation. "I'm so embarrassed for her."

"What? Why? I don't understand."

"She probably feels so foolish and humiliated right now." Katherine blushed. "I actually feel bad for her."

"I wasn't trying to be rude to her..."

Interrupting him, she said, "But you were, I'm sure not intentionally."

"Listen, she interrupted our conversation. Anyone could clearly see that we were engaged in a deep conversation. I politely told her to wait. She then gives me her card, for what? She wants me to call her for a date? That's so disrespectful to you, me, and actually to herself," he stated, almost a little heated that she would disregard worth.

"Why do you say that?"

"We clearly look like we're on a date." David laughed, then said, "And we've already established we are clearly not on a date."

Katherine chuckled, sipping her champagne, allowing the bubbles to dance on her tongue.

"But she didn't know we aren't on a date. She couldn't care less that you were being polite by calling her over and taking a picture for her. That's disrespectful," he stressed. "She clearly has no respect for herself. She basically was telling me she is willing to be used for whatever, that it didn't matter if I was with you or not."

"Okay, I agree with you, but how were you being disrespected?"

"She assumed I'm the type of guy who would cheat and stoop to that level. And I'm not!"

"Just like the woman from the furniture store today," Katherine said. "You did the same thing to her."

"Exactly," he said.

"Alright, I get it, but why put her on the spot? Why call her out? Why not just let it go?" Katherine asked seriously.

Shrugging his shoulder, David said, "I don't know. That's a good question. It just comes out like that. It's just me."

Lighting up brightly, she said, "Oh, my gosh you are my dad! My mom and dad debate this exact subject. She thinks he's too direct, and he thinks she's too subtle. But they don't argue, they analyze it, eventually laughing over their conversation."

"That must be why we get along so well," David announced.

Katherine didn't know if he was referring to her or to her father.

The Exposure

Their eyes twinkling at one another, charmed by their connection, sipping on the imported wine and French champagne, Katherine looked up when the server asked, "Would you like to hear our specials for tonight?"

Picking up her menu, she said, "I guess we should order."

David looked at the server, kindly saying, "I'm in no hurry."

Katherine blushed. He truly was direct.

343

"Neither am I, sir. It's my pleasure to serve you, and I want you to enjoy your time with us," the young man replied.

"What's your name?" David asked.

"Alexander, sir."

"You can call me David and this is Katherine."

"Nice to meet you both," Alexander said.

"It's our pleasure," David replied.

"Are the patrons bothering you too much?" Alexander asked, refilling both their glasses.

"Katherine, does it bother you?"

"No, I'm enjoying it."

"No, Alexander. It's fine with her. Thank you for asking," David said.

"If it gets too much, please let me know and we will put a stop to it," Alexander assured.

"Thank you, I appreciate it. Can we have a plate of carpaccio? Do you have that?" David asked, not cracking open his menu.

"Yes, sir, we do."

Motioning to Katherine, David said, "That's one of her favorites."

Katherine turned red. She didn't know he knew how much she loved that appetizer.

"I'll place the order now," Alexander replied, hurrying away.

Taking a sip of his wine, David said, "Okay, tell me the story about Rose."

Katherine took a couple of sips of champagne before starting. "Well, James and I would come here maybe a couple times a year."

"I can see why. It's a great place," he said. Watching her face fall sadly, he knew this story was sensitive from the change in her demeanor.

"Well, we were here one evening celebrating my pregnancy. And it was a little late, but not too late. Usually, when we went out to dinner, we would complete our evening in about an hour."

He understood then that this was a new experience for her. David had made this an event, not just dinner.

"It was a really nice, sort of a magical evening for us. We talked about baby names. I talked about the design of the nursery. We even decided that we would put a crib in his office." Katherine chuckled a moment. "Anyway, it was time to go home, and we said goodbye to Rose, who again congratulated us." Katherine stared off in the distance while she spoke. "We got on the road and it had been raining. We started driving home when the next thing I remember is standing on the side of the road and Rose in my face, screaming my name."

Tears moistened his eyes. He felt her pain seeping into him.

"Rose wouldn't allow me to look at the car. She took me to the sidewalk and held onto me." Making eye contact, she admitted to David, "I was in complete shock. I still to this day don't remember a thing." She took a deep breath to prevent tears from falling. "I'm so thankful I don't remember anything, and I'm so thankful that Rose prevented me from looking at the accident."

David reached out for Katherine's hand, but she pulled it away, showing she would break down even more. He understood. Sometimes a single touch could be the breaking point in maintaining one's composure.

Katherine took a sip of champagne, then finished with a little laugh. "Then, I have no idea where this guy came from, it was like out of thin air. He was a reporter. He shoved a camera and microphone in my face, asking me how I felt about the accident."

"There's just no way!" David said, so intent on her story that he was angry on her behalf.

"Yeah." Katherine nodded. "Rose was trying to get him to leave, but I all heard was, 'How do you feel? How do you feel?'" Breathing a little heavier, she continued. "And then I don't know what got into me—I have no idea—but I just hauled off and punched him right in the face. And I'm not saying I slapped him. I mean, I literally decked the guy right in the nose."

Looking at her hand, she said, "James had just bought me a beautiful ring to celebrate our pregnancy, and it was large. I couldn't bear to look at it afterwards, so I gave it to charity." Taking a sip from her glass to gather a little courage, she went on. "Anyway, I not only broke his nose, but that ring cut his face severely. He needed stitches."

"He deserved it," David stated.

"Well, wait, there's more," she said, enjoying a little more of champagne. "A couple days after the funeral, I got served with a letter. That reporter was suing me for hitting him, breaking his nose, and leaving a pretty significant scar on his face. He was claiming not only monies for missed work because of his condition but also future earnings because he could not work, citing his face was his calling card."

"You cannot be telling me the truth."

"I couldn't make this up if I tried."

"What happened?" David encouraged.

Katherine could spot someone coming over to their table for another autograph.

"Can you give us another ten minutes," David said without missing a beat.

"It's fine, David. It's not like the other conversation. We needed to finish that one so we could continue this one with no problem," she sweetly assured him.

While he signed autographs and took pictures, Alexander brought their carpaccio, refilling Katherine's champagne and water.

"Will you please bring me some lemon for my water?" she asked kindly.

"Alexander, it would probably benefit you if you just brought her a pitcher of water with no ice. She drinks a lot of water and doesn't like it too cold."

"What is with you?" Katherine chuckled. "Am I that picky?"

"No. You just like what you like," David said, signing another autograph.

Katherine took some more pictures while Alexander brought the water pitcher. "Thank you, Alexander. I'm sorry to be so selective."

"David's right. The more I know your desires, the easier it is for me to meet them," Alexander replied.

After the crowd left and they ate the scrumptious appetizer, Katherine picked up her glass, savoring another taste of the golden liquid as David said, "So continue. You said this guy was basically taking you to court for breaking his nose and leaving him with a scar."

"Well, it was a pretty large gash. It looked horrible," Katherine confessed.

Making a fist, David said again, "He deserved it!"

"Easy tiger, let me finish the story." Katherine grinned.

He settled, loving that she called him a tiger once more because he genuinely felt that way around her.

"Well, as you can imagine, I was not in good shape and I told my Dad to settle," Then, bright-eyed, with a glint of mischief, she said "And you know my dad. There was no way that was happening."

"Yes, I do know your dad. I'm surprised he didn't go after that guy and literally kill him."

"Yes, but you are forgetting about my mom." Katherine grinned proudly.

"Yes, your mom. Of course she would be the only one who could reason with him."

"God alone gave her strength during that time," Katherine said with tears in her eyes that threatened to brim over. "She was holding me up, and holding back my Dad, and comforting Lana."

David understood why Katherine couldn't hurt her mother by taking her own life as she had wanted at that time.

"So my dad got the absolute best lawyers and we were getting set to go to court."

"You? You went to court with that guy?" David asked.

"My dad was not settling anything with him. And he was determined not allow me to do that either."

"How was it even possible for you to sit in court and deal with all that while you were still grieving?"

"Well, things sort of took an interesting twist, at least to me."

Katherine waved over some patrons who were waiting and David happily autographed a Cleveland jersey and football.

"Word must be out that you are here if people are now bringing you personal items to sign," Katherine said, smiling.

David smiled too but urged, "So go ahead, what was the interesting twist?"

Katherine drank the rest of her champagne and David refilled her glass.

"Well, since James was in this business, he knew many athletes and media. The funeral was packed with hundreds of people. The amount of flower arrangements was overwhelming. To this day, I hate the smell of flowers. It reminds me of a funeral," Katherine admitted.

"I'm sorry to hear that," David whispered.

"Actually, I really never liked flowers anyway. They are pretty for the first day but they die off quickly, start shedding, and the water gets all moldy. It becomes a complete mess that I have to clean." Katherine grinned trying to lighten the mood.

David understood she wanted to avoid talking about the funeral.

"I do think there's something quite sexy about getting a single rose and pretty, petite box of dark chocolate truffles. You know, just a small enough box to feed to one another."

David lovingly said, "I'm sorry that you will never have that with James again."

"Oh, that wasn't something we did together. I just thought of it when you were describing how you wanted to outfit your master suite," Katherine confessed.

David looked at her, astounded.

"Wow. Okay, this is exactly why I can't have more than one drink. I know my limit," Katherine said, pushing her glass slightly away. "I'm sorry, I usually don't drink this much."

"Katherine, please don't apologize. This is an extremely difficult conversation. We don't need to talk about it today," David said tenderly, waving Alexander over to the table.

"You are right, and I haven't talked about this in years. Plus, coming here, maybe I wasn't ready for this."

"Really, when would it ever be a good time to come here?" David asked gently.

"You are so sweet. I really enjoy your company. Thank you so much for everything you have done for me," she said genuinely.

"Yes, David. What can I get for you?" Alexander asked.

"Will you please take this? Katherine is through with the champagne," David said, handing him a nearly empty bottle.

"Is it not to your liking?" Alexander asked Katherine.

"No, she loves it, but she just knows her limit," David stated.

"Yes, I understand. I'll remove it for you immediately. Anything else I can get for you?" Alexander asked.

"Katherine, do you need anything?"

"No, thank you." She blushed, waited for Alexander to leave, then said, "Thank you for having that removed. I'm sure it would have been a temptation as I continued the story."

"It's completely understandable," David said affectionately, then excitedly added, "Wait a minute. You just gave me a kiss without a kick!"

Chuckling, talking out of the side of her mouth, she asked, "What are you talking about?"

"You told me I was sweet, that you enjoyed my company, and said something about doing something for you, which I admit I'm not sure what you meant."

Katherine licked her lips, enticing him with those magnificent eyes.

"Look, bottom line, you gave me a kiss and no kick," David said, all cocky.

Then Katherine got that unknowingly sexy grin on her face. "You know, I'm actually quite tipsy right now, so I'll probably say just about anything nice to you." And then she winked at him.

"What?" David asked with an answering grin.

Leaning into the table, she challenged, "You heard me."

Accepting her dare and placing his elbows on the table, he asked, "Are you telling me you can't give me a kiss without being tipsy?"

Raising one eyebrow, she toyed, "Oh, one of my kisses would be too intoxicating for you."

David moved closer. Deadlock eye contact, he was ready for her, and when he went to take her on, he heard that still voice command, "Deflect."

Pointing, she teased, "I see some more women want your autograph. Would you like me to call them over?"

Warning, he practically growled, "Don't you dare."

Katherine chuckled and leaned further into the table, ready to play.

"Deflect," that familiar voice warned David again.

"Let me get this out of your way," Alexander said, removing the empty plate of carpaccio.

Nothing was said for "deflect" wouldn't leave his mind. He knew it was God's voice. Without breaking eye contact with Katherine, David said, "Alexander, I would like to visit the terrace. Could you please make sure we aren't disturbed?"

"Let me walk you over to our VIP section," Alexander responded.

"Thank you, Alexander," he replied, staring at Katherine, placing out his hand saying, "Come with me."

She felt weak for he was intense and so manly.

Alexander walked them to a secluded area of the terrace. They leaned against the railing overlooking the beautiful city lights looking deeply into each other's eyes with neither of them backing down.

"Katherine," David said, holding both of her hands.

She wasn't tense in the least bit. Their bodies faced one another, almost touching.

"You are so beautiful," David continued. "Your eyes can just about melt my heart. And when they start pleading with me, I'm like putty in your hands. I would never want anything to destroy that."

Her unknowingly signature grin displayed as she remained silent.

Lightly touching her lips, he said, "And this sexy grin of yours just fires up the passion inside of me like you can't even imagine."

Katherine's breath was heavier.

Passionately, he said, "It's so pure and so raw."

Katherine licked her lips, never breaking contact with his blue eyes.

Kissing both her hands, he said, "I know you so well. It's like you were created just for me."

This time Katherine wasn't fearful of David's gesture, nor did she wish to run away. Though she could say it was the champagne, it really was David's romantic poetry that had lowered her guard.

"I would fight endlessly to make sure nothing ever ruined that for us." He stroked her face lovingly. "I wouldn't even allow my own desires to ruin our story by rushing whatever this is between us. And even though I can't wait to find out, I love you too much to dictate the path."

Katherine continued to look directly into his eyes.

"You are so intriguing. I love to study you. And I know you are a woman worthy of respect," David said intensely.

Katherine didn't blink.

David then brought both of her hands up to his mouth again, gently kissed them each, and said, "I know you are deflecting. I've never seen you drink more than a glass of champagne. I can only imagine how devastating it must have been for you to be at your husband's funeral. And now to begin to relive the memories. We don't need to talk about it today. But please don't run to this."

Tears welled up in her eyes. He understood her with sincere compassion.

David continued tenderly. "I know you are afraid. I know that you are afraid of me. And I can see you opening up with me and I know that scares you. I know that you are doing this to actually push me away.".

A teardrop fell from Katherine's eye.

David wiped the tear away, saying, "You must really trust me to test me like this. I know that if I would have taken your bait, you would have lost all respect for me and our story would have come to an end. I know you are trying to push me away and protect yourself."

Another tear fell.

"Let's let God direct this, okay? I'm not ready and neither are you. We have the entire football season to discover each other in a wholesome and pure way that would honor and respect us both. I don't want any unnecessary human desires to defile that," David said fiercely.

He wiped away some more tears as Katherine confessed, "I'm afraid."

"So am I," David answered.

"I'm so tired of being afraid," Katherine cried.

"I know," David assured. "So am I."

Katherine looked down, not knowing what else to say.

David gently lifted her head and looked into her eyes. "We both know the sudden pain that life can bring. Let's enjoy each day and each moment. When it gets scary, we need to talk about it. Let us happen naturally. Okay?"

"Yes." Then she turned away from him slightly, looking at Cleveland's lights. She could see the stadium lit up. "Isn't this an amazing view?"

"It sure is," David said, never taking his eyes off her.

Katherine faced him, lovingly kissing his cheek, and gave him a tiny hug. "Thank you for being a gentleman and treating me like a lady."

David wasn't expecting either the hug or the kiss and was taken back. Even though he couldn't return her hug, it felt warm. Confessing, he said to her, "It's a pleasure I didn't even know I would desire."

They continued to look deeply into each other's eyes, and David could feel himself being pulled to her like a magnet. He wanted to kiss her, but somehow he knew the time wasn't right, so he said, "So do you want to finish telling me about that prick news reporter?"

"Easy tiger. Just relax," Katherine said with her sexy grin.

Automatically David growled very low…very sexy.

"Easy, tiger!" Katherine warned. "You are bringing out the tiger in me."

David stepped back, looked up to heaven, saying "Okay, I can't handle anymore."

Katherine chuckled, asking, "Who in the world are you talking too?"

David smiled. "Apparently God."

"Oh. He will never give you more than you can handle," Katherine replied seriously.

"Eat" came to David's mind. "Look, we need to get some food in your stomach. You probably are tipsier than we both realize."

Chapter 56

The Defender

Walking back to their table feeling a deeper connection, they saw a crowd of fans waiting to get David's autograph and picture. Alexander stood guard at their table, however, to ensure they weren't being disturbed.

"Alexander, will you please share your dinner recommendation and put in a rush order for us? I know for sure Katherine likes lobster and filet, but whatever you recommend is fine with me. I completely trust your taste," David said while seating Katherine.

"Absolutely, David," Alexander replied, getting the temperature of their meats before rushing away.

"Excuse me," David said to a couple sitting nearby.

"Yes?" the man answered.

"Are these guests coming to our table disturbing your evening? If so, we can have them stop."

"No, we are enjoying it ourselves and are glad you are here," the man said, smiling.

"So am I," David replied.

David signed autographs with Katherine taking photos until their dinner arrived.

"Alexander, will you please make sure we are not disturbed while we are eating?" David asked.

"Yes, of course." Alexander said, ever the host.

Rose had made an incredible plate of surf and turf for them and they enjoyed every morsel. About halfway through their meal, Katherine volunteered, "Let me finish the story. I just want to get it out of the way so we don't need to revisit it one day."

"Okay," David said, placing down his utensils, giving her his full attention.

"You can eat," she giggled.

"I know, but I would rather just listen." He smiled.

"But your meal will get cold."

"I don't mind. Alexander can warm it up for me," David said dead serious.

Katherine smiled, tearing up from his overwhelming love.

"So you ended with telling me there was an interesting twist and you were heading to court," David reminded.

She smiled, loving his selfless quality. "Well, since James knew so many athletes and media personnel in this town, when word got out that guy was taking me to court, it started a huge debate."

"What kind of debate?" David asked.

"Do you mind if I continue to eat? I don't like cold food. I mean, I can wait until we finish our meal and then tell you the story," Katherine said, feeling selfish.

David demanded, "Please, you need to eat and I want to hear this story."

Katherine blushed. David truly made her feel like she was the only one who existed in the world. Taking a bite of her filet, she continued. "Well, you know how popular Trino is in Cleveland. He has a huge following. When he heard that guy was taking me to court to sue me, he exploited the entire story."

Pounding his fist on the table, David reacted instantly. "I can't stand him. He was just trying to get ratings."

"Easy tiger. Let me finish," Katherine teased, obviously still drunk.

David allowed her comment to go this time.

"At first glance, you would have thought he was doing this for ratings, and I admit that's what I thought, but he was absolutely brilliant, and as a result I have so much respect for him. Not many people understand just how clever he really is. He knows exactly what he's doing and he does it with flawless perfection," Katherine stated.

David eagerly listened, too interested to even want to eat his meal.

"Trino completely exploded the story. He told his audience every account of the event. Pretty much the story I told you up to this point without getting into the details of the funeral," Katherine said, reaching for David's wine glass, taking a couple of sips.

David said nothing, allowing her to drink his wine, but he wanted to laugh since anytime she tasted the wine a look of disgust played across her face. Katherine was a champagne lady, not a wine drinker.

Pursing her lips with a sourpuss's face, she rejoined her tale. "He told his audience that I lost my baby and that in my grief I would need to go to court and be forced to look at pictures from the scene of the accident."

David watched, realizing she needed to multi-task while telling her story to distract herself from her heartbreaking loss. Just as she had allowed the fans to get David's autograph when she first began, she was now eating. The story was too intense to share it straightforward with no interruptions. And anytime it got too emotional, he noticed she drank his wine.

Finishing her meal, she said, "And Trino, who is so incredibly brilliant at his trade, told them who I was; that I was the daughter of Michael, highlighting all the charitable events, community outreach, and our love for Cleveland."

Amazed, David said, "He told his audience the truth, painting a picture so they would fall in love with you and your family."

Katherine nodding. "We've known Trino for years. We are involved in charity events with him. His wife died of breast cancer and he was absolutely in love with her."

David hurt for the man he thought of as heartless.

With tears, Katherine said, "He understood firsthand what it felt like to lose a spouse and the pain I was experiencing, and there was just no way that he was going to stand for some guy to do this to me or my family."

"That is so amazing," David said awed, resting his hand on his chin, mesmerized by the turn of events.

Katherine took another couple of sips of wine as David covered his smile. "He whipped the audience into such a frenzy that the local media and newspaper had to pick up the story. It had a shelf life longer than four days." Katherine drank, remembering. "Now anytime the local news aired or someone saw me, they knew me as the woman who lost her husband and baby. I couldn't go out in public, but I had to because of the case. I started reliving all the events with the lawyers. Even Rose had to get involved."

Katherine finished the rest of his wine, taking a bite of bread after. "But Trino was relentless in his pursuit, making it so intense that Cleveland residents actually started stalking that guy. And this was all within a three-week time frame of James's death."

She held up his glass, looking for David to refill it.

He called over Alexander and handed him the wine bottle, saying, "This is too much of a temptation. Will you please take it away?"

Katherine smiled lovingly, piping up. "Alexander, will you please bring him a new plate of food? He doesn't enjoy eating cold food. I'll take that plate to my dad. He doesn't mind eating his food cold." Pointing to David's plate, she added, "And you can put that on my bill."

"Certainly, Katherine," Alexander said.

"Alexander, don't separate the checks. Your tip depends on it," David warned sternly.

Katherine was dying inside. He was so manly.

"Alexander, I don't remember because it's been so long since I've been here, but do you still have those dark chocolate molten lava cakes?" Katherine asked.

"Yes, we do."

"I know those take a while to make, so will you please put that in for us?" she said.

"Would you like just one to share?" Alexander asked Katherine, not even looking at David.

"Yes, please," Katherine replied and quickly added, "Do you also have some type of lemon dessert, preferably low fat?"

"Yes, Katherine, we do. Would you like that as well?" Alexander asked.

"Yes. I would like David to taste that too," she said with that sexy grin that always got him.

"Uh, no thank you. Alexander, please don't listen to her. I have no desire to taste that type of dessert." David said, never taking his eyes off the beautiful vision before him.

"Yes, sir," Alexander replied.

Katherine was very aroused by David and having a tough time not flirting with him. But David read her so well now that he changed the mood, asking, "So the residents came to your rescue with the reporter?"

Instantly her demeanor changed back to the topic at hand. "Yes, he couldn't go anywhere. Even some national news outlets picked up the story. It got to the point where they were picketing him. He couldn't go anywhere without the residents attacking and humiliating him. So he dropped the case and left town. I'm not even too sure where he is these days," Katherine said, looking away, lost in wondering about whatever happened to the man who wanted to take her to court.

"That is truly, truly astounding!" David marveled.

"It could only have been God's doing," Katherine said sincerely.

David nodded, clearly seeing God's hand in the events.

"So after that was over, I just completely lost it. It was just way too much for me to handle, and I checked out of life," Katherine said, picking up David's empty glass, trying to drink the last drops left.

Alexander brought David's new plate of hot food.

"Thank you, Alexander. I hope we aren't taking up too much of your time tonight," Katherine said sweetly, concerned about his feelings.

Smiling, he confessed. "I wasn't scheduled to work tonight, but they called last minute, asking me to help. I really didn't feel like it, but had this nagging feeling I should work." Looking at David he said, "I'm a huge football fan. If I found out you were here and I hadn't worked because I didn't feel like it, I would have been so mad at myself."

Katherine smiled.

Blushing somewhat, Alexander admitted, "I know, it's pathetic, but to serve you is such a great story and the highlight of working here while I'm trying to get my degree."

Katherine lovingly touched their server's hand, saying, "That's beautiful, don't say that it's pathetic. My husband—well, late husband— went to school and worked. I know firsthand how difficult it is. There's a lot of pressure. What are you studying?"

"I want to be a CPA," Alexander proudly announced.

"When do you graduate?" she asked.

"This coming June."

"Here," she said, reaching in her purse. "Here's my card. I know plenty of firms. I can help get your foot in the door. You've given us excellent service tonight, but I can tell it's your natural work ethic. Call me a couple months before you graduate and we will have lunch with some of my contacts."

"Oh, thank you so much." His entire face lit up with a sense of excitement that she would help him carve out a new path.

"She's serious, Alexander. I have seen her do this with others," David reassured him.

"Thank you again. I will call you. Now, let me let you get back to your meal."

Chapter 57

The Grooming

David had been eating while Katherine talked with Alexander, but now put down his utensils, saying, "Continue your story."

She shook her head no, insisting, "You are eating or I'm not continuing on with the story."

"I'm not eating until you finish your story," David countered.

This fired Katherine up and she leaned into the table, warning in a low voice, "I will get up right now and walk out of this restaurant and take a cab home if you don't eat while I continue the story."

David pushed his food aside, taking on her challenge. He leaned back in his chair. "Go."

She was so aroused. Tilting her head, grinning brightly, and making eye contact, she threatened, "I won't come over your house tomorrow and help you with the furniture."

He crossed his arms. "I'll call your mom. I know she will come and help me."

David wasn't allowing her to control him and she loved it. They stared at one another, but she truly wanted him to eat because she cared that he didn't like cold food. Pleading, she extolled, "Please, David. The story is almost over and I really want you to enjoy your meal. It was so thoughtful of you to stop eating while I ate, telling you my story. That was a little rude of me."

He absolutely couldn't resist her pleading. She wasn't being fake or trying to control him; she was sincere from her heart. Once again, he needed to break the sexual tension. "Katherine, you weren't being rude. You were being yourself. When there is a topic or subject that is either emotionally heavy or makes you nervous, I know you need to do a few things at the same time to help you through it."

Sitting back, she almost shouted, "What?"

"You do! It's the way you hold back your emotions. I've seen you do it a hundred times when we've worked together."

"Wow! You need to go. I'm now on a mission to get you out of Cleveland by the end of the season. I promise you, you will get the best contract and the most beautiful sunny weather." Even though her tone was light hearted there was a sparkle in her eyes.

David laughed, taking a bite of his food. He knew he had her; she'd just announced she would do anything to push him away.

She sighed with relief. "Thank you for eating."

David smiled while he ate, finding her concern over his well-being tenderly speaking love to his heart.

"So basically, I was in my old room at my parents' home for a couple months. My mom basically was feeding me to sustain my life," Katherine said, fidgeting with her napkin, restless.

Motioning with his fork, he said, "Drink your water. You will get dehydrated from all the alcohol if you don't."

Taking a sip of water, Katherine said, "I didn't want to go on any medication because some from the Christian community condemn you, saying you are relying on medication rather than God."

"Really?" David asked oddly.

"Yep. But you know what's interesting?" she asked, taking another sip of water. "I'm glad I didn't take medication because I believe for me— and this is only for me— I think I would have stayed in bed longer. I don't know if that makes any sense."

"Yes, it makes total sense to me," David said, recalling his depression after breaking his collarbone.

"I realized sometime later that I understand why someone would use medication. God created each person differently, and I'm not a Christian who is opposed to anyone using it, but it wasn't needed for me." She grinned for she loved how God interacts with each person uniquely as He created them.

David understood her point.

"Anyway, when my dad told us my mom had breast cancer, all I could think of was Trino's wife. And I had this fear, which actually motivated me, if that makes any sense at all," she said, sipping more of the lemon water.

David understood. "I think I know that fear but can't describe it right now."

"So I literally got out of bed that day and started taking care of my Mom, which eventually led me to helping my dad at our company,"

Katherine said, finishing the last of her water. "And mostly, it was a pretty smooth transition to be part of the organization and media. I think since Trino put a spotlight on me, they welcomed me into their world."

David nodded, it making sense.

Pushing away her empty glass, she smiled brightly. "But Trino gave me the hardest time. Most were pleasant, but I think it was because they knew my story. But Trino was almost ruthless with me." Flirting, she added, "Sort of like when I first met you."

David smiled, blushing, but continued to eat.

"And I hated it because it was so confusing." She chuckled. "How could he be what seemed so loving only to be a complete prick to me when I entered his world."

David laughed, taking the last bite of his food, thinking she must be drunk since she never spoke of anyone with ill intent, especially using that language.

Katherine smiled brightly of the memory of Trino. "And it took me a long time to realize what he was doing."

"What was that?" David asked.

"He was teaching me how to stay in this game long term. See, everyone else was being kind to me because of what I went through. But once they realized I was a serious contender, they became competitive. And by the time that happened, I was well groomed." Joking around, she alluded to being a quarterback herself. "When they tried to sack me, I scrambled. And at times they knocked me down, but I got back up, and eventually we built a good game. I actually enjoyed the intensity of it."

"I love to watch you work. It's elegant," David confessed.

"I love my job. I absolutely love my job!" She smiled since it was such an energetic and electrifying career. James once believed God had created him to do and now Katherine believed she was to continue on in James's place.

Chapter 58

Pull My Hair?

Alexander brought the couple the luscious, dark chocolate lava cake with real whipped cream and two spoons, placing it in the center of the candlelit table. Both their eyes went wide with anticipation.

"Isn't this the most beautiful dessert you have ever seen?" Katherine asked, licking her lips.

David didn't take his eyes off her. "Absolutely."

Each took a bite, rolling their eyes as they tasted the hot, dark chocolate ganache center melting in with the whipped cream.

"I can see why you love this dessert." David went in for another bite.

"You know, there is something about eating a dessert with a spoon that translates romance to me."

David smiled. He loved her description of enjoyment.

"I love cake. It's great because it's a dessert that represents a celebration—birthday, graduation, baby shower," she said, scooping up some ganache.

David agreed, although he felt bad. She had lost her baby.

"But you eat it with a fork. And it's usually served at a party with a crowd of people having a slice too. Now, don't get me wrong, I love celebrating, and I love what the cake represents, but it's not as, I don't know, romantic as this dessert. People usually don't share a slice of cake," Katherine romanced.

With fiery, passionate eyes, he said, "Well, you are forgetting the wedding cake. It's the trophy, the most romantic of all desserts. The married couple feeds one another. What can truly top that?"

Katherine's heart raced; she actually felt it pounding ferociously in the middle of her chest. David was speaking in a way that seduced her emotions. "Yes, but most couples smash it in each other's face," she deflected.

"That's disrespectful. I wouldn't do that, and I can guarantee you wouldn't either."

Katherine blushed; he was right. She tensed slightly with fear again.

David sensed it in the way she edged back in her chair gradually. "Go on with your analogy about desserts," he said, walking them to safer territory.

Katherine couldn't look into his eyes. She was falling for David and needed to stop herself. "A desert with a spoon is more suited for sharing. You usually use a spoon for eating something that is hot and melts part of the dessert. Like crème brûlée or a hot apple cobbler with ice cream."

"True, but those can't hold a candle to this dessert."

"Yes," Katherine agreed.

Then their spoons touched across the plate and a feeling like an lightning bolt ran through both of them. David and Katherine were deeply connecting with each other and having difficulty not wanting to take it to the next level.

"This is like sex on a plate," Katherine said.

David smiled and agreed, but he wanted more with her than sex. He wanted to eat wedding cake with her.

Sitting back, blushing, Katherine said, "Okay, really, I had no intentions of drinking as much as I did. I don't think I realize just how drunk I must be."

"You are fine. You don't need to be concerned. I will be a complete gentleman, I promise you that," David said seriously.

"Just how much can I trust you?" Katherine asked, dead serious.

The question threw him off. "What?"

"Really, just how much can I trust you?"

Not breaking eye contact, he said, "I promise I would do anything to protect you. I would lie down my life for you."

"Down tiger," Katherine warned.

David realized he was getting too close to her core like at the hair salon. Intrigued, he asked, "What do you have in mind?"

"I'm just about drunk enough to be almost completely honest with my feelings." She flashed a sexy grin.

"Okay," he said, ready for the honesty.

"I've come to a restaurant that I haven't been to in five years. I've had more to drink tonight than I've had in probably that same time frame. I've talked about a horrible, tragic story that I really had no intentions of ever reliving or retelling in my life."

David listened.

"Now, I weigh maybe 115…okay, honestly, it's probably more 117-118." She laughed.

The sound was like bells in the air. David loved this.

"I am very, very drunk right now. The food, even though fantastic, hasn't really taken the edge off enough to sober me up."

"Well, that's because you drank my glass of wine," he playfully teased.

"I know, I'm so sorry!"

He looked away. He couldn't take those deep, dark eyes. "Okay, go on."

"Look, I'm sick and tired of talking about myself. I really don't like to spend this much time on myself," she confessed.

"I know that's true about you."

"And we can't start talking about you because I know I have the ability to lead our conversations back to the cat-and-dog game we play."

"You think?" David asked, riled up and ready for another round of their playful bantering.

"I just did. I did it with dessert too. Do you really want to test me?" she teased, challenging him.

Agitated that she was right and that he was having a difficult time resisting her charm, he said flatly, "Just continue."

Her tipsiness showing, she gushed, "You are so awesome. I just love spending time with you."

"Boy, you must be drunk to tell me that!" He laughed.

"I am! That's my point. I know I can continue leading you down this road and eventually I will get my way. You were absolutely right about me out on the terrace. You know exactly what I'm trying to do. And if anything happens, even just a kiss, you will be working with my mom tomorrow."

"Are you challenging me?" he asked, fired up.

Dead serious, she Katherine said, "No, I'm warning you. Please know that I'm in a state of mind that I would look at you as a challenge tonight, as a toy, as something to play with, and treat you accordingly."

"You are drunk." He grinned since he was intoxicated by the natural sensuality that spilled out of her.

"I told you that I am." She smiled looking so deeply into his eyes that his heart felt like it fluttered to his stomach.

"So what do you want from me?" David asked.

"I have a tremendous amount of respect for you, and I don't want to treat you with any disrespect. It was killing me to see you hurt by so many others."

"Thank you," David said lovingly. "So why don't you let me just take you home so that there are no temptations."

"Thank you for being such a gentleman; I love it. But actually I need to have fun right now. It's been too much emotion for far too long and I have been feeling caged, and I hate that feeling."

"I understand. What do you want to do?" he asked.

"I need to play what Lana and I call "pull my hair", Katherine said dead serious.

"What?" David asked, tickled.

"Okay, first let me ask you this. Are you in any rush to get home?"

"Not in the least bit."

"Then I'm trusting you to let me take down my guard for the night," she said.

"But what does that have to do with pulling your hair?" David replied.

"Being a woman of God, we have to watch our character and keep certain things about ourselves in check. Being married, I didn't need to worry about that. I could just be myself with James."

"That makes sense. I understand."

"Now, being single, I have to constantly watch everything about myself. The way I dress, the way I talk, the way I walk.

"You can't be yourself."

"Exactly! But the truth is, I don't want to be myself with just anyone. I really don't mind that I have to shield that side of me, but lately, and specifically tonight, I want to let down my hair," Katherine admitted, relieved to put the need into words.

"Alright, so what do you want from me?"

Katherine lowered her voice. "See that table of guys over my right shoulder?"

Not even looking in the direction she referred, he said, "Yes."

"There is a guy over there I know is interested in me," she stated.

"The guy wearing the brown suit?"

Raising her eyebrows, she said, "How did you know?"

"How did you know? Your back is to him," David inquired.

They looked deeply into each other's eyes, smiling, and she broke the mood by saying, "Okay, this is where "pull my hair" comes in."

Leaning into the table, he said, "Boy, am I intrigued."

"Let's just say without getting into a lot of details that I can tell when a guy is attracted to me without ever looking at him," Katherine said.

"Cocky, aren't we?" David said with his sexy grin.

"Confident," she corrected. "Let's test out my theory. I'll walk up to the bar and I'm sure within five minutes he'll follow me."

"And what if you are wrong?"

"Oh, I'm never wrong. But if I am, you have a great story to always keep me in my place, wouldn't you?" she asked, teasing and tempting him.

Completely into her, he asked, "So what does that have to do with pulling your hair?"

"Well, I want to go out and have some fun."

"You aren't having fun with me?"

Katherine reached out and touched his hand, lovingly. "I haven't enjoyed myself this much in the past five years."

David smiled, holding her hand before she pulled it away.

"But I can guarantee," Katherine continued, "if you continue holding my hand, we will never come to this restaurant again."

David knew they had an intense attraction between them and wanted to protect their working relationship and respect. "Well, I wouldn't want that. Continue."

"So that group of guys dressed up in suits has to be having a bachelor party. Why else would they come to a nice restaurant with no dates? They certainly wouldn't have selected this place to meet single women. I mean, sure, over at the bar they would, but they are having dinner."

Chuckling, David shook his head. "I love how you think."

"Anyway, I want to take my hair down for the night and just feel a little sexy and not have to be concerned with it going anywhere, and that's where you come in."

"Huh?" he asked.

"I want to be able to feel like a woman and flirt and have some fun, but the moment you see that he's trying to touch me or kiss me, you need to step in by physically pulling my hair if necessary," Katherine said.

"Wait a minute, what?" David asked again.

"You don't need to be concerned about me trying to kiss him. I won't do that. I can be aggressive, but I think it's a turnoff when the woman takes the lead role in dictating the first kiss. It's up there with the wedding cake," she said.

"Wait a minute," David said, trying to get her attention.

"And don't pull my hair too hard, because I might just like that," she seriously warned him.

"Okay, stop. Stop talking," David said. "I have so many questions I don't know where to begin."

She smiled with the grin he loves so much.

His eyes loved on her. "You never cease to amaze me. First, tell me where this whole pulling your hair thing came from."

"Well, in college, Lana and I went to the bars together. We went strictly to dance, not because we were looking at finding men. Eventually, we became friends with a large group of men and women who wanted to enjoy hanging out." Katherine put down her head, laughing. "I can tell you so many stories from those days."

"Maybe I can hear them some time."

"Well, anyway, at times there were guys outside of our normal group who asked us to dance and we would. But we watched over one another, and if at any time it became a little too tempting and one of us was going down a path we shouldn't, we would literally pull each other's hair it get us back on track." She grinned at the cleverness of it all.

Burrowing his brow, David asked, "But aren't you being a tease?"

"Sure, I guess you can call it that. But pretty much as soon as the guy knew he wasn't getting laid, he looked for someone else," Katherine said.

Shocked she would act as such, he asked, "But wouldn't you be leading this guy on?"

"Let me tell you something, by the time we are through with the night, that guy will not be interested in me anymore and I will leave him with a great story. He'll feel more confident than he has in years," she said.

"How do you know?"

"Because I'm still who I am to my core. I just have the need to bust out of this cage for tonight. And I need to trust you enough to make sure that I don't take it to a place where I would regret it. Are you able to do that?"

David thought, not answering her. Was this right?

"David, there's no pressure. You can take me home and I won't be offended or upset or treat you any differently."

Still thinking, he wasn't sure what he wanted to do.

"David, I'm so sick and tired of always doing the right thing! Believe me when I say that for the first time since my husband died…I…I just have some passion inside that has been building and I need to release it somehow. I'm so tired of feeling dead. I promise I will make him feel like a man when it's all said and done. And it won't be because he laid a finger on me. It won't be about sex at all."

Shaking his head, his competitive nature emerged. "I'm not sure you can do it."

"Do what? Make him feel like a man or not do anything sexually with him?" Katherine asked.

"Oh, you have both those in the bag. But you are forgetting one thing."

"What's that?"

"Me!"

Grinning, looking deeply in his eyes, she said, "I can never forget you!"

"Well, right now I'm his competition. Do you think he can handle that? He may not attempt to go up against me."

Katherine closed her eyes, licking her lips unknowingly. She loved David's confidence. "It's like the woman who gave you her card... Acrylic Nails."

"Now I'm so intrigued. I have to see this with my own eyes."

"Yes! Thank you so much!" She smiled victoriously. "Here's the plan. Let me first use the ladies' room and when I come back to the table, I'll make eye contact with him."

"Haven't you already?"

"No, I haven't. I'm extremely careful with men. I hardly ever make eye contact with a man I don't know," she stated.

"I understand. You don't want to give off any false impressions," he said.

"Exactly!" She smiled, happy he got it. "Okay, how about you go sign some more autographs? There is a slew of people waiting for you."

Chapter 59

The Alignment

Even though David couldn't take his eyes off her, Katherine waved some fans over, but just as before, he noticed that guy checking her out, and he hated it.

"Here, I'll take pictures for you," Katherine said kindly, taking a phone. "Isn't he handsome, ladies?" Not even looking at David, she handed the phone back to the woman, taking another from the next person waiting. "He has the bluest eyes you've ever seen. Kind of makes your heart melt, doesn't it?"

They all agreed.

"And that head of hair. Makes you just want to run your fingers through it," she said, riling up the women. Her playfulness intrigued David. She was giving compliments by using the women as a buffer. His dad did the same with Michael.

A young woman avoided Katherine, baring her stomach and asking David, "Can you sign this?"

David wouldn't look at the girl, raising his voice. "Katherine, just so you know, I will never sign any skin or clothing that any woman is wearing. Do I make myself clear?"

Katherine understood. "Yes, you can count on me to take care of that for you."

"What about undergarments?" the girl asked.

Looking up from the phone, Katherine said, "If I see anything like that, I can assure you you won't be getting an autograph or picture. Got it?"

David grinned, loving her possessiveness, saying, "We want to keep this a family-friendly environment."

Katherine agreed as she blushed.

The Preserver

After he finished with the fans, Katherine announced she was going to the ladies' room. While she was gone, David checked out the guy. He'd seen him watching Katherine as she took the fans' photos. Did she do that on purpose to get his attention? No. David knew Katherine wasn't that type.

The guy wasn't even that good-looking. He was almost bald with a five o'clock shadow from his ears to his chin. His eyes were dark brown; nothing too exciting. He was pretty tan and sort of built, though. Nice suit, but not of the quality Katherine had selected for David.

Upon her return, Katherine stopped before sitting at the table, bending down slightly to pick up her purse lying on the floor. That's when she made direct eye contact with the guy. She didn't make a big deal of it, only enough to get his attention.

"Wow! I'm not sure if I like this side of you," David confessed.

"Why?"

"I'm not sure," he replied truthfully. "I can't pinpoint it."

"Interesting," she said, thinking, although they didn't discuss it.

"I'm going to the restroom," he said.

As he walked to the restroom, of course, someone asked him for an autograph. Happily, he signed a jersey, and when he turned to get his photo taken, he saw the guy at his table talking to Katherine. He couldn't believe it. Katherine was completely open, speaking freely. And then he watched as she stood to speak with him, being somewhat seductive. He didn't like that picture at all. There was no way he was going to let this go any further.

He walked straight toward Katherine, forgoing the restroom, and when she saw him, fear filled her core. David's eyes were intense, just like her father's when he needed to protect his family. She froze helpless since she had brought this on herself and knew her game had ended, for she would have never been able to play this silly game in front of her father and since David was like him, she couldn't with him either.

Stepping right in between them, not acknowledging the guy, he growled to Katherine, "Come with me."

"Hey, I didn't realize you were on a date," the guy said, challenging David for breaking up his conversation with Katherine.

Facing him, David asked, "What would give you the impression that we aren't?"

"Because how many dates would offer to take pictures of other women hanging on her man?" the guy said.

David hung his head, smiling. Of course, Katherine would know this guy was full of confidence. All evening he'd been checking her out, making it so apparent that Katherine couldn't help but notice. She even knew the moment she gave any indication of her interest, he would approach her.

"You are absolutely right," David replied.

The guy didn't answer. He wanted to talk to Katherine. So David moved, standing next to him. He wanted Katherine to have a clear comparison of them both.

"Are you guys celebrating anything tonight?" David asked friendly.

"Yes, my buddy is getting married."

"Great! Congratulations to him!" David said.

"Yeah, I guess."

"You don't sound too happy for him. My name is David Mann. Have you met Katherine? She is my manager, my business manager. What's your name?"

"Nice to meet you, David," he said, shaking his hand. "Thanks, I hadn't had time to get her name yet. I'm Gary." He said this while only looking at Katherine.

She grinned politely now trying to think quickly of how to get out of the conversation and, more importantly, the situation she had placed all three of them in.

"So Gary, you don't sound too thrilled for your friend's marriage. Why not?" David asked.

"Well, I got divorced not too long ago and marriage isn't what it's all cracked up to be. Have you ever been married, David?"

"No, I haven't."

"Katherine, have you been married?" Gary asked.

"Yes," she replied.

"Oh, so divorced too. You and I can understand one another," Gary chuckled.

Katherine looked down, chuckling. She then looked at David with all his brilliance and majesty, comparing the two men, and was forced to take a deep breath. "I'm sorry to be rude, Gary, but we are having a celebration for what our partnership has accomplished to date," she said pleasantly.

"Not to be rude back, but he's only won one game—the last preseason game with hardly the first team playing," Gary said.

David was amused that the guy was bold enough to rip on him while standing right next to him.

Katherine wore her sexy grin and whispered to Gary, "I believe he can take us to the Super Bowl."

Gary snorted, moved in closer, and spoke lowly in her ear. "I'm sorry, I don't mean to laugh, but we've heard that same old story so many times before, haven't we?" Slowly backing up and winking at her, Gray flashed a condescending smile, mistaking Katherine's sexy grin to be for him when in reality it was for the belief she had in David.

"You know, Gary, you have such a great amount of confidence I'm sure women probably fall head over heels in love with you quite often," Katherine stated truthfully.

"Well, what about you? Do you want to fall head over heels in love with me?" he asked.

Despite the fact that Gary had just hit on Katherine right in front of him, David was starting to like this guy since he reminded him of Jordan with his quick pick-up lines. And since Katherine's demeanor had changed. No longer seductive, she was showing her normal and professional side, not the private side she shared with David or her family. He stepped aside, folding his arms and bringing his hand to his lips, trying to hide his smirk.

Katherine smiled at David. They understood one another. They were more than a team where she was his manager and he her client. They protected one another. They knew each other's heart, their core being, almost seeing their souls. David knew that Katherine couldn't play with Gary's emotions and Katherine knew David wouldn't allow her to lead anyone on for she wasn't that shallow.

"You know what, Gary. I was married to a pretty amazing, loving man, but he passed away pretty tragically. I'm still not quite over the heartbreak. It's been a long time, but, well, I'm still dealing with the pain," Katherine said sweetly.

"Well, maybe I can help you along with that," Gary suggested.

"Gary, trust me when I tell you that I would use you like a toy and then spit you out."

"You can use me anyway you want," he replied.

Seeing David get agitated, Katherine gave him a look that she would handle the situation, saying, "Gary, you are too good for that. You are obviously still hurt from your divorce. I know you just want to have fun tonight and forget about the pain. I completely understand that more than you can realize. But you and I could go out, have fun, and you will end up being more hurt than you already are. I'm sorry your marriage didn't work out. I'm sure you had such amazing aspirations for it. But God always uses our pain to bring us closer to Him, and if you would just allow Him to speak to you, He will heal you too."

Now turned off by her rhetoric, Gary began looking for a way out. "Um…yeah…hey, do you want me to take a picture of you two? You've been taking everyone else's picture, how about one of the two of you?"

"Yes! That would be a nice switch," David said, happy Katherine was able to be herself, involving God in part of her everyday conversations.

Both gave their phones to him and posed for a photo. Afterward, they thanked him politely and walked him back to his table, where they congratulated the bachelor on his upcoming nuptials as well. The men were in for a night on the town, having rented a limo to party all night. David bought them a round of drinks to help them celebrate. Once they returned to their table, Katherine whispered, "Thank you."

"Is that what you wanted to do?" David asked.

"Well, that's what I would've ended up doing, but I was going to ask if we could tag along with them and go dancing. I wanted to dance with him," she said.

"How do you know he dances?" David asked.

"It wouldn't have mattered. I would have gotten him out on the dance floor and just did my thing," she confessed honestly.

"Oh, I've seen you do your thing Katherine. And if you thought I would have just stood there and allowed that to happen, then you really don't know me," David stated in no uncertain terms.

"I know you. You're just like my dad. I realized when you interrupted us that there was no way you would stand around watching me dance with someone else," she replied.

"I don't even like you talking to another man," David told her, a possessive edge creeping into his voice.

"David, I can't take much more. Please stop," she begged. "It's too much. I'm sorry, I can't. I'm going to do whatever I can to push you away."

Knowing she was being truthful, he said, "I understand. I do. But you have to understand that I don't like being caged either."

"Yes, but I have a lot of plays in my game book. I've been doing this for years," she teased.

Even more determined, he said, "Yes, but you forget that I've spent my entire life studying defense."

Katherine placed down her head, not challenging him this time.

Driving home his point, David threatened, "Do you want to go back on the terrace?"

"No."

"Then let's get you home."

"Okay," she replied, sad. She didn't want to go to her home. Lately, it felt cold and empty.

Chapter 60

The Purse

Once Alexander brought the bill, Katherine reached for her purse. David halted her motion, insisting, "Katherine, if you think I'm going to take your money, you really don't know me."

"Well, I thought it would be nice if I paid half."

This time her large, honest eyes didn't work. "Please listen to me and put your purse away," David said.

Knowing he was serious, she listened and placed her purse down.

"Rose comped the complete meal!" David announced when he opened the bill fold.

"Really?"

"Yes, she listed the amount and deducted it so I know how much to tip."

Looking around the restaurant, Katherine said, "Well, this place is pretty busy. She must be thankful for the additional business you brought."

"Yes, maybe," he said leaving a $800 tip.

"Wow, David! Really, that much?" she asked, surprising herself that she would even question his decision.

"I love excellent service and I pay well for it. I like to be treated like a king and Alexander did just that."

For some reason, she blushed. She had also enjoyed the service immensely and liked being pampered.

David stood, going over to Katherine's side to help her with her chair as she thanked him sweetly. Before leaving, he noticed her purse still sat under the table. Reaching down, he grabbed it and handed it to her, saying, "You forgot your purse."

She stumbled back and life left her face as she fought back instant tears. It reminded her so much of the last dinner she had with James. She moved to rush away but she saw Rose and knew she couldn't go without saying goodbye. "I had an absolutely fabulous time!" Katherine said, hugging her as tears leaked out.

"I'm so glad you came back again. David brought us a lot of business tonight. We had to call in extra help!" Rose said, laughing. "Will you come and visit me again?"

Looking at David, she said, "Yes, most certainly."

Rose grabbed David, hugging him tightly while whispering, "Please take care of her."

"I will take care of her the same way you cared for her that evening," he replied gently.

Rose looked at him with tears in her eyes, then laughed. "Go win us some football games!"

"That's why I'm here!" He smiled, caring affectionately for this woman. "You are as beautiful as your name, Rose."

"Oh, Katherine, he's a tiger, isn't he?" she chuckled.

"Yes, that's why I keep running away from him."

Leaning over, he whispered in her ear, "You must be still very drunk."

Chills ran through her body. She couldn't take much more and wasn't sure they could manage being alone together in the car.

"Katherine, do you have your purse?" Rose asked.

"Yes, thank you. David reminded me," she replied.

The Thunderstorm

David thought it was odd of Rose to ask but couldn't question it because more patrons wanted his autograph and photo. He even was asked for a quick interview before leaving. While in the elevator, Katherine, who was still clearly drunk, began with her bedroom eyes. David was having difficulty keeping his arousal in check. Looking for anything to prevent enticement, he found his target, asking, "What's the story about your purse?"

Katherine straightened up, her bedroom eyes now filled with painful tears and a slight tremor shook the purse in her hand. David wanted to hold her and comfort her so much, but because of her condition, he knew her guard was down and it would likely lead to a place he would regret the rest of his life. Instead he said, "It's okay, you've already told me plenty tonight. We don't have to talk about it."

Looking to make light of the situation, she said, "Really, outside of some other things that I haven't told you because not even in my drunken state am I ready to talk about them, this is one of the final pieces to the story."

Stepping off the elevator, walking out to some light rain, David handed the valet his ticket as the familiar fear came over Katherine. David opened her car door, helping her in, but his gentlemanly action did nothing to soothe her. When the rain came down heavier, her anxiety took center stage. As he pulled away from the restaurant, the windshield wipers hardly cleared the view. It was too much. Katherine couldn't hide her fear any longer; she was practically hyperventilating.

Seeing her state, David grew alarmed. "Katherine, what is it?"

"David, I'm so sorry. I'm so sorry," she cried.

Feeling helpless, he asked, "What's wrong?"

Balled up on the seat, burying her face in her hands, she was unable to control her emotions and she wept loudly.

"Look, I'm pulling over." He decided the Cleveland football stadium parking garage would a provide a private place where he could comfort her. He parked his car, got out, went to her side, picked her up, and sat on the ground as she cried uncontrollably in his lap.

"I'm so sorry. I'm so sorry," she sobbed into his shoulder, her sides heaving.

Stroking her hair, David soothed, "You have nothing to apologize about."

Again, she attempted to stop the tears, but all she could say was "I'm sorry. I'm so sorry."

David prayed because he didn't know what else to do. He asked God to help Katherine in this moment because he truly loved her and hated to see her hurt. Then David thought about Michael and how often he spoke about God to him. It was uplifting, so he preached to her, wanting the words to carry all his love. "Katherine, what you described tonight is tragic beyond anything I could ever imagine. And I know there are details that are just too overwhelming for you to even think about."

Holding her like a baby, sitting on the garage floor, leaning up against the car door, he said, "Even though you thought going to the restaurant wasn't a good idea, I'm so thankful we went and you showed me this side of you."

Only moments before, Katherine could hardly breath from crying but David's words stilled her to a few last sniffles.

Holding her lovingly, pressing his cheek into her hair, David told her, "I love how you feel absolutely free with me and trust me enough with your inmost thoughts. That you feel comfortable enough to show me the real you, to let down your guard with me."

She relaxed in his arms while the sound of the thunderstorm filled the background.

"I know that you needed to feel like a woman by flirting with Gary, but I know you would have felt bad and cheap if that had succeeded. That game worked when you were in college, but you are a completely different person now." He held her a little closer to infuse her with his warmth. "I know you are tired of doing the right thing, always guarding yourself. I know how many men find you attractive, and I know that you are conditioned to level with them, and you do so flawlessly."

She rested her head on his shoulder.

David's eyes grew moist. "I don't know God the way you or your family does, but I can't help but see just how much He loves you, and that honestly brings tears to my eyes."

Katherine started crying again, shaking her head no and in an instant David knew she didn't believe God loved her.

He held her a little tighter, rocking her back and forth as she cried. "Katherine, I don't know a lot about God, but if I can see He loves you, then clearly those who know Him see it plainly. I know your parents tell you repeatedly how much God loves you. Don't you ever doubt His love for a second. I'm sure through the devastation of losing your husband you questioned that constantly, but His love for you is so evident."

Katherine stopped crying altogether for she longed to hear the only words that would ever give her peace.

"I think that's why Brooke is so threatened by you. Who wouldn't want that type of love from God? I can't help but be drawn to it, even though I don't understand it. Look at all those people God moved in order for you to be able to stand back up and get out of your bed? You said yourself that you didn't need medication, but why? It was because God was moving in and through you. Gosh, I want that so bad for myself."

David knew what he was saying was truth for Katherine because she completely went limp in his arms.

He reassured, "I realize there are a lot of rules or whatever that you have to abide by, but as hard as it may seem at times, you are better off for it in the long run."

Melting together, unable to distinguish their own body parts, he held her even tighter.

"I know firsthand how hard it is to stay disciplined and not cheat by taking drugs or quitting when it gets so rough and lonely. But look at where we are now. We both know we are on the verge of something," David said, thinking. "I'm not even too sure that a single word can describe it. But it can only be from God."

Katherine was completely putty in his arms now. Feeling it, he stroked her hair, kissed her forehead, and looked deeply into her eyes. "Thank you for making love with me tonight. Thank you for allowing me to feel this with you. Thank you for allowing me to love you and to care for you. Thank you for again giving me a pleasure I didn't even dare desire. Thank you for completely surrendering yourself in my arms, just for tonight, just for a little bit. This is what you needed. This is what makes you feel like a woman. I know because it makes me feel like a man."

Katherine nestled her head deeper into his shoulder, falling asleep, exhausted from all the emotions she'd experienced throughout the night. David cried as she slept because he loved her so much and was so thankful to God for bringing him to Cleveland.

He remained that way with her for over an hour, holding her, sitting on the ground of the private Cleveland football stadium parking garage, leaning up against his car. He didn't want to let her go. He knew tomorrow would be back to business as usual. So he did what had been working and prayed. "Lord, I have no idea where any of this is going. You know my love for her is real. I can only think that you are involved with this, so I pray you help me understand how to love her the way you created her to be loved. Please show me."

And even though he didn't want to let her go, he knew it was time, so he gently got up and placed her back in his car, buckling her seat belt around her while she remained sleeping peacefully. He drove them to her parents' home, holding her hand the entire way as the thunderstorm slowly came to a still.

Chapter 61

The Profession

As David pulled into the driveway, he could see lights on in the house, so he opened the garage door, parked the car, and carried Katherine inside. She was so exhausted from emotion that she didn't stir. When her parents saw her, they rushed to his side, alarmed. David tried to put his finger up to his mouth for them to keep quiet since she was completely, soundly asleep.

Sharon whispered, "Is she okay?"

David nodded.

"Let's take her upstairs." Sharon pointed out the way.

Carrying her the whole way, he followed them to her room. There he laid Katherine on the bed, removed her shoes, covered her with a blanket, and kissed her forehead. He stood a moment and looked at her lovingly before he left with her parents. They kept the door slightly ajar and tiptoed downstairs to the kitchen.

"What happened?" Sharon said.

"We went out to dinner," David answered. "We went to the Top of the Town."

Sharon immediately hugged David and cried. He hugged her too, crying himself as Michael wrapped his arms around both of them with tears. Eventually, Sharon motioned for them to sit at the table, and they sat as a family at the familiar location which had hosted countless honest and heartfelt conversations. That was the reason why David purchased his table. He wanted the same setting, that same life.

"What happened? How did you get there? How was she?" Sharon pelted him with questions.

And David confessed from his heart, "I'm in love with your daughter!"

And all of them cried anew, even Michael, though each had their own reason for their emotion. And no one spoke because they weren't too sure what to say. David let go first saying, "I think I've loved her from the moment I met her."

Michael and Sharon made eye contact with each other.

Tears pouring out, confused as could be, David let it fly. "I don't even understand what it means. I'm not sure what to do. It doesn't even matter to me if she loves me or not. Maybe this is God's way of showing me how to love. I have no idea. But all I know is that I love her and I don't want anyone else other than her. It's like she was specifically created for me, which is odd because she's already had a husband who she is still clearly in love with."

They watched as he rubbed his face, leaned back in his chair, and placed his hand over his eyes to stop the tears. "I'm not even too sure why I'm crying."

"It's because you are experiencing God at His finest," Michael loved.

And David wept. He just wept. He didn't even know if he could talk about his feelings, and Michael and Sharon didn't ask him to. They didn't ask about the evening, but they allowed him to expose his emotions, his genuine feelings, in a circle of love and safety.

Finally pulling himself back together, he grinned. "Gosh, I'm so sorry. I always cry around you people."

Sharon patted his hand. "It's truly our pleasure for you to open your heart to us."

Looking directly at Michael, he asked. "Would you mind if I sleep on her bedroom floor? I promise I won't touch her. She had a pretty emotional evening and I want to make sure I'm there for her in case she wakes up."

Tears instantly poured out of Michael's eyes and he could hardly speak. "Thank…you…for protecting…her."

"I know my parents are asleep, but I want to check in on them before I head upstairs," David said.

The Provider

As soon as he left, Sharon cried. "Michael, I know Katherine. She'll do whatever she needs to do in order to push David away. I know she doesn't feel worthy to have this again."

He cared for her concern. "Sharon, God has always been faithful to our family. Let Him take care of this. I think it would be in our best interest to remain quiet in prayer and be here when they need to talk."

She nodded, knowing the truth of her husband's words.

"Besides, look at what God did for our marriage. He'll provide like always," Michael said, getting up and coming over to her side to nestle her in his strong, warm arms, the place he knew she truly felt comfort and safety.

The Love

David tiptoed into his parents' house. The nurse was up and she pointed to the bedrooms to signal that his parents were asleep. He crept to his mother's room and slowly opened her door, then cried upon seeing his father sitting in a chair next to her bed, his head laying next to hers. They were both asleep and holding hands.

It was a clear picture to David. He was his dad. His father had an intense love for his mother, and his mother had been afraid of it. But now, she was open to his father's love. It took a stroke and partial paralysis for his mother to accept his father's love.

David knew his game plan with Katherine had to be perfect. But somehow he knew he wasn't capable of doing it alone. Without a doubt, he would need God to walk him through each and every encounter with her. He was determined to know God deeper so that he could clearly understand His direction.

"Do they sleep like that every night?" David asked.

The nurse smiled. "Yes, since the day he came here."

David thanked her and returned to the main house, kissing both Michael and Sharon goodnight before going to Katherine's bedroom. Sharon had thoughtfully placed an air mattress, blankets, and pillow for him next to her daughter's bed. David quietly removed his shoes, suit coat, tie, and vest, then settled onto the air mattress and listened to her breathe. It comforted him.

He lay awake praying to God to help him with Katherine, for this was more significant than any football game he could ever play. And as much as he loved football, he would give it up to marry her. But something inside told him he needed to love God first and foremost.

He didn't understand what it meant, but now he understood his father's obsession with his mother and understood how it could have ruined his life. David loved his father more than ever, and he knew he would learn from his father's mistakes and not head down that same path. The only way to ensure that was to love God first. And David was determined to do just that. He would study God and His Word with the same intensity and passion he did with football and with Katherine.

David felt entirely at peace, falling warmly to sleep with his heart settled. His last thought was of thanking God for the most beautiful evening of his life.

The New Path

Slow, deep, tranquil breathing gently stirred David awake though it was so early in the morning that the sun hadn't shown its rays yet. His heart raced as he thought how much he would treasure awaking to the sound of her sleeping and her unique, natural scent every day if the Lord allowed it. David was ready to meet God on His terms, but as with any path he walked in his life, he knew he couldn't achieve it alone and needed help. Quietly, he got up from the air mattress, located a Bible (one was in every room of the house) and grabbed a notebook and pen from the desk. Before leaving, he checked on Katherine, seeing her snuggled cozily in her blanket sound asleep.

David tiptoed down the stairs and entered the kitchen, finding Sharon sitting at the table reading her Bible in usual form. When she looked up, her motherly eyes became wide with curiosity in seeing David so early, holding a Bible with a notebook and pen. "I want to learn about God," he said.

Looking out the large sliding glass doors, Sharon pointed to Michael on the patio reading his Bible and said, "I will bring you a cup of coffee."

David nodded and opened the door, hearing the birds sing out their praise and enjoying the gentle breeze, the faint smell of Lake Erie, and the warmth of a late summer new day. He pulled out the table chair, sat across from Michael, and opened his Bible to the ribbon marking the page. Looking over the verse, tears misted his eyes knowing he was on the right course as he read Proverbs 3:5-6: "Trust in the Lord with all your heart and lean not on your own understanding; in all your ways submit to Him and He will make your paths straight."

He could not have received a stronger message.

Acknowledgements

Psalm 139:13 NIV

"For you created my inmost being; you knit me together in my mother's womb."

Lord, for most of my life I struggled with why I was born, and to think I was created with any purpose was a joke that wasn't funny. But as I began the long and tedious work of cleaning out sin from my heart, You revealed such richness that an addictive path was laid before me. Thank you for my relationship with You. Thank you for its unimaginable depth, its unquenchable intimacy, and its laughter which overflows with joy. Though I know as I walk through this tempting, sin-filled life I won't always be filled with gratitude, love, or faithfulness, we've journeyed long enough together that I know I'll eventually come running back to You desiring to feel Your presence. I pray I always remain Your humble servant and that I'm able to share the saving grace of your Son, Jesus Christ, in the way You created, which I believe is deep, raw, and with much fun. In your name Jesus, Amen.

John 10:10 NKJV

"I have come that they may have life, and that they may have it more abundantly."

To the abundance of my life—my party. My husband, the life of the party. My oldest daughter, the party waiting to happen, and my youngest daughter, the party in and of herself. As we journey together through life, each growing according to God's purpose, there is no party to celebrate without each one of you.

Psalm 94:19 NIV

"When anxiety was great within me, your consolation brought me joy."

To Martha—a wonderful pastor's wife. Thank you for teaching me the power of forgiveness and the true riches of Romans 8:28. I believe with you wholeheartedly, although not always readily, that God works all things for good of those who love Him who have been called according to His purpose.

Matthew 7:7-12 NIV

"Ask and it will be given to you; seek and you will find; knock and the door will be opened to you. For everyone who asks receives; the one who seeks finds; and to the one who knocks, the door will be opened.

To Michelle Schacht, my editor. When I set out to find an editor, my must-have was to find a personality full of life. I wanted a woman who would teach, coach, mentor, and analyze my words, bringing out of me what I didn't know I possessed. God answered in a way more than I could have asked by leading me to you. I've enjoyed our conversations, shared teary-eyes, and delighted in so much laughter along the way. Thank you for bringing this story to life and pushing me in a way that grew what God created within.

Philippians 1:3 NIV

"I thank my God every time I remember you."

For the many men and women God has placed in my life, both the saved and unsaved, thank you for investing your time into me. Some were lasting friendships and others were mere words that helped guide me on God's path, but each of you are truly treasured for loving me enough to speak truth.

About the Author

Up before the sun rises, alone with God and her thoughts, Shenlee Luketic prays for wisdom as she navigates life in a world that doesn't always seem to remember Him, for discernment in raising two young ladies, and for enlightenment in the many seasons of marriage. She also cherishes God's unique creativity as she explores Scripture preparing fun and joyful Bible lessons for Sunday school where she teaches Jesus Christ is the Savior. Her favorite moments in life include time with family and friends, laughing and sharing heartfelt conversations, cheering on Ohio's hometown teams, and savoring a gourmet meal and an occasional glass of champagne.

CPSIA information can be obtained
at www.ICGtesting.com
Printed in the USA
LVHW042241300922
729679LV00001B/46